PERFECT

UNYIELDING BOOK TWO

RUIN

NEW YORK TIMES BESTSELLING AUTHOR

NASHODA ROSE

Perfect Ruin
Published by Nashoda Rose
Copyright © 2015 by Nashoda Rose
Toronto, Canada

ISBN 978-1-987953-05-3

Copyright © 2015 Cover design by: Louisa Maggio at LM Creations
http://lmbookcreations.wix.com/lm-creations

Cover Photo by CJC Photography, www.cjc-photography.com/

Model: Assad Shalhoub

Content Edited by Kristin Anders, The Romantic Editor
www.theromanticeditor.com

Editing by Hot Tree Editing, www.hottreeediting.com

Formatted by Champagne Formats, champagneformats.com

*Any editing issues are my own. I'm Canadian and on occasion I may use
Canadian spelling rather than U.S.

Kai

There is nothing I care about.
No attachments.
No connections.
Outwardly, I'm a perfect gentleman
until my target sees my knife.
I fear nothing, not even death.
In my world, death is considered a privilege.
But my life comes with unbreakable cruel strings and
when I met her, I should've walked away.
I didn't.
I was too selfish.
And that sealed her fate.
Because one week with me led her into the hands of ruin.

London

We all have unique layers that make up who we are.
What makes us vulnerable or strong.
What we fear and what excites us.
But peel back those layers and you're left naked and exposed.
They did that to me.
Each piece was slowly stripped away then burned.
I merely existed.
But there was one layer they overlooked.
The most important of them all—the tie to one man.
The man responsible for me being this way.
The man who found me.
And the killer who would do anything to protect me.

Perfect Ruin is the story of Kai and London.
Their beginning.
And the continuing story of *Vault*.

Must be read in order:
Perfect Chaos (Unyielding, #1) Deck and Georgie
Perfect Ruin (Unyielding, #2) Kai and London
Perfect Rage (Unyielding, #3) Connor's story (early 2016)

*This book contains offensive language and sexual content. 18+

Books by Nashoda Rose

Seven Sixes (2016)

Tear Asunder Series
With You (free)
Torn from You
Overwhelmed by You
Shattered by You
Kept from You (Kite's Story) 2016

Unyielding Series
Perfect Chaos
Perfect Ruin
Perfect Rage (Early 2016)

Scars of the Wraith Series
Stygian Book #1
Tyrant Book #2(2016)
Untitled Book #3(2016)
Take (standalone Scars of the Wraiths)

www.nashodarose.com

Author's Note

Thank you to the readers, for giving me my dream and for keeping it alive.
And now #meetKaiifyoudare and his braveheart, London.

PROLOGUE

Present Day

France

Kai

"HELLO, MOTHER." I strode into the room. The two white candles perched on pedestals at either side of the door flickered as I passed, causing a glimmer of shadows to dance along the stone walls.

"Darling," she cooed, as if pleased to see me.

We both knew different. She hated me, but the feeling was mutual.

Bitch had kept me waiting three weeks in France before giving me an audience. Finally, I'd been summoned like a fuckin' pet to its master by one of her minions. The waiting was a ploy to unnerve me. Unfortunately for her, it failed. Patience came easily to me as I'd spent my life having to live up to the word.

As a child, I'd been kept waiting for food, for sleep, for the pain to end. I'd learned that time was better off being nonexistent, to never wait for something to occur, but instead, to ensure that anything I

1

wanted would happen and that time had no significance.

There'd been a glitch in that way of thinking—London. Time suddenly mattered and that fucked with me.

She didn't bother rising from behind her large mahogany desk that faced the ornate, stained-glass window. She merely tilted her chin at an upward angle to glance over her shoulder at me. Her slender fingers went to the pearl necklace around her throat and she caressed the beads.

"A shame I missed you on my last visit to Toronto. Brice told me you were in New York checking up on Dr. Westbrook. I hope all went well."

This was complete bullshit. "Yes, of course." It hadn't. I'd been in New York, but I'd been searching for London, not checking up on her father, Dr. Westbrook. London had been at my house, a house no one knew existed; at least, I'd thought that was the case. Now, I knew different.

"How have you been? Are you staying in the city?"

Her slow interrogation was meant to sound like casual conversation, but there was always a purpose to every word out of her mouth. To an outsider, it would sound like a loving mother. To any who knew her, it was a manipulative way to try to obtain information without appearing like she was doing anything but chatting.

I reached the desk and bent to kiss the cheek she offered. My lips barely touched her cool skin before I straightened. I nonchalantly leaned against the desk beside her and crossed my arms. "I've been well, Mother." I had no intention of offering anything else.

I'd been staying at a quiet inn just outside of Paris where the goats bleated all day and the linen sheets smelled like they'd been doused in lavender. Actually, the entire house did, but it was the last place Mother would expect me to stay and the bonus was the owner cooked brilliant meals.

I'd paid for a room in a five-star hotel in the city and had all my messages sent there. I did wonder how long it took them to discover I wasn't staying there.

"Your flight was good?" She raised her brows that were beginning to thin out as she aged. The creases around her mouth and the corners of her eyes were more pronounced than the last time I'd seen her. But instead of making her look frail, as it did most people, the wrinkles hardened her appearance.

I chuckled. "Yes, three weeks ago, when I arrived."

She smiled, unaffected by my slight. "I apologize. I had a few delicate and time sensitive issues to deal with."

"Anything I can do to help?" I glanced at her computer screen and the security camera of the entrance to the front door was up. She'd been watching my arrival.

"No. No. A mere nuisance that I've dealt with." She clicked the ESC button at the top left of the keyboard and the screen went black. "How is Georgie? What's she go by? —Chaos? A shame about the Tanner situation. He was a great asset."

Her comment was like a burr against my skin. That tiny prickle of warning to be careful as to what I said. But then, I was always careful around the bitch. It was best to follow what was expected of you when you were planning the unexpected. "Tanner was too attached to her and required elimination."

The kid, Tanner, had been assigned to befriend Georgie and her brother, Connor, over a decade ago. It was before Connor was taken by Vault; he was now one of us—with a little coercion, of course. Never thought I'd give a fuck who Vault tortured, manipulated, or conditioned because I'd been one of them. But London changed that. She changed everything.

Mother nodded and a strand of blonde hair, streaked with grey, slipped out of her tightly woven bun and she pushed it back behind her ear. "Yes. You did warn us he could become a problem. But, he had his usefulness." She paused, her eyes drilling into me. "And Deck?"

There it was. What she really wanted to know. I kept my eyes on her, unflinching under the cold severe stare. "Placated and more focused on Georgie than on finding Connor. The note was a nice touch." A note written in blood from Connor warning Deck to stop searching for him or he'd go after Georgie.

She looked away as she shuffled the stark white papers in front of her—long, red fingernails like daggers. Daggers that would pierce your heart if she was in the mood to inflict pain. "Good. It was the right time. With Connor's threat and Deck close to her, his meddling into Connor's whereabouts may be discouraged now." Her movements were precise and delicate, as if she were handling valuable documents. But from my quick glance when I'd kissed her cheek, the papers were nothing more than expense reports. "Unless you think he is a risk?"

She was talking about killing Deck. I took my time answering; a hasty reply would be ruled as suspicious. "No. I think that would be foolish when we may be able to use him yet."

She pursed her red, drawn-on lips together. "Yes. True. I hate to eliminate potential operatives. Once the drug is stable, then we can reconsider our options. Connor has become very... reliable and we need more like him."

I laughed to myself. Operatives? It was a kind way of saying killers.

"What about the farm?" The compound where I'd grown up. Where kids were conditioned to be like me—cold killers. We needed the fuckin' location. We didn't even know what country it was in.

I waited while she toyed with me by remaining quiet. The bitch liked to constantly test me, but the handlers at the farm had trained me to be patient, emotionless, a machine that had no attachments and no feelings.

The pits were the worst. Thrown in a deep hole in the ground for days with no food, or water, freezing at night, sweltering during the day, never knowing how long you'd be there. I'd learned to escape into my mind and not return until the ladder lowered and I was taken out. The 'pit' was worse than any physical torture, and the faster you conquered the test, the less time you spent there.

"The farm is none of your concern."

But it was. She just didn't know it.

Only three board members knew its location: Mother, a Las Vegas hotel mogul, Peter Dorsey, and one other I didn't know. He'd remained anonymous, and I was betting he was responsible for overseeing the farm.

The man had been at my sister's public torture a few years earlier when she tried to disappear after an assignment. He'd kept in the shadows with a hat low over his face, but I recognized the two gold necklaces he wore. One had a cross on it and the other a large emerald. I'd seen a man wearing the exact same necklaces when I was eight or nine years old while living at the farm.

He'd stood looking into the pit, hat low to shield his identity. I remember his hand at his side, index finger and thumb rubbing together the entire time he watched me. I also remember the necklaces swaying side to side as he leaned over the pit. I'd been pretty delusional after three days in the pit, hot as hell, barely able to stand. But when I saw the same necklaces years later, I knew it was him.

"We won't need the farm if we have the drug," I said.

"We will utilize both." *Fuck.* "Children are easy for him to acquire and he uses them for another purpose. The arrangement works nicely. The farm will remain."

"And who is *him*, Mother? Don't you think it's time I know who all the board members are?"

She licked her lower lip, eyes narrowed as she contemplated. "That's not my decision. It's his."

"So, he calls the shots. Not you." Her back straightened. I knew she wouldn't like that. Mother always wanted to be the most powerful.

"Of course not. But he runs the farm and other rather delicate activities. It is better he remains anonymous for everyone. We'd rather not have to relocate the farm again after the last breach."

Tristan had been the breach. The fifteen-year-old kid who escaped the farm was now the multi-billionaire owner of Mason Developments, who had worked his entire life to get to this point and take Vault down. It was his jet that waited at the airport in France, pilots on standby to get us back to Toronto as soon as I was done here.

I couldn't press the issue. I needed something more important from her.

She pushed back her wooden chair with the plush, blue velvet backing, and, in a slow, elegant glide, she crossed her legs. I learned her movements and I was a lot like her, playing the cool unaffected person with genuine charm. Except, I did have charm. She was just a bitch playing the part.

Finally, she said, "You're here because of the girl."

It was a statement and the correct one. I *was* here because of London. I'd never willingly see Mother unless I had to and she knew it.

I'd still be the numb, unemotional killer the farm made me if I hadn't met London. Mother thought we were more dangerous if we had no attachments, no feelings toward anything or anyone.

She was wrong. I was a lot more dangerous now because I had something to lose.

"Yes. It's time we get this out in the open, Mother." *Because it may be our last opportunity.* "I clearly remember telling you a few years ago that I'd look after the situation and I did. She wasn't going to the police. But you had to go behind my back and make it your situation. I gave her father two months."

"He knew the deadline and he was delaying. And Kai, that was years ago. It no longer matters."

Oh, it fuckin' mattered. "We needed the drug. He needed two more months. You agreed to give him that." She didn't say anything. "Then after a week, you took his daughter and shipped her off to Raul. In fuckin' Mexico. Dr. Westbrook was under control."

The corners of her lips curved upward and despite the urge to smack her across the face, I met her with a smile of my own.

"I didn't realize you knew where we sent her. Interesting." She full-out smiled, flashing her pearl-white teeth that matched her choker necklace. "Did you go see her, Kai? Fuck her as a slave?"

I did go to Mexico and try to get her out, but shit went wrong and I lost her then spent the next two fuckin' years searching for her again. Of course, Vault didn't know that. "We don't deal with men like Raul. And you don't interfere with my work."

"You fucked her, Kai."

"I fuck lots of women. I'm a man," I said.

"For a week."

I shrugged. "She was good." I suspected it had been my frequent flights from Toronto to New York that had tipped her off. Even though

I'd been assigned to watch London's father, Dr. Westbrook, I'd gone more often than necessary.

"And better now, I imagine. Or at least obedient."

Fuckin' bitch. I resisted taking my knife and gutting her. Instead, I chuckled, but it was harsher than I wanted and I suspected she knew she'd gotten to me. "Why did you do it?"

But I guessed the answer. Because I'd been with London. I hadn't just fucked her. I'd been with her for a week and Mother had found out and didn't like it. So, she wanted to destroy London, and she had succeeded. She'd stripped her dignity and left her broken, a shell of a girl with nothing remaining of the woman I'd been with.

Mother would've thought that was the end of it. Another girl lost in the sickening world of sex trafficking. Vault was rarely involved in that type of criminal activity, except to take out the individuals who became problematic. I volunteered for those jobs.

I'd never fuck a girl who was trained to please me and I certainly didn't get off on forcing one to suck my cock. I got off on a girl begging for it with desire smoldering in her eyes.

Mother tapped her finger on the top of the pile of papers. "You're a lot like your father. Intelligent and arrogant. Women are drawn to you… like this girl."

"London." She really had an issue with London.

She shrugged her slender shoulders draped in a black suit jacket. "Her name is no longer significant."

Fuck. They were going to kill her. I kept my face impassive, the way I'd practiced in the mirror a million times before when I was a kid.

A branch scratched against the stained-glass window to the right, and then I felt the slight breeze as the air leaked through the seams of the window. Still leaning against the desk, I crossed my ankles and lowered my head, appearing not to care about what she just revealed, but inside I was a crackling fire. The building rage played with my control, but if I reacted I would destroy my chances of getting what I needed from her.

"She must have been good in bed for you to come here and beg for her life."

I scoffed, shaking my head with a half-smile. "I don't beg."

I knew her all too well. The way her spine stiffened, indiscernible to most, but it was there all the same. Fuck, I'd been studying her gestures at every opportunity since the day she brutally killed my father in front of the Vault board members, my sister and me. It was that day I realized the core of her was far worse than an unloving mother. She was pure evil.

She'd shoved her knife up between his ribs and watched him die. And the entire time, her face remained the same—expressionless. But there was one thing that gave her away… the twitch of her right leg. She did it when she was upset. Not sad. My mother was incapable of sorrow; no, it had been disappointment in my father.

"Are you sure about that? Seems to me like you may… care about her."

She was suspicious, but I expected that. "She was an exceptional fuck."

That splintered her stone expression and she smiled. "I'd prefer if my son didn't end up like his father over a woman."

And there it was, why she hated me. I had parts of me that reminded her of him. My father fell in love with another woman, but that wasn't the only reason Mother killed him. It was just her excuse to kill him. She thrived on power and control and when she killed him, she took his place on Vault's board. Then everything changed.

No longer nine board members, but five. Two of whom she brought into the organization, Peter Dorsey and the man whose identity I had yet to figure out.

"Tell me, Kai, what makes a killer like you fuck a weak woman like her."

London was anything but weak; at least she wasn't until the violent and cruel men, Jacob and Alfonzo, broke her. It was time to end this bullshit. I had one chance at this and if I failed I was sealing London's fate. "Your cruelty knows no bounds, Mother. And it was stupid of you to ruin a potential asset. I told you she was valuable and to leave her alone, but you couldn't trust me."

She leapt to her feet, her composure breaking. "How dare you!" Her face contorted into the bitch sneer that always lay just beneath the surface.

I met her eyes, steady and calm. "I dare because you're getting old. And you made decisions based on assumptions." Her cheeks were red and her face a mask of fury, but this was exactly what I wanted, to turn the tables. "She is young and intelligent. A scientist whose father developed a drug you want more of. Sorry, you *need* more of. We agreed on this after she was brought back from that shit you put her through. We were going to have her take over for her father." It had been my only way to make certain London stayed safe. Make her valuable to Vault.

"She was useless after her… experience." I wanted to rip her cold heart out from her chest with my hand. London had been broken, destroyed, ruined after two years lost in that cruel world. "And I recall telling you to bring her in, but instead, you hid her away in a house we didn't know about."

I smiled because if I didn't, I was going to kill her before I had what I came here for. It was time for my ace. "Dr. Westbrook is dying of cancer." That got her attention. "Doctors give him six months. From my last visit, I'd say closer to three." The ruptured steadiness began to crumble as her eyes wavered from mine.

"Another scientist can easily take over his work."

"We could have used *her*," I said. "Why do you think I fucked her for a week instead of torturing her like you suggested? Why do you think I came to you and suggested we use her? You agreed. It was so simple and you fucked it up both times." I slammed my fist into her desk. "I needed her to finish school. I needed her sane. We *needed* her." I lowered my voice, pushed off the desk and stepped close to her chair. "But you always *need* to destroy and break when there are times we need to fuckin' cultivate."

"We will—"

I raised my voice. "I had her, Mother!" I took a deep breath and turned to look at the fireplace, feeling as if the flames were slowly eating away at my skin. "She trusted me. She would've done anything

I asked of her and you completely destroyed that. And for what? Because you were afraid I was getting too close to her?"

"You were. And you did," she replied, her voice quiet.

"I was fucking her. She was an acquisition. Torture isn't the only way to make people do what you want."

She was silent as she considered everything I told her. Whether to believe me or call me out. Perhaps even have me beaten until I broke, but there was nothing to break of me anymore and she damn well knew it. They'd already done their damage to me.

It took everything I had to remain standing where I was when all I wanted was to take the wire out of my pocket and wrap it around her throat; to watch her eyes bulge out of her head while she thrashed around struggling for air. I couldn't decide if it would give me more satisfaction though to plunge my knife up under her rib cage like she'd done to my father.

The farm made me numb to everything, including my sister, and the hate I had for my mother had lain dormant for years until I began to feel again. Until death suddenly mattered. Until a girl weaved her way into my heart and made it beat again.

I walked over to the fireplace where shimmering specks of light shone onto the white shag carpet laying before it. When I was a kid, before I was sent to the farm, before my father was killed, before Vault was on this path, I used to sleep beside the fire and listen to it crackle, and my father would read to me.

Now, I hated fire. I hated what it had almost killed.

I casually sat in the antique purple velvet chair, crossing my bent leg over the other and leaning back. I rested my hands on the padded armrests that had carved lions' heads at the base. My father used to relax in a chair like this in the evenings, although it was in England where we grew up before my mother sat on Vault's board.

His glasses would perch on the bridge of his nose, and he'd have to keep pushing them back while he read. He could be deadly, but he also had a lightness to him that made my childhood a little easier. He'd often sit me on his lap and talk to me about Vault and how it all started. A secret government that didn't follow the laws, but had laws of its own. Its purpose had been to take out individuals that governments couldn't due to laws, politics or resources.

But that had changed when Mother took over.

She would never admit to missing him, but I knew parts of her did. She had to because she made one fatal mistake the day she killed him—she *killed* him.

Instead of years of torture, she gave him mercy. He knew it, too. They were the last words whispered from his lips. I couldn't hear him, but I knew what he said, 'Thank you.'

But none of it mattered anymore. All of this was ending. I was taking out Vault's foundation and that included Mother.

"I don't like her."

I sighed. "You don't like anyone. And you're making this personal."

She turned and her heels clicked evenly on the stone as she walked over to the window. "It's too late. I told Brice to get rid of her."

Bile rose in my throat and my heart thudded against my rib cage. *Fuck. Fuck. Fuck.* Brice looked after Vault's Toronto house and was a cold son of a bitch. "A shame." *I'm going to gut you.* I stood and headed for the door like I didn't give a shit. Like I wasn't being torn apart inside by a dull, rusted blade.

"You really don't care about her? You were using her for Vault?"

I closed my eyes briefly before I turned and faced her. "No, I don't care. You taught me better than that. But like I've told you before, I would've utilized her brilliance."

It was like something flashed in her eyes, a greedy bead of hope for using another person for her own benefit. "And you believe she can take over her father's work? The girl was rather pitiful and didn't finish her schooling."

And whose fault was that? I had no idea if London could, but it didn't matter, none of this did. I was here to get my sister, Chess, out of prison, convince my mother London was valuable again so she'd drop any security on London's cell in Toronto, and to find out what I could on the farm as well as details about the anonymous board member. It didn't look like I'd get much out of her on the farm, or the board member, but there were other ways.

"Yes, I do. She's been working beside her father since she was able to hold a test tube. I wouldn't have gone to so much trouble for pussy, no matter how good it was. That was a mere bonus." It was my best lie yet and there wasn't even a flicker of suspicion in my mother's expression. "But you've had her imprisoned, and torture has a way of destroying the mind."

"Kai, you know the protocol. It's not torture. Merely methods to persuade that have been used for centuries." Torture. I knew them because I experienced them.

"And what do you need to persuade her for if your plan was to kill her?"

She laughed, a mild, frilly sound that didn't match her cunt attitude. "I'm certain you're aware, your loyalty was unclear. We required a test."

I fuckin' knew it. "And did I pass?"

"Not with flying colors, son." I couldn't stop the twitch in my jaw when she called me that. I wasn't her son; I was a product of Vault. "Regardless, the girl hasn't been touched in weeks. She was rather feisty until you saw her. What did you say to her?"

And of course Mother had looked at the security feed that day I went to the Toronto house to erase the email Tanner sent. I'd been walking down the dark, cold basement corridor when I heard her— London. I'd kept walking, even made it to the door, before I turned back. I had to see her even though I knew I couldn't get her out. That day destroyed me. What I had to say to her was worse.

Luckily, I'd been at an angle where the security camera feed wouldn't catch my expression. Because if she had seen the look in my eyes, London would be dead by now. "Exactly what she needed to hear." What I'd said to London had its purpose because I had no idea when I'd be able to get her out, and London... she had hope. Hope that had to be crushed.

"You better be right about her, Kai. The other board members might not be as forgiving as I am." I chuckled because she didn't even know what the word forgiving meant. "She trusts you. We can use that."

"Trusted. Past tense. She hates me now. But I can be very… persuasive." Love and hate were complete opposites; and yet they intersected so frequently, changing paths often until they collided and made one big mess as they became parallel and found peace within. With London, my path had never strayed, but hers had been tested again and again.

She walked over to her desk and sat. "I'll inform Brice of the change in plan. I want you both in France. I have the copies of her father's formula and she can start to work on the drug here once I have a laboratory set up. When I know she can do what we need, then I'll decide whether she is valuable enough to keep."

I listened, but remained impassive.

She typed on her keyboard, and with each tap of her long, slender fingers, she sealed her fate. "I'll lift the security on her cell."

Bitch. But exactly what I needed to know and one purpose for my visit. If I had attempted to use my fingerprint on London's cell weeks ago, the place would've gone into lockdown and an alert would've been sent out. A test and one of the reasons I'd had to come to France first. But each piece was falling into place. "So mistrusting. I've been loyal my entire life."

She failed to look up as she continued to type. "Yes. But women are a man's weakness."

Like my father. "And would you have sent someone to try to kill me if I failed your little test?"

"No, Kai. I'd have tortured the girl and made you watch. Then I'd have killed her. And you'd live the rest of your days with that image in your head."

Evil was too tame of a word to call her. "I don't have a weakness. You made certain of that." I kept my voice even and neutral as I set in motion the final plan. "I'll fly back this afternoon."

"Are you going to visit with your sister before you leave? I'm sure she'd be pleased to see you." I was doing a lot more than visiting. "I've allowed her some freedom and I think in a few years, perhaps she can be utilized again. Of course, the farmhands would have to make the final decision."

I hid the swirling anger with a soft chuckle as I walked back toward her then kissed her cheek, my eyes briefly going to the screen of her computer. Almost there.

"Mother, you know I don't give a shit about that traitorous bitch." The words were laced with a sneer, but it was a lie. If she knew I cared even the slightest for my sister, it would be used against me. I made a point to never ask about my sister and never attempted to see her.

She tsked, but by the way her blue eyes sparkled, she was proud of my words. She hit Send on her email and closed the lid on her laptop. "I've removed the security on her cell and Brice is expecting you."

That was all I needed.

It was done.

She reached over and put her slender hand on my arm. It was as if a shark latched onto me. My stomach curdled in disgust. In a slow, gentle caress, she ran her hand up to my shoulder and back down again. "And you're right. I grow weary. I'm hard on you because I have to be. I want you to be prepared for anything."

I was.

Emotionless.

Detached.

I'd slit the throats of men who had families. I'd destroyed lives. I'd been groomed to ruin and not care how I did it as long as the job was done.

But what Mother didn't know or understand was you never stole or harmed the girl belonging to a cold ruthless killer.

Flecks of who they made me into had begun to chip away the day I'd met London, and what leached inside me was a slow acting poison. One that ate the numbness, brought in the light when all I'd seen was dark.

I leaned closer to her, my hand on the back of her neck as I whispered in her ear, "Maybe I am like my father. Because I'm a man who *will* do anything for the woman I want." She tensed and the creases around her mouth accentuated as she frowned. "I wish I had more time to do this justice."

I had my hand out of my pocket and the piano wire around her throat before she had the chance to take a final breath.

She looked like a fish out of water, flailing against me as she struggled to breathe. I held the wire tight, no mercy, no feeling toward what I was doing. Her fingernails ripped her own fragile skin as she tried to loosen the wire.

Her legs gave out.

Her wild, horrified eyes went dead.

Her body fell limp.

I dropped her to the floor and put the wire back in my pocket. Then I crouched down beside her lifeless body. "London is mine and you fucked with that. Vault is going to pay for what it's done."

CHAPTER
ONE

Four Years, Seven Months Ago

London Westbrook

THE BROOM HANDLE dug into my back and the scent of bleach burned my nostrils. I'd knocked over the disinfectant spray bottle when I'd heard the voices and the pungent liquid leaked from the nozzle onto the tiled floor.

The storage closet door in my father's laboratory was ajar. I hadn't turned on the light when I'd come to grab a roll of paper towels, so I was partially concealed in darkness. That was if I stayed out of the stranger's direct line of sight. I prayed my drumming heartbeat or my ragged breathing suffocating behind my hands wouldn't give me away as I watched him glide his finger over the shiny surface of his knife. And it was not a butter knife. It was a six-inch blade with a serrated edge and it completely contradicted his look of a businessman as he held it in his hand in front of him.

The stranger casually strode closer to the closet then stopped a foot away. As I inhaled, the scent of his expensive cologne filled my lungs and I gasped. *Holy shit.* The familiarity of it sent a wave of comforting heat through me. I knew that scent. I'd never forget it, but it was obvious this man was anything but comforting or safe.

He wore an immaculate black suit with a light blue, pin-striped dress shirt that had the top two buttons undone. No tie, and for some reason that seemed appropriate, as if a tie would be too constricting.

He looked in his early thirties and probably over six foot two. From the way he carried himself, there wasn't an inch of him that wasn't muscled, although it was more toned than bulky. Regardless of the threat he conveyed, he appeared completely relaxed, as if he were caressing a kitten and not a deadly weapon.

I waited for him to see me. Hear me. To turn and throw the knife and pierce my chest to silence my racing heart. But what I was more concerned about was my father who was in the room with this guy.

God, Dad, what's happening? Who is he?

Ever since I could walk, I used to help my dad in the laboratory. Although, at that age, I wasn't much help, but my dad never seemed to mind. I knew the periodic table before I knew my times tables and was conducting experiments all through high school instead of joining any team activities. Science was my passion and there was nothing that drove me more than to experiment with different compounds and research the effects.

When I hit college, my workload became too heavy and I spent less time at my dad's laboratory and more time in the school's lab with my head in my books.

But lately, I noticed my dad appeared off—agitated and tired. I decided to drop in at the lab after seeing him at dinner on Sunday. He'd been pale with dark circles under his eyes and he'd lost a lot of weight. When I'd asked if he was feeling okay, he said 'of course,' then got up from the table having barely touched anything on his plate.

"They were rather… displeased with your last email." The stranger's smoky voice triggered shivers to trail down my spine and my toes to curl in my running shoes. His tone was calm with a hint of a British accent, almost bored sounding. But underneath, it was threaded with danger. I bit my lower lip so hard I tasted blood.

He tilted his head in my direction and I held my breath. I waited for him to kick the door the rest of the way open and drag me out. I prayed the shadows kept me hidden enough, but if he turned his head a little more….

He didn't. Instead, he tipped his head down to peer at his knife, causing a few strands of his dark russet hair to fall forward and brush his defined cheekbones. There was no question he was attractive, but if there was ever a time to use the idiom 'looks were deceiving,' it was now.

"It's delicate and the resources are difficult—" My father's voice cut off when the man abruptly interrupted.

"Excuses are not an option."

I had the urge to burst out of the closet with the broom and smash the guy over the head. But I'd never been a fighter and I sure as hell couldn't take on a guy like this. But no matter how senseless it would be to try to get a knife from a deadly man who obviously handled one like it was part of him, I was not going to stand here and do nothing if he went for my father.

I eyed my phone sitting beside the computer across the room. Even if I had it with me, he'd see the light on the screen the moment I pressed any buttons.

He lowered his knife to his side then slowly turned his head and his piercing green eyes locked on the closet. I quickly squeezed my eyes closed, afraid he'd see the whites of them blazing in the darkness. My muscles cramped as I tensed, fear seizing every nerve in my body.

Oh, God, don't see me. Don't see me.

I squinted to peek at him and was greeted by a mild twitch at the corner of his mouth as if… as if he knew I was here.

But he didn't drag me out; instead, I heard a mild chuckle as he walked away.

I opened my eyes and inhaled quiet gasps of air. The quivering in my body was so bad that the broom pressing into my back vibrated. I quickly stepped away and my legs buckled. I placed my palm on the wall for support while I looked at the shelf across from me, searching for anything that I might be able to use as a weapon if I needed to.

Shelves of paper towels. Containers of hand soap. Bottles of disinfectants. Where were the hammers and nail guns when you needed them? Shit, I'd have to resort to using the broom if necessary and no doubt get myself laughed at, then killed.

I stepped a few inches forward to peer out the door and saw him leaning up against the counter where there were several computers. He crossed his ankles and arms, the knife gone or at least hidden from my line of sight. My gaze hit the purple leather bag right beside him.

My purse. Shit.

Okay, it could belong to anyone. Except my dad would know it was mine. Had he seen it? Did he know I was here?

"Kai, please. I need more time to come up with that much."

Kai? I'd never heard my dad mention the name and I sure as hell never heard my dad's voice tremble before. He was always quiet and steady, solid. My mother had been the unstable and flamboyant one from what I remembered of her. She'd died in a fire when I was fourteen years old and her vast amounts of wealth were left to my dad, which he used to start his own lab. But he was never the same after she died, becoming more and more reclusive and spending most of his time in the lab while a nanny raised me.

"They're tired of waiting. You knew the deadline."

"Please." My father's voice rose with panic. "I need two more months."

"You've had years. Your time is up."

What? My father had been working on something for this man for years? How many years? Why? What was he working on? It had to be a drug, but what kind of drug?

Kai reached inside his suit jacket and removed his knife. My heart raced and I wanted to look away, but couldn't. With the tip of his blade, he put it under one of the straps of my purse and with a mild upward jerk, he cut the leather.

Oh, fuck.

He raised his chin and looked toward the closet, his brows rising with a slight grin. I heard my father sputtering on about testing, but the words were lost to the fear that skipped through me. My nails dug into the drywall as his gaze remained locked on the closet.

Striking was the word that came to mind when I looked at him. The second word was lethal. Intense, sculpted jaw and matching cheekbones—chiseled and flawless, just like his expensive suit.

There was an old world look to him that matched his confident expression. No, it was more than confident. It was fearless, as if he had nothing to lose, nothing could touch him. And even if I could by some miracle reach my phone and call the police, I suspected he'd merely laugh at the inconvenience of having to take his suit to the cleaners after killing anyone who tried to stop him.

But it was his eyes that captivated me, and wouldn't let me go. A deep jade that held amusement mixed with a dangerous glint, which completely contradicted one another.

And just when I thought he'd walk over and drag me kicking and screaming from the closet, he put his knife away and directed his eyes back on my father who I couldn't see. "You have one week."

My dad sputtered, "Kai, that's impossible. Please, you have to tell them I can't have it ready by then. Make them understand—"

Kai laughed and the sound was magnetic, as if his voice alone could kidnap you and make you do anything he asked. "Your misconception of the situation is rather amusing, Dr. Westbrook." He pushed away from the counter. "Have a shipment of the drug ready within the week."

I swallowed as his gaze turned toward the closet again and I leaned back further into the shadows, only able to catch a glimpse of the side of his face. My heart thudded so loud I swore he had to hear it.

"Walk out with me, Doctor." He moved out of sight and I nearly collapsed to the floor as every muscle relaxed and the trembling took over. Okay, he wouldn't hurt my dad, at least for now, and we could call the police and they'd deal with him. "You have a beautiful daughter by the way."

My head smacked into the wall. Oh, God, he had seen me. But how did he know I was Dr. Westbrook's daughter?

"Don't you dare touch her," my dad shouted.

My father never raised his voice in anger, he rarely became angry. He'd claimed the emotion was weak and failed to accomplish more than acting irrational.

Kai's voice lowered. "If this goes wrong, it won't be me touching her… unfortunately."

My breath hitched.

I heard the automatic door glide across with a hiss then close again.

I collapsed against the wall then slowly slid down until my butt hit the hard linoleum floor. His words repeated over and over in my head. 'It won't be me touching her… unfortunately.'

I waited five minutes for my father to come back, but he didn't, so I grabbed my cell and my purse with the sliced strap and left the lab.

As I passed familiar faces in the building, I asked if anyone had seen my father. No one had and my fear intensified with each rushed step out to my car.

I searched the parking lot for his silver Mercedes, but it wasn't in the usual spot. Did he go home? *Please, let him have gone home.* I jogged the rest of the way to my car, dialing my dad's cell for the fifth time, but it kept going straight to voice mail.

Dad, come on, pick up. But it was usual for him to have his phone off. That was why if I ever needed him, I just came straight to his lab because he was always here.

I lowered my phone and pressed unlock on the doors of my car. I glanced at my hand and saw the trembling. I was normally steady and calm like my dad, but there was none of that in me at that moment. I felt like a slow-burning firecracker ready to burst into sparks of emotions.

I jumped in the car and shut the door, tossing my purse and cell on the passenger seat, then leaned my forehead against the steering wheel as I tried to get back some of the calm that had been smothered by that man's haunting image.

I was good at figuring things out, connecting puzzle pieces, but none of this made sense. How could my dad be working on something for years and never say anything? Why would he work with a man like Kai?

I stiffened and froze as the hairs on the back of my neck rose like little warning soldiers and my heart skipped a beat.

Oh, God.

That scent. It was in my car. *Him.*

I slowly inched my hand toward the door handle.

"Not a smart idea," he drawled. "And I know you're a smart girl, London."

I jerked into action, diving for the handle with both hands, but his knife was under my chin before it unlatched. The emerging scream locked in my throat as I stilled, breathing harsh, chest rising and falling rapidly as I waited for the slice of the blade across my jugular.

"Start the car and drive nice and easy out of the parking lot."

The knife left my throat and I glanced in the rear-view mirror as he leaned back against the seat looking as if he were going for a ride to the grocery store. He didn't appear angry, merely annoyed at this inconvenience with his lowered brows and lips lightly pressed together.

I started the car and let it idle for a second as my brain calculated my options.

"Seatbelt, my dear," he said.

'Never let them take you to a second location' kept repeating in my head.

I reached over my shoulder and pulled the strap across my body. I pretended to fumble with the clip and tilted my head slightly to see if he was watching me. The bastard was texting. Texting. As if he were making dinner arrangements or chatting with a friend about the ball game.

I let the belt go and it hadn't even snapped back in place before I had my door open and one foot out of the car. He was halfway over the seat when his arm hooked my neck.

His grip wasn't strangling, but it was firm and I was forced back in the car. His icy words bit into me as he whispered in my ear. "You want your father to live?"

I swallowed and nodded.

He slid the flat side of his knife over my chin. "Good. So do I."

I swallowed and the pressure of the knife increased as he caressed my throat with it. I'd seen how easily it sliced my purse strap. I knew with little effort he'd cut open my delicate skin.

He released me and the seat leather creaked as he sat back again. "Shut the door and let's go for a drive."

"What do you want?"

"Oh, there will be plenty of time for questions, London."

The way his accented voice dragged out my name it was as if I'd heard him say it before. But it wasn't my name; he'd called me something else. But that was impossible; I'd never met this guy before and he wasn't someone you'd easily forget.

"Where's my dad?" Had he hurt him? Maybe that was why he didn't come back to the lab. My grip on the steering wheel tightened as did the ache in my chest at the thought.

"I suspect on his way home to pour himself a drink."

"My dad doesn't drink," I blurted. He hadn't touched alcohol since my mother died. I think it was because he felt responsible somehow for her death, although he wasn't. My mother was a heavy drinker and a careless smoker. According to the fire department, the carelessness killed her. But my dad took responsibility on his shoulders for everything.

I glanced in the rearview mirror and he met my eyes like he'd been waiting for me to look at him. The corners of his mouth curved up. "An intelligent man. But I already knew that." He leaned closer so his elbows rested on the back of my seat, lips inches from my ear as he whispered, "Drive, my brave little scientist."

How did he know I was a scientist? Or rather, studying to be one.

I slipped the gearshift into drive and slowly pulled out of the parking lot. The automatic gate arm lifted to let us pass and I wished there were old school security guards instead of the transponder on my dashboard.

So many thoughts whirled in my head. I could steer us into a tree and hopefully escape. That was if I didn't kill myself. Or if I went over the speed limit, maybe we'd pass a cop and get pulled over. Or I could....

"You're beautiful." His deep voice caused me to jump and the car lurched forward. "But when you're contemplating escape, it's rather... adorable."

Adorable? I didn't even think that word was in his vocabulary. "What do you want with my father?"

"Aren't you concerned about what I want with you?"

"No." I was, but he was so arrogant that I had no intention of giving him the satisfaction of knowing I was completely terrified of that exact thing.

I caught his reflection in the mirror and he grinned. For a brief second, a flicker of relief warmed me because his grin was mesmerizing. Not evil or malicious, it simply made him look engaging. And that was why he was even more dangerous—because it was deceiving.

"And you heard enough to know what I want. You're clever, London. Maybe even too clever for your own good. And, I understand, about to graduate with full honors in pharmacology and toxicology. Impressive. Following in your father's footsteps. I'd advise not to follow too far."

Whatever the hell that meant.

I glanced at my speedometer, slowly pressing on the gas and now going twenty over the speed limit. I needed to keep him talking so he didn't notice how fast we were going. "I'm going to be late for class."

"Classes are done for the day."

I stiffened. How the hell did he know that? "It's a yoga class."

He chuckled. "You don't take yoga."

Holy hell. Who was this guy? "Well, I didn't, but I do now." Of course, that was a lie, because I could barely touch my toes never mind curl into a pretzel.

"Mmm, I do believe you are lying, but I'll let it slide... for now." He moved and it was quick, agile like a sleek panther. Deadly. He had his hands on my shoulders, squeezing, but it wasn't painful. "Slow down and take the dirt path up there on your right."

Path? It was hardly a path, more like a parting of trees that led into the woods. All I could picture was my body being found in the middle of nowhere, ripped apart by wild animals. I wasn't ready to die. I wouldn't. I may not be a fighter, but I sure as hell would fight with everything I had to survive. "Are you going to kill me?"

He sighed. "You're letting your imagination run away with you. I have no intentions of hurting you—unless of course you hurt me first."

I inwardly huffed at the thought. I couldn't imagine anyone being able to hurt this man.

I did as he instructed and the car bounced as it crept along the wooded path until I saw another car parked ahead. "Pull up behind it, then give me your keys."

As soon as I did, he got out of the back seat, but didn't shut the door and I knew why, so I didn't lock him out. Not that it would stop him for very long as he had the keys.

I did have my cell though. I quickly reached for it just as he politely opened my door as if he were my date. "Out." He held out his hand to assist, but I ignored it. He took my hand anyway, his fingers curling around mine.

When I stood, I almost collapsed—my legs were shaking so badly. He must have noticed because he leaned me up against the car.

"Toss the cell back inside."

I gritted my teeth, but I did what he ordered and he shut the door.

"Don't move," he said.

He strode to his car, his expensive suit making him appear completely out of place in the middle of the woods. I glanced toward the road and wondered if I could make it before he caught me. He was wearing dress shoes and I was in my running shoes.

I could make it.

"My knife is faster than you," he said without even glancing over his shoulder at me.

Shit.

He opened his car door, bent and reached inside. I expected him to pull out a gun, but instead, he held a cell phone—another one. He'd had one in his pocket that he'd been texting on in my car. He tapped on the screen then placed it to his ear.

"He wants two months." He slowly walked toward me and with

NASHODA ROSE

every step closer, my heart pounded harder. "I know what I have to do." He stopped in front of me and so did my breath as I stared up at him.

God, there wasn't a flicker of uncertainty in him. It was like the world worked around him. He owned it. Owned me. Owned my father. Owned the bloody ground.

He stood inches away, his eyes locked on mine as he listened to whoever was on the other end. I couldn't hear what was being said and his indifferent expression failed to give away whether he was pleased or pissed off at their words.

"I have her already," he said in an abrupt tone, his eyes darkening. "I'll deal with the situation like I always do." He stiffened and his jaw clenched.

I licked my dry lips, refusing to look away, but the nerves in my body sparked off in warning. Of what, I wasn't sure of yet. And I think that was his intention.

He reached out and before I could move, his hand curved around the back of my neck, dragging me closer. I tensed as the warning sparks turned into emergency flares and my chest rose and fell erratically.

He scoffed then said into the phone. "He'll get the message."

His fingers tightened when I tried to move back and I winced under the pressure. The look in his eyes changed to amusement again as his hard, muscled body closed the space between us.

It pissed me off and I didn't care if he tried to kill me, I was running. I raised my elbow and hit his arm as hard as I could, dislodging his grip on my neck. I ducked and dove under his arm.

He dove for me, his fingers latching onto the sleeve of my shirt. The material gave to the pressure and ripped, but I was free.

I ran toward the road.

My heart slammed into my chest and I stumbled on my trembling legs. I was not a runner, but my life depended on me being one.

The sound of his footsteps chasing me was one I'd never forget. It was my life flashing before me. The choking reality that he would hurt me. That I may die. I waited for the pain of his knife to take me down. I waited for his body to tackle me to the ground. What I refused to wait for was to become some statistic. Some chick who didn't run, who didn't fight.

He was right behind me.

Oh, God.

His steps closed in and I heard his breathing.

Closer.

I choked out a scream as his arm hooked my waist.

"No. Let me go," I yelled as my legs continued to run even after he'd easily plucked me off the ground.

His arm tightened as his lips came up against my ear as he drawled, "Now, I respect you."

What? Was this guy fucked? I kicked backwards and for once, wished I had on heels as my running shoe hit his knee. He failed to flinch, but he did slide me down his body until I was able to stand again.

"I don't give a shit, asshole." I stomped on his foot as hard as I could then shoved my elbow back into his side, but he held me so close that it had no momentum behind it.

"I like you. But then I already knew that."

"Well, I don't like you."

He laughed. "I don't want you to. That would be dangerous for us both. Plus, my advantage would slightly diminish if you did."

What a bastard.

With his chest hard against my back, he guided me to the car. He was gentle as he pushed me against the side of it then bent and picked up his phone, which he'd obviously dropped when I ran.

Water dripped from the device and I bit my lip when I saw the shallow puddle it had landed in.

He wiped it off on his pants, fiddled with it a second then sighed. He opened up the backing and took out the SIM card then dropped the phone on the ground and smashed it with his heel. The plastic cracked under the force.

I glanced off to the side. Maybe I could lose him in the woods. I was smaller and—

"Run again and respect or not, my knife will be the one chasing you next time." He kicked his busted phone into the bush. "And I never miss my mark."

I raised my chin and crossed my arms over my chest. "What do you want with me?" I hesitated then added, "Kai."

He grinned when I said his name. It was a slow forming grin as if he was pleased with me. "I don't want anything from you." He paused as if waiting for me to do something. I didn't. "Except your complete cooperation, of course."

"Why are you doing this? Why are you threatening my father?"

"The less you know the better. Keeps you alive." I swear my heart dropped to the pit of my stomach. "And I'd prefer if you lived."

"Why? You obviously brought me out here for a reason."

"I did."

"Are you going to tell me?" Fear catapulted to another level while I waited for him to tell me, or not. Either way it wasn't good.

"I've been put in a difficult position." Did I care? Well, I did if it meant he had to kill me. "I wanted to keep you clear of this, but your father has made that impossible."

"If he says he needs longer for whatever he is doing for you, then he does. My dad doesn't lie."

"I never claimed he was lying."

"Then why not give him more time?"

He shrugged. "It's not my call." Then as if something came to him, a flash of amusement hit his eyes. "Perhaps, you can help him."

"Me?" I probably knew enough, but I had no intention of assisting in whatever illegal drug my dad was making. And I was pretty damn certain it was illegal and that was why he'd never mentioned it to me—for years. "I'm not experienced enough."

"Oh, I think you are, London." My breath hitched as he stepped closer so he was a mere arm's length away. God, he sounded so certain. What pissed me off was that he was right. I'd do anything to help my father. "And if he doesn't have something ready for us in a week, there will be consequences."

I stiffened. "What kind of consequences?"

"If I told you that, then you'd have time to prepare for the... unpleasantness."

Holy shit. What the fuck? Who was this guy? "Will you kill him?" My stomach lurched as I said the words.

He watched me for a second not saying anything and I held my breath waiting for his answer. "That isn't my decision to make."

I wasn't so sure about that. Kai seemed like the type of guy who did whatever he wanted.

I was calling the police the second he let me go. I didn't care what he threatened me with. He couldn't get away with this. Whoever he was or whomever he worked for, the police could deal with it and my dad and I could go in protective custody or something.

The warm breeze played with his dark, thick strands causing them to fall in front of his right eye. He didn't bother to push them away as his eyes narrowed in on me.

"I can see your brilliant mind working hard at trying to come up with something, but there is nothing you can do here. If you decide going to the authorities is a wise choice, then by all means. Except know it will snowball into something you and your father won't like. Consequences, London… and there is nowhere you can hide where you can't be found." He sighed. "I'd rather this end nicely for you."

My fingernails curled into my blouse so hard I heard a tear. I believed him. I believed every terrifying word out of his mouth. But I had to help my father. He was all I had left. No other family. No close friends since all I did was focus on school. I'd had my nanny, Lila, who lived with us after my mother died until I was eighteen. Lila hadn't been much of a communicator as her English was poor. But she loved to cook and let me do what I wanted, which was spend time with my head buried in my books. When I was eighteen and started university, she moved back home to Sweden and I never heard from her again.

"What will help him?" The man had to want something else.

"Nothing."

"Why the hell would you kidnap me only to tell me I can't do anything? Why bring me out in the middle of nowhere?"

"I knew the police would've been the second call you made after your father. As I said, that is not in your best interest and you needed to be warned of that. Besides, this is not a kidnapping, merely a business meeting."

I huffed.

He laughed, the green in his eyes lightening and a mild wrinkle appearing around them. I was betting he was one of those guys who became better looking with age, if that were possible; he was already very attractive—unfortunately.

All laughter left his face. "Be careful, London. You are a pawn in a dangerous game that can get you hurt. And when I say hurt, it is beyond anything you've ever imagined."

"Then why not just kill me now?" I shouted.

"I told you, I'd prefer if you lived."

"What am I supposed to do, damn it?"

"Nothing. You need to do nothing, London. That's the point. You mention this to anyone, including your father, this will not end well. I need you to stay as far away from this as you can." He tossed my car keys to me then said, "I can't protect you if you don't follow the rules."

Protect me? What was he talking about? And why the hell would he want to protect me?

He turned, walked to his car, and folded in. Not once did he look back at me. I could've had a gun in my car—which I'd never have as it was highly illegal—and shot him in the back, and it was like he didn't care.

Regardless, I wasn't a killer. I'd never held a gun, never threatened anyone, and I never would. My whole life was about studying science in order to help people. To save lives. I volunteered at one of the homeless shelters at least once a week. I'd even gotten to know a few of the less fortunate, those like Ernie who I saw every day near my building.

There had to be something I could do to help my father. Were they worried he'd not finish whatever he was working on? Why not give him the two months he required? And what happened when he was done? Would they kill him because they had what they wanted?

His car started and I had seconds to decide if what I was thinking was a good idea. But it was all I had. God, I knew nothing good could come of what I was about to do, but my dad's life was at stake and I'd do anything to help him. And despite what Kai said, I think he could make decisions if he chose to.

The car rolled toward me and I stepped in front of it. I almost dove out of the way when he didn't stop at first, and then at the last second, he slammed on the brakes. The bumper lightly hit my thighs sending me back a step.

The front windshield was shaded from the overhanging trees, but I caught a glimpse of his narrowed, piercing green eyes.

I stepped back as he got out of the car and shut the door—hard.

I stepped back again as he stalked toward me and didn't stop until he was inches from me.

He wasn't touching me, but it sure as hell felt as if he was. I went to back away a little more when he said, "You want to be brave then be fuckin' brave. Don't just piss me off."

Jesus. Warmth flooded my cheeks at his harsh words. I swallowed, my throat tight as I tried to get the next words out. "I think you *can* make the decision to give him more time."

He didn't say anything.

I swallowed the lump in my throat. "If you're worried he'll not finish whatever he is working on for you or he'll run away, then take me. Insurance until he finishes, then you let us both go."

By his widening eyes and lifting brows he appeared surprised, and no matter what I'd just bargained, that pleased me. Then any amount of confidence I had washed away when he laughed. His head tilted back and the husky sound echoed in the isolated woods. Birds scattered from the treetops and I didn't blame them. I would have liked nothing better than to fly away.

"What makes you think I want to fuck you? Or that you're worth it."

It was as if he hit me in the stomach with a baseball bat. "God, that's… that's not what I meant. I just meant keep me… until he's done."

"I know exactly what you meant," he drawled with a playful grin.

Anger blanketed any sensibility I may have had as I raised my hand and slapped him. He didn't move. Not even a jerk of his head from the impact. But his eyes narrowed and his lips pressed together in a firm line.

"You're an asshole. Do you enjoy scaring women? Bringing them out into the woods thinking that they are going to be raped and murdered? You're disgusting." I raised my arm to slap him again and he latched onto my wrist before I made contact.

"Stop pretending to be brave, London. I'm letting you go with a warning when my associates want something very different. Don't make me regret my decision."

My blood rushed through my veins as our gazes locked. "So, you *can* give him more time if you want?"

He didn't say anything, eyes driving into me. I *was* trying to be brave. God, I'd never been braver than I was right at that moment, but I was still terrified.

"Don't hurt my dad. Please. You can have me…" I briefly closed my eyes as I continued, "in any way you want."

His grip loosened on my wrist, but he didn't let me go. "I don't fuck unwilling women."

I stiffened. "I'd be willing. I'm willing."

He moved quick as he grabbed me by the shoulders, spun me around and shoved backwards a few steps until my legs hit the bumper and I fell back so I was lying on the hood of the car. I pushed up on my elbows to get up, but that was as far as I managed before he leaned over me, hands on either side of my head.

"Are you? Because I think you'd say or do anything to protect him. That's not willing. That's simply stupid."

I was stunned by his words because I saw it in his expression—the desire.

My palm stung like hell from the slap and yet I wanted to hurt him again. But I doubted this man could ever be hurt.

"If you give me time, I can get you money instead." I had a trust fund from my mother, but I'd need a few days to get access to the amount of money he'd want.

"Don't need money."

"What do you need then? There has to be something."

I heard him swear beneath his breath and the frustrating sound didn't suit him. He shifted his weight to one arm then raised the other so his hand came to my face. I tensed, but didn't move. He slowly stroked a finger over my parted lips. "Being with me… you don't know what you're bargaining."

I didn't, but sleeping with this man was a sacrifice I was willing to make. "I'm fully aware of what I'm bargaining."

He paused, watching me—assessing. "I'll consider it."

I breathed frantically in and out as the reality of what I was doing hit me. It was as if I couldn't find enough air. "And then you won't hurt him? Even after he gives you what you want?"

"No. I'll only hurt you, London." His tone was laced with amusement, as if he was kidding, but there was truth in what he said. Because what I offered would hurt me. But I'd repair. I'd forget. What I'd never forgive would be walking away and doing nothing.

"Can you get off me now?"

He didn't move.

I collapsed my elbows to lie flat on the hood of the car then placed my palms on his chest and shoved at the same time as I lifted my knee and tried to nail him in the balls. I failed. "I can't breathe, damn it. Get off."

"You've run from me, slapped me, and just attempted to knee me in the balls. I've killed for much less. I'm not a nice man, London. It's best for you to understand that now."

I had no doubt that he was ruthless.

"Hurt me then if that's what you want."

He laughed and I felt the rumble in his chest against mine. "You're extraordinary. And no, I don't ever *want* to hurt you…." He paused as if he had all the time in the world. "London."

Again, the way he said my name caused a wave of familiarity to filter through me and it wasn't fear I felt, but protected. How was that even possible?

My palms pressed into his dress shirt and I felt the hard contours of his muscles beneath the material. But there was far more than his hard muscles under my touch. There were raised lines, like welts or maybe scarring.

"I'll never lie to you, London. And I don't *want* you to fear me." His grip lessened when I stopped pushing at his chest, but instead of moving his hand away, his thumb casually stroked back and forth over the cleft in my chin.

I didn't understand him. Why did he care? He spoke as if he knew me and I felt…. Why did I feel like everything he said was true? "Well, you're doing a piss poor job of convincing me of that."

He sighed. "Perhaps that is for the best." He stroked a finger down my cheek.

I closed my eyes, unable to watch the satisfaction in his eyes when I said the words to try to negotiate the deal. "One night and you give him the two months he needs and promise not to hurt him."

"Hardly seems like a fair deal," he said.

I looked at him and met his laughing eyes with a glare. "I'm worth it."

He grinned. "I'll be the judge of that."

Jesus. What the hell was I thinking? He was toying with me and wasn't going to accept any deal. "Let me go." I struggled when he cupped my chin, fingers harsh.

"Shh, I'm merely teasing." His grip lessened when I stilled, but his brows were drawn low over his eyes, all amusement gone. "One week. And he'll get his two months."

"And you won't hurt him."

"He won't be harmed." He paused, frowning. "But let's be clear here. This is your choice."

Oh, God. How could I be with this man when he was threatening my father? Maybe I should've let him drive away. How did I even know anything he said was true? I had nothing except his word.

But there was something more to Kai. I couldn't put my finger on it, but it was the same feeling I had when I first smelled his cologne while in the closet. "How do I know you're telling the truth and you won't kill us both?"

He leaned forward until his mouth was so close to mine I could taste the scent of him on the tip of my tongue. A scent I recognized from a night I'd nearly died.

"I'll always look out for you, braveheart," he whispered.

I gasped, eyes widening, fingers tightening in his shirt, heart racing. Oh, my God. Oh, my God. It was him. He'd called me that.

It was like my mind was on rewind as the memory came whirling back. I'd been lying on the cool damp grass coughing and sucking in fresh gulps of air. My mind a fog, vision even foggier as I struggled to breathe. A shadow of a man leaned over me as he swept my hair away from my face with the tip of his finger. My eyes flitted open for a brief second, but everything was hazy and dark.

It was him.

I stared up at Kai, my mouth gaping. "It was you." He scowled and started to draw back, but my fingers held onto his shirt. "It was you that night. You pulled me from the fire."

He grabbed my wrists and clamped down on them so hard I was forced to let his shirt go. He pushed away from me.

I darted upright. "You called me braveheart. I remember." The smell of his cologne. The sound of his voice. But it was him calling me braveheart that triggered the connection. "You said…. Oh, my God, you'd said you'd always come for me." What had he meant? Come for me when? Why?

My mind spun out of control as the memory continued to replay. The fire was in the house I shared with five other students during my second year of university. It was deemed an accident, faulty wiring in an old house. We all got out in time, except I should've been dead. I'd passed out from all the smoke in my bedroom upstairs. All I remember was waking up on the neighbor's grass with a man on his knees beside me. It was pitch dark and I couldn't see his face, but I remembered the scent of his cologne mixed with smoke. And then his words when he said, "I'll always come for you, braveheart."

I thought I'd imagined him. The smell. Those words.

I'd dreamed about those words for months. I'd dreamed about this man—Kai. *Holy Jesus.*

I stared at him, my heart racing, emotions sparking off in every

35

direction. He terrified me, threatened my father, was not a good man and yet... he was. He'd saved my life. Why would he do that? Why had he been watching me? "I don't understand."

"There is nothing to understand. Go home, London." The air around him was dangerous, as if the moment you stepped close enough there was no escape from him and what he wanted.

He strode back to the driver's door and opened it, his form elegant and at ease again. Casually, he took off his suit jacket and tossed it inside his car. "I'd advise keeping our little meeting from your father and the police. I'll be in touch."

"Our... our deal?"

He didn't turn around as he said, "Anything for you, braveheart." He bent his tall frame into the luxury car and shut the door and then, while I stood to the side of the path, he drove away.

I watched until the car turned onto the road and disappeared before I dove into my car and found my cell between the console and the seat. I tapped my code then dialed the police, his license plate embedded in my mind.

"Nine one one. What's your emergency? ... Hello?"

Shit.

"Sorry, I hit the emergency button by mistake."

I hung up.

CHAPTER TWO

London

I JERKED UPRIGHT, THE pale green sheet slipping from my
shoulders and pooling at my waist. My heart raced and my skin
was flushed from the vivid dream—of him. Kai.

Three nights.

Three nights haunted by dreams of him. Sometimes he'd be holding me, gentle and sweet, and other times, he was terrifying as he held
a knife to my throat. There were parts of me that believed Kai saved
me from the fire because there was good in him. That he wouldn't hurt
my father or me. That maybe Kai wasn't as bad as I thought.

"Jesus. I've lost it." What was I thinking? He had a knife. He held
it to my throat. He worked for people who were obviously dangerous.

And he hadn't been in contact in three days. I was worried he'd
decided to forgo the deal. What then? What would happen to my father?

I'd called my dad numerous times a day, trying to sound normal while inside I freaked out. Kai had given him a week, that was if he decided not to take my deal. That meant my dad was safe for four more days. But it didn't stop my anxiety. Everywhere I went, I constantly looked over my shoulder, wondering if Kai was behind me or around the next corner; if he was watching me.

God, I was driving myself crazy.

Outside was dark, but the moonlight filtered through the sheer white curtains into my loft. It was an open-concept apartment with fifteen-foot ceilings, exposed ducts, brick walls and no partitions except for the bathroom. My father had insisted I live in a secure, newer building after the fire, so he bought the loft, which was within walking distance to school. An investment, he'd said. I'd argued that it was too much even though he had the money. He'd pointed out the fact that I was on scholarship from all my hard work in high school and he hadn't paid for my university.

And I loved my loft. It was close to school in a small, six-story, quaint building with security guards, and was quiet so I could study.

Not wanting to go back to sleep and slip into another Kai dream, I slid my legs over the side of the bed to get up and that was when it hit me. His cologne. The scent I'd never forget. Never. It lived inside me, whether I wanted it to or not. Now that it was connected to Kai, it made it that much more powerful.

And it lingered in the air.

I quickly flicked on the bedside light then stood, letting the sheet drop. I wore my usual boxer shorts and a spaghetti-strap pink night-shirt, but suddenly I felt... exposed.

Numerous emotions flooded me all at once. Fear took the lead, but a close second was the fact that my body was hyperaware of him. After three nights of dreaming about him, thinking about him, the heightened awareness amplified.

I stepped off the platform my bed was perched on and the hard-wood creaked beneath my bare feet. The sound echoed in the silence and I shivered as my eyes scanned my loft.

Had he been here and left? But how could he get into my place?

I listened for movement, while my gaze searched the shadows. My pulse throbbed beneath the thin layers of skin on my wrists and throat as I waited for the moment I saw him.

But there was no sign of him and the only sound was the streetcar squealing on the tracks outside my open window.

I walked into the kitchen, my heart finally settling back to a quiet rhythm. I reached into the cupboard and took out a glass then set it on the counter. Maybe the stress was making me imagine things. I was on the sixth floor, and we had security. There was no chance he could get into my loft without me knowing.

I laughed to myself as I opened the fridge and the blaring light flickered once before it turned on. I leaned over and shuffled containers around until I found the orange juice. I pulled it out, stepped back and went to close the fridge with my foot when hands settled on my hips.

I screamed, the juice carton slipping from my grasp and landing on the floor. The orange liquid splattered the stainless steel fridge and pooled at my feet.

My pulse raced and nerves sparked. His scent was magnified a hundred times stronger as he stood directly behind me, his breath a warm caress against the back of my neck. Goose bumps were having a field party.

"Kai."

"Mmm," he murmured next to my ear. "Were you expecting someone else?"

The fridge suctioned closed and with it, the light it offered. "No."

"Good to hear." His grip tightened on my hips and my breath hitched when one of his fingers slipped beneath the elastic of my boxers and made contact with my skin.

Holy shit. I stopped breathing. Why did I feel something? No, it wasn't just something. It was my body reacting to his touch, liking his touch.

I swallowed. "My father? You'll give him the time he needs?"

"Yes."

"And you won't hurt him even after he hands over whatever he is working on for you."

"He won't be harmed."

"How do I know you're telling the truth?" Because the reality was, Kai could tell me anything he wanted and it could all be a lie.

"I told you, I'd never lie. At least not to you." His finger stroked back and forth over the tiny inch of skin that was exposed to his touch.

"I think you'd say whatever you needed to in order to get what you wanted."

His chest vibrated against my back as he chuckled and the sound trickled through me like a heated waterfall. "True. But with you... just the truth." His voice lowered. "Unfortunately, you won't always like what you hear, braveheart."

I tensed, heated waterfall gone. "And why am I the lucky one to be honored by your honesty? You don't know me." But maybe he did? I had no idea how much Kai knew about me, and he'd saved my life. He'd been at the house that night. He'd somehow made it to the second floor of a burning house and carried me out. No matter how dangerous he was, this man risked his own life to save mine. And it made me feel... secure in his arms. It made me feel protected.

It was such a contradiction. *He* was a contradiction.

He pushed me forward so my palms lay flat on the cool, smooth surface of the humming fridge. Chilled orange juice pooled between my toes and there was a mild stickiness on my legs where the splatters landed.

"Oh, but I do."

"You've spoken to me once."

"Perhaps. Yet, I've known you for years."

I tried to turn around, but his hands locked down on my hips hard and he used the fridge and his body to keep me from moving. "Kai?" My voice trembled when I said his name and I knew he had to have heard it.

"Shh." He ran his hands down my naked arms until his hands curled around my wrists. Then he slid my arms to either side and above my head.

"Kai...."

He pressed his body into mine so I was between the humming fridge and the heat of his body. It was a weird sensation of the vibrating fridge against my front and his hard warm body against my back.

Holy shit. I could barely breathe and every time I did, my breasts pressed painfully into the hard surface. My head to the side, cheek against the fridge and all I saw of him was the sleeve of his white dress shirt, cuff unbuttoned and rolled once.

"Do you want this?" he asked.

No, my mind screamed and yet my body screamed something else entirely.

"Do you?" he repeated.

"I… I don't know." I was confused by my body's reaction to him. The fear lingered, but since finding out about the fire, it was intermeshed with other emotions.

"If there was no deal, would you want me? Do you want me?" he drawled.

Did I? Yes. I wanted the man who had held me in his arms and told me he'd always come for me. I wanted him. I'd always wanted him. "Yes," I whispered.

"Good. Then this is day one," he murmured against the back of my neck as his lips made contact.

"Please. Tell me… I need something to make this… okay." Nothing would make this okay. I knew that. This was a deal and I was trading my body for my father's safety to a man who was obviously dangerous.

It was just sex. That was all.

But no matter what I told myself, I knew sex with Kai was more than the act. I felt it the second my body reacted to him and my mind fought him.

He suckled on the lobe of my ear and desire spread like wildfire. "You're safe with me. Always."

"And if I don't believe you?" But the fucked-up part was that I did believe him.

He pulled back slightly, just enough so I no longer had the heat of his body against me, but still felt the closeness. "That's up to you. But your body trusts me and if there is one thing in life you should trust, it's your body."

He released one of my wrists. Brushing my hair aside from my neck, he replaced the touch of his finger with his mouth. His lips trailed a path of gentle, light kisses of heat over my skin and some of the tension left my body.

"What if my body is wrong?" I closed my eyes and curled my hands into fists, unable to move. Afraid to. Wanting to.

"Your body doesn't know how to be wrong. The only lies are the ones your mind feeds it."

"I'm scared," I admitted.

"I'll make it go away, baby." He leaned back into me and with him came comforting heat. "Are you wet for me, London?" he whispered.

"Yes." It was humiliating. Degrading. Because I *was* wet and it was for a man who was threatening my father. I hated myself, but he was right, my body told the truth.

"Then you have nothing to fear." He ran his hand down my side while he continued to gently kiss the crook of my neck. "I can't wait to taste you. The silky wetness on the tip of my tongue, the sweet scent of you as I lick your pussy."

"Jesus." I hadn't meant to say it aloud, but it was erotic. I'd never had any man speak to me that way. My belly swirled and the clench between my thighs ached for what his words declared.

He toyed with the thin strap of my top then kissed the spot, his tongue circling before his teeth nipped, only to ease the pain with his tongue again. He moved to the other shoulder and did the same thing.

The second his hand splayed over my abdomen desire shot through me and I had to clamp down on my lip to stop myself from gasping and arching back into him.

"Don't hide from me. Show me what you're feeling."

I couldn't. It was a betrayal of who I was. It was wrong. I shouldn't enjoy any part of it.

His hand slid up beneath my shirt and hesitated just below my breast, his finger trailing a path under the crease. My nipples hurt. They burned for his touch. *I* burned for his touch.

But he wouldn't. He moved to the other breast and continued to draw paths of heat just below my breast. I had no control as I curved into him, my head dropping back onto his shoulder.

"Oh, God, Kai." It slipped out, but I couldn't help myself. I needed him to end the torture. With the vibration of the fridge and him behind me, his cock pressed into me, his teasing… My body won the battle.

"Yes," he whispered. His hand cupped my breast, finger flicking over my erect nipple causing my body to shudder. "That's it. Let me have all of you, London."

I tensed, jerking my head up straight and he immediately pinched my nipple until I cried out.

"Let go," he ordered. The pressure on my nipple increased the pleasure, sweet pleasure as he eased the pain with gentle circling.

"I need you right now. I need to sink my cock inside you." His hand went to the elastic band of my boxer shorts. "And this is the last night you'll wear clothes to bed." He backed away for a second while he tugged my boxers down. "Lift." I lifted one foot then the other. He walked away, and I shifted to turn when he said, "Don't move."

It was said with a casual air, another order, yet there was gentleness in his tone. Regardless of how he said it, I wasn't going to move. I glanced over my shoulder at him and saw him open the cupboard below the sink and toss my boxer shorts into the bin.

His brows rose when he met my eyes as if daring me to object. I didn't.

I noticed he was wearing jeans with his dress shirt and it almost gave him a sexier appeal. The suit had been sexy, too, but this made him more… approachable, if that were possible. His hand went to the button of his jeans and I heard it pop as he undid it.

I watched as he unzipped them next and the material parted making a V. Shit. A man, a hot sexy man, with snug faded jeans low on his hips was mouthwatering. But add in jeans undone, it was sexy as all hell that surpassed all other levels of hotness.

I had my hands still above my head on the fridge, my bottom half naked, my body tingling with anticipation and a sexy, and yet still scary, man a foot away from me.

A man I knew was dangerous. A man who could hurt my father. A man who I had no misconceptions had killed another human being at some point. But he was also the man who saved me. That I'd dreamed about holding me in his arms. Who had held me in his arms.

"Stop thinking. I know that's difficult for a brilliant mind like yours." He smiled and I couldn't help but admire the beauty in him when he smiled. But I definitely didn't feel any of my brilliance coming into play when it came to this man.

With each step toward me, his jeans opened a little more and I caught a glimpse of the fine trail of hairs leading down to his cock. When he reached me this time, he didn't press against me. Instead, he ran his hands down my back to my butt where he squeezed. "Mmm…. Perfect," he murmured.

I'd been with a few men, but nothing was like this. God, I'd only had sex on the floor and in bed before.

Kai slid his finger down and I stiffened.

"A virgin ass." It was a statement and the correct one.

His finger circled my sensitive puckered flesh and I was about to wiggle away, but he must have sensed my discomfort because he curved his arm around my waist, keeping me still. "Shh, relax. I won't go there until you're ready. And you're not ready." He continued to stroke the area until I slowly relaxed. "That's it." He trailed his finger down further into the wetness and then back up again.

I moaned. I couldn't help it as he played with me, my body needing more, aching for it.

I rested my forehead against the fridge as quivers shot through me. I panted with need for him to be inside me. I hated myself for it, but there was no going back. I needed him desperately.

He suddenly grabbed my hips, turned me to face the granite island opposite the fridge and shoved me against it. "Bend over. Hands above your head."

His hand came down on the back of my neck as if to make sure I followed his orders, but I didn't need guidance as I lay over the counter, my hands able to just reach the opposite side and curl around the lip.

"You have to use…." I stopped when I heard the plastic rip. I peered over my shoulder and saw him rolling on a condom.

He glanced up at me, brows raised. "I'll always look out for your best interests, London."

He moved in and I gasped when his cock slid back and forth through my wetness. He kept one hand on my neck, a firm grip with strands of my hair wrapped around his hand.

"I'm going to fuck you. And I want to hear you scream when you come and I won't stop until you do." He leaned over me. I couldn't see his face, but I felt his breath against my ear as he said, "And I can fuck you for a very long time."

The weight of his body left me, but not his hips as he placed his cock at my entrance. I expected him to thrust hard inside me, but it was agonizingly slow, inch by inch, as if he wanted to savor the first time his cock slid inside me.

My grip on the counter intensified and I bit my lower lip so hard I tasted blood. It was frustrating the way he did it so slowly and yet it was sensual, too. His hand left my neck and slid down my back across to my hip where he tightened his hold. He was deep inside me and hadn't moved. It gave me a minute to adjust to his size and yet, at the same time, I was sparking with need. A need so intense that I pushed back against him.

"Not yet." He ground his hips against me in a circular motion, his cock buried deep.

"Yes, yet," I said.

He chuckled and put his other hand on my hip. His fingers dug into my flesh painfully, perhaps a warning as to what was to come.

And it was.

He pulled out then thrust back into me, hard. Once. He stopped and I waited for him to do it again, but instead, he rotated his hips while sunk deep, his hands keeping me in place.

"Fuck, you feel good." He glided out then shoved inside again. My fingers curled around the edge of the island kept me in place as he thrust.

In. Out. Hard. Slow. Gentle. Never knowing what was next until my body screamed for him to just fuck me. I throbbed. Pulsed. But when I moaned, that was when his hand came between me and the counter and he played with my clit.

"Oh, God," I panted. "Kai."

He groaned and thrust faster, harder to match his finger flicking back and forth. My body trembled and shook until it reached the pinnacle.

Then my body tensed.

Clenched.

Quivered.

And I screamed as he made me come apart. Waves of pleasure shot through me.

I released the edge of the counter and my body rubbed back and forth on the hard smooth surface as he continued to thrust inside my sated body until he groaned, shoving hard into me one last time.

He stopped.

Everything stopped.

I lay silent and still, his hands no longer holding my hips, only his pelvis against my ass and his cock jerked a few times as it throbbed deep inside me.

He pulled out and I heard the roll of the condom as he took it off. Then his footsteps before the cupboard opened and the bin lid opened and closed.

I straightened and went to grab my boxers, but remembered he'd thrown them out. I wanted to dart for the cover of the washroom, but pride wouldn't let me. I wasn't running from my own choices. I never had and I wasn't starting now.

I'd fucked him.

This was my deal.

I made that choice.

"Go shower, London." He leaned up against the counter, his jeans zipped but the top button undone. His shirt was rumpled, but he still looked like he could walk out the door and attend an opera.

I reached for the dish cloth hanging over the tap to clean up the orange juice, but his hand latched onto my wrist. "Do what I tell you."

My spine stiffened and I was about to tell him to go fuck himself when he gently eased the dish cloth from my hand. "Are you going to be here… after?"

His eyes locked on mine and they were cold, unlike anything I'd seen in him before. Shivers raced through me and my stomach dropped. The fear that had been extinguished by the lust came alive again.

Those piercing green eyes were the ones his victims witnessed before he… killed? Tortured? I didn't know. Maybe both. Probably both.

Jesus, I'd had sex with a killer.

His brows rose as if he knew exactly what was racing through my mind.

I was going to be sick. I spun around, ran into the washroom and slammed the door.

CHAPTER
THREE

London

HE WAS GONE by the time I came out of the shower. The orange juice had been cleaned up and my washing machine was running. I walked over to the laundry closet and opened the doors. My green sheets from my bed were covered in suds, swishing back and forth in the circular window.

Why would he wash my sheets? I glanced over my shoulder at my bed and saw the spare white sheets now perfectly fitted onto the mattress. He had even neatly folded down the duvet on the side of the bed I always slept on.

I could somewhat understand why he'd put the sheets in the wash if we'd had sex on the bed, but we didn't. He'd obviously gone through my stuff to find the extra ones, then took his time fluffing up the pillows and tucking in the sheets.

I noticed the noise from the city streets was gone and realized he'd closed my bedroom window. I always slept with it open. I had since the fire.

I remembered the panic of yanking up on the window that night and it wouldn't budge. I struggled and struggled until I collapsed on my knees as the lack of oxygen became suffocating. With the hallway engulfed in flames there'd been no other way out. I'd crawled across the floor to my desk chair thinking I could use it to smash through the glass.

I never made it.

I should've died.

Ever since that night, I've slept with the window open. I'd never be trapped again.

I walked over to the window to open it and a small piece of paper, which had been wedged between the window and the sill, fluttered to the floor. I bent and picked it up.

I'll always come for you.

My breath stopped as I stared at the neat handwriting. Kai.

I peered out the window then turned and searched the shadows of the loft for any sign of him. But I felt the emptiness. Kai's presence filled a room and that feeling was gone, just like him.

Relief and disappointment rolled into a tight little package in my head. Logically, I was glad one night was done, yet the illogical side, which was my body, hung on to disappointment that one night was done.

I crumpled up the note and tossed it in the trash, then walked to my bed, placed a knee on my mattress about to crawl into bed then hesitated. My gaze dropped to the crisp white sheets. Sheets he'd run his hands over while smoothing out the creases. Sheets his strong hands had gently tugged on before he tucked the excess material under the mattress. Sheets his palms caressed like he'd caressed my body.

Damn it.

I backed away from the bed, grabbed a throw blanket from the chair in the corner, walked to the couch in the living room, and flicked on the TV. I curled up into a ball and watched an old black and white movie until I finally fell asleep.

I woke with a cramped neck and the enticing smell of coffee.

Coffee?

I threw off the blanket and jerked upright. My nose guided my eyes to the brown paper bag and steaming coffee cup, which sat on the granite island right where I had lain hours ago while Kai thrust inside me.

I stood and walked over to the counter. No note. But I knew it was from him, although how he broke into my loft twice now was concerning. I'd have to speak with security.

I opened the bag and the scent of a freshly baked cinnamon croissant wafted into the air. It was my favorite from the bakery a block away.

How did he know it was my favorite? How did he know that was where I went every morning before classes and picked up my coffee and croissant? But it started to make sense. Kai did know me because he'd been watching me.

I shivered, rubbing my bare arms. Why would he do that? I could understand my father, but why me?

I crumpled the bag closed and shoved it away.

I didn't like it. I didn't like any of this.

But last night… I'd enjoyed it. Last night, he'd broken down my defenses. Last night, he'd made my body his.

My gaze caught the blaring yellow on the microwave. Crap, it was already nine and I had a lab in fifteen minutes.

I quickly brushed my teeth and hair, threw on my jeans and a T-shirt and was ready in five.

I grabbed the coffee and brown paper bag, my laptop, and ran out the door. As I passed the security guard, Derek, I said, "I need to talk to you later."

"Sure thing, Miss Westbrook."

I hurried out of the building then down the sidewalk one block. I stopped at the corner where the homeless man sat with his empty cup begging for money. He was talking to himself like usual, and without looking up, he held out his paper cup.

"Change for a…?" He tilted his head and his eyes met mine. He smiled. He had perfect white teeth which was unusual for many of the homeless living on the streets. "Mornin', beauty." I'd told him my name several times, but he never used it.

I held out the paper bag with the croissant and steaming coffee. "Morning, Ernie." I bought him a coffee from the bakery every morning since I moved here after the fire.

His bushy salt and pepper brows lowered as he gave me a puzzled looked. He set down his empty cup and took the coffee and paper bag from me. "I was right here. Know I didn't miss you walkin' by earlier."

I laughed. "Don't worry. You didn't. Someone bought these for me," I explained.

He nodded with his lips pursed together as if he were thinking about something. Ernie was an attractive man, maybe late forties, but it was hard to tell with the layer of dirt on his face and hoodie he wore. Weird thing was his fingernails were always clean, except I'd noticed his hands were calloused as if whatever he used to do for a living had been rough on his hands.

The man rarely said much to anyone except the same sentence

over and over again, 'Change for a coffee.'

His eyes locked on me before he said, "Be careful, beautiful."

And that was it. He went back to rocking and holding out his cup to others who passed by and ignored me. I wondered what he meant, but Ernie could be cryptic with his words. Once he'd told me to 'Stay away.' I didn't know what he meant, but the next day he was across the road and when I started toward him, he began ranting and raving about a devil following him.

"I will. See you tomorrow," I said then jogged across the street before the light changed, not bothering to go to the bakery and getting something for myself.

All day.

All day I was distracted thinking about Kai. I never saw him watching me, but maybe he was. Maybe I'd been so oblivious to my surroundings that Kai had been following me for years?

I did hope he'd seen me give away the coffee and croissant this morning. It was my statement that I wanted nothing but to fulfill my part of the deal. It was a small inner victory on my part yet if he had seen, I was pretty sure he wouldn't care.

When I came home from school, the thoughts of Kai magnified. I paced my loft, pasta left untouched on the kitchen counter, bottle of red wine almost empty. Sleep eluded me, while my body betrayed me and my mind sparked with all kinds of irrational thoughts about him. I realized that any control I thought I had over this situation was false.

Kai controlled it.

Every sound made my heart leap as I waited for him. I was curious as to how he got in last night and again early this morning, and the security guard Derek wasn't at the front desk when I came home from school, so I hadn't been able to ask him if he'd let Kai in.

Would Kai knock if he knew I was awake? No, I couldn't imagine

Kai asking for permission to do anything.

It was two in the morning when I realized he may not come at all. We'd agreed upon a week, but we'd never discussed if it had to be seven days in succession. God, was he going to drag this out for months? Slip into my loft once a week… me never knowing when.

My breathing picked up at the thought. Because no matter what my mind tried to fight against, he was right. My body knew the truth and it craved his touch.

I climbed into bed, tipsy from too much wine because I rarely drank. I punched my pillow until it indented then curled my hands under my cheek and finally drifted off to sleep.

I moaned, parting my legs further as the sweetness of his cock pressed into me, slow and gentle, agonizingly slow. I arched my back, tilting my hips to meet him. His scent filled my lungs with every ragged breath.

"Kai," I whispered.

"Mmm."

My eyes flashed open to the deep, graveled sound of his voice right next to me and I met Kai's piercing green eyes.

He was fully clothed, lying on his side with the sheet pulled back and his finger lightly caressing the spot just above my breasts.

I was so shocked, I froze for a second, my heart racing to match my breath. "What are you doing?"

"Waiting for you to wake up."

Oh, my God. How long had he been here? And I'd been dreaming about him. Heat burned my cheeks at the thought of what I'd been dreaming.

He moved, quick and agile as he straddled me, hands grabbing my wrists and pulling my arms above my head and locking them down. He tilted his head toward me, and his lips gently kissed where his fingers had been moments before.

His hard thighs clamped my hips and with his weight there wasn't a chance of getting him off me if I wanted.

"Kai, please. I don't like this." It was scary to wake up with him in my bed. I had no time to get ready for him and it wasn't a 'put on makeup and look nice' get ready, it was get ready as in prepare my mind, so I had some control over what was happening. Instead, my mind was still groggy from sleep and my erotic dream.

He loosened his grip on my wrists, but he didn't release me. "You will, baby. I promise." He bent and licked my nipple through my T-shirt. "I want you naked when I come to your bed."

"I can't. I can't sleep naked." I hated it. After the fire, I wanted to be ready. Be prepared to escape if I needed to.

He raised his head and looked at me. The moonlight revealed the left side of his face, unshaven for a couple days, with brows low over his eyes—contemplative. But there was the intensity of a blazing fire of desire in the glass pupils staring back at me.

It set me aflame to see that and my body relaxed into him. He must have noticed because he let go of my wrists, then took hold of the bottom of my T-shirt and slowly pulled it over my head and tossed it on the floor.

"There is no debate here, London. Until we're done, you'll be naked when you slip beneath the sheets." He cupped my chin, so I was forced to meet his penetrating green eyes. "And if you give away what I buy for you again, I won't hurt you, but I will most assuredly hurt them."

I gasped, eyes widening as fear scintillated into me. "You didn't…." Oh, God. Ernie. "Please, you didn't hurt him."

"That was a warning."

He didn't say anything more and instead, took my nipple in his mouth again. I couldn't react. I was freaked out, scared at what I'd gotten myself involved with. Scared he'd hurt a defenseless man because I'd given him the coffee and croissant.

I lay still as he trailed kisses to my other breast. My body reacted to his kisses, his touch, but my mind was elsewhere.

"Fuck." He pushed away from me and climbed off the bed. He tossed the sheet aside so it went up in the air like a parachute catching the air then collapsed on top of me as the air suffocated beneath it.

I stayed where I was, not looking at him, but I heard him stride across the room then the light to the washroom blared and the tap turned on for a minute then shut off.

I sat up as the light turned off again and his bare feet padded back toward the bed. I bit my lower lip when I saw his narrowed eyes and dipped brows. Angry. And he'd obviously washed his face because moisture clung to his skin. Water from a few strands of hair near his forehead trickled onto his shirt.

"Get up."

I jerked at his harsh voice. I grabbed the sheet and held it to me like it was a shield against his anger.

"Do you want to find out what I'm like when I'm really pissed off?"

I didn't. I really didn't, but everything in me rejected the idea of being ordered around. My dad thought my stubbornness was cute. But at this moment, my stubbornness was going to get me hurt or worse, killed. No. That wasn't true. No matter how dangerous Kai was or what this was, I knew there was something in him that was good. That Kai wouldn't hurt me... at least not physically. Emotionally, I wasn't so confident.

I swallowed my pride and stood, taking the sheet with me.

"Leave the sheet."

I clamped my teeth together and dropped it. I stood half-naked in front of him.

I raised my chin and refused to cover my breasts with my hands as I faced him. His eyes flicked over my chest for a second before he held out his hand. When I didn't take it immediately, his brows raised in warning.

I put my hand in his and he led me into the living room. He lowered onto the couch, his back against the armrest, then he urged me down, so I sat between his legs lengthwise.

He put his other leg up on the couch so I was trapped between his thighs. "Lean back."

My heart slammed hard into my rib cage as I leaned against him, the heat of his chest instantly warming my back.

"Lift your leg." I did and he moved it so it rested over his and even though I wore boxers, I felt completely exposed.

"Not fucking a girl who doesn't want to be fucked. So, we're not." He leaned over and grabbed the controller and turned on the TV, flicking through channels until he found a late-night movie, an erotic late night movie. *Jesus.* He tossed the controller on the floor and I expected him to touch me.

He didn't.

He did nothing. I lay with my legs slightly splayed, breasts naked, while he watched the movie.

He had one arm around on my abdomen, while one hand rested on my inner thigh, doing nothing. Not even a finger twitch. Nothing.

I lay stiff in his arms, his steady heart beating against my back and I listened to his calm, even breath, and on occasion, the mild chuckle when something funny happened in the movie. And the funny was some ridiculous bad acting. But I heard the moans. The slapping of naked bodies. The screams of pleasure.

I shifted uncomfortably as mild tingles between my legs became intense tingles.

His arm tightened. "Stay still."

I did.

"Relax and watch the movie."

How the fuck could I? I sat on my couch with parted legs, his hand inches away from my throbbing sex while we watched a porno. I was tense, confused and desire pulsated through my entire body. I kept thinking about him holding me in his arms after the fire, and how it had been gentle, caring. Protective.

He continued to ignore me and after a while my body grew weary from the constant tension and I slowly relaxed and stopped fighting the sensations tap dancing through my body.

It was when the credits rolled that his hand moved and it was to cup me between the legs. The second he did, I moaned. The barrier of my boxers doing nothing to stop the intense pleasure.

I was wet, throbbing. And there was no question I wanted him to fuck me. I was completely willing and wanted him to.

He rested his hand on me for a long time. No words. Nothing.

I breathed erratically. He didn't. But I did feel his hard cock pressed into the small of my back, so he was turned on too.

Just the touch of his hand cupping me was going to make me come. I'd been worked up sitting with him, his increasingly familiar scent in every breath I took and the fear I'd felt dissipating and changing to want, *need*.

"Baby," he whispered and I jolted with pleasure at the sound of his voice against my ear.

His hand slipped inside my boxers and I gasped as he ran his finger through the wetness. He then withdrew it and brought it to my mouth. I eyed the pad of his glistening finger. "Taste how amazing you are."

I'd never tasted myself. I'd never even considered it, but with Kai, it was so hot that my insides clenched.

He placed his finger on my lower lip and traced a slow path across the sensitive surface. He repeated the process with my upper lip. I tilted my head to look at him and my lips parted. But he didn't put his finger in my mouth; instead, he slipped it into his.

Jesus. My body tensed as I watched him slowly suck on his finger. A charming gleam of amusement lit his eyes then a slight twitch played at the corner of his lips.

He withdrew his finger. "I knew you'd taste amazing, braveheart."

His hand slid down the front of me, between my breasts, over my rib cage to my abdomen then under the waistband of my boxers. His finger rolled over my clit and my hips rose to his touch.

He began circling, slow and gentle at first while his other hand played with my nipples. My body heated, overheated. It craved more. Needed more.

It didn't take long as my body had been anticipating his touch for an hour.

"Kai," I moaned as his fingers quickened back and forth. "Oh, God." I was on the cusp, ready to fall over the edge when it all stopped.

His hands went to my hips and he plucked me off his lap and set me down on the couch away from him. He stood and towered over me, and I saw the bulge of his cock against his jeans, but it didn't match the look in his eyes.

"You want to fuck me, great. But baby, if you don't… you damn well better fuckin' tell me. Don't ever lie there and say nothing like you did tonight in bed."

My mouth dropped open.

I pulsed. Throbbed. I ached for him to finish me, but there was no question he had no intention of doing that. By his grating tone and glaring eyes, Kai was seriously pissed off.

He strode into the bedroom and snagged his suit jacket off the chair. When he turned and came back toward me, I saw the leather holster dangling from his hand with the familiar knife and a roll of what looked like strands of wire peeking out of his pants pocket.

I stiffened, getting ready to run for my life, but he didn't stop walking, nor did he look at me as he opened the door and left.

Jesus fucking Christ.

What the hell had I gotten myself into?

CHAPTER
FOUR

London

I LAY IN BED feeling stupid, weak, and completely vulnerable.

I was unable to concentrate at school.

I was unable to stop thinking about him.

And for two nights… nothing. Not since he'd left me on the couch. He'd disappeared and that spiked my unease because Kai didn't seem like a guy who'd back out of a deal. I should be glad he'd voided two of our days because if I saw him again, I was going to make that clear. A week meant seven days in succession, not seven days whenever he felt like it. If he wanted to waste his nights, then that was his problem. As long as my father had his two months, I didn't care if I ever saw Kai again.

That was what I tried to convince myself of.

I shut off the light then curled up onto the leather chair beside the couch. I couldn't sit on the couch or sleep in bed because all I thought about was him. Even looking at the island in the kitchen made me imagine him taking me.

At school that day, I'd broken three test tubes, spilled my lunch down the front of my lab coat and barely passed my quiz in microbiology because I was so absorbed with what was happening with Kai.

He was a virus. The plague. And I had to find a vaccine to stop him from leaching any more of my thoughts. I sure as hell wasn't following his stupid rule of sleeping naked and since I wasn't in bed, then I wasn't really breaking his rule.

And why should I follow his rule? That wasn't part of the arrangement.

The distinct sound of the lock clicked and I darted upright, my heart slamming into my chest. He had a key? Oh, my God, he had a key. Shit, of course he did. He'd probably stolen my key that first night and made a copy then returned it the next morning when he brought the coffee and croissant.

For being a straight A student all my life, I was falling short.

I had my legs tucked beneath me on the chair and the wool blanket up around my shoulders. The door opened and for a second before he stepped inside and closed it, I saw his handsome face under the hallway light above my door.

He may be a dangerous man, but there was no question he was a gorgeous one. He could wear the rags Ernie did and still be the most charismatic man in a room. He owned who he was and that made him all the more threatening, because I had a feeling he'd risk everything in order to get what he wanted.

The door closed behind him.

He stood watching me and I suddenly wished I was naked. That I followed his rule. But then he did something that didn't suit him. He ran his hand through his hair as if agitated. Kai exuded steadiness and patience, and the gesture was unlike him.

God, I was thinking as if I knew him. A completely false perception because I doubted anyone did.

His next words blew any thought of him being agitated up in flames. "Take off your clothes and come here."

Butterflies lifted and fluttered at the sound of his voice then land-ed heavy in the pit of my stomach. Uncertain. Confused. Complete chaos of emotions. "How did you know I wasn't naked?"

His brows rose. "Because you're stubborn and rebellious. Al-though, it's in a rather passive way."

It was unnerving that he read me so well. As a child I'd never outwardly shout or throw a tantrum; instead, I'd be quiet and subtle about it. The silent treatment was a usual occurrence in my early teens.

"You're not mad?"

A slightly amused grin and the butterflies lifted again into perfect formation.

"No," he drawled.

"Why not?"

"Do you want me to be?"

"Well, no. It's just that I thought you would be."

"And yet, you still refused to follow the rule." He nodded to me. "Clothes. Let's try and live up to your nickname, braveheart."

I thought about refusing for about one second. But I'd made this deal, not him.

I uncurled my legs and stood. The blanket dropped to the floor. I crossed my arms, grabbed the bottom edge of my T-shirt and pulled it over my head. My nipples were erect and aching as was my already pulsing sex.

His eyes traveled down my neck to my breasts, hesitated, and then went to my over-sized boxers. He sighed, but he had a mild grin on his face. "A beautiful woman should never wear anything as unflattering as those. I suggest you get rid of them."

Maybe I'd purposely worn my most unattractive boxers that should've been burned years ago. It was a quiet rebellion, but I'd never been one to give in to anyone easily.

What was surprising was that he obviously had a sense of humor, although I was aptly aware that this man could change to a deadly adversary in a flash.

I walked into the kitchen, pulled off my boxers, then opened the cupboard and pitched them in the trash.

When I turned back around, he was leaning against the door with his arms crossed. Casual. Patient. God, it was like he owned my place, owned everything in here, including me. Maybe he did… at least for another three nights.

I slowly walked barefoot across the hardwood floor until I was a foot away from him.

"Undress me," he said.

My eyes narrowed for a second as I considered his order. And it was an order. The uncertainty was what would happen if I refused.

But no matter how this started out and how it would end, I wanted him. I was turned on by the way he was. I liked that he was so confident that nothing could touch him. I liked how sometimes his eyes lit up with amusement. I liked how his hands felt on me and how he made my body submit to his.

And most of all, I liked that when I breathed in his scent, it comforted.

I also had no delusions as to what this was and once I fulfilled my obligation, Kai would disappear and I'd move on with my life without him invading my every thought.

I lightly placed my hands on his chest then undid the tiny buttons of his pinstriped dress shirt. When I reached the bottom, I had to take off his belt that had a leather casing attached to it for his knife.

I unbuckled it and it slipped from his waist, the weight of it hanging in my hand. I'd never held a weapon before. Any kind of weapon, and it felt powerful and magnetic and scary as hell to know that in my hand I held something that had more than likely killed. Or maybe it hadn't. Maybe it was all a game. No matter what it was, I didn't like the knife and I tossed it on the floor. It made a loud clunk as it landed.

I untucked his shirt from his dress pants then undid the last three buttons so the material parted.

My breath stopped when my gaze hit his chest and his name tumbled from my parted lips in a breathless gasp. "Kai."

Angry, cruel, scars crisscrossed his skin. Some were raised white lines, others faint, but as my eyes trailed from one to the other, I couldn't stop the tears from welling.

What had been done to him? Who did this? Why?

I slowly ran my hands up over the blemished skin, touching the horror of what looked like…. It was torture. It had to be. There was no other explanation for it. I shuddered at the thought as I traced one line after the other with the pads of my fingers.

When I finally looked up at him, he watched me, expression hard and unflinching. I didn't understand what was happening. It was a clash of my fear, my desire and my compassion colliding.

"Kai… what… who did this?"

He didn't say anything.

"Why? How could anyone do this to you?" A tear slid down my cheek and his lips pursed together, eyes darkening as his gaze followed it until he raised his hand then gently wiped it away with the pad of his thumb. "Kai? Please, tell me this won't happen to my father."

He didn't say anything for a minute and my worry escalated at the thought of the danger my father was in. "No one will touch him. Or you."

He said it with such certainty that I believed him. He'd kept his word so far and there'd been no reason for him to. He obviously worked for some powerful people who had no qualms about hurting or killing anyone. But Kai was protecting me. I knew that with every part of me.

"Finish what you started, London."

I slowly ran my hands up his chest to his shoulders then slipped off his shirt. I turned to place it on the back of the chair when his arm curved around the waist. He swung me around so my back was against the door and the shirt fell from my fingertips, forgotten as his body pressed into mine.

That was it.

All control faltered for both of us as I fumbled with the button on his pants while his hands were all over me, scorching, hard and unforgiving. I unzipped his pants and they fell to the floor. He stepped out of them and kicked them away while he kissed my neck.

"Fuck." He breathed against me. "I need to taste you, London. I can't stop thinking about tasting you." Then he did what was totally unexpected and dropped to his knees. He picked up my right leg, put it over his shoulder then lowered his mouth to me.

My head jerked back hard against the door, my hands weaving into his hair as I moaned. "Holy shit."

He parted my throbbing lips with his fingers then flicked his tongue over me, suckled, and tasted every inch. There was no forgiveness as he played and teased. When he was too rough, he'd ease the discomfort with gentleness until I arched with intense need.

I'd never felt so out of control.

My body was his.

I had no recourse, but to let go and give in to him.

My body tightened as I came to the edge of the cliff. There was a mild fear that he'd stop again. That he'd leave me, but even if I wanted to, I couldn't control the building, the burning inside me that mounted as his tongue drove me to the peak.

My fingers dug into his shoulders as my body clenched. "Oh, God. Oh, God." I didn't slip over the edge. I leapt and he was there to catch me as he held my hips steady while his tongue lazily brought me back down from the shuddering waves of pleasure.

I sagged against the door while he unhooked my leg off his shoulder, then grabbed his pants off the floor while rising to his feet. He reached into the pocket and pulled out a square gold package and held it toward my mouth. I kept my eyes locked on his as I gripped the corner of it with my teeth and tore it open.

He pulled the condom from the package, yanked off his boxer-briefs and rolled it on. Then his hands came under my butt and he hitched me up off the floor.

"Put me inside you," he ordered.

I hooked my ankles around his hips then reached between us and held his cock. It pulsed and throbbed in my hand, the veins expanded with rushing blood. I squeezed, watching his face and the flicker of satisfaction as his eyes briefly closed, lips parting.

It felt good to give him that look. To have some control over his expression because I doubted he allowed anyone to have any power over him. I ran my hand down the length of him, my thumb stroking the tip. I wrapped my fingers closed again and jerked up at the base and he grunted.

"Stop fooling around. Put me inside. Now," he growled.

Yeah, he definitely didn't like anyone having control.

I locked eyes with him and guided his cock to my entrance. I didn't have time to move my hand away before he pushed inside me. My spine pressed hard into the door and when he pulled back, I moved my arm from between us and cupped the back of his neck.

He arched his hips then thrust forward again, and my body hit the door. Again and again.

"Neighbors," I panted.

"I don't give a shit." He slammed into me.

I thought I'd split apart but at the same time, I wanted it harder. I'd never experienced such raw unrestrained sex before. It was without boundaries as he grunted and pounded into me, hands gripping my ass so hard I knew I'd have bruises.

I didn't care. I was catapulting over the edge with him. His grunts and my moans unleashing an angry, wild need that both of us craved. Wanted.

"Fuck, London. Fuck." His body stiffened at the same time as mine. I clenched around his cock as the pulsing exploded into a frenzy of sparks as I came hard. Quivers darted through me for an intense few seconds before my final shudder and I sagged in his arms.

Kai thrust once, twice more, then stopped. I closed my eyes and rested my forehead on his chest, hearing his racing heartbeat next to my ear.

We stayed like that for a few minutes, not speaking. Unmoving.

I unhooked my legs and he slowly lowered me until I stood.

"Dangerous," he muttered.

I had no idea what he meant by that and I didn't have time to contemplate or ask him as a knock sounded on my door.

"You okay, Miss Westbrook?"

My head jerked up. *Fuck.*

More knocking.

"Miss Westbrook, we tried calling, but there was no answer."

The phone rang?

"We've had a complaint about banging."

My mouth dropped open and eyes widened as I looked at Kai.

He slowly grinned.

I didn't. I pursed my lips together then scrambled around for my clothes. "Yes. It's… a… Yeah… it's fine, Derek. Thank you." Shit, where were my boxers? Damn it, the garbage.

"Do you mind opening up? I have to check. Someone reported screaming, too."

Jesus Christ. I'd lived here for almost two years, was quiet as a mouse and suddenly, I had a complaint about screaming and banging. I snagged my shirt off the floor and pulled it over my head while I ran into the bedroom and grabbed a pair of yoga pants from the dresser.

"Yeah, sure. I was just…."

I heard the deadbolt click and the door open.

Kai had his shirt and pants on already. "She's fine."

I glanced at the floor a few inches from the door where his knife lay. If Derek looked down, he'd see it. *Shit.* I ran for the door, kicking the knife to the side as I greeted Derek.

"Sorry. I didn't realize how late it was. We were hanging—"

"Ah yeah… a *painting*. Your boyfriend said." Derek chuckled and winked at me. Oh. My. God. My face felt like it was on fire. "Hey, you watch the game yesterday?" he asked Kai.

Boyfriend? The game? "No, unfortunately I had business to attend to."

"Oh, man, you missed a good one. The Raptors totally kicked ass…." I looked from one to the other as they chatted about the basketball game.

Kai put his arm around my shoulders and dragged me in to his side. "Right, hon?"

"Huh?" I was still reeling that one of the security guards spoke to Kai as if they were friends. A man I was sleeping with in order to fulfill a deal.

"Well, keep the ah… hammering down?" Derek wiggled his brows at me.

Jesus. I'd been the quiet geek in loft 607 and now I was... God, I didn't even want to know what the security guys would talk about now. I'd never be able to look them in the eye again. I'd have to run for the elevator or better yet, come in through the parking garage and avoid them altogether.

Kai shut the door. I pulled from his snug embrace and walked into the kitchen. I grabbed a bottled water from the fridge, cracked it open and chugged it back.

By the time I'd set it down on the counter, Kai stood next to me, eyes twinkling.

"Boyfriend?"

He didn't say anything.

"The game?"

Again, he didn't say anything.

"What are you doing? You have two more nights then this is over."

"Four."

I glared. "No. Two. You didn't show up for the last two nights. That's not my fault."

He gently took the water from my hand and took a sip before answering. "Four, London. Actually, five because tonight isn't over."

"That's not the deal. It was one week."

"Yes. Seven days."

I wasn't giving in on this. I couldn't let him win. He was taking advantage and I couldn't do four more nights. It was... it unhinged me. I lost control and I didn't like it. I didn't like any of this because the truth was I did like it and it was wrong.

I marched to the washroom then glared over my shoulder at him. "Two more nights and then our association is over." I slammed the door.

I leaned over the sink and splashed cold water on my heated cheeks, brushed my teeth and hoped by the time I was done, he'd be gone.

He wasn't.

He was lying naked in my bed.

I crossed my arms. "What are you doing?"

"If you insist on two nights, I plan to make them last."

"You can't stay the night." Shit, this was backfiring. I expected him to fuck me and leave, not lie next to me all night.

One leg was bent and the sheet pooled at his hips, dipping where there was a light trail of sparse dark hairs. He was half-perched up by two pillows under his shoulders and I hated that he looked hot in my bed, relaxed, as if he belonged there.

"You going to throw me out, London?"

I crossed my arms over my chest and stared at him. "I'm not sleeping naked," I grumbled as I walked to the bed and climbed in with my yoga pants and shirt on.

"We'll see," he said and pulled the sheet up over me. His thigh landed on top of my thighs. Then his arm came around my shoulders and tugged, pulling me back against his chest.

I fumed.

Because I liked him wrapped around me. I liked the feel of him. I liked him in bed with me.

And I'd never felt so protected in my life. The irony was I had the feeling that Kai could very well destroy me.

CHAPTER
FIVE

London

TWO MORE NIGHTS.

I paced back and forth. Tonight, I had dinner at my dad's and I hated not being able to say anything to him. But what made this all feel like it was worth it was that the worn, worried frown he'd had for months had eased, although he was still pale and looked tired.

Even though I wanted to ask him about Kai and the drug he was working on, I couldn't. No matter how old I was, I'd always be his little girl and he'd want to protect me. Finding out Kai and I were sleeping together would be catastrophic.

Kai was someone my dad couldn't protect me from. Although with each encounter, I felt more and more like Kai was the protector and not the threat.

By one in the morning, he still hadn't shown, but it was nothing unusual. I realized this was how he liked to play it. Keep me waiting so I was thrown off. I poured myself a glass of wine and tried to study, but I read the last paragraph four times and still didn't take in what I was reading. I listened for the key in the lock and every time I heard the ding of the elevator, my heart raced.

It was the weekend and I didn't have classes, but still, staying awake all night waiting for some guy wasn't something I did. I laughed to myself because this wasn't just some guy or some usual night.

I stood, parted the curtains and looked into the alley. I had no idea why. It wasn't like he'd be down there. I couldn't picture Kai standing in an alley. He wouldn't sneak around. He'd go wherever he wanted.

My phone rang and I nearly dropped my glass of wine at the sound. I hurried over to my desk, set my wine down, and glanced at the display, *Unknown Number*. I normally avoided answering calls like this, but in my gut I knew it was him. Who else would call at this time.

"Hello?"

"London."

"Kai."

"Baby, I need you to do something for me."

I remained quiet. I didn't like the sound of that.

He continued, "I will forfeit one night if you do what I ask."

He was willing to forfeit a night? A hint of disappointment hit me. Whatever this was, I wanted to have sex with him and I had to accept that. But he didn't need to know.

"Agreed?"

My stomach dropped and goose bumps popped up along my skin. I didn't like agreeing to something I didn't know what I was agreeing to.

"Does it involve hurting anyone?"

He laughed. "No, baby. That's my job, never yours."

I was also uncertain how I felt about him calling me baby. It was different than his nickname for me. It was personal and familiar, like we were something more than a deal.

"One less night. And no one gets hurt."

"Yes," he drawled.

"Fine."

"Good girl. Go to the freezer." I frowned, holding the phone to my ear as I walked into the kitchen and opened the freezer door. "On the bottom shelf. Metal container."

My eyes scanned over the frozen corn, the Häagen-Dazs ice cream, then stopped. I swallowed as I slowly took out the metal container and peered through the small window in the lid. It had a dildo with a blue embossed swirl around it.

"You have it?"

I nodded.

"London?"

"Yes."

"Take it out of the box." I did. "Now get into bed. And take off your clothes."

Shit, he knew I broke the rule once again and was wearing pajamas.

Once in my room, I slipped them off and crawled onto my bed.

"Prop yourself up and bend your knees," he instructed.

Oh, Jesus, I knew exactly what I was supposed to do with this. The most experience I'd had with sex toys was a tiny clit stimulator.

"Need you to talk to me, London."

"Yeah. Okay, but—"

"Legs apart." I swallowed. "Wider," he growled into the phone.

To my mortification, tingles erupted between my legs. A man on the phone was telling me what to do with a dildo he'd put in the freezer.

"Now, rub it between your legs." I stared at the toy in my hand and thought about it. It was cold. Really cold. I didn't like jumping in a swimming pool below eighty. I was one of those people who took their time inch by inch and if it was too cold, I didn't even bother.

Could I pretend to do what he said and not do it?

"Never hesitate, London. Hesitating will get you hurt," he said. It was like he was warning me, not because he was angry, but for my own good.

I switched hands with the phone and the dildo, as it was already

71

too cold in my hand. Then I closed my eyes and lowered it between my legs.

My breath hitched as the hard cold met my heated soft skin.

"Slide it up and down your pussy. Get it wet, baby," he directed.

The phone crackled with my heavy breath when the pain from the cold sifted through me. "It's too cold." I pulled it away.

"That's the point. Your body will warm it enough to put inside you."

I didn't want to. I didn't like being cold and I didn't like doing this. I felt awkward and silly.

I tossed the dildo aside and yanked the sheet up over me. "I'm not doing this."

I hung up and shut my phone off.

I sat up against the headboard, my knees to my chest, arms around them. My pulse raced as I wondered what the hell I was thinking considering shoving a freezing cold dildo up inside me.

It was only five minutes before I heard the dead bolt click, and the door opened. Kai stood there, looking larger than life. He was larger than life—at least in attitude.

"Kai," I breathed as he stalked toward me, his cell still in his hand. "I thought…." I clamped my mouth shut as he tossed his phone on the bedside table, grabbed the sheet and yanked it off me to pool on the floor. His gaze scanned the bed then stopped on the dildo where I'd tossed it.

He took two steps to the right, leaned over and picked it up. Only then did he look at me.

I was terrified by what I'd see, but he didn't look angry. But he wasn't happy either. I couldn't tell what he was feeling and that bothered me more than anything because I had no idea what he'd do next.

"Don't ever hang up on me."

Yeah, Kai wouldn't appreciate that. I held my legs closer to my chest protectively. Despite my balled-up shielded appearance, I met his eyes and refused to flinch or look away.

"You don't want to do something, say it. But don't ever hang up on me." He grabbed my ankle and a small scream escaped as he yanked and I landed flat on my back.

"You can't tell me what to do."

He completely ignored what I said, dropped the dildo between my legs and it bounced once on the mattress. He unclipped the belt on his stylish charcoal grey dress pants and pulled it through the loops. He held onto the buckle and wrapped the leather around his hand twice then left the rest dangling.

My eyes widened as they went from the belt then back at him. "You can't," I stammered.

His brows rose. "No?"

Holy shit. He was going to spank me for hanging up on him? *Shit.* I dove for the side of the bed. "You're crazy," I shouted as I scrambled to my feet and ran for the door.

I heard him come after me, but he took his time and I realized why. I was naked.

This was why I slept in clothes. This. An emergency like this. Okay, not like this, but an emergency and this was an emergency and now I was naked because he told me to be.

I had my hand on the doorknob wondering if I should scream bloody murder running naked through the hallway and then have to move out of the building or… or what?

I turned around and he stood watching me while leaning against the large wooden beam between my living room and my bedroom. He still had the belt in his hand, arm lowered to his side.

"What are you going to do, London?"

"I'm not into that stuff if that's what you're planning. I don't like it."

"Have you tried?"

"I don't need to try something to know. My *body* knows," I threw back at him.

He half-smiled. "What did I tell you?"

I frantically searched my brain for what he was referring to. "Don't hang up on you."

"Yes," he drawled. "What else."

"Be naked in bed and I was."

"Yes, but you weren't until I told you to."

I swallowed, my hand reaching behind me to undo the dead bolt. The sound of it clicking was like an elephant just burst through the door.

"What else?"

He was so fucking calm it was maddening. I was betting his heart rate was non-existent while mine ran a marathon, and I hated running. I was a bookworm, not a sports person.

"Are you going to spank me?" God, that sounded... pathetic.

"London." He shook his head back and forth and slid the leather across his palm on his other hand. My eyes kept going to it. "Baby, what else?"

Him saying baby made me a little calmer. "I... you said...." The leather slipped from his palm as he lowered his arm. I looked back up at him. "You said to tell you if I didn't want to do something."

He gave a subtle nod.

"I don't want you to spank me," I said. "I'm not into that."

He tossed his belt on the couch. "Good girl. Lock the door again." Then he walked back into the bedroom and undressed.

It took me a few minutes before I was able to walk across my loft to the bed. My legs were still shaking and my heart had slowed to a half-decent beat. Naked, Kai sat with his back up against the head-board, the vibrator beside him.

Before I joined him, I asked, "Where were you when you called?"

He answered immediately, "In the lobby."

"The lobby? My lobby?"

"Yes."

"Why did you call me from the lobby?" I frowned. Why would he be in the lobby calling me?

"I wanted to see if you'd do what I asked."

I narrowed my eyes on him, spine stiffening. "What? Why the hell would you do that?"

"A test. To see how far you'd go without me. And because I want you to learn that if you ever don't want something, you need to tell me. That's twice now."

"God, you're an asshole." This was an arrangement for seven days, not a relationship and yet I couldn't help but feel like it was more. "This isn't some game. I don't need testing and I sure as hell don't need you telling me what to do."

He laughed. The sound vibrated through the loft, a deep, gravelly sound that sent shivers across my skin. "I love your courage, sweetness. I've had few…" he paused, "… no. I've never had a woman speak to me as you do." He patted the mattress. "Lie down. I want to try this on you." He picked up the dildo.

"You've got to be kidding me?"

But from his relaxed expression and shrug, he wasn't.

When he merely ran his finger down the length of the toy. I scrunched my nose to match my frown.

"I don't want to do that."

"Now, you're lying," he replied. He placed his finger in his mouth, wet it, and then ran it down the shaft of the glass. "You didn't want to do it because you were alone. Now, you're not."

I shifted, putting my hand on my hip and wishing again that I had clothes on. My sex pulsed as I watched him.

"I'll make you a deal," he said.

"I think one deal with you is enough."

He quirked a half-smile and lowered the dildo to the mattress. "If you're wet, I get to use the toy. If you're not, I'll get you wet and fuck you with my cock."

Jesus. It was like he had no filter, which was a total turn on.

"I know you're wet, London. I can see your pussy swollen and glistening from here." God, I hadn't even caught him looking at my sex. "I would never make you do anything you didn't want to."

I thought about it for a second. It was a dildo and probably not cold anymore. I wasn't that much of a prude, was I?

"Fine."

"Good." He nodded to the mattress and I knelt on it. A little self-conscious, I was uncertain what to do. "Thought it could end," he said, shaking his head while watching me, piercing green eyes intense. "It can't."

I was uncertain what he meant, but when I opened my mouth to ask, he said, "Lie down. Do exactly as I told you on the phone." He held out the vibrator to me.

"What?" I tried to sit up, but he put his hand on my neck and kept me down. "Kai. I thought… I thought you were going to do it."

"Now that would be too easy. Let's see how brave you are." He went to the end of the bed and came to his feet, then walked over to the dresser and leaned up against it. I could barely see him in the shadows, but what was clearly visible were his green eyes and they were focused on me. It was disconcerting having him watch me because, like it or not, I wanted him to see that I was brave.

"Pick it up, London."

I glanced at the dildo he'd dropped between my legs. Brave. I was brave. I wasn't afraid to try new foods. I went bungee jumping with a group of school friends from my chemistry class a few years ago. When I was picked on by a bully in eighth grade, I punched him. I was a geek, but it didn't mean I didn't have backbone.

Fuck it.

I grabbed the dildo, bent my knees, widened my legs and pushed it inside me.

My breath locked in my throat as the cool met the heated wetness and I closed my eyes at the strange sensation. Shit. It felt… good. I slid it out then pushed it in again. A thrill of excitement soared through me not only from what I was doing, but that his eyes were on me. Actually, that was a bigger turn on because I liked his eyes on me.

I parted my legs further, arched my back and moaned as I pushed it in and out. My sex tweaked with need and I lowered my other hand and circled my clit while I continued to push the cool dildo in and out.

"Fuck."

He came out of the shadows and was on the bed within seconds. He grabbed the toy and threw it across the room so hard it made a dent in the drywall.

He was already wearing a condom as he slid his cock up and down between my legs once to get it wet before he pushed inside me—hard.

But I was ready for him as he ruthlessly took me. His hands

grabbed my wrists and locked them down on the mattress on either side of my head. There was a wild look in his eyes as he hovered above me thrusting with his hips. His lips pursed together, brows lowered as if he was angry.

"Christ," he growled.

I was already close to coming before he entered me and it wasn't long before I went over the edge and came violently around him. "Kai," I gasped as shudders tore through me.

"London," he shouted as he pumped hard and fast a few more times before he groaned low in his throat and came too.

It was several minutes of him on top of me unmoving, eyes closed, hands still locked around my wrists. He finally rolled to the side, releasing me. We were both breathing erratically with the smell of sex and sweat in the air.

Unrestrained. That was what it had been. I didn't pretend to know this man, but I suspected he rarely lost control—until me. I saw it in his expression, the furrowed brow, the unsettled look in his piercing eyes.

I perched up on my elbow, my head resting in the palm of my hand as I faced him. I reached out and trailed a finger down his chest. His arm was thrown over his face covering his eyes and one knee was bent as he lay on his back beside me.

"Kai?" I traced one of the scars that went from his pectorals down to his abdomen. "Who did this to you?"

He moved his arm from his face and tilted his head to look at me. When I saw the darkness in the depths of his eyes, my heart jumped with a tinge of fear.

"We fuck, London. Not share fairy tales of our past."

I yanked my hand away and despite his words feeling like a slap across the face, he was right. But from the look in his eyes and the depth of his scars, his past was no fairy tale.

Why did I care anyway?

Because I did. I cared about everyone. It was the type of person I was and I couldn't help it. I saw the good in people even when most saw none. I had no doubt the scars contributed to who Kai was and it saddened me to think that someone hurt him so badly it had molded him into a man who was dangerous. I wanted to know more. I wanted to understand him because Kai wasn't all bad. If he were, I'd be either dead or he'd have beaten me out in the woods as a warning.

But he was right. None of this mattered and the less I knew about Kai, the better. One more night and he'd disappear from my life. I'd get my head back into my studies and pretend this never happened.

But I knew pretending I never met Kai, never having had him inside me, pretending he never existed was never going to happen.

I turned over on my side and closed my eyes.

At some point, he curled his arm around me, tugged me back against his chest, and then gently kissed my neck.

CHAPTER SIX

London

H E WAS EARLY.

Hours early.

Like it was still daylight early and I'd just walked in the door from school. "What are you doing here?"

Kai was different. He wasn't wearing a suit or even a dress shirt. He was in a black T-shirt and jeans, snug jeans that hung low on his hips and made him look hotter than usual, which was seriously hard to do.

I watched him walk into the kitchen and help himself to a bottled water from the fridge. There was something else that was different. He had barely looked at me. Normally, his eyes trapped mine the moment he entered my loft. But today… he ignored me.

He was tense, on edge. Kai had that in him, but it was not in a threatening edge. It was like he was uneasy about being here.

"What's wrong?" I asked.

He didn't say anything, merely leaned against the kitchen counter and chugged back the water. And he looked sexy as hell doing it. *Shit.*

He finished the water and tossed the bottle in the recycling bin under the counter.

If he didn't want to talk, that was fine with me. It wasn't like we had anything to talk about anyway.

I tossed my purse onto the coffee table and walked into the bedroom, rummaged through my dresser for clothes, then went into the bathroom and shut the door.

I'd just climbed into the shower when the bathroom door opened. And shut.

Our eyes met through the fogged glass and my pulse shot off like a bullet. The sprayer hit my chest, hot water pouring down the front of me as I stood unmoving. He kept his eyes on my face, not once wavering to my naked body even though I loved how his eyes trailed down my body like it was something to devour.

Hawks dive bombed in my belly.

Then I watched as he slowly undressed, his movements unrushed and smooth, just like him. He folded each piece of clothing as he removed it and placed it on the counter beside the sink.

I wanted to look away, but I couldn't. The reality was, Kai captivated me.

Remember who he is, London.

I glanced at the sheathed knife he'd put beside his clothes. Did he go anywhere without that thing? I shivered at the thought of blood being wiped clean from its blade. Had he killed? How many people? Were they good people like my father?

Bile rose in my throat. I was having sex with this guy. I let him use my body and I liked it. I was turned on by him. That made me just as disgusting and vile as him.

The shower door opened and I stepped back.

He scowled as I looked for an escape, but he blocked the only exit and by his unyielding expression, I wasn't going to get by him.

"What's changed?" he asked as he stepped under the spray and I backed up against the tiled wall. "I see it in your face, London. What's changed?"

He kept approaching until his body was up against mine. His hand cupped the back of my neck while his other curved around my lower back. With one rough tug, he had me pressed against him.

"Answer me," he shouted.

It was the first time he'd raised his voice and it wasn't race cars of goose bumps shooting across my skin, it was fighter jets.

"The knife."

His fingers tightened on my neck. "What about it?"

His cock was pressed into my abdomen. "You've… killed people with it?"

There was no hesitation as he said, "Yes."

"Good people?"

"Does it matter?"

Did it? Killing wasn't right no matter who it was, no matter the reason. I wanted to save lives and Kai took them. But yeah, it still mattered. "Yes."

I tried to look down, but he wouldn't let me. His fingers grasped strands of my hair and firmly pulled my head back. "I've never pretended to be anyone else, London." True, that was all me. I saw him as the man who saved me. I'd convinced myself that Kai was good. "Has every person I've killed deserved it? Probably not." I swallowed. "Were they upstanding citizens? No. But I won't apologize for who I am. Not to you or anyone else."

"I don't like you. I don't like this."

"Baby, if you liked me, we'd have a problem. But make no mistake, you do like this." With his mouth to my ear he said, "Nothing wrong with that, London. You can't control it, so accept what this is for one more night. Forget that I'm a killer and I'll try to forget that you're a scientist."

I huffed.

He grinned and his grip loosened on my hair as his other hand came up to cup my chin, thumb stroking back and forth. "The rule comes into play at any time, London. Always."

I frowned, uncertain what he was referring to. "What do you…?" Then it hit me. His rule. If I didn't want something, all I had to do was tell him. "But the deal."

"Always." His thumb played with my lower lip and the action didn't match the serious look in his eyes.

It was the same word he'd written on the note. The same word he'd said to me after the fire. He'd always come for me, whatever that meant. I didn't understand him. But I suspected he liked it that way.

One more night. We had one more night and then he'd leave and the *always* wouldn't matter anymore. I trapped his thumb with my teeth and then slowly dragged it into my mouth. His eyes blazed with desire and I liked that I could do that to him.

He released me, reached up onto the tiled corner ledge and grabbed the soap bottle. Then he passed it to me.

"Wash me."

I swallowed, staring at him while I took the bottle.

He stood like a stone statue in the rain, the water dripping over his shoulders down his length, trails of heated moisture. Kai was lean and there was not an ounce of softness about him. Agile, like a deadly black panther. No, he was rarer than that, a solitary Amur leopard.

"Water will be cold soon." His voice broke through my thoughts and I noticed the lightness to his tone had returned and some of my uncertainty dissipated.

I squeezed soap onto my hands. "Umm, you'd be better to stand out of the spray."

He shook his head, sighing. "Don't say umm, London. It doesn't become you."

I went to retort something back at him, but I clamped my mouth shut and bit the insides of my cheeks instead. He wanted me to react. What pissed me off was that he was right. I never said umm. It was an ugly filler sound. If I couldn't find the words, I hesitated, not filled the silence with umm.

I slid the soap along the surface of his smooth skin, his muscled arms, the tattoo on his right shoulder that gleamed black under the wetness. Then I moved to his chest and my hands roamed over the story of his past.

The knife.

Was that why he carried one, because a knife had wreaked havoc on his body? But some scars looked like burns and others were wider than what a knife would leave. Torture. It was impossible all the scars were from an accident. God, who would hurt him like this?

As I finished his upper body, I hesitated when I reached his pelvis and his cock. It was hard and erect, and like the rest of him—commanding.

I glanced up at him.

He arched a brow and took the bottle from me and tipped it, squeezing out more soap. I put my hand out to catch it and the white thick gel suddenly didn't look like soap anymore.

"You can clean it with your mouth if you prefer?"

My heart jumped and I swallowed, my eyes going back to his jutting cock. I took hold of the base and heard him suck in air. I inwardly smiled. Then with the soap, I stroked the hard surface up and down while I continued to fist it. Once he was covered in soap and now breathing hard, I used one hand to wash his balls. Gently, rolling them like delicate jewels between my palms before slipping my finger between his legs along the crease of his ass.

His hand latched onto my hair then shoved me to the back of the shower, so he stood under the spray to wash the soap off. Then he turned to face me again.

"I want to… taste you," I said.

His eyes blazed with desire, heightening the inferno of heat roaring through me.

I dropped to my knees and he blocked the spray with his back, but water trickled over his shoulders, down his chest.

The tiles hurt my knees, but when I wrapped my mouth around him, I forgot all about the bruising pain. He tasted like soap and water and… him. It was the smell of him that I'd never forget. It couldn't be washed away or overlooked. It was in him. And it was in me.

He groaned as he pushed his hips forward, his hand on the back of my head to keep me in place. I gagged when he went too far down my throat, but I didn't stop or pull away. I sucked on him harder, taking all of him then drawing back again, my tongue circling the tip.

"That's it, braveheart," he said as he widened his stance and tightened his grip in my hair. "Fuck. Yes."

He began to push his hips forward again. "Take all of me."

I tried to relax my throat as he withdrew then pushed to the back of my throat again. I sucked at the same time, loving the taste of him. His cock jerked and his hand tightened in my hair. Then his body tensed.

He groaned as he shot down my throat.

"Fuck, baby."

I swallowed then gently licked the remnants from the tip.

He helped me to my feet and smoothed the wet strands away from my face. "Better than I ever imagined."

I bit my lip, liking the thought that he'd imagined me sucking him off.

It was another ten minutes before we came out of the shower because he washed every inch of me paying special attention to between my legs, which ended up having me quivering and crying out his name.

The look he'd had earlier had left and he was the man I was beginning to understand… well, understand small pieces of.

He had kindness in him that I hadn't expected when I'd first seen him through the crack in the closet. But it was there, lying dormant most of the time, but like when he washed me and then toweled me off, it was with gentleness and care.

Then I'd caught the reflection of the knife in the mirror and wondered if maybe it was an act. The kindness he showed my body.

Maybe I was fooling myself to think I knew even a piece of this man. Did any of it matter? This was the last time I'd see him.

Then my thoughts were quickly set aside as he fucked me on the bathroom counter then again in the kitchen from behind like he'd done the first night a week ago. I did notice he never kissed me on the mouth. Not once. I wondered why he didn't, but maybe it was better. Less… personal.

When he suggested we order in something to eat, I thought it odd and… well, normal. He dressed but insisted I remain in only panties and a spaghetti strapped camisole. I argued at first, but then stopped because I realized it was hot being half-naked with him dressed.

I ordered in Thai food and when I'd asked what he wanted to eat, he'd told me he'd like whatever I did. It was sweet and I liked that.

While we waited for it to arrive, he was on his phone. He kept his voice quiet, but I heard him say the name Chaos a few times as if it were a person. Who was Chaos? Or had he been referring to a situation? But it sounded like he was saying a name.

I placed plates on the small round glass table with white napkins. I used chopsticks, but I wasn't sure if Kai did, so I put out cutlery, too. Then I placed the two candles in silver holders I kept for special occasions in the center. When I stepped back and glanced at the table set for two, my heart sped up.

What were we doing? What was I doing?

Then it hit me.

Oh, God, I liked him here. I liked that he stood in my living room. I liked that his scent was everywhere. I liked how he made my body feel and how he took any sexual inhibitions and smothered them.

I liked how he was so sure of himself. I liked that he pushed my boundaries. Challenged me.

Jesus, I liked Kai.

And that terrified me.

I glanced up at him and our eyes locked. He was no longer talking on the phone, but was watching me. Nothing else existed except us.

My breath stopped.

He must have seen it. Seen the realization. Seen something in my eyes because he did what we both knew was the only option.

He walked out.

CHAPTER SEVEN

Kai

FUCK, ONLY THREE weeks.

Three weeks since I walked out of her loft and took the first flight out of New York to Toronto. I'd met up with Chaos and went over a new assignment, went to Vault's Toronto house and saw Brice and Glen, emailed Mother, because I didn't care to hear her voice, plus it was easier lying in an email.

But I was distracted. Uneasy. The cool steady calm that normally filtered through me had slowed to a trickle and instead, I was on edge, the sensation of sandpaper being constantly rubbed against my skin.

Unable to sleep, I stayed up and read about fuckin' chemistry. Chemistry. I had no interest in chemistry, but it linked me to her. To London.

I followed my gut instinct because that was always a certainty. Most people ignored it, but if that became a habit, a person would slowly become numb to what their instincts were telling them.

I didn't. I listened to every single one. Maybe because I had nothing to lose by taking a chance. Maybe because I'd never given a shit if I died.

But at that moment, my guts were speaking loud and fuckin' clear. Something was off, but I didn't know what. It had been that way ever since I walked out of London's door after seeing her face. Fuck, I told her it was better she didn't like me.

I had to leave and never go back for her sake more than mine. I'd already risked a lot by being with her. Selfish. That was what it had been. But I hadn't been able to resist her after feeling her beneath me on the hood of my car. After finally touching her.

It was pure lust when I'd seen her picture for the first time two years ago when I'd been assigned to her father. She had an innocence about her, a quietness that played across her face, but there was also a stubborn quirk that lay beneath the natural beauty. It was cute and refreshing. I was never attracted to that type of woman because the quiet, innocent ones would be terrified of me. I fucked women who wanted what I did… no strings.

It was when I saw her in person that everything went to shit. I'd flown to New York to check up on her father and went to the house she shared with some other students.

I'd been sitting outside at a café sipping an espresso when she emerged from her house across the street with one of her roommates. I knew the other girl was a roommate because I'd checked into everyone surrounding London and her father.

London's head was tilted back as she laughed at something her friend said, neck exposed, eyes bright and filled with lightness. A lightness I wanted to grab and hold onto. She gently laid her hand on her friend's arm and the sweet gesture was like being wrapped in her warmth. As she walked in my direction, her hips swayed, not provocatively, naturally.

Her smile was genuine and filtered into the passersby as if it were infectious. I found myself smiling too as I sat back in my chair, legs out, ankles crossed as I watched her.

Then I saw her stop and crouch in front of an old woman sitting on a subway grate, bags all around her and a shopping cart filled with garbage. Well, what I considered garbage, but I was certain the homeless lady didn't think so.

London reached in her school bag and pulled out what looked like a sandwich and passed it to her. The old woman, who had been moaning and frowning, looked at London and smiled revealing her rotting teeth. London smiled back then put her hand on the woman's arm and said something to her. And still to this day, I wanted to know what she said. Not that the words were important. But because that single moment changed the course of my life.

I never gave a shit about the homeless. Never thought about them until that moment. I didn't know what it was, maybe the simple, quiet gesture. Her softness. Her caring. It was something I completely lacked and London's compassion fed me lightness that filled the dark rift inside me.

It began my need to watch her. I pretended it was to make certain she didn't become a by-product of Vault's needs, and it was partially, but it was far more than that. I was addicted to her.

I found myself coming to New York more than I needed to, just so I could feel that lightness again.

But London played with my control even though she didn't know it. I was on a tether being pulled tight, waiting for it to snap. And it fuckin' had snapped when I finally had a chance to have her. Taste her. And for the first time in my life, I was uncertain what I'd have done if she'd said no that first time when I held her against the fridge.

I was a bastard for accepting her ridiculous deal. But I'd thought if I had her, tasted her, fucked her, then my constant need would finally be sated and I could forget her.

It didn't. My need strengthened. Insatiable. And it was dangerous.

Reading people was part of my training, their eye movements, gestures, the slightest shift in weight, and London was an open book with the pages filled with big bold writing.

The last day I'd been with her… her standing beside the table at her loft, me standing on the other side of the room having just gotten off the phone with Chaos—Georgie. I saw the realization in her eyes that this was more than some deal.

It was the end to what never had the chance to begin. But fuck, for a split second, I wanted to hold onto her and stay.

But staying was never an option. I'd already broken the cardinal rule and become too close.

I leaned forward, the black leather couch crinkling and rested my elbows on my thighs and put my head in my hands, gripping my hair.

"Shit." This wasn't supposed to go down like this.

Mother had wanted London 'hurt' as a warning to Dr. Westbrook. I said I'd look after the situation and I had, just not how she would've liked or expected. I hadn't planned on what happened between us. I was simply going to scare her into remaining silent because there was no way in hell I'd do what Mother wanted.

The ties surrounding me were cruel and unbreakable, and London's fate was already balancing on a tightrope because my gut was telling me that Mother knew what I'd done.

I came to my feet and paced the length of my study. The warning siren blared in my head getting louder and louder each day I stayed away. It was the same feeling I had when the fire went down in that shitty house London lived in with her friends.

I'd been on my way back to the airport after checking on Dr. Westbrook's progress on the drug and then spending a few hours watching London as she studied in the library. I'd followed her home and waited until I saw her light turn off in her bedroom before I drove off. Maybe it was purely instinct, maybe it was my obsession getting stronger. Whatever it was, I turned the car around twenty minutes later and went back.

The entire way I was convinced it would be the last time. I'd say goodbye. I'd stop coming to see her. But when I was a few miles away and saw the smoke, I knew. In my fuckin' gut, I knew it was her house and for the first time since I was a kid, my heart raced so fast it hurt.

I drove like a maniac.

I swore and cursed.

I didn't stop when I pulled up to the house. I drove right through the back fence and used the hood of my car to reach the ledge of her window and pull myself up to where her room was located. I heard the fire trucks screaming as they drew closer, but the crackle of the fire roared in my head much louder. I wrapped my hand in my shirt then smashed my fist right through her window.

I climbed inside, the jagged pieces of glass cutting into my arms, chest and thighs. For a minute, I couldn't see a fuckin' thing as I was engulfed by smoke and heat. But I didn't have to see or go far when my foot hit the body. I crouched. The smoke wasn't as thick lower down and that was when I saw her. It was the first fuckin' time I cared if someone lived or died.

It was the first time I felt as if I had a heart because the thing stopped. It stopped until I pressed my palm to her chest and felt her heartbeat. I picked her up and went out the way I came in.

I carried her to the neighbor's backyard then gently laid her on the grass. Her eyes opened briefly and if I hadn't been on my knees, I would've been brought to them just seeing her look at me.

I held her for a minute, my finger brushing her hair from her face. She coughed and coughed and I held her, rubbing her back as she sucked in the fresh air. When she finally caught her breath, she tilted her head and our eyes met. That was when I said, "I'll always come for you, braveheart."

Her brows lowered and she tried to say something before she coughed again and closed her eyes, lying limp in my arms. I noticed a fireman look in my direction, so I let her go, jogged back to my car and left.

That was when I hired Ernie to watch her. Of course, the only way to appear as if he wasn't watching her was to be disguised as a homeless guy.

My cell vibrated on the coffee table, jiggling a few inches across the smooth, hard surface. I stared at the blinking screen, unable to see the number, but I didn't have to. It was the cell phone I had that only one person had the number to.

I reached across, picked it up and then pressed the green circle on the screen before placing it to my ear. "Ernie."

"No show this morning, boss."

The storm pushed into me and my hand tightened on the phone. If I were forced to trust anyone, it was Ernie. He wasn't part of Vault, but knew about them. As an ex-Navy SEAL, he knew about loyalty. Plus, I paid him a shitload of money.

My jaw clenched. "She sick?"

Ernie hesitated; he was a straight-up guy so this cemented the fact that what I was about to hear wouldn't be good. "Got that feeling. No movement in her windows all morning. Got here around six and left last night after eight. Boss, the window's closed."

Fuck.

I stood. "Get in there. Don't care how you fuckin' do it." I strode out of the living room and into my bedroom and threw my bag on the bed. "I'm on the next flight."

I hung up.

I've never felt fear before. Had nothing to fear since it was beaten and tortured out of me when I was a kid. But suddenly that catapulted into me because I didn't need to take a flight to New York in order to check what was up with London.

I knew.

I'd made a fatal error. I'd spent a week with London and Mother found out about it.

No attachments.

Mother was making sure of that and now London was paying the price.

CHAPTER
EIGHT

London

"**F**UCK. YOU!" I screamed.

His beefy arm raised and then his hand smacked me across the face so hard I fell to my knees. I put my palm on my throbbing cheek, the impact like I'd been hit with a wooden paddle.

I would never submit to these assholes. They could beat me until my last breath. I wasn't giving in to them.

"No. You're the one who will be fucked." He laughed and the sound was like fingernails running down a chalkboard. I wanted to take his fingernails and rip each one off and shove them into his eyeballs. I had no idea where that came from because I wasn't like that. I always tried to find the good in people. But this man grinned and looked giddy when he inflicted pain. He liked hurting others. He enjoyed it and that wasn't just mean-hearted, it was evil and cruel.

I didn't know how long it had been since I'd been kidnapped. But I was taken a week after Kai walked out and I knew that because I couldn't stop thinking about him. I'd counted the days, hoping it would get easier, every morning when I woke. It hadn't.

I'd tried to get back to my routine, but I'd been in a daze, unable to sleep or study. Even Ernie noticed a change in me and asked if I was okay.

I told him I was stressed over school, but that was a lie, and I think he knew it by the way he shook his head and frowned as if disappointed in something.

I hated myself for thinking about Kai and yet no matter what I did, he was there in my thoughts. Maybe that was how they kidnapped me so easily. I'd opened my door to what I thought was my order of Thai food and the next moment, blackness. I hadn't even had time to scream.

And since then, I'd been drugged with some kind of sedative. I was transported in a windowless van and switched vehicles several times, but I couldn't tell who moved me or what anyone looked like because my vision was all fucked up. I was force fed and had to pee at the side of the road before being thrown in the van again.

Finally, they stopped drugging me and I started to process the reality of the situation. And it was so terrifying that I wanted the drugs back. I wanted to stay in the fog and not wake up again until I was back home. I cried for hours in the van, quietly so they wouldn't hear me, but they were choking sobs of fear. The unknown gripping my chest so tightly I hyperventilated.

Once the tears were gone, the anger rose and that was where I was emotionally when the van stopped. I was angry at them. Angry at myself for crying. Angry at opening the door in my loft. Angry at feeling helpless.

I was dragged from the van, and taken inside a massive house. I only had a second to process it, but the place obviously belonged to someone exceptionally wealthy with the elaborate front hall that had beautiful paintings on the peachy-brown stucco walls. I heard voices approaching and they weren't speaking English. It sounded like Spanish.

The bruising grip on my arm tightened as he yanked me forward and I stumbled. "Move."

He pulled me down a hall, opened a door, and I was dragged down a flight of stairs. A few more steps and another door, which he opened, then shoved me inside. He stood in the doorway as I did a quick scan of the room with cement walls and no windows. The anger had invaded, but the fear was fighting for the top position because being locked in here... it was my worst nightmare.

I swallowed back the bile as I faced the man. "Whatever you plan... it will be by force because I won't do it any other way."

He smiled. It was a cruel, malicious smile that revealed his one crooked, lower front tooth. Despite the sweltering heat, shivers ran through me and I crossed my arms in an attempt to control my shaking.

"We'll see." He slammed the door and the lock clicked.

Oh, God.

Even though I knew the door was locked, I still tried it. I even attempted to undo the screws of the doorknob with my fingernails, but I broke all ten of them in the process.

Not that I'd be able to escape once I was out of this cell, but trying was a hell of a lot better than sitting and doing nothing while hoping someone would find me. Anyone.

But after days, my hope shifted from being found to being given water and food for my cramping stomach. My throat was so dry that I could no longer swallow and my lips were cracked and bleeding. But the worst was being trapped, no windows, being below ground and feeling like I never had enough oxygen.

I was sitting on the floor when the lock finally clicked and the door opened. I scrambled to my bare feet, spine against the wall. My plan had been to jump whoever walked in. That plan slowly diminished over the days as I grew weaker. No doubt it was their plan. Make me submit by doing nothing, by just shutting me in a room for days until all I could think about was begging for someone to help. Begging *them* for help.

But I wouldn't. I couldn't do that.

The man in the doorway wasn't the same as the one who brought me to my cell, but I'd caught glimpses of him in the van through my drugged fog. I never heard him speak, smile, or do anything. His expression had been cold and blank. No smirk. No scowl, just blank and unreadable. The unknown.

He was tall and bulky, a muscled bulky, with dark, almost black hair and naturally sun-tanned skin. It was his beady, brown eyes that were the scariest though because they stared at me like I was nothing more than an inconvenience, a piece of garbage he had to deal with.

"What do you want? Who are you? Why am I here?" In the back of my mind, I couldn't help but think of Kai and the scars across his chest. Were these the people responsible for that? Were they the ones he worked for? Had I become insurance anyway? Did they have my father, too? "My father? Where is he?"

"At home, I imagine." I sighed with relief. Okay, my dad was okay.

The man raised his brows as he examined all the scratch marks on the doorknob, then he looked at me and gestured with his chin to the cot. "Lie down."

My heart pounded wildly. "No," I retorted. No way in hell was I lying on the cot. Only one thought came to me why he wanted me to. No. I wouldn't.

"Are you sure you want to take that approach?" He stepped further into the room and my eyes narrowed as I watched him. He was confident, and he should be. The asshole had all the power against a defenseless woman.

"Are you sure you want to?" I stupidly said back. But he'd left the door ajar and I was thinking about escape and not what I was saying.

I never saw it coming, how could I? His gun was in the back of his pants. He pulled it out and shot me in the thigh.

I fell to the floor clutching my leg, blood seeping between my fingers. The sharp pain went right through my body and I rolled on the floor trying to stop myself from screaming and giving him the satisfaction.

"On the cot."

"You shot me!" I'd been shot. Oh, God, I didn't want to die. No matter where I was or what they did to me, I wanted to live.

He raised the gun. "And I will again if you don't do as I say."

I had no doubt he would. I also had no doubt that the situation I was in could be my last. I pressed my palm to my leg as I crawled to my feet then limped to the bed. He obviously didn't want to kill me; he could've done that days ago.

"Hands above your head."

Shit. I didn't want to do it, especially when I saw the rope in his hands. But I wouldn't give him the satisfaction of me begging. Never. I may have been the quiet geek in school, but I was also stubborn and determined.

But I wasn't stupid and had to be careful what I said next time.

I screamed as the gun went off again. This time, he hit the cot and stuffing billowed out into the air beside my left leg.

Oh, God. Help me.

I gritted my teeth against the throbbing pain pulsing in my thigh and raised my arms above my head, fingers curling around the metal bar. He walked over, his steps quiet and slow, the opposite of what was happening inside me.

He stopped beside the bed and I glared at him, refusing to flinch under his stare. "I have a feeling we're going to be here a while."

"What are you going to do? Why are you doing this?"

He leaned over me and wrapped the coarse rope around my wrists then to the cot's bedframe. The tiny hairs of the material cut into my skin and I sharply inhaled when he yanked and the rope tightened.

His eyes traveled the length of me, hesitated on my thigh as if assessing whether I was going to bleed to death or not. He crouched, elbows casually resting on the cot beside me.

This time I did flinch when he reached out and pushed my hair back from my face. Then he said in a low, calm voice, "My name is Jacob and I'm your worst nightmare."

Dust. That was what I'd become. A speck of dust, floating, falling, fading. Something to be wiped away with a swipe of a finger and disappear.

Physically I existed, but the remains of who I'd been had been erased. The fight to hold onto who I was slipped away. That five-year-old girl who told her teacher she was going to stop people all over the world from getting sick had vanished.

Day by day a layer of me was peeled away and I was left raw and exposed. I never thought I'd ever choose to die. But I did. I begged for death. Not to them, I wouldn't give them that, but when I was alone in the darkness.

But I didn't die. So I existed.

I survived. And within the speck of dust, I had a speck of hope.

Maybe that was how I survived. Because without hope, there was nothing.

I sat in the corner of my room, my legs to my chest, my palm on the floor as my fingers scratched slow and methodically back and forth on the cement. I no longer had a bed frame, just a thin ragged mattress on the floor. They took that away after I used it to try and get out of my cell.

The door opened and I didn't look up, merely continued my rhythmic movement.

"Get up," Alfonzo ordered. After two months of being here, I'd discovered his name. He was the one who handled me when I'd been kidnapped and brought here. He was also the second worst next to Jacob.

Alfonzo liked sex. Jacob liked pain.

I stood, kept my eyes on the floor and followed him out the door. He didn't have to make certain I was behind him. He didn't have to force me. He didn't have to do anything because I wouldn't disobey him.

Not anymore.

Alfonzo was my trainer so to speak. Jacob hurt me, terrified me, he made me submit. But Alfonzo… he humiliated me. He treated me like an object and after a while, I became an object. I was nothing more than an expendable item to give pleasure to him and I wore a collar around my neck to prove it.

We walked upstairs, through the dining hall and out onto the terrace. I hadn't been outside in weeks. The heat felt good on my skin, even with the welts scoring across the backs of my thighs from a few days earlier.

I stepped on a sharp stone and it dug into the sole of my foot, but the pain was minimal to what I was accustomed to. I did my best to keep my steps even and quiet like I was taught—compliant and invisible.

I stopped when Alfonzo did, keeping my eyes down.

"Leave us," a voice ordered.

Alfonzo pushed by me and I was left standing on the hot patio stones, the soles of my feet burning. I closed my eyes and gritted my teeth trying to numb out the pain. I was good at numbing out the pain.

I recognized Raul's voice. He owned the compound and he owned me. I'd seen him a number of times at meals when I was in the dining hall, not eating but being played with.

"Come closer."

I took several steps forward until I stood under the shaded canopy and kneeled. I'd never been brought to Raul before. Fear crept across my skin as I wondered what he wanted with me. It was insane to feel this way, but comfort came with routine, with knowing.

And this was unusual.

"This is the girl. Raven. Of course, that's not her real name. Alfonzo named her. Said she reminded him of a raven because she is so intelligent. A problem solver." He chuckled. "She pushed her bedframe up on its edge against the wall, then climbed it so she could reach the ceiling. Then she used the sheet wrapped around her hand to dig through the plaster between the wall and ceiling. Smart. She knew when she could do it and when my men would be checking on her even without a window to tell the time." Every day I dug a little further until Alfonzo walked in unexpectedly one day and saw me. That's when they took my bedframe away. "Raven is the daughter of a well-known scientist."

I inhaled deeply to try and settle my nerves and that was when his scent hit me.

A slight whimper escaped and I started to look up, but stopped myself. I couldn't breathe because I knew that scent. I'd never forget it. My heart pounded and sparks darted over my skin.

I wanted to fall on the ground and sob, but I was too scared to do anything but keep my head down and remain as still as I could.

So many emotions traipsed all over me and through me. It was like my adrenaline had been drowned and now it was being pulled from the depths of the ocean and given life again.

Kai.

Maybe I was wrong in assuming he was here to save me. Maybe it was the stupidest thought I'd ever had. But it was *all* I had.

"Obedient. Now. Took Alfonzo and Jacob weeks to break this one." Raul laughed and it crackled as if he smoked too much.

"She's a risk," Kai said.

I choked on the sob as his voice blanketed me. I dug my cracked, split nails into my naked thighs to keep myself from looking up at him, to see for myself that it was really him.

"Perhaps. But my understanding is you enjoy risk, Kai," Raul said.

I heard the click of a lighter and then the smell of cigar smoke billowed in the air.

"A high-profile missing girl is a liability." Kai's voice was controlled and casual. What was he saying? It sounded like… no. No. It wasn't true. "No matter how beautiful."

Raul chuckled. "True, but you wouldn't have come if you didn't want her."

I squeezed my eyes shut to keep the tears from forming. Emotions ran rampant like I was being tossed and turned in a tidal wave. I didn't know what was happening. He'd been told I was here? Raul told him?

Kai knew Raul?

"She's too skinny and I'm betting if she looked at me right now, her eyes would be dead. Your men have broken her already. I prefer to do my own breaking, makes for a loyal slave."

Tears filled my eyes as I listened to his words. It was the last layer of me being slowly peeled back, but it wasn't thrown away. I wouldn't believe it. I'd seen something in Kai. I'd felt it. And if there was any part of the girl I'd once been left inside me, then I believed Kai was here to help me, not to destroy me. I saw the good in him. I felt it. I wasn't wrong about him.

"Raven." I stiffened as Raul spoke to me. "Get up."

I stood and he grabbed my wrist, yanking me close. My thigh hit his knee and I nearly fell into his lap.

My heart pounded erratically as I sensed Kai's eyes on me. Eyes I liked watching me a couple months earlier. Green eyes I'd been captivated by. Eyes that I dreamed about until that memory was beaten out of me.

Raul released my wrist and his harsh fingers dug into my chin as he raised my head. "She is striking, no?" Raul forced my head to the side so my face was directed at Kai.

I slowly raised my eyes to Kai's and everything stopped as our gazes locked. It was like when I'd last seen him in my loft, when nothing else existed except for us. No pasts. No pain. It was knowing that despite our beginning, there was more than the lust. More than a deal. It was the reason he walked away.

And looking at him now, I knew it was also the reason he was here. His words resonated, 'I'll always come for you.'

Oh, God, Kai. I wanted to fall to my knees and cry. I wanted him to pick me up in his arms and carry me away from this place like he'd carried me from the fire. I wanted Kai to save me because I couldn't save myself. Not from this.

"Yes," he drawled.

He sat with his legs outstretched, one hand curled around a frosted glass which he casually turned and the ice clinked against the sides.

My eyes darted to it and I swallowed. I was never given anything cold to drink. I was given room temperature water and at meals, Alfonzo would on occasion offer me a sip of his wine if I was good.

I'd do anything to slip an ice cube in my mouth. To have it clink against my teeth as it melted slowly on my tongue, the sweet moisture drizzling down my dry throat.

I'd have begged for it if I could.

God, how did I sink so low? How did I become a pathetic girl who had lost all dignity?

But my fairy tale had ended. Like a book thrown in the incinerator, pages of my life had been burned into ash then re-written into a girl called Raven.

Raul's hand dropped from my chin. "Go to him," he ordered.

I hesitated, unable to take my eyes off Kai. Not wanting to drop to my knees in front of him, but knowing I had no choice. Then I realized what bothered me the most about this. I didn't want Kai seeing me this way.

I stepped toward Kai and began to kneel at his feet when his arm snaked out and latched onto my wrist. He tugged and I half fell into his lap, my palms landing on his chest.

His heart beat steady and slow under my touch and I wondered how he could be so calm, so in control. But this was Kai. He was fearless even when in some criminal's compound, who I suspected had more power than the government.

And maybe that was because Kai's friends were like Raul. Maybe Raul was a friend.

Kai turned me around, so my back was against his chest then settled his arm on my abdomen. His heated breath swept across the back of my neck and I clasped my hands together in my lap as the tears formed again.

Raul's voice broke through the momentary silence. "She'll have to be kept hidden, but it is always invigorating to have something everyone is looking for. Si?"

"Mmm, perhaps."

I stiffened as his hand slid over the top of mine that were currently clasped together so tight the tips of my fingers were white. He gently squeezed, his entire hand encompassing both of mine.

I dropped my head forward, letting the small comfort of his hand settle over me and, for the first time in months, I felt safe.

The two men spoke about the upcoming fight between a guy named Sculpt and another man. From what I picked up on, that was why Kai was here. Raul had invited him to the fight and that meant they knew one another. I'd suspected Kai's circles were dangerous, and maybe I was deceiving myself to believe Kai had good in him, but Raul... he was malicious and cruel.

"Touch her," Raul said. "I've not tried her, but Alfonzo says she is tight."

Kai's comforting hand left mine and trailed slowly down between my legs.

I knew his touch. His familiar long fingers that had caressed every inch of me and made me ache and beg and shudder with release.

"Open for me, braveheart." His mouth was against my ear as he whispered the words.

My spine straightened and I chanced a glance at Raul, wondering if he heard what Kai said and not understanding why Kai would take the chance that he would overhear. But maybe Raul knew Kai and I had been together. No, he'd introduced me as if it were the first time Kai had ever seen me.

I opened my legs knowing I couldn't refuse with Raul watching. I closed my eyes as his fingers touched me.

"Beautiful, si? Alfonzo has told me she is one of his best. I suspect he'd keep her if he could."

"Disappointing."

"You don't like her?" Raul's voice was abrupt.

I tensed at his tone. Oh, God, no Kai. What was he doing? Raul would have me beaten if I didn't please Kai.

"On the contrary. She is remarkable; however, I'm disappointed she's not wet."

Raul laughed, slapping his knee. "You demand too much. Slaves who get wet are difficult."

Kai's finger didn't go inside me. Instead, he merely cupped me.

"Do you like me touching you?" Kai said, this time it wasn't a whisper and I knew Raul heard.

I'd been trained to give the right answer even if it was a lie. "Yes, master."

I heard him swear beneath his breath and his body stiffened. His breath wafted across my ear as he whispered so low that I barely heard the words. "Fuck, London."

I sharply inhaled at the sound of my name. It had been months since I'd been called that. I was Raven now, but my real name passing his lips was like he'd given me a piece of home.

Tears welled and this time, I couldn't stop one from slipping down my cheek. I quickly tilted my chin down further so Raul wouldn't see it. I saw it drop onto Kai's arm, soaking into his white dress shirt and leaving a round wet mark.

Kai withdrew his hand from me then reached for his drink. I had the urge to grab it from him and chug back the cool liquid, but his arm around my waist jerked as if in warning, like he knew exactly what I'd been considering.

I drew my eyes away from the frosted glass, but I heard him swallow the liquid and then he put it in front of my mouth. I parted my lips and he tipped the glass and the cold gin and tonic hit my parched mouth. It was like being handed heaven and it didn't matter if I hated tonic and its bitterness. It was the best thing I'd ever tasted.

He causally set it back down on the patio table. "How did you acquire this one, Raul?"

"I was paid a great deal of money to take her, have her trained and advised to get rid of her as quickly as possible."

"It's been two months."

"She's been difficult."

Kai chuckled and I felt the gin come back up. I quickly swallowed several times. "But they are usually worth the most."

Raul laughed. "True. But I have potential trouble with my son and his slave. I prefer neat and tidy."

"And yet you kidnap a high-profile girl."

"I was paid four times her worth or any other slave's in order to take her."

"And you don't find that peculiar, Raul. Paid to kidnap a girl?"

Raul chuckled. "Money keeps me safe and my business thriving. And we both know that whoever wanted her to disappear could've had her killed, but they paid a great deal of money to keep her alive. They wanted her to suffer."

"And you heard I was looking to acquire a slave and thought I could be appeased." I stiffened. Kai had been looking for a slave? No, that didn't make sense. Kai would never be with a woman who was forced.

"Yes."

"Let's be honest here, Raul. You used her as a lure to get me to your fight."

"You have many friends, Kai."

"I wouldn't call them friends," Kai replied.

Raul laughed. "You are a fascinating man. Perhaps you would consider staying a few days?"

"No. I am a very busy man." He gently urged me off his lap and I knelt on the unforgiving cement at his feet.

"A shame. Perhaps another time."

Kai stroked my hair. "Mmm, yes. A shame." There was something about the way he spoke that made me think he was angry. No, not angry. Furious. But Kai was an enigma and even after spending several nights with him, I didn't know his true emotions except perhaps when he desired me. His hand stilled on my head. "This girl... Raven, who paid you to take her?"

Smoke drifted into my face as Raul held his cigar between his fingers on his lap. "Anonymous. But nothing to be concerned about as the transaction was clean. No ties. The girl belongs to me. You will have a taste of her tonight after the fight."

"I do not taste, Raul. I fuck and I fuck girls who belong to me and I don't do it publicly."

Raul laughed and slammed his hand down on the table. I jumped at the clash of his glass as it tipped over.

"Then she belongs to you now. And I hope this will strengthen our relationship and perhaps we can do business in the future."

Kai's voice grated out, "I don't believe our businesses have the same interests. But of course, I appreciate the gift and it will not be forgotten."

I barely listened as I watched the cool liquid slip over the edge of the table and drip to the patio stones. I thought about licking it off the cement where it puddled in front of me. I even took the chance of shifting slightly forward on my knees until Kai's foot slid out in front of me blocking my path. He rested his heel in the puddle and I dared a glance up at him.

He was already looking at me and his dark brows lowered over his narrowed eyes in warning. I cast my eyes down again, my shoulders slumping forward in defeat.

Kai's chair abruptly pushed back and he stood. "I'll leave directly after the fight. Have her ready."

"No. No. You will come to the dinner party afterwards and meet Sculpt." Raul's tone hardened. "I insist. The girl will be brought to your table."

"Fine," Kai said and then walked away.

CHAPTER
NINE

London

I WAS DRESSED IN a sheer red bra with gold sparkles and thin, interlinked gold chains dangling from the underside. It didn't cover my nipples and its purpose was solely to push my breasts up. I didn't have much, but by wearing this it looked like I did. I had on matching panties minus the dangling chains. My discomfort sleeping without clothes had been obliterated the first month of my captivity. Or rather, my ability to be embarrassed had been obliterated. I was numb to everything.

Except Kai. He had awakened the hope that I'd escape this hell.

Alfonzo brought me to the dining hall an hour ago and I'd been kneeling on the floor beside a table before Kai strode into the room. Even with my eyes on the floor, I knew he walked toward me because, like always, when Kai entered a room, he owned it, even one filled with powerful criminals.

He sat in the chair beside me while he chatted with Jacob who had accompanied him. He had yet to touch me or acknowledge I was even there, and for a moment a wave of doubt flooded me. Maybe he wasn't going to get me out of here. Maybe he'd changed his mind. Maybe I'd missed reading the signs he gave me this morning.

As if sensing my unease, his hand lowered onto the back of my neck and he gently squeezed before pulling away. I closed my eyes, shoulders sagging.

"Raven!"

I jerked as Jacob's harsh voice shouted my name. Oh, God, I hadn't been listening. I had no idea if he asked me to do something. Fear clamped down on me and I trembled, fingers digging into my thighs as I stayed frozen, uncertain what to do. I knew better. I'd been taught better. Always listen.

"Do what you're told and please your new master."

Kai's hand pressed hard onto my shoulder, forcing me to stay in place. "As I told Raul, I do not publicly have sex. That includes having my cock in a girl's mouth."

There was a moment of silence before Jacob said, "She gives you trouble, let me know. We will exchange her for another. Enjoy your evening." I caught a glimpse of Jacob's white shoes as he turned and walked away.

I inhaled a deep breath of relief. Jacob told me the truth. He was my worst nightmare and there was no one I feared more. The man was psychotic and enjoyed watching pain and suffering.

Kai's hand cupped my chin and he tilted my head so I met his eyes. They were soft and yet beneath there was swirling anger, but I knew it wasn't directed at me. "Remember what I told you?"

My mind spun as I thought of our time together, before any of this. It seemed so long ago, almost as if it hadn't happened. As if my life hadn't happened before this place.

His thumb stroked back and forth. "Only willing, braveheart. No other way."

I had no response and I knew he didn't expect one. He released me when a girl was pushed down beside me. I kept my eyes on the floor, but caught a glimpse of her from the corner of my eye. I felt her gaze on me. Stupid. You were beaten if you dared to look at anything except the floor unless you were told to.

I'd seen her the day she arrived. She belonged to the fighter, Sculpt, and hadn't been here long. I'd also heard her screams in the room beside mine after she foolishly spit in Raul's face and called him a disgusting parasite. Alfonzo was giddy with excitement that the girl would be taken to Jacob. No one wanted to spend time with Jacob.

"Sculpt. Good fight." Kai's tone was controlled and cold. The mild amusement often attached to it was gone.

"Kai," Sculpt said.

Kai's leg brushed against me as he leaned to the right. "I have no interest in the fighting circuit, but I was rather impressed by your ability. And I lost a lot of money tonight."

"Raul mentioned your name in passing," Sculpt replied. "I'm curious, why is it that you've travelled all this way for a fight you're not interested in?"

Kai reached toward me and grabbed my chin, raising my head. "Her. I was curious when Raul sent me the invitation to the fight. I declined, however. Raul must have known I would, and he is intelligent. He also knew if I refused to come, many other of my acquaintances wouldn't either, so he offered me her. Alfonzo's latest."

From the corner of my eye, I noticed Sculpt's slave put her hand over her mouth and her eyes widened. I remained impassive. Nothing bothered me anymore, not her reaction, not what would happen to her tonight. Every emotion was ripped out of me except one… that flicker of hope that sparked the moment Kai showed up.

Sculpt nudged his girl with his leg, and she lowered her hand from her mouth. "He is giving her to you? Raul doesn't like to give anything away."

Kai chuckled. "No, but I required a new girl, and Raul knew that. When I saw her picture, I had to have her."

Kai grabbed me by the collar and jerked upward. It was meant to look aggressive, but his other hand had slipped down onto my hip so the pressure on my neck was minimal. He pulled me onto his lap, my back to his chest and then his hand reached around and played with my nipple, pinching and circling hard then soft. "He knows my type and this one is… is special."

I remained in his lap while he chatted about the fight, but despite appearing relaxed, I felt the tension in him.

He fed me parts of his meal and let me sip his wine and ice-cold water. The usual sounds in the dining hall were the same as every night except louder and filled with excitement over the fight.

Kai kissed my ear and it appeared as if he were enjoying himself, but the tension pulsed in every muscle in his body. "Baby," he whispered. His voice was so low that I had difficulty hearing him. "Raul is watching us."

I lowered my chin in a subtle nod so he knew I heard him.

"She is stunning." Kai nodded to Sculpt's girl. His hand rested between my legs, not doing anything, merely cupping me like he'd done that night on my couch.

"Hmm."

"Dinner appears to be over, and my understanding is Raul likes to play afterward. Care to indulge?"

This is what Raul's parties were about and even though I'd only been to a few, I was experienced enough to know that the best chance of survival of what was to come, was to be obedient and quiet.

"Not really."

Kai's finger twitched. "Then why bother having her? My suggestion is tame, nothing to frighten your little slave. She does look like she wants to be swallowed up by the floor." Kai reached over and stroked the side of the girl's face. "Look at me."

"I don't share," Sculpt said abruptly.

"Neither do I," Kai said, and his hand dropped from her face to stroke my inner thigh. "But watching the women together. Two beauties… now that I would enjoy."

I knew exactly what Kai was doing. He'd never fuck me. Not now. Not when I was being forced to. But there had to be a show for Raul so he was using Sculpt's girl as a scapegoat.

"No." Sculpt raised his voice.

"No, what, gentlemen?" I stiffened at the sound of Raul's voice and couldn't help but lean further into Kai's embrace.

He was right, Raul was obviously watching us.

Kai spoke, "I suggested a little play between the women. Sculpt has declined."

"I never said that."

"I had something else in mind for tonight," Kai said.

He put his hands on my hips then shoved me off his lap. I landed hard on the floor and quickly righted myself and knelt beside Kai. I didn't have any doubt about what he was doing. We were going to get out of this place and Kai was making certain it happened. He'd do whatever it took, and so would I.

A feminine hand reached out to me and my heart leapt and my eyes widened. Stupid girl. She was going to get us both beaten with Raul watching. I sidled up to Kai's leg like I was taught to do and turned away from her.

"I'd be interested in hearing this," Raul said. "Kai, Sculpt has been hiding this gem away for over a week now. I was beginning to think that she'd escaped him." Kai laughed. "She was rather… disobedient when she arrived. I was anticipating Alfonzo having to train her as he did your new slave. But, she has been reined in. After being away from us for so long, I was thinking Sculpt had become soft."

"Then what do you have in mind for this part of the evening, Sculpt?" Kai asked.

That's when I blocked their words out. Blocked everything out. I became numb and cold and prayed for the evening to be over and Kai to get me out of here. I silently sang to myself, voices becoming a blur of rough sounds.

Kai reached down and put his hand on the back of my neck, his finger slowly caressing back and forth. It was soothing. Comforting. Then he bent down, his lips close to my ear as he whispered, "Always, baby."

The words were spoken so low I barely heard them. But I did and the overwhelming emotions crashed down on me. It was only his comforting hand that kept me from collapsing to the floor in a heaping mess of sobs.

Always.

Always.

He'd always come for me.

A tear slipped down my cheek and dripped onto the back of my hand. Then another. Oh God, I couldn't let Raul see. I couldn't falter now.

Sculpt said something, but I was so focused on Kai I didn't pay attention, but I saw Sculpt get up and leave with his girl in tow.

"As I told you," Raul said, "he is too attached to his slave. I will have to put an end to that."

Kai chuckled, but it was laced with a grated tone. "She has spirit. Something I admire. But, yes, attachments are dangerous. Better to kill her or sell her."

"Killing her loses money. Perhaps you'd be interested in acquiring her as well?"

"Perhaps," Kai replied.

I stayed at his feet while he chatted with others for what seemed like hours. I kept a part of me touching him at all times or rather he did, I wasn't sure which.

"Look at me…" he hesitated then whispered, "London."

I slowly raised my chin and the flicker of life singed my skin for the first time in months. My throat tightened as our eyes locked. It was with that one look he'd wrapped me up in a warm blanket and held me. Protected me.

Bang.

Bang.

Bang.

I jerked my eyes to the terrace that led out into the gardens. Kai bolted out of his chair and it tipped over backwards.

Several more gunshots rang out.

He pulled out his knife, grabbed my arm, and shoved me under the table. "Stay there."

Raul's men ran through the dining hall shouting while some guests took cover, and others ran toward the gunshots with weapons drawn.

It was complete chaos as men panicked because sure as hell this place was filled with illegal substances, activity and more than likely, wanted men.

Kai took out his cell, tapped a few times then put it to his ear and started shouting at someone about getting the Jeep. He shoved the phone in his pocket then crouched in front of me, his knife in his hand between us. "Keep down and out of sight."

My heart raced and my stomach tightened with dread. "Don't leave me."

He reached out and stroked the side of my face with his knuckles. "Baby, I'll be right back. I need to see what the fuck is going on." He stood, nodded once then jogged off in the direction of the gunshots.

As he disappeared around the corner, cold shivers coursed through me and my stomach flipped. I screamed his name because I knew, I knew he wasn't coming back. It was the feeling of dread like I was trapped in an ice cube, unable to escape the cold that sank into every part of me.

He wasn't coming back.

No.

No.

No.

I crawled out from under the table and ran.

I made it ten steps before an unforgiving hand latched onto my arm and yanked me to a stop. "Where do you think you're going?" Jacob said then locked his arm around my chest and started for the basement. "Looks like he doesn't want you. Guess you're staying with us."

I flailed.

I fought.

I screamed for Kai.

But there was nothing I could do to stop Jacob as he dragged me downstairs and threw me into my room. I fell to my knees. The door slammed and then the finality as the lock clicked.

I collapsed.

I sobbed.

And I begged for Kai to come back.

But hour after hour, day after day the lifeline slipped further and further away until any hope for Kai returning finally extinguished.

My end had begun. I became Raven.

CHAPTER
TEN

Kai

SEVENTEEN MONTHS, ONE week and five days. That's how long it had been since I'd left her under the table at Raul's in Mexico when the fireworks of gunshots went off. Raul's business acquaintances had shot at anything that moved thinking the compound was being raided. Most of them were on the wanted list and weren't going down without a fight.

And that was the reason I hated guns. Bullshit like that. Getting shot for no reason because some asshole was shittin' his pants and shooting at shadows. I'd seen Sculpt, the fighter, shooting at Raul's men. I didn't know what the fuck was going on, didn't care except to make certain I got London out. But I never made it further than the front steps when an agonizing pain hit my chest.

I remembered one thing as I fell—London. Just her. Only her.

The agony of the gunshot was nothing compared to the agony of what I knew was going to happen. I thought I heard her scream my name before I hit the ground and everything went black.

Then nothing for fifteen days. Fifteen fuckin' days.

I ended up in some Mexican hospital with Ernie sitting at my bedside looking as haggard as I felt. Then minutes later, I found out why he was so haggard when he told me the shit that went down at Raul's wasn't the FBI or DEA or anyone else, it was Sculpt causing a distraction.

For a brief few minutes I was relieved because that meant London would still be there. But Ernie wasn't done. I found out that while I was lying in a fuckin' hospital bed, Deck and his men raided the compound and took out everyone who needed taking out. Then blew it up.

But Raul escaped, along with Alfonzo and Jacob.

I didn't have to say her name. Ernie knew what I'd want to know. London.

Ernie's hooded eyes and grim expression said it all.

That's when I freaked. Never freaked before. Never cared enough to give a shit about anything to lose control like I did that day.

I'd ripped the IV from my arm and yanked the heart monitors from my chest before knocking over the machine that screamed a loud warning signal. Took me three tries to get my legs moving and over the side of the bed and I was so frustrated that I threw the IV stand across the room and it smashed into the television.

Nothing mattered except getting the fuck out of there and finding her. My head was so drugged up on painkillers that I didn't even see or hear Ernie as he tried to keep me in bed. All I saw was London on her knees. London submitting to those fuckin' disgusting bastards. London. London. London.

I finally made it to my feet and found out why. Ernie was no longer holding me down. He was at the door with a needle in his hand. A nurse stood beside him, eyes wide and terrified. He came at me. I made it one step from the bed before he tackled me to the ground and shoved the needle in my arm.

For another week I was kept sedated, unable to do more than curse Ernie when I briefly opened my eyes before I passed out again. They were probably smart to keep me that way until I healed, because if I hadn't been, I'd have never stayed in that bed. I'd have been out doing what I was doing now, searching for London.

At another fuckin' auction. This time in Germany.

I'd been to at least a dozen of these with no sign of her and I was beginning to wonder if she'd ever show up, but I had nothing else and I refused to believe she was dead. I'd know if she was. My gut told me she was alive and I wasn't giving up until I found her.

I'd used contacts that weren't associated with Vault to keep what I was doing quiet, and there were only two people who knew I was searching for her, Ernie and London's father.

I'd gone to see him, but not by choice. Since I'd been out of commission for weeks, Vault, meaning Mother, had been looking for me. I went off the grid plenty of times when I was on assignments, so it wasn't unusual to disappear for a month, but she wanted Dr. Westbrook looked into. Threatened was really what she wanted because the drug he'd given her was causing a zombie-like state on her test subject, Connor, and she was pissed.

I'd flown to New York and left Ernie in Mexico searching for any info on where Alfonzo and Jacob could've gone because they were my only lead to what happened to London.

When I saw her father, I told him what happened to her. I'd seen men cry, beg for the torture to stop. I'd seen them drool and flounder under my knife, but never had I seen a man fall to his knees in racking sobs of grief. I stood and watched, unemotional. Cold. Allowing nothing for what I was feeling about London in. Because if I did that, I'd go insane with rage.

But I did give her father one thing before I left him in his lab on the floor, a promise to find her and bring her back.

Now, as I stood in a private room in Germany watching a television screen as girl after girl was brought on camera, I faltered. My easygoing casual persona was cracking at the edges because I was cracking. It had been too long.

I'd dealt with the lowliest scum of the earth all my life and yet these men were worse. Even Vault stayed clear of this side of the underworld, because like me, they had no respect for men like this. They weren't strong. They were weak and used slaves to make themselves feel powerful.

I barely watched the screen. It was sick. Dogs were treated better than these girls. I closed my eyes and took a few deep breaths as I tried to control the anger throbbing.

Then it happened.

I didn't have to open my eyes or look at the screen. I just knew it was her.

Goose bumps popped up along my skin and my stomach lurched. Everything inside me stilled. It stilled and then it began its climb toward her. It's need.

I slowly raised my head and finally looked at the screen. Every muscle tensed, my fingers curled into fists and for the first time in almost two years, I let myself feel.

"Fuck, boss." It was Ernie who was standing by the door, doing what I was doing—watching.

She was barely recognizable as she stood on stage, her hair hanging limp and dull over her shoulders. Shoulders slouched, thin; the notches of bone prominent. I clenched my jaw, the rage rising as my eyes traveled down her bruised, barely-clothed body.

Her head was lowered, eyes downcast just like every other girl brought before the camera. Submission, and I'd expected it, but expecting and seeing were completely different, and I wasn't prepared to see her broken.

My brave scientist ruined.

They'd ruined her.

She'd been fuckin' perfect. She was brave and cute and caring and fuckin' perfect, and they'd ruined everything she was.

I snapped.

Ernie saw it coming and was on me, but it was too late. My fist went through the television and then he was hauling me back.

"Boss, let's go. She has to be in one of the rooms."

London. Fuck, she was here. So close I could feel her. Blood dripped from my hand that now held my knife. "It's been too long." I kept thinking of her on the TV, a girl I no longer recognized. "It's been too fuckin' long."

"Boss." Ernie had the door open, his gun out, but he wasn't looking at me. He was looking down the corridor. "Fuck. Deck."

I ran to the door and just as I careened around the corner, I saw Deck glance over his shoulder at me. What the fuck? Why was he…?

But then I knew.

One of his men, Vic, came out of a room to the right with a body over his shoulder. A girl. My fuckin' girl.

Deck and his men were here for my fuckin' girl.

I started toward them, blood dripping off my fingertip leaving a trail of blood.

Ernie was right behind me and I heard his gun cock.

I stopped ten feet away from Deck. He was dressed in combat gear as were his men. I knew of them, Vic, Tyler, Josh, because I knew everyone associated with Deck.

Deck had his hand on his gun at his hip, but he hadn't withdrawn it—yet.

My eyes went to Vic who stood with London's limp body over his shoulder, unmoving. Not fighting.

I stiffened. "Jacob and Alfonzo had her?"

"Yes," he replied. Deck said something to Vic who turned and jogged down the corridor then disappeared around the corner. With London. And yet, I didn't move.

"Boss?" Ernie questioned.

But I couldn't do it. Deck wasn't like me. He had morals. He was good and he was here because he was getting London out probably because Sculpt or his girl had told him about her.

He was getting her out.

My vicious, cruel strings were tied to London and I had to break them. I had to make her valuable to Mother and Vault then stay the hell away from her. It was the only way for her to stay safe and alive.

I had to let her go.

I nodded to Deck, then turned and walked away.

CHAPTER
ELEVEN

France

Kai

"HOW COME DR. Westbrook's daughter is in Toronto, Mother?"

This was how I had to play it. Like I hadn't found London in Germany and seen Deck get her out. Any suspicion of me having an attachment to London had to end today. The second Deck took London back to New York, Mother would know about it because I'd have to tell her. It was much more productive to tell her before the fact.

"She is?" She straightened, scissors in one hand and three roses in the other. I'd found her outside in her garden, an area of land that had more bushes than actual flowers.

Mother looked surprised and that gave me an advantage. "Yes. Chaos called me." And she had. Told me Deck had a girl, Raven, staying with her. "Said her name was Raven, but I checked into it and it's London Westbrook." The lies were becoming easier.

Mother's thin brows rose. "Deck is resourceful, isn't he?"

"Deck is good at what he does and one day we may be able to use that." She nodded with a slight shift in weight. She liked that idea, just like I had to make her like my next idea. "And we can use her."

Her eyes narrowed and any hint of a smile faded. "I don't see how. She's a weak, pathetic—"

"Scientist," I interrupted. "She's brilliant and knows how her father works." All of that was true, but Mother's face was tense and I knew she still wasn't convinced, so I threw in, "We can send her to the farm until we need her." No way in hell I'd let that happen, but Mother didn't know that.

She turned back to the rose bush and snipped off another bud. A drop of blood dripped down the pad of her finger from a thorn, but she hadn't even flinched at the prick. She sifted through the flowers, ignoring the scratches to her hands as she cut more and more. She wasn't even collecting them now. Instead, she merely cut the red flowers and let them fall to the ground.

Killing them for no reason.

She continued, ignoring me until the rose bush was bare of all buds then she slipped the scissors into her pants pocket. "Dr. Westbrook got the message." The message being his daughter disappearing for two fuckin' years. "Maybe he will be more productive if we allow his daughter to return. The drug needs some adjustments."

I kept completely still, not even a facial twitch. "How is the drug coming along?"

"It's useful. It's been rather... difficult to come by one component of the drug." She waved her hand as if to dismiss the conversation. "You will continue to monitor Dr. Westbrook. I will consider his daughter. For now, she isn't going anywhere. I suspect she is in a rather... delicate condition anyway."

Ruined, mother. You fuckin' ruined her.

I nodded, then moved in and kissed her cheek. "Good to see you again, Mother."

"Son," she replied and turned back to her rose bush.

I had one more thing to do before erasing London from my life. Hunt the bastards who destroyed the girl I'd once known. Because the girl I saw on the camera at the auction wasn't London. She was a ghost of the girl I'd been with.

And Jacob and Alfonzo were responsible. And there was nothing I wouldn't do to kill them for what they did to her. Nothing.

CHAPTER
TWELVE

Toronto

Kai

IF I BELIEVED in fate, it was seriously enjoying itself fuckin' with me. Despite trying to keep my distance from London, I was thrown right back in her path within two weeks. But this time, it wasn't me stalking her or searching for her, it was because Deck had yet to take her back to New York and she was still in Toronto.

And also in Toronto was the bastard, Alfonzo. And I knew this because I was hunting Jacob and Alfonzo. No lead on Jacob, but I'd tracked Alfonzo here.

In my fuckin' territory.

I thought he was in Toronto for London. As it turned out, he wasn't. He was using London to get to Emily, Sculpt's girl. Sculpt and Emily had been the reason Deck took down Raul and the compound, and now Alfonzo wanted payback.

Well, so did I and I was using anyone in order to get it. Alfonzo was a dead man, but first I needed him to lead me to the elusive bastard, Jacob, and to do that, I had to use Chaos.

I walked up to the gate of Chaos's backyard where I'd agreed to meet Alfonzo. As far as he knew, I'd come to buy Raven since he claimed he owned her still. Of course, it was all bullshit.

What I hadn't expected when I strolled into the backyard was Chaos and Alfonzo rolling around on the ground fighting over a gun. Fuck. Already this situation was volatile and Chaos was a live wire.

"Jesus," I muttered, diving for Chaos before she got herself shot, and dragged her off Alfonzo.

I wasn't nice about it either. Alfonzo had to be played. He was already uneasy about meeting me, but word was he was also a greedy fuck.

What the fuck was Chaos doing? This had to play out my way or Jacob would slip away like he and Alfonzo had done with London for years.

Alfonzo scrambled to his feet and went to punch Chaos's face when I caught his fist in my palm and shoved him back. What I wanted to do was take my knife and gut him like a fish, but that had to wait.

I heard the commotion inside and shoved her forward into Alfonzo. "Hurt her and I hurt you." Then I walked inside the house, saw the girl, Emily, on top of London, and a gun inches from both their hands.

I had no idea what the hell was going on except Alfonzo had lost control of the situation and I had to get it back in order for this to go down like I needed it to.

I grabbed Emily and hauled her off London.

"Stop," I ordered as she struggled against me.

London's breath hitched and her eyes flew to mine. Then, as if she were terrified to look at me, she dropped her gaze to the floor.

"Raven!" I used the name Alfonzo called her because I wasn't supposed to know her real name.

Alfonzo yanked Chaos back inside and Raven quickly kneeled, head low as she came to my side. *Jesus. Fuck.* Seeing that, seeing London on her knees and so submissive and terrified of doing anything except what she'd been beaten into doing, it was like setting my insides on fire.

"Where's the transporter?" I ground out. Jacob, I wanted Jacob. The bastard who was in charge.

Alfonzo kicked Chaos in the back of the legs, and she fell to her knees. I clenched my jaw, but didn't say anything. I needed to be un-emotional. I needed all I'd been taught, because if I slipped, then Jacob would disappear and my chance was gone.

I knew the second I put a call in to Deck about what was going down, the guy was going to go ballistic. Chaos and Deck had history and it was history that connected all of us, although Deck didn't know it.

Alfonzo tied Chaos's wrists behind her back and I saw her wince. This shit had never bothered me before. I wasn't attached to Chaos, even though I'd been assigned to her since she was sixteen.

No attachments. It was simple. I kept it that way, but there was nothing simple about it now.

Alfonzo picked the gun up off the floor. "I promised you Raven. You have her. That's our deal."

"Our deal has changed," I said. No matter what, Alfonzo was dying today even if he refused to lead me to Jacob. I excelled at 'convincing' men to do what I wanted and if need be, that was my next option. "What are you doing with that one?" I nodded to Chaos.

"She's coming with us. And that bitch"—he nodded to Emily—"escaped Raul. No one escapes Raul and lives."

"Raul's dead." *Pathetic asshole.*

Alfonzo kicked Chaos in the lower back, and she grunted and fell forward. I had my hand on my knife ready to gut him and screw the plan. It took everything I had to remain calm and steady.

"Once I'm done with their training, they'll go to auction and never be found again. That's if they live through it."

I glanced at Chaos. Fuck, she was pissed and I knew what she was going to do before she did it. She slammed her head backward into Alfonzo's knee.

I heard the sound of her skull hitting his knee cap; then Alfonzo yelled in agony.

Jesus Christ.

"No!" Emily yelled as Alfonzo raised his gun to Chaos.

"Killing her is a waste," I said, careful to keep my voice calm. "Take me to the transporter. I need to see him."

Alfonzo had his gun to Chaos's head, his fingers weaved into her hair. "I can't do that. That wasn't the deal. Raven and the money. That's it."

"It's the deal now," I said.

Alfonzo's face turned beet red. "I'm selling you the girl for half her price."

"I could have easily found Raven myself. I found you, didn't I? What I want is the transporter."

"No one gets to meet him. He doesn't meet with anyone. Ever."

I shrugged. "He will meet with me. Call him."

Alfonzo blanched. "You just don't call him. It's been set up already—"

"Raul is dead. That means you and your transporter no longer have a main source. Call him. Now. Or I kill you and take all three girls myself."

"Fuck." Alfonzo's fat fingers twitched on the gun, and his eyes shifted side to side. Alfonzo raised the gun and hit Chaos on the head when she tried to get up.

"Georgie," Emily cried and tried to pull away from me. "Please don't hurt her."

I tightened my hold on Emily's arm and said in a low and almost inaudible voice, "It's better this way."

And it was. I'd dealt with Alfonzo's type. If Chaos pushed it much more, he'd put a bullet in her head. Of course, I wouldn't let that happen, but protecting her would blow my cover. I'd been forced to learn a lot at the farm. One of those things was to be unreactive even when shit went bad.

Alfonzo tied a strip of cloth around Chaos's arm and pulled out a syringe. I knew what it was and it was going to keep Chaos alive because being drugged meant she'd stop fighting until I got to Jacob.

Emily struggled against my hold. "Please, don't. Georgie."

"Stop." I yanked her arm to the side and she cried out in pain.

Alfonzo glanced at me and grinned. I was thinking about stabbing my knife into his eyeballs then cutting off his dick while I half-smiled back at him. He slid the needle into her vein, and within seconds, Chaos's body relaxed and her eyes closed.

Alfonzo took out his phone, tapped a few times and then put it to his ear. He kept his voice low as he mumbled my name and something about a warehouse and meeting.

He hung up and nodded to me.

Finally.

Jacob.

"Let's go," I said. I guided Emily out the door ahead of me.

Alfonzo slung Chaos over his shoulder and I heard him order Raven to follow.

Like a fuckin' dog. And the worst was watching her do it. My stomach curdled.

This shit was ending.

I leaned against a large piece of machinery with London kneeling beside me, her hands in her lap and her head bowed.

Chaos was still drugged and Alfonzo paced back and forth looking anxious. His eyes kept shifting to the warehouse door then to his phone. It was obvious the guy was nervous and, from when I'd met Jacob in Mexico, he had every right to be. It made me sick to think that London had spent two years with these men. No wonder why she was nothing of the girl I'd known.

Finally, the metal door slid on its tracks and opened.

Jacob.

There was no hesitation as he advanced toward me. No gun in sight. Arrogant and sure of himself. I was going to enjoy watching that flicker of life in his eyes fade away to nothing when I slit his throat.

He stopped in front of me, but when he spoke it was to Alfonzo, who had followed along beside him like a puppy dog.

"I don't like changing plans," Jacob said to Alfonzo. "It causes mistakes."

I kept my eyes on Jacob as I said, "Raul's right-hand man. I thought you were dead," I lied.

"So does everyone." Jacob nodded to Raven. "You've travelled a great distance for one girl. She doesn't look worth it."

"Where are the other girls?" I asked. There was no way he came to Toronto for simply one girl. Even two. He had to have more and I took a chance asking, but I needed him to think I wanted to go into business with him. What I was doing was delaying. I was waiting for Deck who I called from my car on the way to the location. I couldn't give it to him before we'd arrived, so he was trying to get here—fast.

Deck had already been looking for Emily, but when I mentioned Georgie, he went stone silent. What was a 'be there in ten,' changed to 'be there in five.'

"Here. Awaiting shipment," he replied.

I tensed. That was what I needed to know.

Jacob's shoulders stiffened and I put my hand on my knife. He pulled his gun, turned, and shot Alfonzo in the head.

Alfonzo dropped to the ground.

I didn't flinch. I remained leaning against the machinery, my hand on London's head, making sure she didn't move.

"I told him, I don't meet clients. He didn't listen," Jacob said.

"So that would make me a liability."

"Your offer piqued my interest." Jacob paused. "I require a base to bring the girls before auction. You can provide me with that."

My hand stilled in London's hair as I heard a footstep. Deck. Time to finish this. "Who has been providing since Raul's death?"

Jacob slipped his gun back into his belt. "No one. This is our first shipment in over a year. That guy Deck and his men have been all over us, and now, Alfonzo screwed up taking that one." He nodded to Chaos. "I don't make mistakes, Kai. I'm careful. Alfonzo wasn't."

"Oh, but you made a mistake, Jacob." I smiled.

Jacob was quick. Before I even finished the sentence, he dove and rolled and my knife narrowly missed his throat. Fuck.

"Raven. Go to the girls," I ordered.

I didn't wait to see if she did because I knew she'd do anything I told her. I kept low as I snuck across the warehouse pausing behind a conveyor belt. I nodded to Deck who was approaching from the back of the warehouse.

Jacob disappeared behind floor-to-ceiling shelves, but I saw his feet as he circled around. And I knew exactly what he was doing and where he was headed. Shit. Keeping low and covered, I made my way back to the girls and came out into the clearing just as Jacob grabbed London hauling her up against his chest.

I came up on his left, my knife at my side.

"Let her go." My gaze drilled into Jacob and my fingers tightened around the hilt of my knife. I was pretty fuckin' sure I could kill him before his finger pressed the trigger.

London whimpered as Jacob's hold tightened.

"In seconds, I can shoot Sculpt's woman and snap your slave's neck."

"Then do it," I said. I never took well to threats and I was betting he wasn't going to kill both girls. If he did, he was dead.

Deck was crouched behind a pile of barrels on Jacob's right. Our eyes met and he chin-lifted to me. I threw my knife at the same time as Sculpt dove out from behind the barrels and took Emily down, protecting her with his body.

My knife sliced through the air and into Jacob's neck, so close to London's ear I saw a speck of blood on the outer edge of the lobe.

Jacob's gun went off, but it was a knee-jerk reaction as his body swayed. London scrambled from his hold and fell to her hands and knees, blood splattered over her face and chest.

Jacob's hand still held his gun while his other went to his neck, blood seeping between his fingers as he tried to stop the flow around the knife.

He was a dead man any second, but I knew why Deck approached, raised his gun and shot him in the chest several times. It was a man's need to put bullets in the guy who hurt his girl.

Jacob fell backwards. The gun slipped from his grasp and clattered to the floor.

I strode over, yanked my knife from his neck, wiped the blood off on Jacob's body then put it in the sheath at my waist. Then I went to London.

She was still on the floor as I crouched beside her. Fuck, I wanted so badly to pull her into my arms, tell her it was over. That the men who hurt her would never touch her again.

But for her, it wasn't over. It was the beginning of finding her way back from what was done to her.

"Baby," I murmured.

She closed her eyes, but kept her head down.

I gently put my arm around her and cursed under my breath at how much weight she'd lost. I felt Deck's lethal stare as he was on his knees beside Chaos.

I turned back to London.

"London." She didn't respond and I closed my eyes as a wave of pain went through me.

Fuck.

Fuck.

Fuck.

She spent years with Jacob and Alfonzo and seeing her like this hurt. No, it fuckin' killed. Torture had nothing on this. The beauty of what London had always given me—lightness—was gone and that destroyed me.

I helped her stand then guided her over to Deck and the others. I saw Deck run his finger over the needle mark on Georgie's arm. "Heroin," I said.

I had my arm around London's waist, and her head was tucked into my chest. Fuck. I didn't want to let go, but I had no choice. There was a chance for her without me. A chance to bring the lightness back, the laughter, the sweetness. I was her destruction and I kept falling back into that rift and suffocating her in my darkness.

Deck nodded. "Probably better. Georgie would've gotten herself killed with that mouth of hers." Deck stood. "Police will be here shortly. You better go."

I peeled London away from me. I hadn't intended on looking at her again. I should've just walked away. Instead, I had to look at her one more time and my heart stopped. Broken. The compassionate, brilliant woman with stubborn determination no longer existed.

Jesus, baby. You need to find your way back. You can't do that with me.

I had to get out of here. "You need to stay with them. Deck will take you home."

Her eyes widened and her face paled. Then she did what I never expected. She fell to her knees in front of me and grabbed my leg. "Please. Please take me with you."

I remained motionless.

Fuck, London.

I'd never cared before. In order to care, you had to give a shit. I didn't. Now I did and it was worse than any physical pain. It was acid eating away at my insides and feeling like there was no way back from the hell I lived in.

I belonged in the darkness and London belonged in the light.

I sighed and then nodded to Deck. He stood, took two steps then snagged London's arm and pulled her away from me. Tears streamed down her cheeks, but she didn't make a sound.

Then I jogged away and didn't look back.

CHAPTER
THIRTEEN

Kai

ERASED.

The word lingered in my head. I became a ghost after ending all communication with London. She was better without me. She was safer.

It had been a year and seven months since I saw her in the warehouse on her knees begging me to take her with me. I pretended it was business as usual, but it wasn't. What I did had nothing to do with business. It was personal as I became the silent killer.

I killed instead of satisfying any sexual needs. I killed to stop the nightmare of seeing her on her knees. And I killed to ease the pain. Weaving in and out of the sex trafficking industry, I killed those who deserved it.

It was my outlet.

My link to keeping my sanity.

Ernie still watched her, but I'd insisted on not hearing updates. He ignored the order and sent me emails anyway, to which for the first couple weeks my finger hovered over the delete button without opening the file. But I always read them.

Shit changed a year ago when she ran away. My first thought had been Vault and after feeling that out, I knew they didn't have her. From Ernie's take on it, London simply left with nothing.

And since she had nothing, there was no trail. No trail meant she was making it one fuck of a job for Ernie to find her. The only good news with her missing was that if I couldn't find her, neither could Vault and they'd been looking because a couple of months earlier, Mother asked me to bring London in. And for the first time, I didn't lie when I told her I couldn't find her.

I had a suspicion that they thought I might even be hiding her. Of course, I wasn't. And even if I were, I'd never bring her in. I was part of Vault, but I didn't submit to them, although they thought differently. I just knew how to play their game and lie really well.

I knew why London ran. She was running from herself from—Raven.

And I fuckin' hated Raven.

My brave London had submitted and that pissed me off more than anything else because they'd broken her so badly that she had no choice but to fracture and yield.

She'd become Raven and Raven was not a scientist. She wasn't strong or stubborn or a smart-as-fuck girl who would do anything to save her father, who cared about others and wanted to save lives.

She'd become nothing.

Her freedom hadn't freed her at all. It trapped her in a world she no longer knew how to survive in and she ran from it.

My disposable phone vibrated and I pulled it from my suit jacket pocket, and then leaned my palm against the glass window as I stared out into the city. "Told you I don't want to know."

"Too bad," he said. Asshole kept me updated on his search for London whether I wanted to hear it or not. "Christie shelter. Found out she often goes there. Although, it's all women, so I can't get in."

For the last six months, Ernie incorporated himself into the streets and lived with the homeless. London had always helped them and no matter who she was now, Ernie and I thought she might gravitate to them, meaning live on the streets.

But the homeless didn't like to share information or were too drugged up to share, and the homeless shelters definitely didn't share. Not when a guy, a guy like Ernie, was looking for a girl who was completely inside herself. It screamed abuse.

"Old man named Donald says he sees her often in an alley behind the Dark Horse. It's a bar near the shelter. Donald says the bouncer keeps an eye on her. Helps her out. Slips her food." Ernie paused and I knew why. His gut said we were finding her tonight and that meant he wanted me there. "You need to deal with this, boss. It's been too long and she's worse not better. Worth the risk."

I curled my hand around the phone. Fuck.

"Boss."

Fuck, London, what the hell are you doing?

I rested my forehead against the cool glass window and closed my eyes.

"On my way." I ended the call.

I pulled my phone out and called Ernie as I drove toward the Dark Horse. "Two minutes out."

"Bouncer says she's in the alley. Not going to like it, boss."

I fuckin' knew I wasn't going to like what I saw. I didn't like what I saw in Mexico, in Germany, in fuckin' Toronto with Alfonzo. "Keep the bouncer inside. Don't need witnesses."

"Got it."

I slowed down when I saw the sign for Dark Horse, a seedy bar that had a scantily clad chick out front and a man loitering, probably selling drugs or maybe the girl's pimp or her potential client.

I pulled down the first alley after the bar, stopped the car then leaned over, reached in my bag and took out one of the syringes. I wasn't taking any chances and didn't need some pumped-up bouncer coming to her rescue and making this turn into something that attracted attention.

The city was alive with sounds, horns, buses, laughter, and shouts and yet, it was my footsteps on the pavement that were the loudest, like the buildup before the climax in a movie. Everything else became insignificant except that moment.

I was like an addict approaching what I'd been denied for years. The need claimed me. She claimed me.

I stopped when I saw her curled up on the ground sleeping, orange peels lying on the pavement beside her and litter scattered around her.

"Jesus." I took the final few steps toward her then crouched. I pushed her limp, dull hair from her face. "Baby." She had dark smudges of dirt on her cheeks and forehead.

I had to make a choice. Ernie was right, this couldn't continue.

Killing her would end her misery.

Slit her throat while she slept and forget I'd ever met her. Wanted her. Fucked her.

Save her the suffering. Save her from me and what I'd have to do in order to stop this.

But I couldn't.

I'd let the monsters invade me. The emotions pulsed and London was mine.

I drew my knife from beneath my pant leg and rested the sharp blade against her collarbone.

It would be so simple.

End this.

End what had become my obsession.

I lay the hard blade flat on the surface of her skin then tilted the tip slightly, the pressure barely there, but enough. With the tiniest movement, my blade nicked her and I watched the pearl of blood rise to the surface, hesitate then trail a path of red down into her torn black sweater.

Her eyes flickered open for a moment and met mine, but they didn't see me. They were dead. She closed them again.

"Fuck, braveheart." But that one bead of blood was my answer to the road I was about to take. "You're going to need to live up to that name now. I can't do this any other way."

Because I wasn't walking away again. And the consequences could get her killed. But she was fading into nothing. She believed she was nothing and London was so much more. She was lost and there was only one way to get her back. I'd have to destroy the girl who'd been running from herself.

Kill Raven.

And hope to find the girl beneath—London.

Her choices had been taken away and she'd been trained to obey. Her survival had depended on being locked inside herself. But she didn't need to do that anymore.

She was trapped, unable to escape the cycle. Afraid to step out of the shadows. According to Ernie, she'd been seeing therapists, doctors, and they had her on medication after medication, but Ernie thought all they did was make her isolate herself more.

Fuckin' Ernie. Bastard knew I'd never walk away if I saw her again. That was why he wanted me here.

Now, there was one option for me… for her. I was going to pull her from the safe, from the shadows and destroy every piece of Raven.

I put my knife away, took out the syringe, and removed the cap. I gently lowered her shirt off her right shoulder, the pad of my finger caressing her skin.

The needle pierced her skin and she flinched, but didn't open her eyes.

"No more running. You're going to have to be my braveheart in order to survive me."

After a few minutes, I saw the tension around her eyes ease and knew the sedative had taken effect. The club door opened and Ernie stood there.

I nodded to him and all he said was, "Finally. This deserves a fuckin' scotch." Then he slammed the door and went back inside.

I huffed and then picked her up in my arms, before striding back to my car. I put her in the front seat, fastened her seatbelt then got in and started the long drive to my house.

I was taking her home, to a place no one knew about except Ernie.

I was finding London and bringing her back to me.

CHAPTER
FOURTEEN

Rules

Kai

I SAT WITH ONE leg crooked over the other, my elbow resting on the padded armrest, thumb lightly stroking back and forth over my lower lip. From across the room, I watched her. It had been hours. It was dark now, but now that she was here, time had no meaning. It was about the present.

London's breathing gradually quickened and she turned over then curled up into a ball, her breath caught in her throat before it changed to deep, ragged inhales as if she were trapped in a nightmare. I didn't bother waking her. Instead, I did what I was good at—watched. Assessed. Planned.

Eight hours we'd spent driving to my house. A house Vault didn't know existed. If they found out my loyalty was compromised, they'd find this place. But for now, it was the safest place I knew to take her.

I'd have to check in with Brice in the city at some point, but Tanner had his eyes on Chaos. The anniversary date was drawing near for Chaos's brother's 'death' and I'd have to meet her in the fuckin' shed.

I did it. I cut Chaos. And I hated it, but it was something she thought she needed. I refused the first time she asked me and she went to Tanner instead. When I saw what he'd done to her back, I beat the shit out of him, had my blade to his throat ready to kill him. But he belonged to Vault and killing him because he hurt Chaos would speak volumes about me. Volumes that had to be buried.

London kicked the crisp white sheet off and it twisted into a pile at the end of the bed. My eyes trailed up the outline of her body and all I felt was disgust. This wasn't the girl I stalked for years. It wasn't the girl I made a deal with and had her silky legs wrapped around me. It wasn't even the girl I'd left in Mexico.

This was Raven.

A girl trained to pleasure men. Ironic that I'd been trained, too, but in a much different way. Vault didn't use sex to break you. Children were molded, sculpted into stone. Conditioned.

And now with the drug, London's father had given them more power. A drug to help them mold men. Men who were already trained killers like Connor.

There was no margin of error allowed. No room for mistakes and yet, I'd made plenty of mistakes in the last few years.

Things weren't so simple anymore.

London had made them complicated.

Her body tensed and fingers curled around the plush pillow beneath her cheek. She was finally waking and what I had to do to her would begin.

She darted upright, her eyes wide and frantic. I waited while she searched the room, trying to figure out where she was and what happened.

Her gaze hit me and I raised my brows, the corners of my lips curving upwards as her mind caught up with what her eyes were seeing.

"Kai—" She abruptly cut herself off, her eyes quickly scanning the room as if searching for someone else. I saw the confusion, the conflict over whether to trust who she thought I was or protect herself and be who she was trained to be, *who* she considered to be the safe option. Well, that safe option was going to be ripped away.

Her brows scrunched together, lips parted with a slight tremble and her eyes… haunted and uncertain.

Then she chose.

She crawled off the bed and slipped to her knees. A submissive position. One London would never do, but Raven would. She had to. It had been her survival.

I'd always come for her, but I'd always walked away too.

Her loft. Mexico. The auction. And then at the warehouse when I killed Jacob and she begged me not to leave her.

I'd left her with nothing of me to trust.

I sighed, uncrossing my legs. Fuck, this was going to be hell for both of us. "Come here."

She came to her feet to do my bidding and walked toward me then knelt. But she didn't stop there. Her hands went to my crotch.

Fuck.

I grabbed her wrist and I wasn't gentle about it as I yanked her hand away, disgust tearing through me. I twisted it slightly so she was forced to shuffle back to alleviate the pressure and only then did I let her go. I knew nothing about therapy, talking bullshit in a room with art hanging on the walls that were supposed to have some underlying meaning other than blobs of colors.

What I did know was how to kill. Break. Destroy. And do it with a smile. That was what I was going to do to Raven. Kill her. And she was going to resist. She was going to hate me taking away her safety.

She ran from home because she was unable to live in that world again. She knew how to be a slave. She knew how to be Raven and being Raven allowed her to avoid facing what happened.

"Never do that again. I have rules and you break any of them I will make you lie in a bathtub of ice water until you're so fuckin' cold you can barely breathe." The threat had to be real. Something I could do if she did it again, because I wouldn't lie to her.

She had to understand that every word out of my mouth was real.

London... no, Raven, she wasn't London yet, sat back on her heels, but a fresh tear escaped her right eye and trailed a path down her cheek. A path because she was filthy and smelled like trash and required a shitload of soap.

I leaned back in my chair. "You're good at following rules." Well, she was now. She didn't used to be. She had refused to sleep naked. "You just heard the first one. Repeat it to me."

"Don't touch you?" Her voice trembled and, if I'd been blind and didn't know London was kneeling in front of me, I wouldn't have recognized her.

"Good. Second rule, I ask you something, I want an answer."

She nodded.

"No, repeat what I just said. I want no misunderstanding here."

"Answer you."

Good enough. The leather crackled as I leaned forward and rested my elbows on my knees. "And you will *never* kneel or avoid looking at me again."

Her breath quickened and her hands lying flat on her thighs twitched. She was debating what to do. Whether to get off her knees now or wait until I told her to. I needed her to think for herself. She was no longer a slave to do what she was told. She had to make her own decisions, even if she thought the consequences were bad.

Eventually, she'd learn the consequences would never be bad, unless she was Raven. This was what she understood—rules. And I'd use them to find London buried underneath Raven.

Her lips quivered and brows lowered as she contemplated.

I waited. Patient.

Then she put her hands on the floor and pushed up and stood. It took longer for her chin to rise and her eyes to meet mine. But she did it and the second she did, I saw the flash of fear over what would happen because she had made eye contact. Then her eyes went dead again.

I nodded with approval. She repeated my words, her eyes staring at me, but she wasn't seeing. Not really. It was a mask. I'd done it myself when I had to take my mind away from the pain that was inflicted on me at the farm.

"Bathroom is over there." I gestured to the left with my hand and she flinched. Jesus, that pissed me off. How many times had Alfonzo or Jacob raised their hand and hit her? "Go shower. There are clothes next to the sink. Come out to the kitchen when you're done and eat something."

I didn't wait for a reply. She'd do everything I told her to.

I stood, brushed by her and left the room.

It had only been eight minutes since I left her before she was walking barefoot across my hardwood floors into the kitchen.

I stood facing the stove, stirring the vegetable beef soup in the cast iron pot, the steam and aroma rising up in front of me.

I refused to direct her on what to do. This was a learning curve for me, too. I was pretty fuckin' sure her normal move would be to kneel on the floor, probably by the doorway. But my rule was blaring in her head.

I swear I heard her heart thumping hard against her chest a few feet behind me as she again had to decide what the next step was. For all I knew, she'd just stand there until I addressed her, but she'd have to wait a fuck of a long time. I'd make her stand there all night if I had to.

I ladled the soup into two bowls then carried them over to the bar stools at the island which was a mere inch from where she stood. The scent of the coconut and mango shampoo mixed with the soup.

I pulled out both seats then sat.

Ask me, London. Fuck.

It was a simple test. I knew she was watching me and from the corner of my eye, I saw her bite her lower lip and her eyes waver to the stool, to the bowl of soup, and back to me.

Take a risk, damn it. Be fuckin' brave, baby.

Ten minutes. Ten fuckin' minutes. I was on my second bowl of soup and hers was no longer steaming.

"May I eat, master?"

"Yes. You can help yourself to anything you want at any time." And I didn't like her calling me fuckin' master. "You know my name— use it."

She sat quietly at the island and ate the cold soup. I restrained myself from heating it up, but that was her fault it took her so fuckin' long.

I never said I was nice.

She was cautious as she ate, and I couldn't help imagining us in her kitchen together. A different arrangement. An entirely different girl.

I looked at Raven. I'd never fuck her.

I shoved back my stool, stood, then went and rinsed out my bowl in the sink, put the rest of the soup in a container and placed it in the fridge. I washed the pot then turned around and she was still sitting there, spoon resting against the lip of the bowl and her head down.

"Go to sleep when you're done, bab… Raven." I strode out of the kitchen, open concept, so I was still technically in the room, and sat on the couch. I put my knife on the glass coffee table along with my rolled-up wire. Then I clicked on the stereo to some jazz, put my feet up, and waited.

I had my head back and eyes closed when I heard her approach. And this is when it fucked with my head because I wanted to look at her, hold out my hand and drag her down on top of me, then undress her and taste that sweetness I'd craved for years.

Years. Jesus.

But I didn't want the submissive, obedient robot. I wanted London.

"Kai," her voice trembled and I stiffened.

I took my time to peer at her standing beside the couch, arms at her sides, fingers gripping her shirt. A scared little rabbit that wanted to crawl in her hole. But I was the wolf and I sat on it, blocking her escape.

"Yes?" I knew exactly why she was here. She had no idea where she was supposed to sleep. Alfonzo, and I was pretty sure he was the one who kept London to himself, may have kept her in a basement, on the floor of a room, fuck, in a closet or cage for all I knew. I'd have liked nothing better than to wrap my piano wire around his neck and watch his eyes pop out as he struggled to breathe. And just for fun, I'd let him take a breath then take it away over and over again.

"Where do you want me to sleep?"

"You may sleep in my bed for now. The guest room isn't set up yet. When it is, you may sleep in there. The choice will be yours."

She hesitated, biting her lower lip as if contemplating what I'd said. But this wasn't about me. This was about her and she had to learn to make choices.

"You have an issue with that, tell me."

That did something. A speck of light hit her eyes and her spine stiffened, not enough for most people to notice, but I wasn't most people.

What I needed was that quiet rebellion. Fuck, I'd take any rebellion right about now. I wasn't getting it, but I would eventually, even if I had to rip Raven apart to get to it. "Go to bed."

She scuttled away and I leaned my head back again and shut my eyes.

I'd give her one week. I was being generous because being nice went against my grain. Then she was going to fight—for London.

CHAPTER
FIFTEEN

Ice Water

Kai

I T TOOK FIVE days before she broke a rule.

I'd expected sooner, but she was meticulous and I could see her mind working on deciding what to do before she did it. The scientist in her was hard at work. Except, it was the wrong kind of fuckin' work.

But when a glass she was putting up in the top cupboard slipped from her grip and fell to the floor shattering, she froze for a split second before dropping to her knees.

Any sympathy for Raven was pushed aside. My rules were fair and they were set up to break through what she'd endured. I'd seen the marks on the back of her thighs. I knew what they were from and coddling her wasn't going to make her any better. She'd had months of therapy, medication and whatever else her father and medical professionals had done to try to help her. Instead, she ran away.

Now we were doing it my way and it was the way that London needed. I knew this because I'd been in hell. Maybe it was a different kind, but it was still hell.

I filled the tub with straight cold water then went to the freezer and pulled out a small bag of ice. No matter how diligent a person was, falling back into what had become a safe place… *that* was human nature. My safe had been not caring. Being unemotional and ignoring who I'd become.

Raven's safe place was on her knees.

Now I was going to re-write that.

She watched me. Sitting on the edge of the bed, her hands wrung together. It was always better when interrogating someone for them to see your torture devices. Let the fear build as your hand hovered over each one, hear their breath quicken while waiting to see which one you'd pick up first.

Of course, this wasn't about torture. Same idea, I had to break her, but with other techniques where she was punished for being Raven.

I could coddle her, wrap her up in my arms and hope she'd find her way back, but I didn't coddle and London was a fighter. I just had to find the trigger to make her fight.

Bottom line, I needed her to get pissed off.

I dumped the bag of ice into the tub and the cubes clinked against the porcelain. I stuck my hand in—yeah, that was fuckin' cold. I'd been in worse.

I'd been chasing a car when it skidded off a bridge into a lake and crashed through the ice. I had to go in after the driver. Not to save him… well, I'd saved him. But after getting the info I needed, I killed him. Bastard was dirty as they came and he was the type of man I took great joy in ending his life.

"Come here," I said without looking over at her.

She stood beside me and there was a twinge of guilt when she started trembling.

"You know why?"

She nodded. "I broke a rule."

"Yes. And why do you think I have that rule?" This would be a hard one for her to wrap her head around. She probably had no idea why, but I expected an answer and wanted to hear what she came up with.

I watched her swallow and I swear I could hear her heart rate pick up. Good. A reaction. "You don't like me on my knees?"

"True. Why else?"

Her eyes darted to me, wide and scared. *Come on, London. Be defiant. Say it.* But when her shoulders sagged I knew I wasn't getting the answer I wanted.

"I don't know why."

I grabbed her chin and forced her to look at me, fingers digging harshly into her skin. "Because you never submit to anyone. Never. You can play. Pretend with someone you trust, but you don't trust me and we're not playing. Did you trust him? Was it all a game with Alfonzo and Jacob?"

Her eyes widened with horror. "No. I… I had to."

She had to. I knew she did. She probably fought like hell at first, that stubbornness causing a lot more pain than most of those girls would endure.

"Yes. But you also submitted to everything." I lightened my hold and stroked my thumb back and forth over the reddened skin. "Submit your body when you have no choice, but protect your mind, London. Never let them have it and right now, they have it."

Tears filled the rims of her eyes, but I didn't want the tears. I wanted the flash of anger.

"In." I nodded to the tub.

She hesitated and I let her. Fuck, I wanted her to hesitate. I would've been ecstatic if she told me to go fuck myself and hit me.

She didn't and I sighed as she undressed then stepped into the tub. I heard her gasp and her gaze went to mine as I leaned back against the bathroom counter and watched.

Hoping. False hope. Something I knew better than to have.

She was too fuckin' skinny. I could see her hip bones and her ribs, and her breasts were smaller. When my eyes finished roaming the length of her body and met with hers again, I almost... almost told her to get the fuck out.

But that was up to her. She may know little about me, but she had been intimate with me. She knew enough that all she had to do was tell me. I taught her that lesson and I wanted her to search her mind and remember. Find those words and tell me she didn't want to do this.

That was all it took.

Her lips parted and she inhaled. I swore she was going to say the words, but instead, she lowered into the frigid water. I dropped my head forward and closed my eyes.

Fuck.

She started hyperventilating, breathing fast and uncontrollably. A body's shock reaction to the sudden cold. I anticipated this and within minutes, it would go away and she'd be able to withstand the temperature for ten to twenty minutes before hypothermia set in. When her muscles weakened, that was when I'd have to get her out of there.

But what I wanted was her to break before then.

My skin crawled and the tension in my chest was so tight breathing became painful. Because watching her was painful. Listening to the ice clink against the sides of the tub was painful. I'd never had this reaction before. Immune to hearing the screams, witnessing torture, death, blood.

But it took everything I had to remain where I was and not drag her the fuck out of there.

She had her legs scrunched up to her chest, arms wrapped around them, her chin resting on her knees that were above the water level. Her nipples were erect, or at least the one I could see, as the waterline sloshed lightly against her breasts as I'd only filled the tub halfway.

Her teeth chattered and she tried to stop the shivering but couldn't, which made the water slosh back and forth more.

"What did they do to you, Raven?" I didn't need to know, but she needed to tell me.

She raised her head and looked at me. "Everything."

Yeah, I had a pretty good idea. "Specifics, please."

Oh, she didn't like that by the way her back stiffened and I inwardly smiled.

"Alfonzo liked sex."

I tensed, knowing what I'd hear, prepared for it. At least, I thought I was. "Did you like it?"

She gasped and her lips pursed together. "No."

"But you let him anyway." I crossed my arms and raised my brows. "You had no choice?"

"Yes," she replied.

"Why?"

"I was tied up."

That was info I'd use later. "Are you tied up now?"

"Umm." I scowled at the word and there was a flicker of something in her eyes. She remembered. I knew she did. That day I told her that umm didn't suit her. "No."

"So, you enjoy the cold water?"

That pissed her off as her spine straightened and despite her chattering teeth, she raised her voice. "You told me to get in the tub."

I shrugged. "True. I did. But if you recall, I once told you to tell me if you didn't want to do something."

Her expression changed from anger to contemplation. Good, I wanted her to think things through. She'd been on auto-pilot for years. She had to flip the switch and take control.

"Can I... get out?"

Finally. That took about three minutes, not bad. I reached for a towel off the rail. She stood and swayed a bit. I quickly stepped over to her, put my hands under her armpits then lifted her out of the tub. I wrapped the towel snug around her shivering body.

After rubbing her down vigorously, I passed her another towel and tucked it in around her. "Get dressed and come out to the living room." I started to leave the bathroom, when her soft voice stopped me.

"I remember."

I put my hand on the doorframe, fingers splintering the wood as my casual manner dissipated. The need to say fuck it and hold her in my arms and tell her it would be all right.

But I couldn't.

I slid my hand down the smooth surface of the doorframe, one I'd put up myself. Every inch of this place was done with my own hands. Took me ten years. Georgie and Tanner thought I went on missions when I disappeared, and I did, but I also came here.

I'd slept in a shed out back for the first five years while I built it. The land legally belonged to Ernie as I put it in his name, and since there were over a hundred acres, I offered him a piece of it. He declined, said he'd rather hear the sounds of the city than the chirping of birds in the country.

Regardless of how careful I'd been though, nothing stayed hidden for long and I was treading dangerous waters with London being with me.

CHAPTER SIXTEEN

Hands and Knees

Kai

THREE WEEKS AND we were making tortoise-pace progress. Raven, and she was still fuckin' Raven, followed the rules so well that it pissed me off because I wanted her to break them. The worst was, she slept beside me and when she thrashed from whatever fucked with her head, I had to hold her and holding her made me think of London.

I was pretty certain she'd have let me sink inside her, but I never would because of that word—let. She'd let me. I wanted more than let and I wasn't taking it until she gave me more than that.

I could be a bastard and cruel when it came to getting what I wanted from my targets, but I didn't fuck chicks who spread their legs because they were forced to. A man who forced a girl was weak and pathetic. I was neither. I also refused to fuck a girl who got paid for it, whether that was their choice or not.

I got hard seeing the desire in a woman's eyes, feeling their pussy clench, hearing their need with their cries, their panting. I wanted them to beg me to give it to them. My life was filled with pain and deceit, but with sex, I demanded real.

I rarely slept after she calmed from a nightmare, and that night was no different. I spent the rest of the early morning sanding the hardwood floors in the spare bedroom.

That was where she found me the next morning.

Ironic that I was the one on my knees.

I tossed the sanding pad aside.

The look on her face was shock when she saw me and it was rather amusing. I pulled down the light blue mask covering my mouth and nose, sat back on my ass, bent my knees and rested my arms over them as I looked at her standing in the doorway. Dust particles fell from the strands of my hair and covered my jeans. A bead of sweat trailed down the side of my face and across my brow. I ran the back of my arm across my forehead.

"You need something?"

She shook her head and her eyes roamed over the newly sanded surface. I'd found an old abandoned barn and ripped out the floor boards and brought them here. They needed a lot of work, but there was nothing like century-old hardwood. I didn't do fake with sex or when it came to building my house.

She bit her lip and then to my surprise, she asked, "Can I help?"

Interesting. "Eat yet?"

"No."

"Go eat then, yeah, you can help."

There. Right fuckin' there. A twitch at the corner of her mouth. She probably didn't even realize she'd done it.

She nodded, left, and I went back to work.

She was back in ten minutes and I had a sanding pad ready for her. I held it up and she walked over and took it.

"You can work on this one." I placed my palm on a wide board. "Ever sand before?"

"No."

I smiled. "Didn't think so. But you're a scientist so you're precise and calculated. That's what I need here. Sand too much in one spot and we get a dip in the wood. Come here, I'll show you." I urged her to kneel beside me and when she hesitated, I realized why. Fuck, right. "You can kneel, London." Maybe she should've figured that out herself by now, but I was feeling generous.

She kneeled beside me and I curled my fingers around her wrist and placed her palm on the floorboard I'd just finished.

"This is what you want." I slowly dragged her palm back and forth over the smooth surface, my arm hovering over hers, bodies moving together in perfect rhythm. "You feel how soft that is? Smooth. Even."

"Okay."

I released her hand and tapped my hand on the board she was to work on.

She crawled over to it and started sanding. I watched her for a few minutes, her hair falling forward and skimming the floor as she worked. She put her back into it and fine dust rose around her. I got up, pulled off my mask and walked over to her.

She stopped, looking up at me. "Am I doing it wrong?"

I smiled. "No. You're good with your hands. But I already knew that." Of course, that had double meaning. She caught it, too, meaning she was letting those memories in.

I crouched beside her, slipped my mask over her head, and put it up over her mouth and nose. I tucked the elastic strings behind her ears and chuckled when I sat back and looked at her.

"Cute." And despite not being able to see her smile, I saw in her that elusive sparkle. I ran my hand over her head, hesitating on the nape of her neck. "Nice to have a piece of you back."

I got up and went to the other side of the room, picked up my sanding pad and went back to work.

Hours slipped by, sweat pouring off my brow and dripping onto the floors leaving a dark stain before disappearing again. I was always aware of everything around me, but I didn't need to look at London to know she was intent on her work, I heard the rhythmic sanding back and forth.

"We'll grab a sandwich." I threw my sander into the toolbox then lifted my T-shirt and wiped my brow. When I lowered it, she was staring at me, at my abdomen. Her gaze darted to mine and a slight flush crept into her cheeks. "Don't you dare look down."

Her breath hitched and her gaze locked on mine. She was still wearing the mask, but London had everything right in front of me blazing in her eyes.

I approached and she climbed to her feet, leaving the sanding pad on the floor. When I reached her, I pulled down her mask so it hung around her neck. Her hair had turned a light blonde with all the flecks of dust. She shifted her weight back and I stepped forward so I was in her space. She'd have to stand on her tiptoes and I'd have to bend my neck in order to kiss her. It was something we'd never done. I'd never kissed her.

"You did good, London." I wasn't calling her Raven anymore. She was ready and tonight, I'd push her over the edge. "We'll finish it tomorrow."

She nodded then said, "Can we do this again?"

"Yeah, baby." I hadn't meant to say that yet. Call her baby, but I saw a piece of the girl I knew and it made me slip.

"This afternoon?"

Cute. She wanted to sand my floors with me. But I had to talk to Tanner then Chaos and see what progress Chaos made with the guy Vault requested she get close to—Tristan Mason. I still wasn't sure why they wanted eyes on him, as Tristan was the owner of Mason Developments. Wealthy. Clean. No political ties. He'd never been on the radar before.

"I have business to deal with this afternoon."

"Okay." Then she tilted her head slightly and asked, "Why by hand? They have sanding machines."

And those were the most words I'd heard out of her at once since I brought her home. The rift in my chest began to fill with light. Jesus, light. It had been years of darkness, killing, blood, destruction, and now the light was beginning to flicker again.

I shrugged. "No reason."

"You don't want to tell me?"

It was like a cool wash poured over me. Refreshing and energizing.

London.

London wouldn't accept my bullshit answer and I grinned because I'd missed her.

"I like walking through my house and knowing every inch of it breathes life because of me. I like the control over building it and I liked when I needed to clear my head, I could come here and work on the house." I ran my hand over my head and flecks of dust rose into the air. "I need to shower and so do you. Go use the one in our room. I'll use the guest." I left her standing in the middle of the room, then went and showered.

I walked out into the kitchen a half hour later wearing a white dress shirt, sleeves rolled up twice, and a pair of jeans. It had become a routine in the afternoons for me to work in my office and she'd read, sitting curled up on the couch, which I could see from my desk because I always left the door open. She'd quietly read with the stillness of a praying mantis while blending into her environment. Probably what she'd learned to do with Jacob and Alfonzo. Hide in plain sight.

I stopped in the archway of the kitchen when I saw her as she reached up in the cupboard and pulled down two glasses. Her hair was damp from the shower and droplets had soaked into the back of the shirt. She was wearing one of my shirts because I'd only stopped briefly at the store on the way here to grab her a few essentials and some groceries. From mid-thigh down, her legs were bare and even from here I could see the moisture still clinging to her skin. I remember running my hands down her legs, feeling her—

"Are you okay?" she asked, glancing up at me while she poured two glasses of water.

Fuck, this was the woman who made death matter to me. "Yeah."

I pushed away from the archway and sauntered into the kitchen. "Grilled cheese sound okay?"

I opened the fridge and took out a block of cheese and a tomato. She came up beside me and placed the cutting board on the counter. I grabbed a knife from the wood block and sliced while she took out the frying pan and put it on the stove.

She worked beside me as she buttered the bread. I stopped slicing and raised my brows at that. Her hand stilled with a glob of butter on the end of the knife.

"Both sides?"

A flicker of pain crossed her face. "My dad taught me." It took her a minute before she continued. "He said if you're going to eat a sandwich with melted cheese, you might as well go all the way."

I chuckled as I sliced into the tomato, the juices pooling onto the cutting board. "A lump of cholesterol between two pieces of bread."

I caught her subtle smile as she went back to buttering. "My dad? Do you know... how he is?"

"He's safe, London."

She lowered her eyes from mine. "I didn't say goodbye."

According to Ernie, she'd run away during one of her therapy sessions. She went in and never came out. Ernie asked the receptionist and she said London ran out halfway through the session through the emergency exit.

"I told him you're here with me."

Her head snapped up. "You did?"

I had and he also knew if he said anything to anyone, he was sealing his daughter's fate. And it wasn't a good fate.

The corners of my mouth curved up as I said, "Need some brownie points with your father."

Her mouth gaped and her eyes widened. Then, she matched my smile with one of her own and I nearly cut off my own fuckin' finger because I was watching her instead of watching my blade. I was never careless with a knife. Never.

Jesus Christ. What the fuck were we doing? I was sick of tap dancing around her issue. I was being a saint. A fuckin' saint. This

155

wasn't me. And this sure as hell wasn't her.

I whipped the knife across the room and it embedded into the cupboard above the oven.

I heard her gasp and there was a sudden stillness from both of us.

It was time. Not tonight. Tomorrow. Next week… right fuckin' now.

"We're done with this shit."

She remained quiet, her eyes drifting to the knife, a butter knife in her hand then back to me. "You going to try and kill me with that?" She shook her head. "Too bad. I'd like a fight. What if I took off my belt? Would you fight me then?"

The color drained from her face. Then she backed away. I undid my buckle and slowly slid it from the loops of my jeans.

"What are you going to do this time? Kneel and take it? Let me beat you?"

I stalked toward her while she continued to back away and she still had that ridiculous butter knife in her hand, but it was at her side, the glob of butter getting ready to drip onto my floor.

"Kai… please. I'll be good."

I smirked. "Now, that is not the response I was looking for." Her chin dropped and I stopped her before she bent to get on her knees. "Don't you fuckin' dare."

Her eyes were wild and uncertain, confused. Fighting against what she'd been conditioned to do in order to avoid abuse. It was the same look before a man debated whether to give me the information I wanted or endure the torture I inflicted.

I either broke them or they died.

"Lie over the back of the couch." Her hands shook and the butter knife clattered to the floor, but she did exactly as I told her. Her hands were on the seat, butt in the air and her hair covering her face, but I saw the trembling. I felt her fear in the air like thick smog.

I approached. Her body tensed but she remained in position. I put my hand on her back and pressed, there was no resistance.

"Is this what they did to you, London? Did they beat you?" Her head bobbed, but that wasn't what I wanted. I yanked her shirt up.

"Answer me."

"Yes."

"Did Alfonzo fuck you?"

"Yes."

"Did you enjoy it?"

"No." Her voice strengthened.

"Are you sure about that?" I snapped the belt over the couch beside her and she jerked. "What else did he do to you? What else gave you pleasure?"

"Nothing."

I stroked my hand over her ass. "Nothing? They did nothing else to you?"

"No. That's not what I meant. He made me… do things. I hated it. I hated him and… I wanted to die."

My hand stopped stroking her ass and my heart raced as a cold rush went straight from my head down my body. "Why?" She didn't answer. "Why, damn it? Fuckin' why, London?"

It happened faster than I expected. I thought I'd have to push her more, but something snapped and she shoved backwards slamming into me as she stood up. With one hand, she yanked down her shirt and with the other she swung her fist at my face.

I took it. And fuck she had one hell of a punch as it plowed into my cheek. Tears streamed down her face, but the blazing fury in her eyes didn't match it as she came at me with everything she had.

I staggered back as she shoved me in the chest with both hands, using her foot on the bottom of the couch for leverage. "You left me." She swung again and I ducked while I backed away. But her fists kept going, hitting my abdomen, my chest, my shoulders, anywhere she could. "You left me," her voice raised, "You gave me hope and then ripped it away. That was worse than dying."

I grabbed her by the shoulders and she kicked out and tried to wiggle free, her hatred raging through every part of her body. But it wasn't just for me. It was for who had done this to her. It was hatred for who she was. And there was no doubt she hated me too right now.

"Let me go, you bastard. I want out of here. I want to go home."

"No, you don't. You ran away. You can't stand being home."

"It's better than being here with you."

I laughed. "Don't lie to me, London."

Her eyes glared, chest heaving. "Fuck you. You don't know what I want."

I raised my brows with amusement. "I certainly know better than you do."

She became a wild cat struggling against me, and I had to take her legs out from beneath her with one swipe. With my arm locked around her waist, I lowered her to the floor with me on top of her.

"What are you going to do, rape me?" Her laugh was cruel and hysterical sounding. "Because it's nothing new. Nothing can hurt me anymore."

Not physical pain anyway. She was past that stage, but she had to learn to deal with her emotional pain. I had her wrists locked in my hands on either side of her head as I straddled her.

"You have that very wrong, braveheart."

She spit in my face and the warm liquid dripped down my cheek. "I hate you."

I smirked. "Yeah, I suspect you do right about now, but not as much as you hate yourself."

That pissed her off and her struggles started again, but I had all the leverage and there was nothing she could do to dislodge me. "I hate you. I hate you. I hate you."

I softened my grip and sighed. "No. You hate what was done to you."

Her eyes rimmed red with tears and rage. "I hate you more."

I gave in to her because she needed it. "Okay, you hate me more."

She pursed her lips together and it was her thinking face, the way her eyes shifted side to side and narrowed. "Why are you doing this? Just let me go home."

"So you can fade away into your nightmares? That option is no longer available to you." I leaned closer so my lips were close to hers and her warm breath brushed across my face. "And I hate Raven. I want London. I want the brave girl who wouldn't back down from a

158

bastard like me. The one that is fighting me right now."

"Why were you there?" Her voice quivered. "Why did you come to Mexico if you were only going to leave me?"

"You know why. For you."

The tension seeped out of her body as she whispered, "But you left me."

I let go of her wrists and climbed off her to sit leaning against the wall, bending my knees to rest my arms on them. "Yeah. It went bad."

"You left me. You left me, Kai. You left me there." Her body tensed. "I didn't think you were a coward."

Normally, I'd kill someone for saying something like that to me, but instead I sighed. "Do you think I'm a coward, London?"

She sat up, her hair a mess from our struggle, but the fight had done her good. I pushed her, knew she trusted me enough that if I did threaten her, she'd push back, and I'd been right.

"No." She raised her chin. "I think you're calculating, cold, arrogant and believe no one can hurt you."

I stilled. "You have most of that right except the last. I do have someone who can hurt me. You."

Her breath hitched and lips parted.

"Baby, I didn't leave you. Not by choice. I took a bullet, and the guy I came with got me out." Ernie saved my fuckin' life. "By the time I recovered, the compound was burned to the ground and you were gone."

"You didn't run." It was said in a whisper more to herself than to me.

I shook my head when she looked at me, tears still leaking from her eyes. "No, baby."

Suddenly, a piercing blare wrenched into the air and I leapt to my feet, racing into the kitchen. "Shit." I pulled the smoking frying pan off the stove and dumped it in the sink. London was right behind me. She grabbed a dish towel, stood on her tiptoes, and waved it in the air under the smoke alarm.

The alarm stopped.

I walked toward her and it was fuckin' nice because London kept her eyes locked on me. No flinching, no tension, and she even raised her chin a bit. And that got me hard.

Because nothing did it for me more than London. The girl who had enough compassion for the both of us. The girl who was brave in her own quiet way.

"The belt. You did that on purpose," she said.

I shrugged and kept coming until I was inches away and she had to crank her neck in order to keep eye contact.

"You were never going to hit me?"

I grinned. "You were ready. So, yeah, I would've if you refused to fight back."

She glared. I grew harder because glaring was good. Glaring meant she had backbone. "And what if I never fought back?"

"Then you'd have a sore ass right now."

Her mouth hung open, then she snapped it closed.

"It wouldn't have come to that though. You were ready to fight me. You were just searching for a way to do it. I gave it to you."

I watched her think about it. London calculated. She wanted every possible solution deliberated before she acted or spoke, except when she got angry. Then she was a missile. I did the same thing. I was dead if I didn't, because in my business, it rarely went the way you anticipated. And outcomes were variable.

Our outcome was one big variable because she couldn't stay here forever, and for the first time I was beginning to contemplate the possibility of ending Vault. How to get my sister out? How to shut down the farm and take out the board members? Because doing all that made London safe. It made us safe.

"So, what now?"

I walked over and yanked my knife from the cupboard it was embedded in. "We start over. Grab the bread, baby."

Then we made grilled cheeses.

CHAPTER
SEVENTEEN

Yellow Sheets

Kai

WITH MY ARMS crossed, ankles matching, I leaned against the doorframe watching her. A subtle smirk played at the corners of my mouth.

I'd been watching her every fuckin' chance I had. It was two weeks after our fight in the kitchen and each day she was getting stronger, not in the physical sense, but emotionally.

She no longer moved tentatively and cautiously. Instead, her shoulders lifted and her hips had a natural, delicate sway again. The magnetic draw of my brave little scientist was irresistible. London was the woman who tested all my control.

She was also the one who could hurt me, who would be used

against me if given the chance. I could never let that happen again. But for once in my life, I had no plan except keep her here hidden until I did have a plan.

"Are you going to stand there or help me?" she said.

I inwardly smiled before pushing away from the doorframe and stalking toward her. And it was stalking because for the first time in years, I was going to taste her again. She may not know my intent yet, but she would soon enough.

I didn't bring her to my home on a whim. There was always a purpose and my purpose was to have London again in every way. To make her completely mine.

With London, I had no need to hide who I was. She was the lightness. She was the warmth that built inside me that had been destroyed by the farm. I'd always have parts of *who* they made me into, just like London would from what happened to her, but both of us were finding a way to live with what was done to us.

She sidled past, completely ignoring me, focused on her project, which was putting together the spare bedroom. We'd finished the floors, sanding, staining, and three coats of varnish. I set up the bedframe and moved the mattress back in and now London was making the bed with fresh sheets.

I strolled over to the opposite side of the bed, grabbed the edge of the sheet to hook it on the one corner while she pulled tight and stretched it to the other.

"It would look much better with yellow sheets. Brighten up the room." She ran her hand over the cool white surface, smoothing out the wrinkles then tossed one of the pillows to the head of the bed.

"You brighten the room enough. Don't need fuckin' yellow sheets."

Her gaze lifted from the pillow sham she was holding and held mine. "Why did you do it? Put new sheets on my bed that first night?"

I bent, picked up a pillowcase and a pillow and then tugged the sham over the pillow. "Why did you sleep on the couch?"

She tossed the pillow to the head of the bed and shrugged, saying, "Good movie was on."

I laughed.

It took her a second and she did, too. She already knew the answer and that was why she'd avoided the bed. I'd done it for the very reason she'd slept on the couch. I wanted her thinking of me when she climbed between the sheets.

"Kai." Her voice was a breathless whisper. "I hated Raven, too."

"I know."

"I never want to feel that helpless again."

"You won't." She didn't ask me how I knew that or argue. She accepted what I told her.

"I want to…."

"I know exactly what you want." Her body twitched like I'd stroked a match and set it on fire. "Take off your clothes, baby." A flush rose in her cheeks and it was cute that she blushed at that. After all she'd been through, that simple ability to make her blush settled deep.

Nothing about us could end well, but time had never mattered before, and now there was a reason… because what I had with London was timeless. There wasn't an end.

Her arms crossed, fingers curling around the bottom edge of her shirt, which was my shirt. With a slow, sexy glide, she pulled it over her head, her hair lifting then falling to settle down her back.

God, I'd missed her. I needed my hands in her hair again, my lips on her skin, her naked writhing body beneath me as she screamed with pleasure.

I raised my brows when she stopped and she got that little defiant look to her face that made my cock jerk. Yeah, she was my braveheart again.

"It's only fair." She nodded to my chest.

I grinned. "Then come undress me, baby."

I remembered how her fingers played with the buttons, fitting them through the holes before they popped out that night in her loft. The way her hands had slid up my chest over my scars without hesitation. How her head fell back against the door, neck exposed as she moaned when I sucked, licked and tasted every inch of her pussy.

"London. Now," I growled.

She crawled across the bed toward me, kneeling on the edge and then reached for the bottom button of my shirt. I couldn't stop myself from touching her any longer. In the beginning, she had been easy to resist being Raven, but over the last few weeks as the pieces of London shone through, it had been hell. And now, seeing the smoldering desire in her eyes, it took everything I had not to just throw her down and sink inside her.

I slid my hand up over her collarbone to beneath her hair, curling my fingers around the back of her neck. It was a power position, holding her like this and I wanted to see her reaction.

But there was no fear or submission as her eyes sparked with need. Her knuckles brushed against my chest as my shirt parted and my skin tingled. "Fuck, I missed you."

Her breath stilled along with her hands and our eyes met. It was the same look as the one that made me walk out on her on at her loft. Beneath the heat was the unmistakable need for something else.

I abruptly grabbed her wrist and put it to my back jeans pocket. "You feel that?" It was the piano wire in my pocket. She nodded, her eyes wide but still burning with desire. "I'm still a part of that."

She pulled her hand away and I let her. "But if you left—"

I chuckled, but there was no amusement to it. She was going to say, if I left the people I worked for. "You don't leave them. If you do, it's in a body bag. Although, that is too polite." I had to be cruel to get my point across. "That is after they've cut you up and made you beg for the pain to stop."

Surprisingly, she took what I said well, but I did see the mild shiver. London had seen and experienced pain and knew that this world wasn't filled with fairies and white flying horses.

Her fingers went back to undoing my buttons until my shirt fell open and she slid it off my shoulders. "Do you... like what you do?"

Hmmm, did I like it? Did I enjoy killing people? A question I never cared to contemplate before. Never cared enough about anything or anyone to consider it. "Yes," I replied and that made her back stiffen and her hands pause. "And no. I enjoyed killing Jacob. I enjoyed watching Alfonzo die and wished I'd been the one to kill him."

She lowered her head. "Kai, why are we here? What happens now?"

I slid my hands down her back to the clasp on her bra and undid it. The white lace slipped forward and dropped between us. "I'm going to fuck you and make you quiver beneath me. A few times." I picked her up under the arms and tossed her down on the bed. "No more questions, baby. Not now."

"Okay," she said. "But you'll tell me about them. About what's happening with my dad?"

"Yeah. London. I'll give you everything."

Maybe I hadn't meant to, but saying those words had more meaning than I intended. There was no going back. Bringing her here… I'd never let her go. And when I gave her everything, she'd know that, too.

I undid my jeans, dragged them down my legs and kicked them aside. I was naked beneath and my cock was hard and ready… more than ready.

I knelt on the bed and straddled her, thighs on either side of her hips. Her breath hitched as I ran a hand up over her abdomen to her breast, cupped it then ran my thumb over the sensitive surface of her nipple. Once. Twice. Then I pinched it before doing the same to the other one.

There was a hint of fear in her and it was something I'd fight to get out of her. I scooted down the bed. Slowly, I dragged her panties down her legs and tossed them on the floor. "Open your legs. I need to taste you again." She did. "Wider." I held her ankles, pushed them open more, and then lowered my head.

The first taste of her on my tongue was like sinking into a heated pool of comfort. Fuck. I'd missed her taste, the scent of her. I'd never forgotten the way she made my insides clench with an intense need, a need that became an obsession. Fuck, who was I kidding? She was my obsession before I even fucked her.

I parted her lips with my fingers and suckled her clit while I teased her opening, not entering… not yet.

She lifted her hips. "Kai."

"Wait. Tonight we take our time. Slow and precise, braveheart. Just like your experiments." She stiffened beneath me and I'd have none of that. I sucked harder and slid my finger through her wetness before slowly circling the sweet spot.

Her body writhed, eyes closed, lips parted as I relentlessly played, tasted and made her forget everything except what I was doing to her body.

"Kai," she whispered.

Her back arched, neck exposed, breathing ragged as she panted. I quickened my movements as her legs trembled and closed around my shoulders.

"Come, baby." My voice vibrated on her sex sending her over the edge.

"Oh, God. Kai. Kai...."

Her body stiffened, hips raised off the bed, thighs shaking violently as she came in my mouth. I pushed two fingers inside her and she screamed with pleasure as she came. She pulsed around my fingers. She pumped onto them and then I slowly brought her back down with a light flick of my tongue.

I raised my head and looked at her face. "Beautiful. Fuckin' beautiful."

I'd dreamed about seeing that relaxed, sated expression on her face again. I couldn't erase what happened to her and I wasn't going to dwell on what had been done to her body. The men who had touched her were dead now.

Her hand slipped into my hair and I moved up the bed to settle my cock between her legs. She frowned as I took hold of it and slid it up and down through her wetness.

"Condom, Kai."

I stilled. "You were checked and your results were clear." That deepened her frown. I raised my brows and half-grinned. "London, do you think I wouldn't check into you once Deck took you from the auction. That you never contacted your friends when you came home or went back to school? That you refused to visit your dad at the lab or be near men? That you went to therapy and were on medication that made you spend days in bed? I know everything about you."

"How?"

Because I had Ernie watching her all the time. Because I couldn't not know. Despite having to stay away from her, I never let her go. She was part of me whether either of us wanted it. But at that moment, I didn't want to tell her about Ernie. And I wouldn't lie so I remained quiet.

"Kai? How did you know?"

Her soft voice drew me away from my thoughts and even my cock wasn't throbbing anymore. I rolled to the side and stared at the ceiling. "I saw the doctor's report. Blood tests."

"But how… that's confidential." God, she really had no clue what I was capable of. When I turned my head to look at her, I raised my brows. "Oh." Yeah, she was smart. Nothing would keep me from finding information I wanted or needed when it came to London.

But there was information I did want regarding Vault and was beginning to quietly check. Location of the farm, the anonymous member of Vault and what the fuck was in the drug London's father developed. Those three answers had power and I wanted them.

"We still need a condom," she said.

"Haven't been with anyone since I was last checked." Twice a year, mandatory physical with Vault, but that wasn't the only reason. I hadn't been with a woman since London. There was no one else. Even knowing I may never see her again, there wasn't a single moment that I considered having sex with anyone else.

I reached over and yanked her up on top of me. "There's no possibility of pregnancy. Ever." All Vault operatives were sterilized since Mother took over and the farm came into existence, a way to make certain no child we fathered or mothered became more important than them.

As she straddled me, her mouth inches away, I wanted to kiss her so fuckin' desperately. I hadn't tasted her lips before. I had never tasted any woman's. It was too personal.

But everything about us was personal.

"That isn't always a hundred percent, Kai."

True. Especially since the doctor they used to do the procedure had been unwilling and under extreme duress. "Neither are condoms." She smiled. "No more talking, baby. Now I want to hear you moan." I reached between us and placed my cock at her entrance then I slowly tilted my hips as I pushed inside her. It was agonizing because my body wanted to thrust when my mind wanted to savor. My mind won.

She was tight as hell and it never felt better. It was like every inch of my body remembered what it felt like being deep inside her and it was screaming yes.

She wiggled a bit and I sank deeper. I grabbed her hips and she latched onto my arms and started moving. "Kai. Why does it feel so good?"

I knew the answer but I wouldn't say it. Not aloud. Never.

"Harder. Kai." I helped her move up and down my cock, while watching her head tilt back, eyes closed.

It didn't take long before I knew I couldn't hold off any longer and it was almost disappointing. But imagining this moment and it being so fuckin' long since I had her, control was not on my side. The sweet flush on her cheeks, the way her lips slightly parted as she panted, it undid me.

"Fuck, London. I can't wait." I flipped her over on her back, still locked inside her. Then I thrust hard and fast as her ankles locked behind my back. "Yes." I groaned as she met my rhythm, our bodies slapping against one another.

"Oh, God, Kai."

And that gravelly voice saying my name had me coming inside her in a violent rush, like a tidal wave crashing down on me and taking every part of me that I had control over and breaking it apart.

I thrust a few more times, her clenching around me, hands on my heated chest, legs now relaxed on either side of me.

Jesus. It was like coming home inside of her.

Her hand rose and sifted through my hair. "You kept your promise."

I leaned in closer, my cock still sunk inside her and kissed the side of her neck then worked my way up to her ear. "What promise is that?"

"Always."

"Yes."

"Thank you for not giving up on me."

I didn't reply because there was nothing to thank.

"Kai?"

"Yeah?" I pulled out and rolled onto my back.

She sat up, holding the sheet to her chest. I liked that she still had that shyness with her nudity despite what she'd been exposed to. "The drug my father was working on, what is it for?"

"Control."

"Over?"

"People, London. Control over people." Except it wasn't just people. It was dangerous men like Connor. I threw my legs over the side of the bed, bent, grabbed my jeans and tugged them on as I stood.

I heard her shift closer to me. "Why?"

I ignored her question because there was so much to tell her and I didn't want to get into it now. "You can't run away from here." I didn't think she would, but I had to say it.

She was silent several seconds before she said, "I couldn't stay there… at home. The way everyone looked at me. My father… everyone knew."

"No. You knew. It just felt that way."

"I couldn't function. I was suffocating. My dad wouldn't let me go back to my loft and the medication was messing me up. All I wanted to do was die. And the doctor… he wanted me to talk about it and I couldn't."

"Because you didn't want to face it."

A tear trailed down her cheek. "I…."

She couldn't say it, so I helped her. "It was easier being Raven than to fight your way back."

She nodded, her chin dropping. "Yes."

"No shame in that, London. You did what made you feel safe."

Being Raven was who she'd become and living as London surrounded by those who loved her was suffocating. Her mind had been trained to submit and suddenly, she had nothing to submit to. She'd been lost, and afraid of facing what happened so she ran.

"No more running, baby."

"Kai?"

"Yeah?"

"Thank you. For what you've done. For everything." Her fingers tightened around the edge of the sheet clutched to her chest and when her eyes met mine, I saw warmth and lightness in the depths. "I know you don't think so, but you have good in you."

I didn't respond to that. I couldn't because my throat was tight and I had no words to give her.

"What happens now?"

"I don't know, London." And I didn't. Nothing was certain, but I'd do whatever it took to keep her from being hurt. If that meant her staying here for years, then that was what would happen.

I threw my leg over her, straddling her, the sheet shielding her naked body from me, but that wasn't lasting long. "I have to leave soon, baby, and I don't know how long I'll be." I lowered my voice. "You need to know that leaving here isn't an option for you."

Her brows rose. "Are you saying I'm a prisoner?"

I smirked. "You can take it any way you want." I drew in closer. "But if you do, there isn't anywhere I won't find you again." I tightened my thighs around her hips. "I found you in an underworld where girls are lost forever."

"Deck found me," she said, trying to hide her smile.

"Mmm, yes. But I allowed him to."

Her breath hitched and her eyes widened. "You were there? Why then... why didn't you take me with you?"

"Couldn't do it, baby. Not then."

"And now is what... more convenient for you?"

My lip twitched. "Yes."

"Why?" she demanded, her brows scrunched together and her supple body tensed beneath me.

Fuck, she was perfect. I grabbed her wrists and locked them together in one hand above her head and grinned. "Wanted to finish decorating my bedroom. Took me a while."

She huffed. I chuckled. She struggled against me, but that didn't last long. Soon, my jeans were back on the floor and she was submitting to me, and it wasn't because I made her.

London belonged to me because she wanted to. And that was a woman's ultimate control.

CHAPTER
EIGHTEEN

Hard Limit

Kai

"BABY, YOU KNOW I love a challenge and if you decide to make a run for it,"—I stalked across the room toward her—"know that I've never lost one." I didn't. It was a fact. Losing was a word I had no experience with because I didn't know how to give up.

Her brows lowered and her nose twitched before she tucked her hair behind her ear. I loved that she was a little uncertain of me, on her guard and yet still her blood rushed through her veins in heated anger. It was the London I'd been attempting to get back, the girl who would stand up to a killer, the girl who challenged me.

My cock strained against my jeans and I liked the discomfort.

I waited. Eager to see what she'd do—if she'd run, fight or submit. I wanted all three in that order. I smiled as I stood a few feet away from her, arms crossed, completely relaxed, at least in appearance, and yet my muscles thrummed, ready to react.

"I don't understand you."

"I'm not meant to be understood, merely… pleased."

"I tried that. You didn't like it," she retorted and I loved that she threw attitude back at me. What I didn't like was what it meant—time for me to return to Toronto and deal with shit. Every night for the last week I went to bed swearing I'd leave in the morning, yet every morning when I woke with her naked in my arms, I said, 'Tomorrow.'

I laughed. "Quite right. But having a woman suck me off because she is trained to doesn't please me. What pleases me is if she gets wet merely thinking about wrapping her lips around my cock. That, my dear, pleases me."

"And if she doesn't want to?"

My eyes roamed the length of her, seeing the slight jerk in her body, the tiny goose bumps on her heated skin. There was no question she wanted me. The question was whether she'd push herself. "Are you telling me you wouldn't want to if I asked you to, right now?"

She hesitated. No doubt contemplating whether to lie to me or not. "No," she replied. Good girl. "But why do you want to do this? Tie me up."

I shrugged. "Push your limits. And because I think you need it."

"I don't like it."

I chuckled. "I know. But you'll do it."

"Are you going to force me?"

"Braveheart, I don't have to force you to do anything. You'll willingly do it because you trust me." I paused, grinning. "And because you're in love with me." Oh, she didn't like that, but the truth blazed in the depths of her eyes. "Come here. Or run. Either way is fine with me."

Her finger tapped on her thigh as she decided. "You're pretty damn confident making that ridiculous assumption." She smiled and mimicked me, crossing her arms then cocked her hip.

Ah, baby, you have no idea who you're dealing with.

"Am I?" I slipped my knife from the holster and dragged it across the palm of my hand.

She pursed her lips together, eyes narrowing, brows low. She was contemplating like she had in the car when I'd made her drive into the woods.

"Fine. I'll do it." Then she added, "But it's not because I'm in love with you."

I shrugged. It was better if she believed that, but she wouldn't do this if she didn't trust me completely. Love? It was an emotion I had no experience with, and I'd said it to see what she'd say.

I stood leaning against the wall, waiting, giving her the time to accept what I was asking. This was more than a challenge. I was rewriting the trauma and my little braveheart was living up to her nickname.

She took a long, deep inhale, her chest expanding and causing her nipples to push against the button-down dress shirt she wore. My button-down dress shirt.

This might be a challenge for her, but it was for me, too, because I wanted to rip my shirt off her, draw her nipples into my mouth until she arched and begged for me to sink inside her.

She walked over to the bed. The mattress creaked as she knelt on it. Crawling to the center, her eyes closed briefly and goose bumps appeared on her naked thighs. This was past her comfort zone, and I was pushing her limits.

She lay back.

When she opened her eyes and looked at me, determination settled within the depths. Then she raised her arms above her head and crossed her wrists.

My girl, so fuckin' brave.

Restraint.

Helplessness.

Vulnerability.

She'd spent years restrained like a dog, an object, something to be abused. Made to feel powerless and worthless. I had to change that. She was no longer a victim and the fear that was hidden behind that stubbornness was still present, lingering like a leech on her skin sucking out the pleasure.

I wanted the fear gone.

I needed it gone.

But most of all, she needed it gone.

I reached into my back pocket and pulled out my piano wire. Something I'd used numerous times to wrap around a throat and end the frantically beating pulse, lungs screaming for the oxygen I deprived.

My eyes roamed down her throat, the beautiful curve so delicate and exposed. I was easily able to end her life and that was why we were here right now. I needed her to trust me completely and put her in a position that made her defenseless.

As I approached the bed, her breath quickened and she tensed. She didn't move although it was a fight, a fight against herself. Because that was what this was. It wasn't me she feared. It was the memories that haunted her.

I leaned over the bed, my hands slowly wrapping the thin, smooth wire around her wrists several times, locking them together. I knotted the ends around the rung of the headboard, not tight, but enough that she'd be unable to move more than a few inches without the wire cutting into her wrists.

Her breath came in short gasps and she paled. I didn't fuckin' like it.

I ran my fingers down her arms to her shoulders then over to her throat, feeling her swallow beneath my touch. "You can do this, London."

She didn't answer. Sitting on the edge of the bed, I continued to trace gentle paths along her neck and collarbone. "You're stronger than what was done to you. Don't let him have you." Him was generic because I didn't know, and never wanted to know, how many hims there'd been.

"I'm scared."

"I know. But we're going to change that." I cupped her chin and waited until her eyes steadied on mine. "No other man is inside you except me. Mind or body." I brushed my thumb across her lips. Lips I was going to finally taste soon. "I need you to give yourself completely to me, not because you're forced to, London, but because you trust me to only give you pleasure."

She pulled a bit on the wire and her eyes widened with panic. "Kai. I don't like it."

I flattened my palm on her chest just above her breasts and felt her heart beating erratically. "Keep your eyes on me. I need you to see me. Know it's me. Only me. Always."

I stood up straight and slowly undressed. Taking my time, I stepped out of my jeans and folded them. I walked over to the chair and placed them on the seat.

I knew what she was doing before I turned. Struggling against the wire. I could hear the creak of the bed, the rustle of the sheets beneath her. "Oh, God, Kai."

I'd release her if she really wanted me to, but I was certain she was strong enough to defeat the panic. "If I untie you, they win. Do you want that?" She bit her lower lip and I could see the imprint left from her teeth when she released it. "Do you want to live with them lingering, sucking the life out of you?" I approached the end of the bed and stopped. "I want all of you, London. Every single piece of you and I want you to give it to me." I knelt on the bed and came toward her until I straddled her body. I leaned over her, my hands sliding up her arms until they rested on top of the bound wrists. "You need to decide whether you want to fight for me, London."

"Fight for you?" Her voice shook and I curled my hands around hers and squeezed.

"Yes," I whispered, leaning closer so my breath swept across her cheek. "Can you do that?"

For once, I was a little unclear as to what was going to happen. I was pretty confident of an outcome before I took a path and if the path changed, I was ready for it. But with London, there was risk because if she insisted I untie her, I had no choice but to do it.

Always follow through with what you say. I was confident that she'd never walk away from me, but I was pushing her. I was taking her fear and putting it in the forefront of her mind.

Then I was cocky enough to say, "Tell me you want to be free. Tell me, London and I will let you go. But if I let you go, it isn't just from the wire, it's from me."

She stilled and so did I waiting for her answer and then she said, "I want to be free." Her eyes closed and she repeated. "I want to be free."

CHAPTER
NINETEEN

My Everything

London

"I WANT TO BE free." I swallowed.

I knew with everything inside me that the second I said the words, there'd be no going back. Not with Kai. He may exude easy charm, but there was nothing in him that would yield. I'd never be able to walk away from him until he let me. He'd own every piece of me. But he made it my choice and that made it even more powerful.

And he knew that.

I took a deep breath and said, "I want to be free of them."

He slowly grinned and the tightly coiled tension in my body sprung. My fingers uncurled from the backs of his hands.

"My braveheart," he breathed.

He'd never kissed me before and I knew he was finally going to as he hovered over me, his lips an inch away from mine. I was desperate, starved to taste him for the first time.

"Do you want me to kiss you, London?"

I nodded, licking my lips with anticipation. The wire, the inability to get away, the fear associated with helplessness, all forgotten.

He kissed the corner of my mouth then trailed a path to my ear and sucked on the lobe. "I kiss you, there is no going back. No changing your mind." He shifted and I could feel his hard cock against my inner thigh. "You'll never be able to leave me, London."

Breathless, I said, "Is that a threat?"

He chuckled. The gravelly sound sank into me and goose bumps rose. "I don't need threats. Just truths."

His hand shifted into my hair to the back of my neck and fisted. "But with me, you'll have to be stronger than you've ever been. I'll do things you won't like and ask of you what you can't understand, but you need to trust every word that passes my lips."

Could I do that? Could I trust Kai so implicitly?

He'd never lied to me. He'd always told me the type of man he was right from the beginning. He'd given me choices. He'd given me the most important thing back—myself.

But I knew the answer. I knew without a doubt that being with Kai was dangerous, but it was also the safest place I could be. And the only place I wanted to be.

I arched toward him. "Kiss me, Kai."

His grip tightened on my hair, and then he groaned before his mouth came down on mine.

It was owning.

It was a judgment.

It was the final knot binding us together.

Our mouths melding became a permanent tether that neither of us could break.

"Fuck, London." He pulled back a second to look at me as if making certain it was real, and then our mouths crashed again, his tongue caressing, tasting, taking. I met his urgency with my own, pulling on the wire that kept me from wrapping my arms around him and bringing him closer.

There was no sweetness as he kissed me, but it was slow and determined, as if he was making certain I understood what all this meant. My body ached and soared, quivers of desire racing through me as I forgot about the wire around my wrists and gave in to him. Gave in to what I needed from Kai.

Everything.

He pulled back as his fingers went to the buttons on my shirt. I wanted him to rip it open, watch as the buttons popped off, and then have his hands on my breasts, but Kai wouldn't do that.

Despite the fire burning in his eyes, he took his time and meticulously undid each little white button. His fingers trailing down between my breasts as he did it.

He smiled and paused. "What do you feel, London?" His fingers moved away from my skin and he merely held the next button between his fingers, not undoing it.

"Desire," I whispered, breathless.

"Specifically, please."

Jesus. I pulled again on the wire, a reminder that I was helpless, yet it was also a reminder that I wasn't. I'd chosen this.

I'd given him my everything.

"Heat. I feel heat all through my body."

"Mmm. What else?"

"A tightness in my chest like... I can't breathe unless you touch me again." He still refused to touch me so I continued, "And tingles between my legs... a vibration of electricity. And wet. I feel wet."

He smirked. "Oh, there is no question you're wet, baby." He undid another button, but this time, he avoided touching my skin before he pushed the material away from my body.

"And a little scared." He nodded as if that was what he'd been waiting to hear.

"Why?"

I thought about it. I was tied up in a bed with a man on top of me and I was completely helpless like I'd been for years, but it was a different kind of fear.

"Because I trust you so much. It's terrifying."

He let go of my shirt and lowered his body until his lips lightly brushed against mine. "I'll never hurt you. But, baby, you know that already."

His mouth lowered to mine and he kissed me again. It was urgent. Bruising. Harsh. His one hand pulled on my hair while the other slowly glided down my body to between my legs.

"Oh, God." Arching my back, I broke from the kiss when his heated palm cupped me. He didn't move his hand, merely rested it there. Claiming. Owning.

"Please," I begged.

He trailed kisses down my neck to the crease between my breasts. He was slow and casual about it, taking his time as his heated breath and moist lips tasted and explored until he finally reached my nipple and drew it into his mouth.

He was gentle at first, the velvet surface of his tongue playing with it back and forth. I wiggled my pelvis trying to get him to move his hand that still cupped me. But his patience was resilient as he just held his hand on my sex with the slightest pressure, causing the anticipation to build.

My nipple slipped from his mouth. Then, he sat up and traced the red surface with his finger while his other hand inside my panties twitched and sent a wave of desire through me.

"Kai. Please."

He unraveled me. Everything he'd done by bringing me here, the ice water, the belt, even tying me up, it was all to bring me to this point. There was no turning back for me now. I wanted only him.

"Pull on the wire, London."

"Huh?"

He climbed off me and lay on his side beside me. "I want you to feel the restraints."

"I do. I feel them."

"I need to know he is out of you."

What he was asking… I'd done everything he asked of me, but what I'd been through would never truly die. It was part of me and with Kai's help, I'd fought back. Now, he wanted me to feel like I had so many times before during those years with Alfonzo and Jacob?

"Fight, London."

"Kai. Why? I don't understand?" Why was he making me do this?

"You said you trusted me." I nodded. "Then I need you to fight. Feel helpless and vulnerable and scared."

"I don't want to." I didn't want that overwhelming panic that suffocated my lungs and gripped my chest so hard that it felt as if a vise was being tightened around me.

"Of course you don't. But you need to." He leaned over me, briefly kissed my quivering lips then got up from the bed.

My heart drummed against my rib cage as I watched him walk to the other side of the room completely naked. His cock hard and erect against his muscled abdomen.

He sat in the chair, leaned back, his thighs parted and his eyes dark and intense as he waited for me to decide what to do.

Kai was an enigma, but there was one trait I knew for certain about him and that was he'd never give in. Never yield if he wanted something. God, he'd searched for me for two years and I was betting he'd have done it for twenty more if he had to.

That was the type of man he was and I did trust him.

So I fought.

I yanked on the wire and I winced as it cut into my wrists. I twisted and turned, the sheet beneath me now wrapping around my legs as I struggled against the bonds, the fear creeping into me as the memory of being on the cot, Alfonzo on top of me, my wrists tied just like this but with the heavy cold weight of manacles.

Panic heightened as the memory grew stronger and I thrashed on the bed. Kai sitting on the chair was forgotten as I struggled to get free.

I couldn't get away.

Trapped.

He was going to leave me here for days.

No.

No.

I screamed as I yanked and pulled as the memories invaded like a black suffocating fog.

"No. No."

With everything I had, I yanked on the wire.

The knot he'd tied in the wire released and my arms shot forward from the momentum as I sprung free.

I lay still for a second, breathing ragged, my wrists still tied together but free from the headboard.

Free.

A cool wave of relief poured over me as the panic washed away. I was heaving in breaths of air from my struggle, but the terror was gone. It was as if the sudden release had re-written the memory. I'd escaped. I'd escaped when for years I couldn't.

"Yes." Kai's voice was a deep resonating sound that was like a blanket of warmth.

"You put a knot that would eventually release if I fought hard enough? You wanted me to break free?"

"Yes."

"You wanted me to feel the fear and escape it myself." It wasn't a question because that was exactly what he wanted.

"You won't always be able to break free, London. That's reality. But if you can't, know that I'll always come for you. Don't ever forget that. You need to know that."

My breath left me as I stared at him, taking in what he said. "I do know." I had no doubt Kai would walk through an inferno in order to get to me. God, he had. "But you're not God, Kai. Even if you think you are."

He raised his brows. "True. But I'm the closest you'll ever get to the big man." I smiled and he said, "Come here."

My legs still trembling, I crawled off the bed and walked over to him. He reached out and undid the wire still around my wrists. Red lines embedded in my skin and he brought my wrist to his mouth, kissing the inflamed skin then repeated with the other one.

My eyes flicked to his cock that was still hard and I wanted to sink to my knees and take him in my mouth. I never thought I'd willingly want to do that again, but the need to taste him on the tip of my tongue, to wrap my lips around the hard velvet surface, to give him pleasure pulsed through me.

I decided right then to break one of his rules and it was without fear. Without uncertainty.

I slipped to my knees on the floor between his legs, my hands on his muscled, naked thighs.

His voice was a low growl as he harshly grabbed my chin and forced me to look at him. "I never want you on your knees again."

I met his fierce scowl, but it was the hint of fear in his eyes that had me softening my initial retort. "You want to give me choices?"

"Yes."

"Then this is my choice. I want your cock in my mouth. I want to hear you groan with pleasure."

"Then we'll move to the bed. I don't want you on your knees on the floor."

It was then I realized that maybe this wasn't just about me. This was about him. He couldn't handle seeing me on my knees. I wasn't sure if it was a reminder of Mexico or something else, but whatever it was he was fighting it every second I remained on my knees.

"Maybe it's time to re-write that memory, too, Kai?" His eyes widened as a flicker of surprise hit his face. "And you won't always get what you want. At least with me."

Then he shook his head back and forth as a twitch of a smile formed while he released my arms. "Mmm, perhaps. But I will certainly try."

Then he picked me up, carried me to the bed and tossed me down. He came after me and settled himself against the headboard.

I crawled between his legs and slid my hands over his knees, up his thighs to his hips.

I watched his expression as my hand lowered to his cock, wrapping around the base of it. He stopped breathing. I trailed my tongue over the tip and his eyes shifted from mine to my mouth and his cock in my hand.

I tightened my grip and before I lowered my mouth to him I said, "You're my everything."

CHAPTER
TWENTY

Hope Destroys

Kai

I LAY IN BED with London curled into me, her cheek resting on my chest, palm on my abdomen covering one of my scars. The most recent, the one in Mexico where I'd been shot, changing the course of London's life.

A stray bullet that cost her more than it did me.

'You're my everything.'

Her words from last night weren't lost on me, but at the time, they'd been pushed aside as she sucked on my cock until I had to flip her over and thrust inside her.

We had to talk. She had to know what we were facing because I had no plan. I didn't know the outcome of what would happen to us.

Her hand slid over my abdomen to a jagged scar left by an iron rod, a red-hot iron rod. She traced it with her finger and I felt the wetness of a teardrop soak into my skin as her cheek rested on my chest.

"What happened, Kai?"

It was time. She needed to know everything before I left. "That was an iron rod when I was twelve." Her hand froze on top of the scar and I heard her sharp inhale. "My mother sent us to a place when we were young after my father died. She called it 'the farm.' A place where you're taught to survive and if you fail, you're dead. Different ages, males, females, it didn't matter. We were there to learn how to kill. But we also had to learn how to write and speak effectively. We learned the ways of the world. Although, their idea of the ways of the world were somewhat distorted." I paused. "If you made it to eighteen, you were sent on assignments."

"How old were you when you went there, Kai?"

"I was seven, my sister five."

She gasped, then after a minute said, "You have a sister?"

I stiffened as a wave of pain gripped me. I'd blocked her out for so long, the farm did that, but over the last few years with the emotions creeping back in, so had my sister, Chess. "She's in France. Mother had her imprisoned."

"But why would your mother do that? Why would she send her kids to a place like that and why imprison your sister?"

I curled my fingers around hers resting on my chest. "My mother is a bitch and she wanted control of Vault." I explained to her about Vault, the board members, what they did, what they stood for then and now.

"Where are the kids now?"

"Some became operatives, others have been killed. Some never made it out of the farm. Kids disappeared in the night and new ones appeared all the time. You never slept well, fearing you'd be next. Disappearing was never good, because we knew those who disappeared weren't coming back and were probably dead."

"Handlers looked after us. Conditioned us, I guess you could say. Pain was a daily ritual. After a while, you grew accustomed to it. Immune. Numb. It's the fear that eats away at you and they were good at making you fear them."

Resting my hand on the small of her back, I softly drew paths going nowhere, meaningless paths. "But it wasn't fear for me. It was fear for my sister." She stiffened. "They knew it, too, and used it against us. It's when I learned that what they wanted was to break me to the point where I didn't care about anyone."

She remained quiet, but her tears said it all. I wasn't telling her so she'd pity me or feel sorry for me. That was the last thing I wanted. I needed her to know, so if Vault ever took her, she'd understand what type of people they were.

"It's why they start us so young, fewer attachments, easier to break and condition us. But my sister… she kept breaking rules. Kept trying to help other kids. When she was about fourteen, she helped a kid escape. I don't know how she did it, but she was taken away and none of us saw her for a long time. That's when we were moved to another place. I guess they were afraid the kid who escaped would tell the authorities."

"Oh, God, Kai."

"When she came back… I don't know why, but she looked okay and she began to learn how to fight like the rest of us. She was compliant. But a few years ago, she went on a mission and didn't come back." I sighed, closing my eyes for a second as I thought about her. "They found her. Brought her back and she's been imprisoned ever since."

"You don't escape them, London. You do what you have to in order to survive. You learn to play their game by your rules."

"Like now."

"Yeah, baby. Like now. You're an attachment and they would end it if they knew you were with me." I cupped her chin and tilted her face to look at me. "If they get to you…." Fuck. I didn't know if I'd be able to save her. Maybe I had lied to her because Vault was the one place I may never be able to save her from.

"How…? God, Kai, how could your mother do that?"

"I may have her tainted blood running through me, but she isn't a mother. I call her that because it's my game. My card to play, so she feels comfort in thinking I'm her loyal son."

"Are you? Loyal?" she asked quietly.

"I have a house they don't know about and I have the daughter of the man who supplies them with a drug hidden in it."

I ran my hand down her spine until it rested on the cusp of her ass. "London, hope is dangerous there. They know how to erase every part of you until you're nothing. And now… the drug your father made for them will only make it easier because they will use men already trained to kill." I paused. "Like Georgie's brother."

She frowned. "Georgie? Deck and Georgie. That Georgie? I don't understand."

I brought her in closer and I told her everything. How Georgie became Chaos, about Tanner getting close to Connor so he and Georgie would trust Tanner. I revealed more than I had to anyone. I did it not to scare her. It was for the opposite reason, because fear came from the unknown. I did it so she could be prepared for anything. To give her power. And to give her what I'd never given anyone, even Ernie—my complete trust.

"Connor was the first to be tested with the drug. I don't know the particulars as anything involving Connor was kept confidential, but he was in an elite task force—JTF2—when he was taken. He had all the skills necessary without the years of training children. But the difference between persuading children to do what you want and someone like Connor, he won't mold easily. And some men will never break."

"The drug." I nodded. "But my father… why would he do that?"

"Your father would do anything to protect you." There was no easy way to tell her what was next, but it was important she knew that her father did what he had to. "The fire you were in… I suspect it was Vault."

She gasped. "But you're Vault. You set the fire?"

"Fuck, no. But Vault knew your mother died in an accidental fire and then for you to almost die in one… I don't believe in coincidences, London."

"But if they wanted to kill me, why wouldn't they tell you. You saved me from the fire."

"I don't kill kids."

"I was eighteen."

"True, and, baby, you were so fuckin' beautiful." I leaned over and kissed her forehead, lips, lingering as I closed my eyes, wanting to take the hurt away, but knowing she needed to hear this. "Your father was delaying. He didn't want to continue making the drug, but then with the fire... he had no choice, London."

I gave her time to accept what I'd told her. To try and make sense of it. Her hand stroked back and forth absently over my abdomen. She didn't sob or break down, but quietly took in what I told her.

Her cheek glided against my chest as she looked up at me. "Mexico was them, wasn't it? Another threat to my father?"

"Yes. And no." I stroked my thumb over her lower lip, still swollen from my kisses. "They had you kidnapped and taken to Mexico, and it was a threat to your father. But it was meant to be more of a threat to me."

She sat up, her body half-leaning over me. "What?"

"I spent several nights with you, but not in the way they wanted."

She reached up and cupped the side of my face when I fell silent. "Oh, my God, you were supposed to hurt me."

"Yes."

Her hand flinched on my abdomen. "And instead you were going to walk away. Let me go."

"Yes."

"But my father—"

"Would've got the extra time he needed regardless."

"But you let me make the deal?"

I raised my brows. "It was a deal I couldn't refuse. I was a bastard for doing it, but I don't regret it, baby. I'll never regret a second I've spent with you."

Her eyes narrowed and lips pursed together before she slapped my chest. "So, I didn't have to sleep with you?"

"I recall you being very willing."

"But I thought...." She stopped, thinking about what to say and I let her. Finally, she said, "Why?"

I flipped her over onto her back and lowered on top of her, grabbing her wrists to lock them down on the mattress on either side of her head. Her chest rose and fell rapidly, her eyes steady on me.

Her heart raced beneath my chest as I moved in closer. "Braveheart, I'd wanted you for years. I knew it was impossible and safer if I stayed away, but when I saw you in the closet and I knew you saw me... I had to warn you. Scare you enough to not do anything about what you saw. But then you came up with that deal." I touched my lips to hers and was disappointed that they were unmoving beneath mine. "I knew it was the only chance I'd ever have you."

"It was wrong," she said.

"Yeah." I got off her, swung my legs over the side of the bed, then leaned over and grabbed my pants off the floor. Fuck, I never cared about wrong or right. I did what I had to do, but this mattered. It had been wrong because my decision cost her dearly. "I have to leave today."

She sat up, taking the sheet with her. "Oh."

I stood, yanked on my pants then picked up my shirt. "Not sure how long I'll be."

"Honey," she whispered and it was as if she handed me the world with that single word. "When are you going to let someone save you?"

Fuck.

I still had my back to her as I did up the buttons of my shirt. My fingers stilled and my back stiffened. Didn't she know? I was past saving; I had the marks to prove it and the history to confirm it.

"Don't need to be saved, London."

When she sighed, I looked over my shoulder at her. Everything inside me fought against leaving her, but I knew there was no other choice.

She sat on the edge of the bed, her hair in complete disarray, and fuck, she was beautiful.

"You were right," she said as our eyes met.

I frowned, uncertain what she was referring to.

The sheet dropped and my cock jerked. This was why I'd protected her. Why I cared. It was right in front of me. London's strength

191

challenged my own. I'd just told her the worst sort of shit possible and she was looking at me with nothing but—

"I do love you, Kai."

Fuck. I closed my eyes a second as her words sank into me. Love. I'd never been loved. Never wanted to be. I was undeserving of love.

I heard her bare feet walk across the hardwood floor and then she was undoing my shirt again. "Kai, you have good in you. I couldn't love you unless you did." Her hands slid down my chest as my shirt parted and my breath locked as I watched her kiss one scar after the other.

I let her. I let her kiss each one before I held her shoulders and pulled her away from me. But what I saw in her eyes was more powerful than anything Vault had ever done to me.

It imprisoned me.

I didn't know what love felt like, but what I felt for her was indescribable with a single word. It was more powerful. It was all consuming. "London, what we are can't be explained with a word, only experienced."

Then I showed her.

"Do they know you came to Mexico?"

"No."

I was dressed and packed to leave. London fidgeted as she picked up her toast and put it down again. She'd spread jam on it twice and tried to put the peanut butter lid on the jam jar. Her legs crossed then uncrossed as she shifted on the bar stool for the last ten minutes.

"You'll be careful?"

"Always careful, baby." She closed her eyes, lips drawn together. I tossed my toast down. "London, someone is always after me. Like I said, I don't have friends and I've made a lot of enemies, but I'm careful and know what I'm doing." Then I softened my voice and stated,

"You're worried."

"Yeah."

Fuck, I liked that.

"What about Deck?" she asked.

Yes, what about him. There was no trust between us, more like a mutual understanding, until he discovered my little secret with his girl, Georgie. Then all hell was going to break loose. I was hoping that wouldn't happen as it could force me to play my hand. Georgie thought I'd kill him, but I wouldn't unless he tried to kill me first, which was a good possibility if he found out everything.

"He won't hurt you." Of that I was certain. Deck was a killer, too, but he had morals and values that rivaled my own. "But he isn't a friend, London."

"Kai, I want to call my dad."

We'd already argued about this. Well, she argued. I simply said no. It was too risky for her to make any contact with him. "No. But when I get back, we'll talk about it and I'll teach you how to handle a knife."

By the spark in her eyes, I knew she liked both those ideas.

"Okay. But maybe it's safer if I go with you?"

I stared at her a second. After all I'd told her this morning, she still wanted me and yet... I was afraid she'd leave. And she'd need to understand why she couldn't leave and why she couldn't go with me.

I grabbed her around the waist, yanked her off her stool then had my knife to her throat within seconds. Her eyes widened and her breath stopped.

"Do you feel the trembling in your limbs, London? The blood rushing through your veins? The tightness in your chest as the edge of my blade rests against your throat?" She couldn't nod because my knife would cut her. "That's fear. And that's dangerous." I stroked my finger down her cheek. "You're not ready to go anywhere with me." And I didn't know if she ever would be. But I couldn't think of that. "I need you to do what I tell you. Stay here, eat a shitload so when I come back, I have some real hips to grab."

I smirked. She didn't.

"So I'm supposed to wait for you to come back or not come back because you're dead?"

"I won't die."

She latched onto my wrist holding the knife, her grip harsh. She was pissed—good. She had to stand on her own and fight for what she wanted... except she'd never win against me.

"You're not invincible, Kai."

No, I wasn't, but I excelled at staying alive. "Arguable." I took my knife away from her throat then pulled her around so she straddled my lap.

When I saw her glare and that stubborn chin lifted, I couldn't help it. I chuckled which caused her to punch my chest. "It's not funny."

"If I die, braveheart, I still won't leave you." And if I died, Ernie had instructions as to what to do about London—Deck. He was to be told everything and London taken to him.

"Death is pretty damn final. I don't see you believing in the after-life."

I nipped the sensitive lobe of her ear. "Hmm, perhaps not." I pushed her hair away from her neck with the tip of my knife then ran my tongue along her slender throat. Her breath hitched and her spine arched. Something about the rush of danger sent all the adrenaline right to my cock. I pulled back so I could see her eyes—flaming desire. I took hold of the collar of her shirt, which was one of mine, then sliced it down the center with my knife.

She gasped.

"If I die," I slowly caressed her exposed nipple, not with my finger but with my knife, "a piece of you dies with me." I laid the flat of my knife against her breast and pressed. "And you will never repair that part of you. But it goes both ways, braveheart."

She moved closer to me, so the flat of the blade was pushed harder into her breast. She reached up and cupped the back of my neck. "I'd like to stay whole, so I'd prefer you to live."

I placed my knife on the counter then undid my jeans and pulled out my throbbing cock. I reached around her and picked her up by the ass. She wrapped her legs around my hips, arms hooking my neck.

"Will you sleep naked when I'm gone so I can imagine you in our bed playing with yourself?" I pushed aside her panties and rubbed my cock through her wet pussy.

Her lips parted as she panted. "Yes."

I jerked my hips forward and groaned as my cock sank into her tight warmth. She cried out at my harsh entrance, hands tightening in the strands of hair at the back of my neck. I buried my head in her shoulder as I whispered, "Don't ever stop believing in me."

Because I didn't know what I'd do if she did.

CHAPTER
TWENTY-ONE

London

THREE DAYS.

He'd left no phone, no computer access and no car. He knew I'd call my father or email him despite saying I wouldn't. So, I was left in the middle of nowhere with nothing to do except eat and watch movies then fall asleep every night on the couch.

I'd never been one to sit around and do nothing; even as a kid I was experimenting with different things to find out what would happen. It was my dad who insisted I learn to ride a bike when I was six years old when all the kids in the neighborhood were already on two wheelers.

I considered myself physically challenged with having played no sports. I'd been forced to play baseball as a freshman in gym and after my first throw, which was underhand and pathetic, I was benched most of the time.

Now, I wished I'd had some sort of natural talent at throwing, but for hours, I'd attempted to hit my mark with the knife. I'd hoped to impress Kai by practicing before he got back and being half decent. With the way it was going, there wouldn't be any impressing.

He said he might be a couple weeks, so I was hoping by then I could at least hit the stupid tree trunk. I raised my arm and threw the knife again. It bounced off the surface of the tree and landed in the long, unkempt grass.

"Damn it all to hell." I trudged across the field at the back of the house, the long grass swishing as the breeze ruffled the tops. I bent and picked up the knife then stabbed it into the bark. "There."

I was frustrated, my arm muscles hurt and I missed him already. I slept on the couch because the bed reminded me of him, the sheets smelled like him and yet I took his pillow and curled up with it on the couch wearing one of his shirts.

I was worried. I didn't like waiting. I'd felt helpless and weak for years and hated every second of it.

But Kai bringing me here had not only released me from that shell I'd been hiding in, he'd made me stronger. I never wanted to be defenseless again. I wanted to be like Kai—fearless without the constant barrage of emotions slamming into me.

Not cold, but controlled.

I walked back to the clearing of trampled grass twenty feet away, raised my arm again, and whipped the blade and it arched through the air in a precise hard line.

"Yes," I yelled as it pierced the tree and wobbled a bit like it was going to fall. I clapped my hands and jumped up and down.

"Impressive."

I spun around so fast I stumbled in the long grass. My eyes hit the man who spoke. He stood with his arms crossed, leaning up against the back door. Everything inside me stilled for a second and then the very reason I was here and not with Kai slammed into me.

Fear.

The man's expression was dead, no smile, no scowl—blank. The strict curves of his face made him appear jagged and harsh. Eyes a brilliant blue, sharp and cold that left no assumptions as to what this man was capable of.

He didn't hide the fact that he had weapons attached to his belt, although none were in his hand, but I was betting he'd have one out before I took one step.

"Who are you?" I was going to ask if he was a friend of Kai's, but I remembered what Kai told me—he didn't have friends and I was never to believe anyone if they said they were.

"I'm here to take you home."

I tensed at the deep, gravelly tone in his voice. A voice that caused the fear to escalate because there was no question whoever he was, he was just as dangerous as Kai, but Kai wouldn't hurt me, this man would.

My fingers curled into fists at my sides. "I'm perfectly fine where I am." I inched back a step and he didn't move. I took another step back. Could I outrun him? Would he shoot me in the back?

"I see that." He pushed away from the door and my heart felt as if it lodged in my throat. God, his arms were huge and if he got hold of me, I'd never get free. I wasn't a runner, but I was small and—

"Please. Do run, little rabbit." My breath hitched and I froze. "My orders are to bring you home alive, but wounds are optional."

"I'm not going anywhere without Kai."

"Ah, yes, Kai. The loyal Kai who is hiding a girl he was supposed to bring in to Vault." He was? "In a house we didn't know about."

"Who are you?"

"Does it matter?"

I glared. "Yes. I'd like to know the name of my executioner."

His brows rose at that. "I told you I won't kill you."

I smiled. "Well, you're going to have to. Because the only way you're getting me to leave is in a body bag." As soon as the words left my mouth, I thought of what Kai said. A body bag was too polite. He'd cut me up first.

A mild breeze ruffled the tops of the long grass surrounding me and the flimsy stems swayed back and forth. I straightened my spine, raising my chin a notch. I'd been afraid of death for so many years, but now… I wasn't afraid of it. I was afraid of never seeing Kai again. Never tasting his lips. Never feeling his arms around me. But most of all, I was afraid of him getting hurt. It was kind of stupid maybe, considering who he was and what he was capable of, but Kai's confidence unnerved me because he was so casual about it, as if his life being taken had no meaning.

But it did. It did to me.

He started toward me, arms dropping to his sides, close to his knife on one side and his gun on the other.

I had to run.

And from his mild shrug and lifted brows, he knew it, too.

I took off, darting to the right and headed toward the side of the house. My feet pounded in my head as I zigzagged across the yard. I couldn't hear him behind me and I didn't dare look. I just ran. I made it to the front of the house. My only chance was the road and hope someone would see me.

I hesitated a second when I saw his black SUV parked in the driveway. I thought about checking for the keys, but he didn't look stupid. Shit, everything about him was the opposite. Cold. Calculating. Unfeeling. A machine.

My feet skidded in the gravel as I hit the driveway and I chanced a glance behind me, but he wasn't there. He hadn't even chased me.

What the hell? Where was he?

I ran as fast as I could, the road only a hundred feet away now. I was going to make it.

The impact of the bullet hit me in the shoulder and took me down. I fell face first into the gravel.

Excruciating pain ripped through my body as I struggled to get to my feet again, my hand holding my shoulder as blood seeped through my fingers.

My gaze darted to the driveway when I heard the crunch of tires. Not from the road ahead, but from behind me. I groaned as the running jarred my shoulder. I veered off the driveway into the brush, but fell as my ankle turned over in the hidden ditch.

I screamed in agony when my shoulder took the brunt of the impact. My vision blurred and I shook my head trying to clear the fogginess. I took my hand off my shoulder and crawled, but every movement was so painful that I was afraid I was going to pass out.

Footsteps sounded behind me. The crackle of twigs snapping under his weight.

I tried to gain my footing, but lost my balance and fell again.

"Are you done?"

I heaved breaths while lying on my side. Blood soaked into Kai's shirt, his nice expensive white button-down shirt. He had so many of them and I hadn't taken them off. I wore one every day just so when I breathed in, it was him who sank into my lungs.

"I'll never be done," I retorted. They may be able to take my body, but like Kai said, never let anyone take my mind.

He bent over and grabbed the arm with the bullet in it and yanked me to my feet. I gritted my teeth trying to stop the scream from emerging, but it came out as a moan.

"You ready to go home now, London? Or do you prefer to be called Raven?"

I glared up at him and spit in his face. The glob of saliva hit his cheek and slid down the surface of his skin to drop off his jaw, soaking into his black T-shirt. "Fuck you."

He hauled on my arm and I had no choice but to stumble after him or have my arm dislocated. I realized I hadn't made it very far from the driveway; although at the time, it felt as if I'd been running forever.

He opened the passenger door. "Get in."

"Where are you taking me?"

Not even a flicker of an expression. God, he *was* a machine. "A new home. One you'll appreciate… in time."

"Vault."

That got a mild lowering of his brows before he leaned over me and did up my seatbelt. Then before I knew what was happening, he had my wrist in a handcuff. He yanked my arm up and attached the other end of the cuff to the handle on the ceiling.

I didn't bother pulling on it because it was my wounded shoulder and there was no point except to cause me pain.

"I'm going to bleed to death."

"Doubt it. We'll see."

He slammed the door and I watched him walk around the front of the SUV. He was terrifying, not like Kai had been when I met him; this was different because it was like I was talking to a wall of blackness. Soulless.

He folded in and buckled his seatbelt before starting the engine. Then he looked at me, his eyes roaming the length of me before settling on my wound. "Put pressure on it."

I glared and didn't want to do what he said, but I wanted to live, so despite the agony, I applied pressure. "Kai is going to be pissed. He'll come after me."

He gave an abrupt nod. "Yes. But I suspect he'll spend months looking for you, thinking you ran away—again." No. Kai wouldn't believe that, would he? He'd know I didn't leave willingly. "And when he does find out, we will then know where his loyalty lies."

I gasped. This was a test. A test of Kai's loyalty to Vault. Oh, God.

He threw the car into gear and started down the driveway. "And my name is Connor."

CHAPTER
TWENTY-TWO

Kai

THE MOMENT I opened the door to the house, I knew. The grin tugging at my mouth that had been there since the plane landed faded, and my stomach dropped.

I didn't need to look around or call her name, I fuckin' knew London wasn't here. Coldness enveloped and the rift split open again filling with black tar and suffocating me.

I took my time, checking room by room, hand on my knife, but the precaution was unnecessary because I knew no one was here. And hadn't been in a while.

She hadn't been.

"FUCK!" I shouted and slammed my fist into the drywall leaving a large dent. The mirror hanging above the hallway table crashed to the floor and shattered.

Rage was an emotion that had played with me, taunted, over the last few years as emotions crept back into me. I'd kept it controlled. I'd kept it blanketed because I'd seen what it did to other men—they made mistakes.

I had been able to smirk through the anger with my casual calm because I never gave a shit.

Now I did.

Now I fuckin' did.

And now I couldn't grin through the anger pulsating through my blood. It had control of me as I strode through the house, a house I spent years building. A house that meant something to me because it lived and breathed London now.

I didn't know why I bothered looking for her. Maybe I was hoping for once my gut instinct was wrong and she was lying in our bed naked waiting for me. Hope. Fuck. Never have fuckin' hope. I knew better.

I kicked open the bedroom door and my eyes locked on the empty bed.

The sheets were tucked into the mattress. London didn't tuck the sheets in. When we went to bed, she always pulled them out from under the mattress so if she made the bed, she didn't tuck. I tucked.

Meaning she hadn't slept in the bed since I left thirteen days ago.

I'd been in Toronto finding info on Chaos's new assignment, Lionel. Vault's email stated Chaos was to get the files on his computer, meaning she had to get an invite back to his place and since he liked to hang out at Avalanche, a bar Chaos knew well, she was going to get his attention and get that invite.

I'd also looked further into Tristan Mason because it didn't sit right that he happened to start showing up at Chaos's coffee shop at the same time as Vault asked to have him looked into.

I hated coincidences.

Fuck, thirteen days. Thirteen days I'd been gone and without contact with London. How long had she been gone? But the bigger question was had she run? Did she regress? Had I left her too soon? Or had she gone home to see her father? I knew she was worried about him, but I'd told her about Vault. She knew how dangerous they were.

My gaze slid to the chair I'd sat in the day I'd brought London here and waited for her to wake. Then to the bathroom where I saw her toothbrush sitting in the holder on the counter. I walked across the room, into the bathroom then ran my thumb over the bristles—dry.

The idea that Vault had found my house, found London...

I swiped my arm across the counter top sending everything flying into the wall then crashing to the floor. I stormed out of the bathroom, pulled my cell from my back pocket and tapped the code then contacts then went to hit Dr. Westbrook's number.

I stopped.

Mistakes. That was exactly what rage did. Reacting without thinking and that was what I'd nearly done. Calling her father was a mistake. Vault knew every incoming number and every outgoing number on his phone.

"Fuck, London. Where the hell are you?"

I switched phones, tapped, and then held it to my ear. He picked up on the first ring. I interrupted his 'what's up' with, "She's gone. Need eyes on the street."

"Okay. How long?" Ernie asked.

I walked into the kitchen, opened the fridge and took out the milk and read the stamped date on the top. Expired six days ago. I tossed it into the sink. "I left thirteen days ago. Could be gone since then."

"She have wheels?"

"No."

"Take me five hours to fly there."

I frowned. "Where the fuck are you?" Since London had been with me, I hadn't spoken to Ernie. He'd said he was taking some time, meaning he was going somewhere hot and lying on the beach doing fuck all except women. "Just get here. I'm calling in my marker with Deck on this."

I hung up.

Deck suspected Connor was alive. Deck, who Chaos was in love with. Deck, who had been a pain in my ass. But Deck had skills and I'd use them. I'd use anyone and anything to get her back.

I walked into the living room, pushed the couch aside and crouched. My palms slid over the hardwood until I felt the slight indent. I pulled out my knife, stabbed it between the two pieces of hardwood where the dip in the floor was and peeled back one of the boards.

I reached inside and pulled out the leather satchel that held my numerous fake passports and all the paperwork I hid from Vault, including the deed to the house. I grabbed the larger knapsack that had a few of my knives, and cash. It wasn't my only cash because I didn't like it all in one place, but it was enough.

Then I grabbed the last bag. A bag I never wanted to use, but the reality was London may not have run away or gone to see her father. There was a third possibility. Despite there being no indication of a struggle, Vault could've found my house. Found her.

I unzipped the last bag and carefully pulled out the device.

No attachments.

No ties to anything.

But it was too late for that. Maybe a couple of months ago this would've been easy, but as I set the device and placed it on the coffee table, tightness gripped my chest.

She lingered here and part of me didn't want to destroy that. No, not part of me—all of me.

I stood, snagged the two bags, the heavy one slung over my shoulder and started for the door.

Tick.

Tick.

Tick.

I threw open the door and walked out.

The sound of my steps on the patio stones were steady and casual, matching the thump of my heart. This is what I needed to do.

I folded into my car, turned the key and the engine came to life. Then I slowly drove down the driveway.

I glanced once in the rear-view mirror just as the ground rumbled beneath the car and there was a loud boom.

Pieces of the house lifted into the air with flames. Black smoke billowed into the sky. I stopped at the road and watched in the mirror as the house burned.

It was the destruction of the rage. Destruction of what one girl made me feel for the first time in my life.

I had to burn the emotions and find the calm again.

Because if I didn't, the rift was going to split and there'd be nothing left of me. The darkness would be all consuming and even London's lightness wouldn't be able to bring me back.

CHAPTER
TWENTY-THREE

Present Day

France

Kai

MOTHER WAS DEAD.

I killed her and all I felt was relief and satisfaction.

Fuckin' dead and maybe I was just as bad as her because I'd enjoyed watching her flounder as she struggled to breathe with the wire tight around her delicate throat. I liked how her fingernails dug into the backs of my hands as she clawed and raked at me, at the wire, at her neck, her eyes begging.

I'd begged at one time, too. As a kid, I'd begged for the pain to stop. Begged her not to kill my father. Begged night after night for my sister to be saved from the farm. Begging did fuck all.

Mother destroyed what a child was born with—innocence. The

power hungry bitch had turned Vault into an organization about supremacy and control using any means to get it and, in the process, changed the beliefs it was built on. Her vision corrupted its path and I'd been a part of that.

I walked down the darkened corridor. My dress shoes a drum on the hard cement floors, like the music before a death scene in a movie. Echoing. Loud. Solitary.

It reminded me of the day I walked the corridor in Vault's Toronto house after Deck, his men, and me rescued Georgie from Tanner in the shed. The day I saw her in the cell. When I heard London's cries.

Unleashed. The snap unclicked and my emotions set free the moment I saw her in that cell. The matted hair, dried blood on her face, eyes dead. And it was then, that moment, when all my training to be unemotional had a purpose—it was to be able to walk away from her so I could stay alive in order to get her out one day.

I'd stared at her, locking away the emotions that fought to surface and gave her the words she needed to hear. Then I left. I fuckin' left with my guise of patience fragmenting and my insides catapulted into a war zone of grated rage.

The 'farmhands' had it right after all. Emotions were the monsters and I'd become one.

London was mine. She'd never belong to them—ever. They should've never touched her in the beginning. Never ruined her. No, tried to ruin her.

I ran my finger along the blade of my knife, watching for any sign that someone had discovered I'd killed Mother, yet appearing like I was out for a stroll—in a dark, musty dungeon. Mother's house was an old castle that had stone walls and sconces with candles to light the halls, but they were only used for visual effect.

I probably had twelve to twenty-four hours before anyone discovered Mother was dead. Not much time to fly back to Toronto and get London out, but it was enough. Deck and his men were on stand-by and Tristan had his private jet waiting at the airport to get us out fast.

I'd taken Mother's cell phone so I'd know if anyone was looking for her and her laptop to hack to try to find the location of the farm, the drug formula, and the anonymous board member. My skills weren't as good as Chaos's, and I knew Deck's man, Tyler, specialized in this shit.

I stopped at the last heavy wooden door on the right with large black iron studs along the edge. Unlike the Toronto house, nothing here had eye scanners and fingerprint access, only old school key and locks granted access, which I'd also grabbed from Mother.

On the other side of the door, I heard my sister's faint footsteps. There was that subtle limp she had from when she was shot in the thigh when she'd tried to escape.

The memories of Chess had been filtering in lately. I'd even told London about her when I'd never told anyone. It was like I was thawing, the ice congealed around my emotions melting a little each day. The constant conditioning to become emotionless and uncaring since I was seven years old had worked—until London.

I put my knife away, inserted the key, turned it, and pushed open the door.

My sister wouldn't willingly leave with me because she didn't trust me. And why should she?

"Francesca." She stood on the other side of the room, stance wide, arms at her side, fingers curled into fists. She was never a fighter and yet she excelled at it.

She was an open book with her emotions, ones that they'd never been able to break her of. No matter what they'd done to her, Chess remained compassionate, but it was now with an edge.

She laughed, but the sound didn't match her hard, sapphire eyes that had once been soft and gentle. "Dearest brother. Are you here to finally lead me to my death? Did Helena send you to do the honors?"

She called our mother by name, refusing the association.

Chess should be dead already. Being the daughter of one of the board members, she'd been given the privilege of remaining alive after her attempt to escape. They caught her. Shot her in the leg then tortured her before she was to be executed. But I reasoned with Mother that execution was a poor example for others. Chess deserved to suffer for the disloyalty she'd shown Vault and Mother. Death was too simple and kind. Too permanent.

I remember Chess glaring at me, her hatred blazing because she wanted to die. But I'd needed her to hate me, so Mother would believe me. It was always about Mother believing me. I realized that I'd never forgotten our connection and even with it numbed and in the far reaches of my mind, the instinct was still there to protect her.

It was the same look she had now as we faced one another. Her hand went to her back pocket and before she had a chance to pull whatever weapon she had, I threw my knife and it sliced through the arm of her T-shirt and embedded in the wall behind her.

I ducked and rolled at the last second as her makeshift wooden spike skimmed my shoulder. It hit the stone mantel and fell to the floor. But she didn't stop as she threw another. I reached into my boot and dove behind the bed as I threw my dagger, my aim off to the right like I wanted. She'd know I'd purposely missed. Everyone knew I never missed my mark.

She stopped, the tension easing from her face. "Kai?"

"It's time, Chess."

I kept my eyes on her. Despite her circumstance, she still had this magnetic quality about her, with her soft features and eyes that sucked you into her warmth when she wasn't pissed at you. Her hair was jagged, shoulder-length black strands, which contradicted her facial appearance. She had broad hips and even wearing pants I could tell she'd been working out with her muscled thighs. I suspected it was to strengthen her bad leg.

She walked to the far side of the room where there was a shelf holding a wall of books. My sister had always been a voracious reader. Fictional romance fairy tales and perhaps the reason she was foolish enough to try to escape Vault, thinking it was possible to do the impossible. Although, we were changing that fallacy.

I remained at the door, listening for any footsteps coming down the corridor, but when I checked the security cameras on Mother's computer, one goon was at the front door and the other was in the garden prowling the grounds. There was also a cook and two maids, but it was highly unlikely they would come down here.

Her head dropped forward and her shoulders sagged. "I don't understand."

"Mother's dead, Chess. I killed her ten minutes ago."

Her head shot up and she spun around, her mouth gaping. "What?"

"It's time," I repeated. She knew exactly what I meant.

As kids at the farm, time had no meaning. There were no clocks, and often we were kept in rooms with no windows so we never saw the sun or moon. Hours, minutes, days, they blended together in the blackness.

After my father was executed, we were taken to the farm and immediately separated. When I did see her, we were unable to speak as the handlers always watched us. They didn't want us forming any sort of friendships, so separating a brother and sister was essential.

But one day, I was left in a hallway while my farm handler took a piss. She was coming out of a classroom with a boy around her age and it looked like she was talking to him quietly, which was breaking the rules. They didn't have a handler with them, probably because they were compliant, unlike me who fought them for years.

At first I hadn't recognized her. She appeared stronger, the baby softness gone from her cheeks, and much taller. She looked to be seven or eight years old then. It was her eyes that were the same, a sweetness lingering within the depths as she spoke to the boy beside her.

I took a chance, knowing I'd suffer worse than I could imagine. I ran across the hall to the classroom and both of them jerked to a stop, eyes wide and fearful. Then Chess recognized me and went to throw her arms around me when I quickly shook my head.

I had seconds.

"I'll kill her, Chess. One day, I'm going to kill Mother. Don't give up on me. No matter what. There'll be a time, Chess. A time to end this."

Seconds and time did matter because I was caught. The handler came around the corner and saw me with her and the boy, and I was taken away to the pit. I didn't fight. I heard my sister's choked sobs so I walked away with my head up. I even glanced over my shoulder and winked at her.

"You killed her." It was a statement and it was like she had to say the words herself to believe them. "What about the farm?"

"We'll find it."

Her eyes narrowed and she stiffened. "You haven't found it though."

"Not yet."

She reached up to the bookshelf and the candlelight caught the edge of her chin where a purple bruise glowed. Vault never marked a face and they'd left Chess alone for years. "Who hit you?"

"Connor." She walked over to her bed, reached under her mattress and pulled out what looked like a necklace. She scrunched it up in her hand and put it in her pocket before I had a good look. "Not his fault. The drug is unstable and Mother knows it. Or she did, that's why they aren't using it on any others yet." That was why Mother agreed to let London live after Deck rescued her from the auction. "He can't control the rage. It's like he's pumped up on something and it has nowhere to go, so he loses it. Not all the time, it's sporadic and, Kai, he has no idea what he's doing. His memories are all screwed up."

"When did you last see him?"

"A couple of days ago. I overheard the guards mentioning Connor leaving for Toronto."

Fuck. We had to get to London. "We need to go, Chess. No one will know Mother's dead until tomorrow. If we're lucky, the next day." I dropped my black bag on the floor. "I have her laptop and we can find what we need on it."

"That's if you can get into it."

True, but it was all we had. "Our flight leaves in an hour. Pack what you need."

She sat on the end of the bed, her hand in her pocket.

I was silent, too. There was no excuse for how I lived my life. I'd accepted my decisions and I'd done what I thought I had to. And now, I was doing what I had to. Chess was alive. My sister lived and breathed and stood in front of me and I wasn't leaving without her. "I did what had to be done, Chess. There is no other reason than that."

Her eyes softened. "I know, Kai. I never asked you to save me."

No, she hadn't.

"You need someone on the inside."

I tensed and a wave of cold shifted through me.

"With Mother dead, the board members will meet here. There's a chance I could—"

"No." I picked up my bag again and threw it over my shoulder. We had until morning before anyone noticed Chess was gone and even then, if the goon who delivered her breakfast didn't pay attention, we had longer. "Put your pillows under your sheets so if they check on you they'll think you're sleeping."

"Kai, he'll be here. I know it's him. I know he's the one who had the farm when it was moved." I knew exactly who she was referring to—the one board member who kept his face hidden. "Maybe I can get a good look at him and sketch him. Then I'll be able to send it to…" she stopped.

"Tristan?" I said, brows rising.

"You know him?"

"You've been feeding him information ever since you got your 'privileges.' It's how he knew about Georgie—Chaos. You're his contact on the inside."

She whispered, "He promised."

I didn't know what he'd promised, but the pieces were falling into place. Chess cared about him. It was all over her with the way her shoulders slumped, her head hanging forward, hair curtaining one side of her face. But the most telling was her hand in her pocket fisting around the necklace.

Tristan had been the boy she'd been talking to that day coming out of the classroom. "How did he escape the farm, Chess? Did you help him? You had to be only what…?"

She shrugged. "I don't know, fourteen, maybe. It was the only way."

"Jesus, Chess. You didn't get out and he did."

She looked at me. "We needed a diversion." *Fuck.* That was why Tristan had spent his life working to get to this point. "It was impossible for both of us to go."

213

"He didn't know that though, did he? He thought you were coming with him."

She nodded.

"Fuck. They put you in solitary."

"It was worth it. I'd do it again."

And that was Chess. Where I had no heart, Chess had two of them.

She sighed, her head lowering. "That look on his face... he was climbing to his feet, ready to run to help me. But we had a pact."

I knew exactly what their pact had been. Instead of never leave a man behind, it was the opposite.

"I was never meant to go with him."

"Is that why you tried to escape a few years ago? Was he helping you?"

"No. He didn't know about it."

"I don't get it, Chess. Why then? Why did you try and leave Vault?"

She raised her chin, eyes hard. "I'm not like you, Kai. I can't do what they want me to."

My sister was stronger than I anticipated, but I understood her. I wouldn't have years ago, but now... I knew what it was like to care about someone. To willingly sacrifice everything for them. Maybe she could never be broken because she'd already cared. Loved. Her feelings for Tristan refused to be buried. I understood that now.

"Kai, get out of here. They'll find Mother's body and the board members will question me. I might be able to find something out. If I do, I have a way to email Tristan."

"And they could simply kill you."

"I'm willing to take that chance."

"No."

"Kai."

"No."

"This isn't your call," she said.

"Fine, it isn't, but I have a feeling he thinks it's his and he won't allow you to stay another second here." I nodded to the corridor. "Either come nicely, or I'll live up to my reputation and make you. Choose."

She stood, eyes narrowed. "He's here, isn't he?"

I smiled. "Down the road. Waiting. Impatiently. I suspect if we take much longer, he'll attempt to storm this place himself and you know how that will end."

That did it.

"We have until mid-morning before they'll notice I'm gone. I'm allowed to wander the property for a few hours then."

I nodded. Cutting it close, but it was enough.

"I hope you have a way out of here."

I grinned. "Front door."

"And you expect to walk out of here with me?"

"No. You'll take a slightly different route." She frowned and had every right to because she wasn't going to like it. "Kitchen. There's a fish truck waiting out back. He just made a delivery and is waiting for the extra cargo."

"You're sneaking me out in a fish truck?"

I shrugged. "He's a greedy bastard. And you might want a sweater." Because she was going to have to hide in a refrigerated container filled with cold raw fish. The fish guy was also the man who removed dead bodies for Mother when needed; except this time, he was removing a live one.

"I really hope you know what you're doing, Kai. Because you've started a war."

"No, I'm ending the war."

She scanned the room as if searching for what to take with her. But she didn't take a single thing except the necklace she still had in her hand. She pushed past me and headed down the corridor.

CHAPTER
TWENTY-FOUR

Tristan

TIRES CRUNCHED THE gravel into the dirt road and my head jerked up. I pushed away from the tree I'd been leaning against for the last two hours and jumped across the ditch to stand on the shoulder of the road.

I'd been calm, steady, determined and confident since I was fifteen and realized Chess wasn't coming with me. I'd escaped the farm as a boy, but seeing her dragged away and knowing she'd sacrificed herself for me... it made me into a man. Age had no factor. I knew what I had to do and despite my world being blown apart, I'd do anything to get there. And I had.

That day was finally here.

My nerves sparked, nerves that had been dead for years. My heart drummed and my hands at my sides curled into fists as I saw the billow of dust in the distance.

Chess.

The fish truck appeared around the corner then stopped a few hundred feet away from my car. Kai pulled past and parked at an angle in front of it then got out. He spoke a few words to the driver then passed him an envelope, which I knew contained a shitload of money.

Kai disappeared around the back of the truck and everything inside me that had been stirring like wildfire—stilled.

The quiet before the storm.

Chess. My best friend, the girl who decided to save one boy. Who *did* fuckin' save me.

Finally it was my turn. I'd waited for this moment. Dreamed about it. Prayed for it. Jesus. None of the money mattered. None of the houses or cars or trips. It was all to get here.

Underneath the truck, I saw her feet as she climbed out of the back. The doors slammed shut and latched, followed by a loud double knock on the back, and the truck rumbled away leaving a trail of dust behind it.

I stood waiting for the dust to settle. Waiting to see with my own eyes that she was alive. Our sporadic emails had been short, formal and gave me nothing of who she was now.

And nothing could've prepared me for this.

We were like an iceberg that had cracked and separated, floating on different currents until years later, the two pieces finally drifted back together and sealed perfectly.

That was us. Chess and I.

I'd imagined her. Every single fuckin' day I imagined her, thought about her. She was what drove me to succeed when all the odds were against a homeless boy with nothing but a handful of change and a cesspit full of nightmares.

For years I hadn't even known if she were alive and there was no way for me to find out if they'd killed her or let her live. But it didn't stop me. I knew about her brother, Kai, from that day at the farm when he approached us. Took me years to track him before I finally found him in Toronto.

I set myself up in the same city. Watched him. Made my money. Made my way in the world knowing that one day, I'd be standing here staring at the girl who risked everything for me.

I walked toward her and it was the longest walk of my life. She stood still, eyes narrowed, arms crossed and her body vibrating from the refrigerated truck.

"You broke the pact," she blurted, lips quivering.

God, the sound of her voice was like sucking in fresh oxygen. All these years I'd been suffocating under a dark cloud, breathing in soiled air. But Chess standing a foot away, stiff, cold and trying to be stoic and brave, was like being woken up from a nightmare.

It was relief.

It was comfort.

It was finding colors in a world of grey.

"Chess."

Her back straightened. "I was better on the inside. Now, we don't have anyone."

"Chess," I repeated.

I stepped closer, so I was inches away. Her breathing was harsh and ragged as she stared up at me. She was trying so hard to be the tough one, just like she'd been at the farm. Always looking out for the younger kids, taking the blame for shit that went wrong. "No more, Francesca." I used her full name because I was making it clear, she didn't need to do this anymore.

"Damn it, Tristan, what about the farm? Kai doesn't know anything yet and he killed Mother and the board will—"

"No!"

She stiffened and I raised my brows, daring her to continue with that line of thought. "You're not being the sacrificial lamb, Chess. Not anymore. Now I have something to say about it."

"But—"

I stepped in to her and cupped her chin. "No." She shut her mouth. "We'll find them. But not with you at risk. That's done."

"If the kids are killed because of this—"

"If they killed *you* because of this, how do you think that would've gone down with me? For once, stop thinking about the farm and think about yourself."

"I can't," she whispered.

Fuck. "I know, baby." She couldn't because she was afraid if she did, she'd fall apart.

A tear slipped down her cheek and contradicted her tense posture. "Fuck, Chess." I went to pull her in to me when she tried to slip away. I caught her forearm then gently pushed her against the side of Kai's car.

She looked at me, strands of hair lying across her face, her eyes blazing with determination. I closed my eyes as the wave of relief hit me full force.

"Chess," I whispered. "God, Chess. I didn't know if I'd ever see you again."

We'd been connected by circumstance, me brought into Vault when I was eight, torn away from my family, scared and alone. And Chess... she'd taught me how to survive the farm. She'd been seven years old and I'd been a terrified eight-year-old screaming and crying for his mom, dad and sister.

"It's time to end this."

She looked at her feet and said quietly, "How can we end it, Tristan? How can it ever end?"

I slid my palms over her shoulders, down her arms, gently unfolded them then entwined our fingers. Her eyes closed and she took a deep breath. "Because I need it to. Because I need you back and I'll do anything to have you."

Her breath hitched just before my mouth came down on hers. I'd never kissed her before, yet it was like finding home. It was never a place; home was a feeling. It was someone you held in your arms.

And for me, it was Chess.

Her quivering lips were cold, but within seconds, they were heated by my own as I kissed her. I felt the moment she gave in to me when her mouth opened and allowed me entrance as I tasted the sweetness of her. It was hard and unyielding then soft and gentle. It was discovery and a yearning for more.

I'd always loved her, but the physical hadn't been there for either of us. Maybe we'd been too young. Maybe because of the situation we'd been in.

But when the fish truck pulled away and my eyes locked on her, I knew. She'd been my best friend for seven years and it was like we hadn't been separated at all.

I pulled back and cupped her now flushed cheek, my thumb stroking back and forth over the smooth skin. "You smell like fish, baby."

She made a half-huff and leaned in to me again and it was the best feeling ever. Chess giving in to me. "I missed you," she whispered into my shirt.

Then she reached into her pocket and pulled out the necklace I'd made for her when I was twelve. It took me months to find the right stones and I stole fishing wire from the storage room. The hard part was finding a cut stone sharp enough to carve with.

She laid it in the palm of her hand and I glanced down at it. I'd carved one stone into a chess piece, a rook, because Chess was so protective of everyone. The other was a heart. I'd told her no matter what happened to us, my heart would always be inside her beating.

"You were with me, Tristan. It's what kept me strong."

I ran my finger over it. She kept it. Somehow she managed to keep it all these years.

Kai's voice was abrupt and cold as he said, "We miss this flight, London is dead. You decide what I'll do if that happens." He folded in the driver's seat and slammed the door.

I knew exactly what he'd do because I'd do the same thing.

"Who is London?" she asked.

I curled her hand around the necklace. "Kai's girl."

"My brother has a girl?" The corner of her lip turned up and her eyes sparked. "Is she willingly his girl? Because I can't see her being with my brother any other way."

I kissed her forehead. "Fuck, I love you, Chess."

CHAPTER
TWENTY-FIVE

Toronto

Kai

I NODDED TO DECK and Vic who stood on either side of the doorway then glanced over my shoulder in the direction of Josh who was on the roof of a neighboring house with his sniper rifle.

Tyler was in the SUV on his computer, taking out the security cameras around the perimeter. Since there were no alarms blazing, he'd been successful—so far. Or we were made to believe that.

Either way, we were going in and coming out with London.

I stepped onto the porch and put my eye up to the scanner. The door clicked and I pushed it open with the toe of my boot.

I had my hand close to my knife as I walked inside.

Two feet into the foyer, I glanced at the camera up in the right corner then crouched to tie my boot. A signal for Tyler to black out the screens for five seconds in the foyer. If he took them all out at once, they'd lock down the basement and we'd never get in unless we blew up the place, and that wasn't happening with London inside.

Deck came in behind me then Vic and we moved in quiet unison across the marble floors to the oil painting. I nudged the frame of the painting with my palm on the frame and it swung open. Then I punched in the code for the door to the basement.

This was our only chance to get her out. Once Mother's body was found, security would be almost impossible to break through and then they'd move London most likely to the one place we had yet to locate—the farm.

But it had to be done this way.

I opened the door and started down the stairs with my back against the wall. I reached up to the bulb hanging in the stairwell. It was hot as hell, singeing my skin as I unscrewed it until it flickered off, masking us in the shadows.

Footsteps came toward the stairs and I held up my hand to Deck and Vic who stopped, and then I walked down the last few steps. Brice appeared around the corner, his gun drawn. He smiled when he recognized me then it faltered when his gaze hit my hand on my knife.

He aimed his gun at me, but it was too late. My blade sliced through the air like a bullet. Brice didn't even have time to pull the trigger before my knife embedded in his neck.

He dropped to the floor, blood seeping between his fingers that were clasped around the handle. Within seconds, he went limp, red-stained skin covering his neck and blood pooling onto the rough cement floor.

I walked over to him, grabbed my knife, and wiped the blood off on his shirt. I had no remorse about killing Brice, because he was responsible for what went down in this place. And that meant he hurt London. I approached the door into the prison, did the retina scan and the lock clicked open.

"Give me five."

I jogged down the sterile, cold hallway to the cell I'd seen London in over a month ago. Fuck. It felt like those two years without her. Except this time, I knew where she was. I just couldn't get to her. That was much worse because I'd had to fight the urge to say fuck it and come here and get her. Would've killed us both the second I used my fingerprint scan with Mother's extra security on it.

I placed my finger against the pad reader and waited for the distinct click. My breath stalled in my throat as I waited, praying Mother had really taken the lockdown code off London's cell.

Click.

Fuckin' Christ.

I kicked the door open and stopped, my gaze skimming the musty cell for London. There was a bare cot, no sheets, no pillow, a toilet, and large metal rings on the damp cement wall with chains hanging from them.

Bile rose in my throat as I was reminded of my childhood because I knew what it was like for London here. I knew the chill in your bones that refused to go away.

It felt like minutes passed before my eyes finally locked on the curled ball in the corner of the room.

"Fuck," I swore beneath my breath.

I knew what I'd see; I'd been prepared for it. I'd witnessed enough torture and despair in my life that I was immune. I'd tortured men to get answers. Killed. Maimed. But the haunting memory of seeing London in this cell had been my own torture. I'd take being physically tortured over the constant images since that day and the echoing sound of my footsteps as I walked away, knowing I had to leave her here.

Knowing what they'd do to her.

I approached the huddled form on the floor. She was filthy, a greyish brown film covering her scantily clothed body. Her long hair hung in oily strands across her face and over her shoulders as if it were her blanket from the chill in the air.

I crouched beside her and was about to brush the hair away from her face when I saw the flash of silver clutched in her hand. "Lon—"

Her eyes flew open at the same time as her fist went for my throat with the small piece of metal. The dull, rusted weapon scraped across my skin and I felt the warm blood trail down my neck.

"London!" I rolled to the side as she leapt on top of me, her eyes steady but glazed over. I latched onto her wrist with the metal and squeezed so hard she screamed. She released the weapon and it clattered to the floor.

"London. Stop."

She continued to fight me, her hair shielding her face as she writhed back and forth. I tried to be gentle, not wanting to hurt her, but I had no choice as I tossed her aside then straddled her before she had the chance to get up. It took me a second to lock down her flailing arms as she tried to punch me. I managed to grab her wrists and used my weight to hold them on the floor above her head.

"London," I shouted. "It's me. Kai."

She stilled, the wild look in her eyes settling as she focused on me. Then her body went limp beneath me. "Kai?"

"Yeah." I released her wrists and brushed her hair away from her face.

She stared at me for a second and I could see her eyes trying to comprehend that what she was seeing was real and not her mind playing tricks on her.

She reached up, her hand quivering as she placed her fingers on my lower lip. Her chest began to rise and fall rapidly and her eyes widened as she finally took in that I was real.

"Kai."

God, she was the most beautiful sight I'd ever seen. The way she looked at me…. Fuck, if I died at that moment, it would all be worth seeing that look in her eyes. I was the reason she was here, the reason for all her pain, and yet I was selfish to keep wanting her. Needing her.

"We have company," Deck said, appearing in the doorway. "Three men entered the premises through the back door."

Shit. Of course, this wouldn't be simple.

London jerked her gaze to him. "Deck?"

There was a puzzled look on her face and I knew she didn't understand why Deck was here with me. She had no idea that this was just the beginning of what we were facing with our fight at taking down Vault.

"Arms," I urged.

She hooked them around me then I lifted her off the damp floor so she stood.

Her forehead rested against my chest and my heart pumped a rush of blood through me as I held her in close. I'd been struggling to get to this day for weeks, and finally, the feeling was as if the endless torture had ended.

She tilted her head up to meet my eyes. "Always," she whispered.

"Yeah, baby, always. God, I missed you."

She stood on her tiptoes. "Then kiss me."

I groaned then lowered my mouth to hers, my grip on her tightening as I tasted her quivering lips.

"Like to get out of here alive," Deck shouted from around the corner.

I pulled back, half-smiled, then grabbed her hand and we ran for the stairs.

"Two SUVs approaching," Deck said, holding the door open. He was wearing a headset to communicate with his men. "Josh counts five in each."

"Give me a weapon," London said, her throat scratchy.

I took the stairs two at a time right behind Deck and Vic.

"I can help," she said.

"We got this," I argued. "Just stay behind me."

"Kai." She jerked back on her hand, but I refused to let go. "Give me a knife... something."

Deck stopped at the top of the stairs and glanced over his shoulder at us. "Josh counts ten entering the front door. Tyler is coming in the back." Glass shattered. "He's taking them out when he has a clear shot."

There was a stampede of rushed footsteps. Coldness drummed into me as if waves pummeled me. It was a roar of need to destroy, to protect what was mine after weeks and weeks of having to keep my emotions locked down. Of pretending shit was okay when London was missing. Having to deal with Tanner, Georgie telling Deck about me, Georgie freaking out that I'd kill Deck.... Another time in my life, I may have, but I needed him to take out Vault and get London out.

225

Something had shifted in me. Even when Deck held a gun on me in his penthouse, I wouldn't have killed him. I did, however, take pleasure in punching him. Landing in the pool sucked, but throwing a few punches was better than a few bullets.

London was the reason for all of this. She was the reason I had to semi-trust Deck. She was the shift inside me.

I looked at London, pale and filthy, and yet she had the same determination in her eyes that I'd witnessed the first day I met her. The day in the woods when both of our lives changed. There had been nothing good about what I'd done, pulling her into my cruel world. But London had survived it. She was still surviving it.

"Kai. Now," Deck growled.

"Give me a weapon, Kai."

Vic yanked a gun from beneath his vest, handed it to her, ignored me, and then moved past Deck to the door into the living room.

"You know how to use it?" I asked her.

She looked at me and I wrapped both her hands around the gun. "Cock it here. Aim and pull the trigger."

I didn't think it was possible after what she'd been through, but the corners of her mouth curved upwards. "I didn't think you knew how to handle a gun?"

Unbelievable. The last time I'd seen her, she looked defeated, her eyes dead and blank. But now, she was fighting. And from her attack on me, she'd planned on taking out whoever entered her cell next—Brice. "Baby, I can handle any—"

"Let's do this," Deck interrupted.

I nodded as I turned away from her and pulled out a knife. Vic gave an abrupt nod to Deck and me, then turned the door handle and kicked it open with his foot. Three men who had been approaching the door, stopped then aimed.

I grabbed London's hand and dove left while Vic and Deck went right, shooting at the men. I threw a knife and it hit one guy in the chest. He went down hard. Deck ran back toward us and Vic took off toward the kitchen where Tyler was.

"Vic, incoming," Deck said in the headset. "Five seconds. Front entrance is compromised. We're headed your way."

I couldn't hear his reply, but Deck shook his head and pointed to the front door. "Josh counts five live. But they're staying clear of the windows. Josh compromised."

"Take her," I said to Deck.

Even though I'd given them the layout, I knew this house blindfolded. I'd made sure I did. I had to take the lead and I didn't want London near me.

"You good?" I asked.

She nodded.

"Okay, let's get the fuck out of here. Give me ten seconds." Without waiting for a response, I dove across the hallway and bullets pierced through the air as Deck returned fire covering me.

I caught a glimpse of a guy with his attention on Deck, firing. I crept around the room, went up behind him and sliced my knife across his throat.

He crumpled to the floor.

I put my back to the wall then peered around the corner into the foyer. There was a guy standing at the front door blocking our escape route.

I heard more gunshots back toward the kitchen where Vic and Tyler were.

I stepped out into view and whipped my knife at the guy. He shouted, but it came out gurgled as my blade pierced his chest. His eyes widened and blood dribbled from his mouth before his eyes went dead and his body crashed to the floor.

I ran over, grabbed my weapon and made my way back to Deck and London. My head snapped to the right over my shoulder when something caught my eye through the east window.

I turned at the same time as a body flew through the glass and slammed into me.

The hard impact sent us both crashing onto the glass coffee table. I raised my knife to stab him in the back when I felt the agonizing pain in my shoulder as he jammed his fist into me so hard that I felt it dislocate.

I gritted my teeth and shoved at him as hard as I could. We rolled and struggled on the floor, the knife knocked from my grip with the arm useless.

I raised my left elbow and slammed it into his face. He fell to the side of me and I heard the crack of bone.

I reached for my knife in my boot at the same time as his kicked me backwards into the bookcase. It came crashing down and I was stunned for a second as hundreds of books toppled over me.

It was seconds I didn't have with him hovered over me, a gun at my temple.

I shoved a few books off then raised my brows at him. "If it isn't their little pet, Connor."

The gun cocked.

"Connor. No," Deck shouted.

There was a flicker of recognition in his eyes at the sound of Deck's voice, but years of being drugged and conditioned in Vault's hands wouldn't stop him.

But Vic's bullets did.

Connor went down as one hit his upper thigh and another in the shoulder. I shoved the rest of the books and shelf off me then grabbed my knife in my boot and went for Connor.

Deck was on me, his gun pressed into my neck. "No."

"He's not Connor anymore. You just saw that. End it."

Connor groaned and moved to get up. Vic came up behind him and grabbed Connor's arms, hauling him to his feet. Deck nodded to Vic, who put his hand on the back of Connor's neck and then within seconds, he went limp and collapsed against Vic.

Deck turned to me, his eyes murderous. "You try to kill him once, just once, and our fragile truce is finished."

I shook my head. "He's not your friend anymore."

"Yeah, well neither are you and yet, I've let you live."

I snorted.

He took the unconscious Connor from Vic and threw him over his shoulder. "Josh. Coming out the front," he said.

I grabbed London's hand, bent to pick up my knife, and followed.

Tyler had the SUV pulled up to the porch. Deck placed Connor into the hatchback and I heard the click of handcuffs. At least he had the common sense to know his friend was dangerous and no longer his friend. The three of us piled into the backseat and we took off, stopping for a second so Josh could hop in the front.

I pulled London in to me, my hand on her head, stroking. The gun lay in her lap, her hand still clutched around it.

I noticed Tyler glance at Deck in the rear-view mirror, his expression grave, jaw tight. "Boss. Is it Connor?"

Deck nodded.

"Not good?"

"Nope," Deck said.

I met Tyler's eyes in the mirror. "He's better off dead."

"We don't kill our men. Ever," Deck stated.

"He's no longer your man. He's theirs."

"He stays alive." Deck slammed his fist into the window.

"I wonder if you'll still say that the day he tries to kill Georgie," I said.

"He won't get near her," Vic replied before Deck could.

I remained quiet because I knew the loyalty between these men was unbreakable. But that cord tying them together would snap if Connor attempted to hurt Georgie. He was a machine, the elements of who he had been reduced to nothing more than a fine mist.

And now, he lived like a trapped animal, chained to who he'd become. I also knew Chaos and there was no chance they'd keep her from seeing her brother.

Tyler pulled off the road into a parking lot an hour later and shut off the engine. Tristan and Chess stood waiting for us, leaning against my car. It wasn't registered, so it was better than one of Tristan's flashy vehicles.

I got out, wincing at the movement.

"Need to deal with that," Vic said, nodding to my dislocated shoulder.

Deck came around to stand beside him. "I'll hold him down."

I laughed. "In your dreams, Deck."

Vic grinned. Probably the only time I'd seen the guy smile. "You'd rather me hold you down?"

London came out of the car and I felt the gentle touch of her hand on my back. "Don't need anyone to hold me down. Just do it," I ordered Vic then dared Deck with my eyes to come anywhere near me. He chuckled and walked away.

It hurt like hell. But Vic was quick, strong and knew what he was doing. When he was done, he patted my now located shoulder—hard. Bastard. I still managed a thanks.

My hand locked in London's and I strode toward Tristan and Chess. "This device better work."

Tristan cocked a brow and picked up a little rectangular black box sitting on the hood of the SUV. "I've been developing it for months. It'll work."

I shrugged. "Not my issue if Deck kills you if your device fails and blows up his buddy."

Tristan gave a cocky smirk. "You think I'd risk using it on Chess? I know what the fuck I'm doing."

After spending some time with Tristan, I hated the cocky bastard at first, but now I was getting that he had the right to be cocky. The guy came from the farm, stayed away from his family, even after he escaped, and spent his life pulling together resources to get Chess out from under Vault's clutches. I'd give him a margin of error even if the device killed Connor.

"I may let you live after all, Tristan."

He huffed. My sister scowled at me before looking to London. She stepped forward, held out her hand and introduced herself. "So, you're the reason my brother finally grew some balls." I scoffed. "Nice to meet you. I'm Francesca, Chess, Kai's sister. And this is Tristan. I'll let Kai tell you about him."

London shook both their hands. It was odd doing something so normal when there was nothing normal about any of us or what was happening.

"Tristan," Tyler called. "We need to do this now. He's waking up."

Chess and Tristan moved to the back of the SUV and I put my

hands on London's hips. "I need to know, baby. Did you run away from me? Did you leave the house and they found you?"

"You know the answer to that, Kai." She reached up and cupped my cheek. "You don't trust anyone and I get that, but you'll need to learn to trust what your body is telling you."

I burst out laughing at her using my own words thrown back at me. Words I said to her our first night together. She looked tired, bruised, and thin, yet she smiled.

I growled before I hitched her up onto the hood of my car where we'd first begun four years ago. "You belong with me, braveheart. That's what my body is telling me."

"Mine, too."

I grabbed her on either side of her head and kissed her.

CHAPTER
TWENTY-SIX

London

IS KISS WAS slow and gentle as if he were afraid I'd break, but then his control faltered and he kissed me like I wanted him to. Owning and powerful, with nothing able to split us apart.

His hands were all over me as he pressed into me until I lay on the hood of the car, his weight on top of me, mouth hard and bruising. My hands on his hips, I pulled him closer even though he couldn't get any nearer. I just needed every inch of him touching me, making this real.

He pulled back, hands on either side of me, resting on the car. My chest rose and fell with ragged breaths and tingles sparked through my body.

He lifted his hand and stroked the side of my face with his knuckles. "A lot of shit has gone down since my house." He hesitated and it was so unlike him. "London, that day I saw you in the cell... I couldn't

232

get you out."

That moment played in my mind over and over again. Before I saw his face through the bars of my cell, I'd known it was him. His scent drifted in to me like a breeze of hope. Then it was like being punched in the gut when I met his hard, cold eyes. I knew then that he wasn't there to save me.

"I know," I murmured.

"And what I said." Kai's one hand rested on my hip, his other cupped my check. "Fuck, I needed you to live and the best way was for you to give in to them. I didn't know when… or if I could get to you."

Kai never experienced love or trust, but I had. No matter what he'd said to me that day, no matter how crushed and angry I was that he walked away, I knew Kai and why he'd said it.

I went dead inside and trusted he'd come back. I gave them what they needed to see, a girl lost and broken with no hope, and I quietly got stronger.

"You never gave up."

He said it as if he couldn't yet believe that I was in front of him.

"I never gave up on us."

I saw the conflict on his face as he looked down at my hand resting on his chest. His heartbeat was steady and rhythmic like it always was. It was the comfort I needed because no matter how I felt about Kai, he would always carry in him a darkness that scared me. But when I touched him, felt his heart beat, it reminded me that he was real, that this man whether I wanted it or not, was inside me. A part of me. We were tied together.

I heard a loud yowl come from the back of the SUV and he stood up straight, bringing me with him. We both looked over and saw the vehicle lurch side to side. Tyler went flying backwards and landed on his butt on the ground several feet from the back.

Through the tinted windows, I saw Deck inside the vehicle kneeling on the back seat, his arm curved around Connor's throat as he continued thrashing trying to break free. He was Georgie's brother, the man they'd been using my father's drug on, the man who took me from Kai's house.

"What are they doing to him?"

"They started placing GPS chips in recruits, operatives, whoever they wanted to track or make certain never escaped them. When Chess was able to contact Tristan, she told him about them and their vulnerabilities. Tristan had someone develop a device to pinpoint its location in the body."

"There are lots of machines that do that, aren't there?"

"Yes. But not ones that won't set them off."

"What do you mean?"

He kissed me lightly on the mouth. My lips were dry and cracked and the sensitive flesh hurt even with his gentleness. "I promise you'll be fine."

"He's going to scan me?"

Tristan walked toward us, his long strides eating up the ground. He nodded to Kai. "Found it. Bridge of his foot." He held a small black box in his hand and it had a little green light flashing on the front edge. "Ready?"

Kai nodded and moved to the side.

"Just going to run this device over your body, okay?"

"I'm not going to blow up?"

Tristan chuckled. Kai didn't.

"Go for it," I said.

Tristan crouched then started at my feet then up my leg and down the other one. The machine started beeping and flashing red when he reached the right side of my pelvis. Tristan placed the machine on the hood of the car and reached for the bottom of my shirt to pull it up.

Kai's hand latched onto his wrist. "I'll do it."

Tristan shook his head, a slight twitch at the corner of his mouth. He let me go then tossed a wad of gauze, a roll of medical tape and a bottle of disinfectant on the hood next to me. "Damage it while removing and both of you will blow up into a million little pieces of flesh."

"Fuck." I stopped breathing.

Kai ignored me and took out his knife. "Then we blow to pieces. No one is touching her with a fuckin' blade except me."

"Kai?" Fear skidded into me. I had a ticking time bomb under my skin?

Tristan shrugged and walked away.

"Don't move," Kai ordered as he pressed me back onto the hood of the car. "I'd like to have a chance at sinking between your thighs again, braveheart."

"Jesus, Kai."

And then I saw his easy-going grin and a wave of comfort seeped into me. He poured the disinfectant over the blade of his knife then I leaned back on the hood and he lifted my shirt. His fingers palpated the right side of my pelvis. I'd never noticed anything there, but then again, I'd been more concerned about my next drink of water than any tiny, unusual lump I may have.

"Here." He pinched my skin an inch away from my hip bone. He raised his head and looked at me. "Try and refrain from moving and killing us both."

I raised my brows. "Maybe you should ask someone who knows how to handle a knife."

He chuckled and I sighed as the familiar sound washed over me. He lowered the blade and sliced into my skin. I bit the inside of my cheeks as Kai carefully stretched my skin apart with his fingers then the tip of his knife sank into my flesh.

I didn't watch, but felt a slight pop when the microchip came free. "Got it." He held up his blade, the tiny device sitting on the flat edge of it.

I pushed down my shirt and sat up. "Now what?"

"Tyler and Josh will take them on a little ride. Should keep any Vault operatives busy for a few days. Then they'll destroy them."

Deck approached us and nodded to me. "Good to see you're okay, London." I doubted that. Our last encounter, I'd been Raven and I'd held a gun on Georgie's friend Emily. He took the microchip from Kai and walked back to the SUV.

Kai took the bandage material and tape Tristan had left and gently lifted my shirt to dress the wound. When he was done, my hand settled over his and heat flared inside my belly. "What's going on, Kai? Your sister is free. You're here with Deck and his men. Who's Tristan? I don't understand."

He caressed the side of my face. "I killed my mother." I gasped. "She was a real bitch."

"Kai…." I didn't know what to say, so I said nothing.

"Been living in a world of black and white. Not caring about anything. Death. Torture. Pain. None of it mattered." He moved in closer, looped his arm around the back of me, and tugged me closer. "Then I met you, braveheart." He lowered his head and kissed me. It was firm yet slow as his lips moved over mine in a deep caress. "We're ending this, baby. We're taking down Vault."

I tensed. *Holy shit.*

That was why Deck and his men were with Kai. He'd always said he didn't have friends and that he didn't trust anyone, but he was putting an awful lot of faith in Deck. "Is that possible?"

He slid his hand down my arm until his fingers linked with mine then helped me off the hood of the car. "I'm making it possible."

"What about… well, my father?"

"Don't know yet."

A wave of fear crashed into me. "We have to help him, Kai. They'll go after him, right? They'll kill him or hide him or… Kai, we have to help him."

He cupped the back of my head, fingers bunching in my hair. "We will."

I gripped the front of his shirt. "Oh, God. Kai, he's all I have left."

He stared down at me, eyes hard and concerned, fingers tightening in my hair. "Yeah."

There was something in his eyes, but I hadn't seen it before. I thought it was concern, but it was more than that. Worry? But Kai never seemed worried about anything.

Kai grabbed me and lowered his mouth to mine and said, "You'll always have me."

He kissed me again. It wasn't gentle and sweet. It was a promise.

I fell asleep in the car and when I woke, it was on a couch with my head on Kai's lap. His hand slowly caressed my hair.

"No. Forget it." I heard Deck saying. "Don't push me, Georgie."

Georgie? She was here? Of course she was. Kai told me in the car before I fell asleep that she was with Deck now. Then he told me about Tristan and Chess. Their story was crushing and beautiful at the same time.

"Vic. Please, talk to him," Georgie said.

"Don't need Vic talking to me, Georgie. I said no," Deck said in a grated tone.

I opened my eyes and Kai must have sensed I was awake as his hand stilled.

"Kai?" Georgie said. "Tell him. I can reach him. I can help."

"Jesus Christ, Georgie, no. Not fuckin' happening," Deck said. "I don't want you seeing him like that."

"He's not who you think he is," Vic stated.

"I don't give a shit," she shouted, her voice quivering and on the edge of tears. "I want to see him."

I sat up and Kai passed me a bottle of water, the cap already off. I chugged it back, the liquid sliding down my throat like cool silk. The plastic crackled as I finished it off and set it on the coffee table.

"Georgie. Stop. Now." It was Deck and his tone was seriously pissed.

I looked over my shoulder just as Georgie went for a door handle on the other side of the kitchen.

Deck was up off the bar stool and behind her before the door was all the way open. He latched onto her arm, dragged her back, then bent and in one swoop had Georgie over his shoulder. He did it so fluidly that it was like it was a usual occurrence.

"He's my brother. He's my goddamn brother," she shouted.

"I know. And that's why I can't let you." He carried her kicking and screaming into another room then the door closed. There was a loud thump, a smack and a few short abrupt words from Deck before silence.

Kai stood and held out his hand. "You need a bath, baby."

I did. Desperately. "How's your shoulder?"

He didn't reply; instead, he lifted me off the couch and set me on my feet. I was guessing it was good then.

"Where are we?"

"One of Deck's safe houses. Although, I don't know if I'd call it safe after seeing the basement."

He didn't let me think too much on that as he urged me in front of him, past Vic who was stirring something that smelled like tomato basil sauce on the stove. He nodded to me and I half-smiled. Vic was super scary and I wasn't sure about him even though he'd helped me escape Alfonzo and Jacob.

We went into a bedroom at the end of the hall and Kai shut the door. The house wasn't decorated and looked rather average, one you'd find in a newly built subdivision. There were no personal touches though; nothing hanging on the walls, and minimal furniture.

Kai walked into the adjoining bathroom. I heard the shower curtain pushed aside on the metal rings and then the water turned on. I walked in to join him and he was leaning over the tub, his hand testing the temperature of the water.

"Close the door."

I did.

Within seconds, the bathroom began to fog up and I closed my eyes, breathing in the heated moisture. I'd been cold and damp for so long, that I feared the feeling of being cold would never go away.

I leaned up against the bathroom door and sighed. It was like I was being clothed in a blanket of warmth that was heating my blood. I felt the moment Kai moved in to me and I opened my eyes. His hands went to the bottom of my long over-sized shirt. He then slowly lifted, the tips of his fingers trailing a path along my sides.

I raised my arms and he pulled it all the way off and tossed it on the floor. I was naked underneath, and my nipples, despite the warm moist air, erect. Goose bumps scattered over my skin.

God, I wanted to succumb. I wanted him to look after me. I wanted to be heated and warm and… I wanted to feel loved.

Kai's hands slid down my body to the edge of my panties. His heated breath swept over my skin as he lowered while slowly dragging them down my legs. I held on to his shoulders as I lifted each foot to step out of them. His warm palms glided back up my legs, over my thighs to my hips as he stood straight again.

I stood naked in front of him, but his eyes weren't on my body. He was watching my expression. My chest rose and fell faster as I anticipated his touch.

He scowled. I was hoping for that amusing charming grin instead. His hands went to the bandage on my hip. "We'll re-bandage it after your bath." He peeled back the tape and gauze, tossed it in the trash, then reached to take my hand.

He stopped. Then his eyes darkened as they landed on the scar on my shoulder. "That's from a fuckin' bullet." His eyes darted to mine. "They shot you?"

"It was minor." Connor had been right. I hadn't bled to death, but I'd passed out in the car and when I woke, my shoulder was bandaged.

"Who?"

The man currently in the basement. The man Kai had no issue killing. And the man Deck and his men would do anything to protect. He also happened to be Georgie's brother.

I wrapped my fingers around his wrist and pulled his hand away from the scar. "It doesn't matter."

His eyes narrowed and he opened his mouth to ask me again, but I stared him down. I saw the moment he gave in to me and I think he knew it had to have been Connor, but if I told him, we both knew what would happen.

"Okay, London. I'll give you this."

I rolled my eyes.

He slipped his hand in mine and guided me over to the tub. "Don't worry, it's warm water."

I snorted at his reference to the ice water he'd made me sit in.

"That was cruel."

"And necessary."

"Necessary in your way of thinking." But it had been. He'd been trying to find a way to break through to me, yet not hurt me.

His hand smoothed over my hair and he was silent. Despite his teasing about the water, there was seriousness in Kai that hadn't been there before I was taken by Vault.

Kai knew me better than anyone. He was in me. I didn't know when it happened. Maybe over time. Maybe the night he'd saved me from the fire. Maybe our nights together at my loft. It didn't matter when, or how or why. He just was and, no matter who Kai had been and who he was now, I fell in love with all the parts of him.

I grabbed his hand before he turned to leave. "Don't leave."

He stared at me for a second then his eyes trailed down my body and my belly whirled. "I can't stay without having you."

"Then have me. They didn't rape me, Kai. I'm not fragile Raven. I'll never be like that again."

His brow furrowed. "London. Fuck."

And then something in him broke. It was like a tree branch under so much pressure that it could no longer resist and snapped then crashed to the ground. He grabbed me around the waist and pulled me into his arms, his hand on the back of my head, pressing me so close I could barely breathe.

There was nothing steady and calm about Kai right now as his mouth took mine in an uncontrolled frenzy. It was so unlike him, a feral need as he forced my mouth open before I even had the chance to react to him.

He whirled me around and shoved me up against the sink and without a second's hesitation, lifted me up to perch on the lip of it. "Legs," he growled.

I hooked my legs around him.

His hands slid down my spine to my lower back, finger stroking the crease in my ass. I put my head back, eyes closed, moaning when he lowered his head and took my nipple in his mouth. It was tender and sweet, licking, suckling. Then his teeth grazed it and I gasped at the sensation coursing through me.

Wildfire. Pain and pleasure. The pearl of ecstasy.

My nipple slipped from his mouth and his hand slid up my body to my neck where his fingers curled around it, not tight, but firm. "No one takes you from me and expects to live."

Something I didn't recognize lingered in his eyes, a rage or maybe it was a hint of fear.

I leaned forward and kissed the corner of his mouth then did the same on the other side.

His grip on my neck tightened as he kissed me again, this time soft and caressing like a silk feather caressing my bruised lips.

"I want you inside me," I murmured.

He groaned then picked me up by the ass. I looped my arms around his neck as he carried me to the tub. "Soon, baby." He placed me on my feet in the bathtub.

I was confused because something had changed in him. He was stiff as he peeled my arms from his neck. "What's wrong?"

He leaned to the right and picked up a facecloth and passed it to me. "Don't like that place all over you." Then he walked out.

I stood in two feet of hot water, staring at the closed door.

Kai had control all his life. He owned it. He was confident at whatever he did because he had nothing to lose. But I felt his loss of control with the way he kissed me, with how he touched me.

He had risked everything to free me from Vault. Free his sister. He was trying to trust Deck and his men when he'd spent his life not trusting anyone. He had his sister back. He killed his mother and was going after the farm. A place that made him into who he'd been for most of his life.

Kai was spiraling into unknown territory. He cared. He trusted.

The reality was Kai had always been the Amur leopard, the solitary hunter, and now he wasn't and he had a vulnerability—me.

CHAPTER
TWENTY-SEVEN

Kai

WE STOOD IN the kitchen going over the possible fall back, one of them being police involvement with Vault's insiders. Deck had already put a call in to the chief of police and a few buddies he knew within the different precincts.

"We take out their strengths," I said. "The farm and the drug. Unfortunately, I have no idea where the farm is or who oversees it, but there may be someone who does. A board member."

"Who?" Deck asked.

"Peter Dorsey."

"Fuck," Vic said, shaking his head.

"Won't be easy getting near him," Deck said. "Take time."

We didn't have time.

Dorsey owned two hotels in Vegas, one in New York and several more across the States. He didn't trust anyone and was a bastard with a dirty hand. I'd met him a few times, even done a few jobs for him a number of years back. He'd also know that I'd turned.

"His weaknesses… greed and power. He wants it all and pretty much has it, except for one thing—he doesn't call the shots with Vault. Mother controlled the drug and another man runs the farm. Dorsey is a minion and if he has an opportunity to change that, he will. Mother's dead. He'll want the control of the drug."

"What about the other members?" Deck asked.

I gave them what I had on them. There were two others, but they were founding members like my father and I suspected weren't fully on board with the direction my mother had taken Vault. But it was the one other member who remained anonymous who was going to be a problem. Our link to him was Dorsey. In order to give Dorsey something he wanted, we needed that something to draw him to us.

"So, we need the drug," Deck said.

I nodded. "I have Mother's files. She claimed she had the only copy of the formula. Knowing her, she did. Mother wouldn't want anyone else to have the power over her."

Vic said, "And Dorsey will want control of the drug now that your mother is dead."

"Yes."

"And the farm? I hate to ask what that is," Deck said.

"It's where Chess and I grew up." Both Vic and Deck stiffened. "Children, like Tristan and Tanner, kidnapped from their homes and… conditioned to do Vault's dirty work."

"Jesus Christ," Deck ran his hand back and forth over the top of his head.

"And you don't have any idea where it is?" Vic asked.

"No. Once you're eighteen, you're removed from the farm, and you never go back. The only one who ever escaped is Tristan."

"If he escaped, then he knows where it is," Deck said.

"Unfortunately, no. He escaped and we were moved within a day. We were blindfolded and drugged, so I can't be sure where the fuck we were taken. Our only lead is the third member, who is unknown. I think I'd recognize him, as he'd been at both locations of the farm, but way more often when I was sixteen at the new location. That's why I suspect he oversees it."

I looked from Vic to Deck. "We find the farm, we find him. But first we need to get to New York."

Deck nodded. "London's father."

The sound of her soft padded sock-covered feet walking down the hallway toward the kitchen hit me and my heart rate sped.

She appeared around the corner, stopping where the ceramic tile in the kitchen met the hardwood in the hallway. Dressed simply in the black yoga pants and a T-shirt Georgie had brought for her, fuck, she looked sexy as hell with her hair wet and messy and flushed cheeks from the heated bath.

The guys were now discussing Connor and what to do with him. I didn't give a shit about him, but there was an advantage with having him on our side. That was if we could get into his messed-up head.

My lip twitched when she caught my gaze on her and I held out my hand. She walked toward me and as soon as she was close enough, I snagged her hand and pulled her back against me. Her ass pressed into my cock and I made a low grunt then kissed just below her ear.

"Better," I whispered, breathing in the fresh scent of soap and… London.

"Thanks for the clothes."

"Georgie brought them."

"Where's your sister and Tristan?"

"Sleeping. Chess is on Central European time zone and exhausted. Tristan won't let her go five steps without him. Never would've suspected the cocky playboy and CEO of Mason Developments would be so fuckin' possessive over a girl."

She placed her hand over mine. "I'm glad your sister's safe."

Vic raised his voice and drew my attention away from London. "He'll kill any of us the first chance he gets. He's a maniac."

"Then we need to find out everything we can about this drug," Deck said.

Deck looked at me.

"Don't know any more than you do. It was kept confidential.

Connor was their guinea pig, but Mother said it's almost stable. Chess says it's not."

"Doesn't sound like Connor's rage is from an 'almost stable' drug," Deck said.

Vic threw his bottle of water into the sink. "So, he stays like that? Chained to a wall in a basement until he dies? He's better off dead."

London shifted in my arms. "It could be withdrawal from the drug." I let go of her hand and slid my palm down until it rested on her hip. "If his body needs it, like an addict's, that might be why he's out of control. When he...." She paused and glanced at me before continuing, "Connor was the one who took me from Kai's house." *Fuck.* He was the reason my girl had been in Vault. "He was calm. Controlled. Almost too controlled. I remember thinking he was like a machine."

Deck crossed his arms over his broad chest. "Okay, he's in withdrawal. Where does that leave us?"

"If I can look at the formula, maybe I can help," she said. "Or not. It's possible he needs the drug or—"

Deck grunted and slammed his fist into the fridge.

She didn't have to say it. If Connor didn't get the drug, it was possible he'd die.

"The lab," Vic stated.

"They'll be watching his lab by now," I said. "And London's father."

"But we need to get to my dad," London said, looking up at me.

Fuck, I had to tell her. Soon. She had to know her dad was dying of cancer, but she'd been through so much already and telling her now didn't seem like the time. I didn't know if there would ever be a time.

"We need the drug for two reasons," I said. "Dorsey will want the formula. We have something he wants, then he may give us what we want in return. And if London is right, it may be the only thing to keep Connor alive. We need to find a way into the lab."

"I can use the old tunnels," London said. "They were used to go from one building to the other in the winter months, but they started to collapse and so they were deemed unsafe and were closed off a decade ago."

"How closed off?" I asked.

"They locked the doors to the stairs, but I don't know what else they did, if anything. I don't even know if they are even passable anymore. They could've collapsed. But if they aren't, I can get into my dad's lab from there without anyone seeing me. If the drug is there, I can find it. I need someone to come with me who can hack into his computer and get the files for the formula." She paused. "And my father. If he's there, we can get him out."

This was my London. She'd been through hell and yet was volunteering to go back into a potentially dangerous situation. But she didn't know the first thing about combat. She was a fuckin' scientist, and I wanted her to stay that way, not become what I was. "You're not going."

She tensed in my arms. "I'm the only one who can get into the lab. I have fingerprint access."

"No."

"Yes. And you have no say in what I do."

Vic cleared his throat and from the corner of my eye, I saw his lip twitch.

"Oh, baby, you are way off base if you think that." She tried to get off my lap, but I tightened my hold. "If Vault is watching the place already, which I suspect they are, they won't hesitate at killing you," I shot back.

Vic said, "She won't go alone. Tyler can go with her. He'll hack the computer."

"Tyler and Josh will be gone for days," Deck said. "By the looks of Connor, he doesn't have days."

There was no chance I'd let her go in without me and I was good with computers, but I knew one person who was better. "Chaos."

All eyes went to Deck. The man had been protecting Georgie all her life and he wouldn't like the idea of her going in. But Connor was his best friend, and Georgie's brother.

Deck shook his head. "That's not an option."

"And this isn't your decision. You forget who's running this operation," I said.

"And you forget you're outnumbered," Deck retorted.

I smiled. "True. But the difference between you and me is that I don't give a fuck if Connor dies and you do. So, I suggest if you want him to live, Chaos goes in."

But what I said sat uneasy with me because I knew Chaos would be destroyed all over again if her brother died. I'd seen her devastation when she was sixteen; although at the time, I didn't care. "We get the drug, the files and then we have something Dorsey wants."

London stiffened. "And my dad?"

Deck met my eyes. There was no love lost between us, but we walked the same path now, although we'd always be on opposite sides of the fence. "It needs to be dealt with," he said.

I knew what he was talking about and it was ironic that he was the one who was being cold about her father's life. I shouldn't care, but I did because London would never forgive me if I killed him. The reality was, her father was a liability because he knew the drug and that meant he could more than likely reproduce it without the files, but Westbrook was also on borrowed time.

"I know." But as soon as I said the words, they felt wrong. For the first time in my life, I wasn't willing to take out a liability and I wouldn't allow Deck or his men to either.

"What does?" London asked.

Deck was quick to answer. "The situation. Connor is in bad shape. We'll leave as soon as Tristan can get his pilots here. A few hours maybe—"

Connor's roar had Deck and Vic running to the basement door. Then there was more of Connor's shouting and what sounded like a body crashing against the wooden stairs.

"We need to get the drug, Kai." She was still looking at where Vic and Deck disappeared. Connor had kidnapped her, more than likely the one who shot her, and put her in hell, and still she cared. She cared what happened to him.

I didn't know how a man like me who never cared about anything was lucky enough to have someone as special as London. I wanted to forget everything and be inside her again. I wanted us to find lightness in all this darkness.

"I'm going to fuck you now. You good with that?" I didn't wait for an answer as I stood, taking her with me.

CHAPTER
TWENTY-EIGHT

London

KAI KICKED THE door closed and before I could take another breath, he had me back against it and his mouth on me.

I quivered under his lips and my belly whirled as he kissed me. He locked my wrists together above my head against the door while his thigh shoved my legs apart and pressed into my sex, sending tweaks of need through me.

I never thought I'd be doing this. Kissing a man as dangerous as Kai.

I never thought I'd love so fiercely that it ruined me. Because no matter how I looked at it, that was what he did to me. Kai ruined me. For other men. For life without him.

I'd hated him.

Feared him.

Desired him.

Needed him.

And loved him.

I'd fallen for him before I was Raven, not loved, but I saw something in him. It was the good in him. The need to protect. The desire to care and yet he couldn't.

Being with him was like breathing in too fast and becoming lightheaded. There were no restrictions as to who I was. Then or now. Kai let me be me and he knew exactly who I was. Sometimes, I think he knew me better than I knew myself. Maybe he did because he pulled me from a place within myself where I'd been slowly dying.

I moaned when his lips left mine then smiled as I ran my fingers through his hair. "Kai." I whispered his name like I'd done for countless weeks after seeing him through the barred cell. I'd been angry, helpless, exposed, but I was never hopeless.

Never.

And Kai wouldn't allow it. He gave me the words to hold onto, the cruel words to remind me to never let Vault see the hope. Kill it. Destroy it and survive.

That was when I shut down, not to die, but to survive.

"I love you," I said.

He tilted his head to kiss me again except this time it was a gentle caress. A velvet touch from his lips reaching deep inside me and taking what I'd already freely given him.

He growled, picked me up and tossed me on the bed then hovered over me, a predator about to devour his prey and I wanted to be devoured.

Kai had found me three times.

He'd found me and brought me back each time. He would always come for me and I wanted to be strong enough to be there for him.

The mattress sagged under his weight as he knelt on it then straddled me. I sighed as he trailed kisses down my neck and toyed with my nipples through my shirt.

I cupped his neck and pulled him in closer. "Show me what you can't say," I whispered.

Kai may never tell me he loved me and I accepted that. I didn't need the words. I just needed him to continue to be the man he was with me.

He stiffened, eyes narrowing as he sat on top of me. Then the corner of his mouth twitched and that playful light reached his eyes. "You brave enough, baby?"

I reached between us and stroked his cock through his pants. "Always."

He laughed then he showed me how much he loved me.

I woke sore but sated between my legs. I'd been brave, but there was no need to be because Kai had been gentle as he made love to me several times over the last few hours. If I ever had a doubt that Kai loved me as much as he could love anyone, it would've been erased last night.

He'd given me the parts of him that I guessed few, if any, had ever seen. The soft, vulnerable parts of Kai. It was why he'd found me. Why he risked everything to get me away from Vault. Why he trusted Deck and his men, and Tristan when he trusted no one.

I reached over to kiss him, but he was gone, the mattress cold where he'd lain with me curled in his arms. I sat up, the sheet clutched to my chest as the bedroom door opened. My heart skipped a beat as my gaze locked on him. God, he always looked so encompassing whenever he walked in a room.

"Tristan says the plane's nearly at Pearson airport and Connor isn't doing so well. He's going to kill himself with all the damage he's doing."

I scrambled to my feet and quickly grabbed my neatly folded clothes off the chair. Kai had obviously picked them up because last night they'd been scattered all over the room.

I pulled on the yoga pants. "I thought you didn't care what happens to him."

He shrugged. "He'd be better off with a bullet in his head, but"— he slowly walked toward me and when he reached me, he slid his hand in my hair and curved his grip into my neck—"he's Georgie's brother."

I frowned as I watched the conflicting emotions in his eyes. He never called her Georgie. He always said Chaos and I think it had been to distance himself from her. But all that was changing.

"Fuck, if I could go back and change how shit went down…. I watched her grieve his death knowing Vault had him."

I remained quiet because this wasn't about me or Georgie or anyone else. This was Kai trying to come to terms with what he'd done for Vault. Forced. Trained. Conditioned. Whatever it may have been, Kai was fighting what he'd done. But there was no going back.

He lowered his head and pressed his lips to mine, his fingers tightening on my neck before he pulled back. "I know why Vault wants us like machines, London. It's because of this. What I feel for you. What I'd do for you." He sighed and whispered, "Anything."

And he had. Kai had kept himself from caring and suddenly, he was surrounded by people who cared about one another and was realizing that this stemmed further than just him protecting me. It was about him breaking free from Vault and letting in what they'd tried to eradicate from him.

He pulled back and slid his hand down my arm until our fingers linked. "Go grab something to eat. I have to help with Connor."

I nodded, watching as he grabbed his bag then left the room.

I slipped into the rest of my clothes, went to the bathroom, and brushed my teeth. As I came out of the bedroom, Georgie came out of hers, pink strands wild and covering half her face, but I still saw the red-rimmed, blood-shot eyes. She briefly looked at me then turned and ran for the basement door.

"Georgie." *Shit.* This wasn't going to be good.

CHAPTER
TWENTY-NINE

Georgie

I PACED THE BEDROOM where Deck had ordered me to stay. I wasn't very good at following orders, but he used *that* tone. The one that made me think twice about disobeying him, not because he'd ever hurt me, but because he'd be disappointed in me and that was worse.

I'd lived for years disappointing him, and pretended not to give a crap, but I no longer had to. He was mine. Deck. My brother's best friend. My brother who I thought was dead then found out he was alive, but wasn't the brother he used to be. The brother who teased me about how perfect I used to dress and how neat I kept my room. The brother who made a grave for my hamster when he died. The brother who protected me in school against bullies who made fun of how I dressed and looked. I was so different, but now, so was he.

And Deck wouldn't let me see him.

I knew he was trying to protect me, but my brother and I had always been close. He'd been my best friend. God, I still had the stuffed rabbit he'd given to me when I was a kid. And I had his journal. A journal that Deck had given me. I'd never read it at the time. Hadn't ever planned on it either, until I discovered Connor was alive. Until shit went down with Tanner. Until Kai told us about Vault.

Then I read it, with Deck. And cried. And it nearly destroyed me because inside the pages was my brother. One I'd lost and wasn't sure I'd ever get back.

I jerked when I heard a deafening roar and then several loud curses came up from the basement.

"Connor." A tear slid down my cheek and I wiped it away with the back of my hand. Pain lacerated my soul at hearing his voice again and yet, it wasn't his voice. It was laced with anger and rage, something Connor never had in him. He'd been calm and easygoing, flirted with all the girls, a cocky playboy who was quick to laugh and hard to anger.

"Christ. Connor. Fuck." I heard Deck shout.

It was his ragged tone as if Deck was about to break that had me running from the bedroom and scrambling for the basement.

"Georgie," I heard London call.

I didn't stop as I flung open the basement door and scrambled down the wooden steps toward my brother.

My brother.

Connor.

"Georgie, no," Deck shouted. "Fuck. Stop her."

"Jesus," Tristan said.

I hit the last stair when Kai stepped in front of me, grabbing my shoulders. "Chaos."

It was like a film in slow motion as I turned and looked over the railing, my eyes hitting my brother. Or a semblance of him.

My heart stopped and bile rose in my throat. I had the urge to run back up the stairs as fast as I could, but I was frozen staring at…. I didn't know what I was seeing. My mind reeled with memories of who he was and what I was staring at, unable to decipher that he was one and the same.

"Connor. No." The words ripped from my throat in a ragged whisper of devastation.

He was chained to the rough cement-block wall, arms out to the sides, feet slightly parted, manacles around each limb.

There were cuts on his wrists and ankles, the blood sprayed across his skin like a fine mist of red paint. His thigh and shoulder were bandaged, but I didn't know why. His chest heaved and there was a wild look in his eyes, expression contorted as if the men were torturing him.

But it was the absence of kindness in his eyes that destroyed me. It was why he'd joined the JTF2, an elite anti-terrorism unit. Why he was the most incredible brother. Why he visited schools and orphanages when he was on tour. Why he was Connor. He may have been cocky and full of himself, but his heart had been filled with compassion and love, helping kids like Tanner who had nothing. Tanner who had betrayed him. Betrayed us both.

There was nothing left of that Connor. There were physically identifiable pieces of him, but what made up who my brother was had vanished.

My gaze darted to Kai. "Get your hands off me," I shouted. "This is your fault." I didn't recognize my own agonized voice as I tried to push past Kai, but his grip on me only tightened.

I never thought I'd do it because despite knowing Kai for years, he still scared me. But so much rage surfaced that I couldn't control it.

I hauled off and punched him in the face. I knew he'd seen it coming by the way he tensed just before my fist made contact with his jaw. I also knew he could've avoided it, but he let me hit him.

"You did this to him. This is your fault you son-of-a-bitch. You destroyed him." I pounded on his chest while Kai stood unmoving. "He was good, damn it. He was good. He was good." And now that was gone.

My vision blurred from the tears and I no longer knew who I was punching and trying to hurt until I heard Deck's whispered words against my ear, his arms wrapped around me.

"Baby. Shh, we'll get him back."

I shook my head back and forth against his chest. "He'll never be the same."

"No. He won't. But he's still your brother. He's alive and that means there's a chance."

Deck had never lied to me. No matter if it hurt, he was honest, and that gave me a sliver of hope because he believed we'd find Connor within that cold, ravaged monster chained to the wall.

"Kai," Deck said. "Give him the sedative. We're leaving." He picked me up in his arms. I closed my eyes, my head against his chest and he carried me back up the stairs. Without stopping, we went to the car.

CHAPTER
THIRTY

London

WE TOOK TWO vehicles to the airport then boarded Tristan's jet to fly to New York. Deck had spoken quietly to three customs officers and since he shook their hands and patted one on the back, I was guessing he knew them.

Tristan's private plane had wide leather seats that swiveled, a bar and a flat screen television. I sat beside Kai. Vic sat facing me with Deck beside him, two round tables separated us. Vic had already carried the sedated Connor onto the plane and Georgie stayed with him.

Chess was about to sit across the aisle from me, but Tristan finished speaking with the pilot and walked toward her and he didn't stop walking when he grabbed her hand.

"We'll be in the back room," Tristan said. "Don't disturb us even if the plane goes down."

"Tristan, what are you—?" Chess started.

He leaned in to her and whispered something. I couldn't see Chess's face but did see her elbow him in the gut. He didn't seem to notice and kept ushering her to the back of the plane.

"I hear them moaning, we're going to have a problem," Kai said.

I smiled. It was odd seeing Kai with a sister, but then it was odd seeing him with Deck and his men.

Vic, who never smiled and was built like a tree trunk on steroids, had his eyes on me and I shifted uncomfortably in my seat. Finally, he said, "You're different. Better."

Yeah, because he'd only seen me as Raven, a girl broken and numb. In a way, I'd been like Connor: a machine that did what I was supposed to except his was mostly drug induced, mine had been a way to protect my mind from what I'd endured.

Once we were in the air it was all business.

Deck placed what looked like a journal on the table and nodded to Kai who picked it up and flipped through the pages.

"What's this?" Kai asked.

"Connor's journal. There are pages ripped out. Looks like five of them in a row. He wrote in it sporadically, so no pattern to it. But according to Georgie the days missing were before they met Tanner. Need you to confirm this."

Kai opened the journal and flipped to the spot where it was obvious pages were torn out. "Looks about right. I was assigned to Georgie after Connor was taken, but Tanner was earlier to befriend them."

"Why Connor though?"

Kai said, "Anything to do with Connor was confidential. I kept eyes on Georgie and Tanner."

Deck chin-lifted to the journal. "We've gone over it numerous times and found nothing useful or unusual. You read it. Might give us a new perspective, catch something we might not have. He talks about ordinary shit. Missing home. His family. Georgie. The deplorable conditions children lived in that we encountered on our missions. I've already looked in to all the places Connor was during the time frames where the pages were torn out," Deck stated and I was getting that Deck was the type of guy who didn't leave any stones unturned.

"Most of which were overseas."

"Maybe you're searching where there is nothing. Torn pages in a journal doesn't necessarily mean anything." Kai shrugged then tucked the small leather-bound book in his back pocket. "I'll look."

"And maybe you haven't told us everything we need to fuckin' know." Deck glared at Kai who merely leaned back in his seat, pushed his legs out and crossed his ankles. "Keeping secrets and lies are your specialty."

"The lies kept your girl out of Vault. How do you think it would've gone down if she were taken by them?" Kai said.

I bit my lower lip nervously. Deck looked like he was going to leap out of his seat and throw Kai off the plane, yet Kai remained relaxed.

Kai continued, "You'd search every single inch of this planet, use every means possible and maybe even resort to torturing innocent people." Deck's brows lowered and Kai smiled. "Don't pretend you wouldn't let your morals slip in order to find your girl." He leaned forward, his elbows resting on his knees and his voice lowering. "I think a couple of lies to keep Georgie safe was the better option."

"I think killing you would've been the best option," Deck stated.

Kai sat back, laughing. "Probably right."

I stiffened at Deck's pissed-off face. I didn't like the direction this was going. Kai must have noticed my discomfort because he reached over and took my hand. There was silence before Vic pulled out his laptop and brought up the blueprint of my father's lab.

Then it was all business again.

I showed them the tunnel and where we had to go in. The tension eased as they quietly discussed the strategies. It was the only time they appeared agreeable with one another.

An hour into the flight, I went and sat across from Georgie at the back of the plane. Connor was breathing heavily, eyes closed as he slept, probably due to whatever they'd given him.

I didn't say anything at first because I didn't know what to say to her. She'd been a pawn in this as well. Kai had told me everything including the cutting in the shed. Parts of me understood why Georgie needed the physical pain in order to try and dull the emotional pain.

I couldn't handle being around people who wanted to coddle me when I'd finally come home. I wanted to be alone. Run from everyone. From everything I cared about. Even from myself.

But like Georgie's cutting, my running didn't help.

Kai had done that.

"I'm sorry. About Connor." He was this way because of my father.

She raised her head, Connor's hand in hers, tears streaking her cheeks and there were mascara blotches underneath her eyes. "He was a great brother." Georgie leaned her head back against the seat, staring straight ahead. "I've wanted nothing more in my life than to have him back." She paused and repeated, "Nothing. And now... he's here, but he isn't."

I didn't respond, my heart tearing at the broken bond between brother and sister.

"I never wanted him to join the military. I begged him not to, but Connor... he told me it was what he was meant to do. It was who he was." She sniffled and rubbed her nose with the back of her hand. "Every time he came back from a tour, he'd walk through the door and despite what hell he'd been in, what he'd seen or done, he'd still smile."

I glanced at her brother who had nothing but ravaged pain etched on his face. I knew the look because I'd suffered, too, and it changed me. You didn't forget. You just learned to adapt with the horror and survive with the black shadows.

I leaned forward and glanced up front. Kai was watching me, no smile and no anger, just watching with interest. There was a slight nod and then he went back to listening to whatever the men were talking about.

"So, you and Kai?" Georgie said.

I nodded.

"Known him since I was a kid. He taught me a lot and he, in his own way, has protected me. Well, I know that now, but damn, he terrified me, too. Never known a man to be as fearless as him and I've been around Deck and his men my whole life. He hides it well. Fucker is as casual as they come." She lowered her voice. "But when you disappeared and he called in his marker with Deck to try to find you…. Kai doesn't use markers. Doesn't need them. And he sure as hell has never been fond of Deck. Shit, Deck still doesn't trust him."

"Do you?"

Georgie shrugged. "Hard question to answer. Not really, and yeah, sort of." She huffed. "I hate the bastard sometimes. For all of this, but a part of me knows this doesn't stem from him. He's a product of what they made him."

I trusted Kai, but I wasn't sure of the lengths he would go to get exactly what he wanted, even if that meant hurting or killing someone on this plane.

Georgie half-smiled. "Sugar, with the way that man watches you he's one-hundred percent into you. Not something to take lightly with him."

"I love him." Her brows rose. "But sometimes… the way he is, his morals, how dangerous he can be, it's a little scary."

"Deck has some big-ass monsters hanging in his closet and I won't even get into what I think delicious Vic has going on in that head of his, but you find the good and you hold onto that because it's what will pull you both through the hell. I think Kai wants to be pulled out, London. I think he's been trying to get unstuck for years and those bastards kept dragging him back down into the sludge. But you and him"—she nodded toward Kai—"you have the rope. Just don't let it go, because my guess, if you do, that guy isn't ever coming back from the darkness again."

I peered over at Kai again as he leaned forward and said something to Vic, that subtle smile barely visible as Vic glared back at him and I knew he'd said something to piss him off. Yeah, he definitely had no fear.

"Prepare for landing," the pilot announced as the seatbelt lights went on.

"Georgie, what happened with Alfonzo at your house—"

"Don't go there. Not your fault. Alfonzo was the lowest of scum and there was nothing you could have done. Kai was handling it and you needed to do exactly what you did."

"Except I should've turned the gun on him," I replied.

She snorted. "Yeah, and then all those girls in that shipping container would be dead right now or worse, for Jacob to ship them off to God knows where." She pushed back her pink strands behind her ear. "Besides, there was no way in hell you would've pulled the trigger." She smiled. "You would now though."

"London." Kai walked down the aisle toward me.

Georgie smirked and leaned over to whisper, "You see… that man has it bad for you. He even wants to hold your hand during landing. You think your cupcake is scared?"

I laughed, glancing up at Kai as he approached. No, he didn't look scared or annoyed. He just looked delicious. I got up. "I don't think Kai has that emotion in him."

Georgie sobered. "Yeah. I didn't either—until you."

CHAPTER
THIRTY-ONE

London

THE TUNNELS WERE damp and cold with cracked cement walls, and I could hear the occasional squeak of mice or worse, rats, but I tried not to think of it as I closely followed Kai. We jogged most of the way with Kai's hand in mine, his other holding a pencil-thin flashlight that gave off a blueish tinge.

Deck took up the rear with Georgie behind me. I was completely out of my element, carrying a gun and wearing a bulletproof vest that Kai insisted on. Georgie and Deck had them on, too, but Kai didn't. He'd said he'd never worn one and wasn't starting now. It made me nervous because, despite Kai being as experienced as he was, I still wondered if he didn't fear death because he didn't care if he died.

And that was the scariest of all because I cared. I loved him and I couldn't bear the thought of being separated again.

Kai's light hit the steel door and we stopped. I was breathing heavily from the jog, but I was the only one. Now, I was kicking myself for not taking some kind of sport or doing an exercise program. But a few years ago, I never thought I'd be holding more than a test tube and sitting on a swivel stool, rolling across linoleum floors as I conducted experiments.

"You good?" Kai asked.

"Yeah." I was as good as I could be breaking into a lab I'd spent more time in growing up than my own house. A lab that had dangerous men watching it. A lab that had developed a drug we knew nothing about, but my dad did. "My dad…" His car was in the parking lot and it was past eleven at night. I was terrified that maybe they'd already gotten to him. That his car was here but he was…. I couldn't say it.

"He's here. We'll get him out," Kai said, knowing exactly what I was thinking.

I nodded then gestured to the door. "There is another door at the top and it opens into a hallway where there are two labs."

"Deck." Kai stepped back, taking my hand and urging Georgie back, too. Deck approached the door and shot the padlock off then unraveled the chain on the metal bar and pushed it open, his gun still drawn.

"Clear."

We ran up the flight of stairs and Deck was already crouched and fiddling with the lock on the door handle. "Need me to do that?" I asked Deck.

He snorted and shot me a scowl. I'd easily picked his lock in his penthouse.

Deck stood. "We're doing this in five minutes." Deck looked at me then Georgie. "You got me, Georgie? No distractions. If London's father isn't there, you get in the computer, find what we need, copy, delete, and then get out."

Georgie sidled up to him. "I get it, baby. A quickie. In and out. You're good at that."

Deck snorted and shook his head. Georgie laughed.

I bit my lip to keep from smiling because Deck wasn't laughing and neither was Kai. He handed me a white lab coat from his bag, which I put over my vest, and Georgie did the same.

Kai put his hand on my hip and urged me toward him then looked down, brows raised. "Gun, London."

Shit. "Right." I put it in my lab coat pocket. Although, if anyone looked close enough, they'd see it. With the weight of it, my coat was slightly skewed, but all of this didn't concern me. My focus was on the possibility of seeing my father.

Vic was on the roof of an adjacent building with a sniper rifle looking for anyone who might be Vault. Since it was so late, there were few people still in the buildings besides security.

Tristan and Chess had stayed at his house to watch Connor. Josh and Tyler were flying in the following morning, which meant the microchips were now destroyed and anyone who had been tracking them knew it had been a false trail.

"Ready?" Deck asked.

I nodded, as did Kai, and Deck opened the door. There was one security guard to pass in order to get to my dad's lab. Kai said he'd 'deal with him.' I didn't know exactly what that meant, but innocent people getting hurt was something I wasn't willing to sacrifice. Most of the people in this building I'd known since I was a kid.

We decided on my plan instead, so Deck and Kai wore suits and ties, teamed with Kai carrying his black bag, which wasn't holding any sort of business-related material, but security wouldn't know that.

We walked down the corridor…Kai beside me, Deck and Georgie behind us. When we rounded the corner a few steps away from my father's lab, a security guard stopped us.

Kai stiffened beside me and I saw the slight movement of his blazer lifting as his hand went to his knife.

I stepped forward, smiling. "Daniel, hi. Nice to see you."

His frown slipped as he recognized me. "Miss Westbrook? Good to see you. It's been—"

"Years," I finished, touching his forearm affectionately. He'd been employed at the lab since I was ten years old and yet he still refused to call me London. "School has been grueling and has kept me away," I lied. "How's your wife?"

I heard Kai curse beneath his breath.

"Great. Still can't cook and still a pain in the ass, but the best, most beautiful, pain in the ass an old guy like me could have." He nodded to Kai, then his eyes shifted to Georgie and Deck before coming back to me. "Your father just told us the bad news. Sorry to hear."

I hesitated. "Umm, yeah." Bad news? What was he talking about?

"How is he feeling? He's looked pretty tired over the last few months, but then your father doesn't know when to go home." He chuckled, shaking his head. "Workaholic, that man. I'm thinking his daughter will follow in his footsteps. Is he meeting you in the lab? I just saw him go upstairs. I thought he was leaving."

"Well, I think—"

Kai stepped forward. "We have a red eye to catch in an hour, Miss Westbrook. Do you mind?" His fingers curled around my arm and I glanced at him with confusion. "Dr. Westbrook," Kai said abruptly.

I nodded. "Right. Yes. Daniel, say hi to Marcy for me. I'll talk to you later."

"Will do." He shifted to the side to let us pass and we walked to the sliding glass door to my father's lab and I punched in the code. I prayed he hadn't changed it as I waited for the red blinking light to turn green.

If it didn't, then Deck and Kai were taking another approach and Daniel was going to get hurt. The three seconds felt like twenty when the doors finally slid open. I waved to Daniel and stood to the side to let Kai, Deck and Georgie inside. Just before the doors closed, I saw Daniel take out his cell phone.

Shit. I didn't say anything to Kai because I knew he'd go deal with the potential issue and it wasn't an issue—yet. Maybe he was calling Marcy to let her know he saw me? I didn't want him getting killed because I saw him with his cell.

I quickly showed Georgie the main computer and she went to work on it while Deck and I scanned all of the shelves and fridge for the drug Connor was on. If my dad was continuing to supply them, there had to be a batch he was currently working on.

Kai kept watch, but I saw him walk over to the storage closet and open the door. Our eyes met and the corners of his lips curved up. So much had happened since he saw me hiding in that closet. I'd been scared and confused, yet his scent had sparked something familiar and comforting about him. Now I knew why.

I found two bottles of pills in the fridge with a label that had no batch code. All drugs had batch codes and they coordinated with files. But the bottles had simple orange labels with the name CONNOR.

I yanked the pill bottles out and took them to Deck who nodded then put them in his bag. Then I walked over to Kai and put my hand on his chest. "Do you know anything about my father? Why Daniel would say that?"

"Yes." He kept his eyes on me as a wave of dread hit me.

My knees weakened and I became lightheaded. It wasn't good. Oh, God, there was something wrong with my dad. "Kai—"

"London, it's not my place to tell you. It's your father's. If I need to, I will, but right now"—he cupped the back of my neck and squeezed—"I need you here, with me. Okay?"

He was right. If the news was bad, now wasn't the time to—

My eye caught the red flashing light on the code box beside the door. "Kai! The door." He turned to where I was looking.

"Deck," Kai said as he grabbed my hand and headed for the door.

That was all he had to say and Deck went for Georgie. "Babe. Need to go."

I punched in the code on the door, but it buzzed and wouldn't open. "It's locked. Security can lock the doors if there is a breach." Oh, God, we had to find my dad and get out of here.

I heard Deck arguing with Georgie as she typed furiously on the computer while Kai took out his knife and jammed it into the top of the black code box, cracking it open.

The cover fell to the floor and he yanked a bunch of wires out and then sifted through them.

"Georgie. Now," Deck ordered.

"I got it. Shit, I need to delete…. Done." Deck yanked her away from the computer as Kai cut two wires and the doors slid open. But it wasn't because Kai cut the right wires; it was because my father overrode security and opened it.

"Dad?"

"London." He stepped forward to hug me when Kai blocked him by moving in front, his hand on my wrist so I couldn't go near him. "I'm not going to hurt her."

"Kai?" I tried to move past him, but he tilted his head to look at me, eyes glaring in warning, a warning I couldn't ignore.

I peered past him to my father and knew something was wrong, not just the concern etched on his pale face, but how sick he looked. Black lines were heavy under his eyes and he appeared ten years older than the last time I'd seen him.

He was sick. And it was serious. My throat tightened as tears welled and a crushing pain latched onto my chest, making my stomach lurch. "Oh, God, Dad," I choked.

"Kai, please," my dad begged. "I'd never hurt her."

"You understand why I'll not take your word on that," Kai replied. "Considering."

My dad peered down the corridor, his feet shifting, uneasy and anxious. "Daniel called me. I was in the car leaving, but... when he said she was here... I had to see her again." He looked at me. "Honey, oh, God, I'm so sorry. I didn't know what else to do."

His eyes filled with tears and anguish pulled at his weary face. "I know, Dad." I did. This wasn't his fault. He'd have done anything to try to protect me.

"I refused to continue making the drug for them, but after the fire...." His head dropped forward.

I turned to Kai, my hand on his arm. He nodded and let me go. I ran into my father's arms and held him tight. "I don't blame you, Dad."

I'd never seen my father cry, even after my mother died. I suspected he did, but he never let me see him break down like he did now and it broke my heart. Why him? He was a good, brilliant man. Why did they have to pick him? But if not him, then it may have been some other scientist with a family.

I heard Deck and Kai quietly talking, but I didn't pay attention to what was being said. I squeezed my dad to me, wanting to take away all the guilt he carried with him.

"We need to go, London." Kai gently put his hand on my shoulder then pulled me back so I was up against his chest then his palm slid over my hip to lay flat on my lower back. "And you need to come with us," he said to my dad.

"They'll send someone after you if I do," he argued. "It's better I stay."

"Dad. No."

Kai shook his head. "You're coming." He grabbed my dad's arm and we started down the hall.

I heard Deck on the headset to Vic, and Kai was asking my dad questions about the drug as he hurried to the door that led to the tunnels.

"I gave them a batch of pills three months ago, but that's all I had. One component is difficult to come by—"

"To who?" Kai asked.

"I don't know. Just some guy." Then he asked, "The guy they're giving the drug to... have you seen him? Do you know what it does?"

"We have him," Kai said.

"He's my brother," Georgie said.

My dad's eyes widened. "He's dangerous. The drug, it clouds his memories and he won't even know what he's done. He more than likely won't know who you are and will do whatever they want. And it also has steroids in it to enhance—"

"Invincibility. Yeah, we figured that out," Deck stated.

My dad continued, "How long since his last pill? He'll have withdrawals and it could be worse. Some of the mice... well, they died when I stopped the drug."

I glanced at Georgie who paled and reached for Deck's hand.

My dad looked at me, the tight expression fading as the wrinkles sagged. "London, you know how this works. He can't go off the drug. Not without severe side effects and maybe even death."

Deck's voice was gravelly and abrupt. "How long?"

"I don't know. The mice, they went into a frenzy, a rage, then after a few days, they began to cramp up then had seizures until... well, until they passed."

"Fuckin' Christ." Deck slammed his fist into the wall.

My dad quickly continued, "But weaning him off it would work. A slow withdrawal and you—"

"Quiet," Kai interrupted as he threw open the door into the tunnel. "Wait here."

I watched as he disappeared into the darkness, the tinge of blue light flickering for a brief second before it disappeared, too. Deck was on edge, but calm, Georgie sheltered by his body, gun in hand. It was only seconds before Kai jogged back up the stairs and snagged my hand and pulled me away.

"No go. Don't know how many, but they're headed this way."

Deck was already moving down the corridor toward the north stairwell. A cell rang and the only one to have a ringing cell would be my dad. All of ours were on silent.

He quickly looked at the screen then stopped, his face paling.

"Dad?"

Deck and Kai looked at one another, then Deck jogged down the corridor a little further and peeked around the corner.

"It's my contact for the drug," my dad said.

"Answer it," Kai ordered.

I put my hand on my dad's arm and squeezed. He looked scared with wide eyes and trembling hands as he tapped on his phone then held it to his ear.

"Hello?" He listened for ten seconds then hung up and turned to Kai. "They know you're here."

Kai half-grinned. "Then they should be worried." He chin-lifted to Deck. "Evac?"

"North stairs to basement. Vic will cover us out the emergency door."

We were moving fast as Deck took lead, Georgie behind, then my dad and me with Kai taking up the rear. Deck stopped, holding out his hand as the elevators fifty feet away dinged.

"Shit. Back," he ordered. "Vic. We need an exit. North exit and tunnels compromised."

My dad ran up ahead. "West. There is a—"

Gunshots echoed down the sterile corridor and Kai grabbed me, shoving me in front of him then pushed me into an alcove.

"Dad?"

"Right here, sweetie," he said.

Deck and Georgie were in an alcove across the hall.

"Can you get us in this lab?" Kai asked my dad.

"Yeah, but there is no way out."

"Do it."

My dad typed in a code and the door beeped but it didn't open. "I can't override the lockdown." He typed in the code again and it beeped, but the door remained locked.

I reached in my pocket and pulled out my gun. Kai saw me do it and nodded once. I heard footsteps and then gunshots, but they were from Deck.

As Deck shot off a few rounds, Kai peered around the corner and the drywall splintered right beside his head. I gasped. Oh, God, they were shooting to kill. They were going to kill us.

Kai stepped back from the door and kicked it. It didn't budge. "Fuck." He grabbed my wrist and pushed me back against it. "Shoot anyone who comes near you. Understand?" I nodded, but I was silently freaking out. I'd seen people shot, murdered, beaten, but it was when I didn't care about anything. Now I had my father and Kai and Deck and Georgie.

Kai looked at my dad. "They're coming from both sides. We can sit here and be sitting ducks or take them out. I don't do the sitting duck thing or surrender, so that means you stay with her."

"What? Kai?" What was he thinking of doing? I reached for him, but he shoved me back with his palm on my chest.

"You need to stay right there."

I jerked at more gunshots. Deck was shooting as was Georgie, but not for long as Deck grabbed her and pushed her back out of harm's way. Deck glanced across the hallway at Kai and raised his hand, indicating five to the right and three to the left.

Kai nodded and Deck pointed to himself and then right. Kai nodded. Oh, my God, they were going to take them out.

"No. Kai." My heart was pumping wildly and I shook so bad, I was afraid the gun was going to accidentally go off.

"No choice here, baby." Before I could say anything else, Kai nodded once to Deck and they both rolled into the corridor.

I stepped forward, my breath locked in my chest as I heard gunshots from both directions. Deck and Kai were out of my line of sight.

I heard groans and bodies hitting the floor, but I couldn't see anything. Georgie was peeking around the corner and shooting. I moved forward, but my dad blocked me with his body.

"No."

"Dad, I can shoot." I couldn't, but I had to do something.

"No," he repeated, his voice firm. "You need to do what Kai—"

A man staggered into the alcove, blood covering the front of his shirt from a knife plunged into his chest.

"London!" I heard Kai shout.

There were a few more gunshots, but everything was in slow motion as the man raised his gun and pointed it at me.

"Deck!" Kai yelled.

I raised my gun, too.

It happened within milliseconds. My dad dove for the guy at the same time as both guns went off. The man fell backward, my dad on top of him.

Neither moved.

"Dad!"

I scrambled for him, dropping the gun and falling to my knees beside him.

"Dad. Dad." I tried to roll him over from lying on top of the other guy. "Dad," I sobbed.

Suddenly, I was being pulled to my feet and arms wrapped around me. "Baby, give Deck a second to help him."

It was then I noticed Deck on his knees beside my father, Georgie standing against the wall her hand to her mouth.

Deck had my dad on his back and there was blood all over his chest. "Kai, let me see him. Let me go." I shoved at his arms and he finally released me.

I fell to my knees beside Deck who was putting pressure on my dad's chest, but there was so much blood. I didn't know if it was just my dad's or the other guy's, but when I saw my dad's face, I knew.

"No. God, no. Dad. No. Please." Oh, God, I was so close to getting him back. After all this time, we had a chance, but it was being ripped away.

"London," he managed and then spurted blood, coughing.

Tears blurred my vision as I watched my dad struggle to breathe. He looked past me and I sensed Kai behind me then his hand was on my shoulder.

"I owe you. For... finding... her. Hiding her from... them." He coughed again and I used my sleeve to wipe his mouth. "For protecting... her when I didn't."

And then Kai did something I never thought he'd do. He crouched, put his hand on my dad's shoulder and squeezed. Then my dad was looking back at me and I took his hand and held it in mine.

"Dad. We can get you out. Just hold on." But I knew that wasn't true.

He half-smiled. "No. Don't... need to hold on... anymore. Just waiting to see you...again. Love...." His eyes glazed over and blood dripped from the corner of his mouth.

"No, Dad. No," I choked out. "Oh, God, Dad." I collapsed onto his neck. "Dad."

I had no idea how long I cried, but it was probably only seconds before I heard Deck.

"We need out. Now," Deck ordered.

Hands peeled me away from my dad and I knew it was Kai.

"Dad—"

"Baby, we have to go."

I knew that logically, but everything inside me wanted to stay with my dad. "I... Kai... we didn't get time."

He wiped the tears with his thumb. "Baby, your dad was dying of cancer. He had months left. Maybe not even. He knew that. He was holding on to see you again."

I swallowed. "Cancer?"

He nodded.

Kai gently urged me further away from my dad, the pain crushing and debilitating.

"He was a good man." Kai kissed the top of my head. "I liked him."

Georgie threw her arms around me. "Sugar, I'm so sor—"

Deck settled his hands on her shoulders then drew her back. "Not now, rainbow. Let's go."

Then we were running for the stairwell. Deck cleared it first and then we took one flight of stairs up before Deck held up his hand and we stopped.

"Vic, we're in position."

Kai handed me my gun. "Baby, here and now. Okay?"

Tears kept sliding down my cheeks, but I nodded. As my shaking hand curled around the hard metal, I heard the gunshots down the hall.

"Vic. He's coming to help us," Kai said.

I was still thinking about my dad, his face, the way his empty eyes stared up at me. God, he'd been dying. And now he was gone and....

Kai's hands cupped my head so I was forced to look at him. "I know you're not good. But I need you to focus."

I nodded.

His thumbs stroked gently over my temples, his hard body against mine, tense and ready to react in a moment. "Answer me, baby."

"Okay." I inhaled a quivering breath. "Okay."

I looked up at Deck and nodded. Then the stairwell door opened and we ran down the hall. We didn't make it far before two men ran around the corner and started shooting. Kai grabbed me, yanked me around the corner and shoved me against the wall, his body protecting me as Deck did the same with Georgie.

The gunshots stopped and Deck gestured to Kai before they both stepped out, Deck shooting while Kai ran and rolled across the hall into another corridor. I couldn't see them anymore, just heard the gunshots.

My grip on the gun was so hard the metal indented my hand.

Georgie had a gun, too, but when I looked at her she appeared pretty steady. She half-smiled at me with reassurance. She had total faith in her man that we'd get out of here.

I couldn't smile back, my fear escalating as I heard footsteps getting closer.

Oh, God, please be careful, Kai.

But this was what Kai did. He'd broken me out of Vault's prison after killing his own mother.

He knew what he was doing.

I heard two loud thumps and a half-shout before the sound gurgled to nothing. "Clear."

It was Kai.

We came out from around the corner and I saw two bodies face first on the floor, blood pooling around their heads from the slices across their throats. Kai had his knives in his hand, blood dripping from the blades.

An alarm blared through the building and Deck said, "Vic." And then Vic was running toward us with one badass gun slung over his shoulder and another in his hands.

"Emergency exit clear. Car waiting," Vic said.

Deck slapped him on the back and they started for the door.

"London." Kai stepped into me and lowered my gun. Then he slipped his knives in his holster and took my hand in his. "It's just a word and I feel so much more than four fuckin' letters. But you need to hear it from me right now, so I'm giving it to you. I love you, London."

He didn't give me time to respond and I don't think I could've even if he did. He linked our hands together and we ran for the emergency door.

CHAPTER
THIRTY-TWO

Kai

FIVE DAYS WE'D been idle at Tristan's place after flying back to Toronto. This one was located on the outskirts of the city and had an elaborate security system protecting what looked like an extensive collection of art hanging on the walls.

As no one from Vault knew of his involvement yet, it was safe enough—for now. But when you were the hunted, staying in one place was never a good idea.

London was being my braveheart, insisting on going over her father's files so she could find out more about the drug and help Connor. But at night when I held her in my arms, her tears soaked into my skin and her body shook as she sobbed.

There was nothing to say and I honestly didn't know how she felt because I'd never experienced a loss like that. I was too young when my father died and we'd been thrown into survival mode at the farm. I remembered being sad and missing him, but it hadn't lasted long.

When I was old enough to comprehend why he died and what happened, I didn't grieve him. I blamed him. He knew my mother was a controlling, power-hungry bitch. He had to have seen what was coming. He had an affair and my mother had her excuse to make her move. It didn't take long before I stopped blaming him because I didn't care one way or another. I didn't care about anything.

It was mid-afternoon and I'd come to check on London, but she was in the shower, so I headed downstairs to make her something to eat. If she ate anything in the last five days, it wasn't enough and I was worried. Fuck, I was worried. That was what it was to care about someone, you worried about them.

Chess came barging into the kitchen, her hands on her hips and her cheeks red. It looked like she'd been arguing. Probably had been with Tristan.

"Why aren't we doing anything? They're going to move the farm, Kai." Tristan strolled in, leaned against the archway into the kitchen, raised his brows and grinned at me. Obviously, he'd already heard this from Chess. "They could have already."

I opened the fridge, took out the leftover piece of salmon Deck barbequed the previous night and put it on the plate. "We don't have a location, Chess." I popped two slices of bread in the toaster. "Can't move on it without one."

She moved in front of me as I went for the fridge again. She glared. It didn't bother me. I was just glad she was standing before me and not in some prison. "And if they kill the kids? What then? Are you going to be able to live with yourself, Kai?" She snorted. "Yeah, you probably can." That bothered me, but she was right to think that. I deserved it. "But I can't. We should be out searching, not sitting here waiting for some prick to call."

We were waiting for Dorsey to call me. We had the drug, the files, and Connor, who was much calmer after being given the drug. But it was the fifth day since we'd given him a pill mixed in the water we gave him and already he was beginning to show signs of rage again. Deck was hoping we could extend the length of time every week, add a few days until eventually Connor was off the drug.

Tristan pushed away from the wall and went to her. I moved back to the toaster and buttered the toast. I looked over my shoulder at them. He was gentle as he came up behind her and settled his hands on her hips. I saw her jerk to get away, but he merely moved in closer and tightened his hold.

"Dorsey may have the location of the farm," Tristan said, his mouth close to her ear.

"What if he doesn't call?" she refuted.

"We give him two more days," I said. "If he doesn't call, we go to him. I have someone on him, if he decides to make a move anywhere." It was always better being the one approached than do the approaching, but Chess was right. If they felt the farm was threatened, they'd move it.

I slapped the salmon on the toast, sprinkled some sea salt and pepper then placed some sliced tomato and lettuce before putting the toast on top. I picked up the plate to take it up to London when my cell rang.

It was my disposable—Ernie. I put the plate back down, leaned against the counter and answered. "Yeah? You have anything?" Ernie was the guy I had in Vegas keeping an eye on Dorsey. If he were going to make a move, it would've been after what went down at the lab.

"Your man is rather stubborn," a heavy, deep voice replied. It was like he smoked too much and his lungs were caked in a layer of black tar. I knew exactly who it was.

"Dorsey." Chess's breath hitched. "This isn't a good time. Just about to eat."

I didn't have to look at my sister to know she was furious at my nonchalance. Tristan no doubt was keeping her from being in my face.

"Ah, well, my sharks are about to as well. They have a feeding frenzy once a week. Tonight they'll have something special." I tensed because I knew exactly where he was going with this. "Unless of course, you'd prefer to have him back in one piece?"

I glanced up as Deck and Vic came into the kitchen, giving me space, but listening. "What I'd prefer is for you to get to the point."

He laughed. "I've always respected you, Kai. Even now, after killing your own mother. She was a cold-hearted bitch."

I remained quiet and he continued, "Dr. Westbrook is dead and his files gone. You stole your mother's files on the drug, you have Dr. Westbrook's daughter, and I assume the famous test subject, Connor, as he's disappeared."

Again I stayed silent. No point denying, he was right on all counts.

"I have a job for you."

It was my turn to chuckle. "As I'm sure you're aware, I'm no longer doing jobs for Vault."

He clucked his tongue and I wanted to reach through the phone and tear it from his throat. "But you'll do this job for me because I know it's what you're after."

"And what is that?"

"The other board member." He paused. "You see, Kai, you killed your mother. You broke out your sister and Dr. Westbrook's daughter, London. You're making sure you have everyone out before you go after the rest of us." He paused. "Or shall I call that girl Raven?" *Jesus fuckin' Christ.* "A shame I didn't have the pleasure of tasting some of that while she was in the… industry."

Keep your shit together, Kai. I normally didn't let words bother me. They were meaningless, but him talking about London was like a knife in the gut.

Deck moved in beside me and I tilted the cell so he could hear.

"Let's get something clear, Dorsey." Any amusement left my tone. "You bring my girl into this, there will be nothing in this world I won't do in order to get to you. And when I get to you, it won't be a quick death. Because like Vault says, death is a privilege."

Dorsey paused, and for a second I thought he hung up, except for his crackled breath. "Feed his finger to the shark," he said, but it wasn't to me; it was to someone with him.

There was nothing I could do. I knew his game and giving in to him would only make it worse. Deck lowered his head and the vibration of anger emanated off him, but he knew it, too. He knew I couldn't give in to Dorsey.

Ernie's fate didn't look good. Fuck. I should've gone myself.

"I'll make you a deal. Give me the drug, the files and the girl, and you can have your man back in one piece. Well, minus a finger." He laughed.

"How about this? I find you, then nice and slow like, cut you up with my knife. And I'll do it for weeks, so your shark has meals for a while. And when you beg me for mercy, shit, right, I don't have mercy. The farm made certain of that."

He didn't laugh this time; instead, I heard shuffling and then his words were muffled as he put his hand over the receiver and spoke to someone else. "You just killed your friend."

"I don't have friends," I replied calmly.

But I did. I did have friends. I had Ernie. *Had.* Fuck, Ernie.

That made him pause and maybe he was getting that I wouldn't give in to anything he said. But it could've been to the sacrifice of Ernie's life. I wanted to lose my shit. I wanted to whip my phone through the window and destroy everything in sight.

The rage burning through me was putting me on the edge of doing something stupid and blowing this all to shit.

"Okay," Dorsey said and it was yielding. "You want to head Vault, I can make that happen."

I laughed. "I don't need you to make that happen. I can do that myself. But that's not what I want."

"You would've been here yourself if you wanted me, so my earlier guess is correct. And I want the same thing, so I believe we can come to some sort of agreement."

"I'm listening."

"Not over the phone," Dorsey said. "Meet me. In Vegas. Without the ex-JTF2 guy."

"I'm alive today because I don't meet my enemies where they choose."

"Who said we're enemies, Kai. We're merely negotiating for what we both want. And I want the files for the drug."

"Okay."

"I give you the information you need and you give me Dr. Westbrook's files." I waited for him to include London, but he didn't. "I can find another scientist, although the girl would've made things easier. But I know you won't give her up. Not after what you've done to free her. But I want Connor and the pills you stole from the lab."

I glanced at Deck, whose scowl was fierce, the lines around his mouth tight. "No Connor. And no Vegas. I'll meet you tonight. Eleven. Should give you enough time to fly to Toronto. Twenty-four hour diner on Spadina at Niagara. Bring Ernie or none of this happens." I hung up, opened the back of my phone, took out the SIM card, and smashed it with the edge of the phone on the counter.

"You trust him?" Deck asked.

"Fuck, no." But Dorsey was all about power and money, which meant he'd probably be willing to give up the board member who obviously had more power than him. "But he wants the drug. If he controls that, he doesn't need the farm. He'll do what was done to Connor. Use it on men who are already killers. Make them into machines. Not sure about the conditioning though. That was Mother's expertise."

"And even more reason to not give it to him."

I grinned. "My morals are more flexible than yours, Deck. I have no qualms about making a deal then reneging."

Deck's lip twitched.

"I want to come with you," Chess said.

Tristan laughed to which she smacked him on the arm. He just laughed harder. "Not happening, babe."

"I have to do something, damn it." Where I had patience, I was learning Chess did not.

"Yeah, you can look after me." Tristan bent, shoulder into her belly then had her up over his shoulder within seconds. She yelled. He ignored her and then they were gone.

"How is she?" Deck asked.

He was referring to London.

Vic poured himself a coffee, but I could tell he was listening by the way his head tilted slightly in our direction.

"Pretending to be good. She needs to be far from this."

Deck nodded. "Georgie, too. Tristan's idea, we need to make happen." An idea that was coming into play if everything went as expected with Dorsey. "Girls won't like it, but if we get what we need from Dorsey, then we have to act. Girls can't be part of that."

Deck and I had our differences, but we had one thing in common now—keeping the girls safe. I grinned. "Tristan is in for a war."

Deck chuckled, a rare sound coming from him. "I've had time with mine. She knows when to fight and when there is no chance in hell I'm giving in to her."

London picked her battles, but I didn't think this was one she'd argue. She wasn't a fighter, despite the fuckin' battles she'd fought in order to survive. She stood her ground when she needed to and believed in something. But her softness and compassion always came through. I saw it with how she'd treated the homeless, the way she moved, quiet warmth emanating from her.

My cock jerked and I grunted, picking up the plate with the salmon sandwich. "Give me an hour," I said to Deck and Vic. "Then we'll go over what needs to go down tonight."

Deck nodded. Vic didn't do anything, but chugged back his glass of orange juice while leaning against the marble counter.

I made my way out of the kitchen and through the living room when I heard the water running through the pipes above. London was still in the shower? It was a fuck of a long time to be showering.

I strode through the living room, went up the stairs, two at a time, went into the guest room, put the plate on the dresser and continued into the adjoining bathroom.

The air was a shield of fog and it whirled around me when the colder air from the bedroom intermingled with the humid moisture. I shut the door.

I couldn't see her, but I heard her. The soft sobs from somewhere to the right and not in the shower.

I made my way across the bathroom and I found her sitting on the floor, leaning up against the wall in the corner. *Fuck.*

I crouched in front of her, my hands settling on her knees that were bent and pulled close to her body. Her hair was wet and dripped onto her naked shoulders then slid down her skin to soak into the blue cotton towel she wore.

"I never should've run away after…." She stopped and I knew why because it wouldn't have changed the outcome. As Raven, she could've done nothing to help her father. She couldn't even help herself.

"Why did he do it? Why did he take the bullet?" Again, there was no need to answer and I didn't think she wanted me to. These were questions she knew the answers to. He was dying and he wanted to do something he'd been unable to do ever since he became involved with Vault… save his daughter.

My thumb stroked back and forth over her knee while with my other hand reached forward and I wiped the tears on her cheeks with my knuckles. She finally looked at me with her red-rimmed eyes, and my heart, one I thought was so tainted and stained it no longer beat, hurt. It was as if someone were squeezing it so hard that it was in agony.

She lowered her head, her hair covering her face.

"He died knowing you're the strong, beautiful woman he raised you to be. You gave him that. His final wish."

She was quiet for a long time before she raised her head and said, "Thank you."

I reached forward, tucked a few wet strands behind her ear and cupped her cheek, my thumb stroking back and forth. "For what?"

"For caring. About him and me." She rested her hand over mine on her cheek then slid it to her mouth and kissed my palm. "They tried to take that from you, but they didn't get it."

They did. They took parts of me that I'd never get back, but she'd given me the greatest gift. The gift of caring for someone so deeply that it lived and breathed inside you. It was so much more powerful than any pain or conditioning Vault had done to us.

She consumed me and maybe it was dangerous feeling so much for one woman, but it was too late. It had always been too late to stop.

"I want you to take the pain away," she whispered. "For a little while, make me forget."

When I failed to move, she pushed to her feet, her hand in mine. I stood and she guided me back to the bedroom where she dropped the towel and lay down.

I stared at her for several seconds, this remarkable woman who I'd go to the ends of the earth for, who I'd kill for if anyone tried to hurt her. I was confident, never thought twice about doing what I wanted, but seeing her lying naked on the bed, her wet hair splayed out on the pillow, her lips still quivering from crying, I was unsure.

And I was unsure because I didn't want to hurt her and I wasn't sure if this was what she needed right now.

"Kai. Take off your pants," she said.

I raised my brows, with a mild twitch at the corner of my mouth. "And if I don't think this is such a good idea?"

She pushed up on her elbows, which pushed out her breasts and my eyes flickered to them for a second before returning to her face. Fuck, she knew what it would do to me. I had been sleeping with her for five days. Held her. My cock rock hard, but not doing anything about it because she didn't need that part of me. She needed a part I didn't know I had. The one that held her close and soothed while she sobbed herself to sleep.

"You do."

"London—"

She interrupted and she never interrupted me. "If I touch you right now and you're hard, then I know you want me and so I get you to fuck me. If you're not hard, then we can lie here until I get you hard and then you can fuck me."

I grinned, shaking my head and she did, too, but I still saw the pain lingering in her eyes. And I wanted to take that away. I wanted to ease her pain. "No need to touch me to know."

My hands went to my belt and I unbuckled it. It clunked to the floor. My pants soon followed and then I lifted my T-shirt over my head and within seconds, stood naked beside the bed.

Her eyes roamed the length of me, hesitating on my throbbing cock, so I reached down and fisted it. Her gaze tipped to my face. "I get hard just thinking about you, braveheart." I kneeled on the bed then straddled her body. "That four letter word isn't enough for me."

"Why?" she asked, breathless, as I settled between her legs that quickly wrapped around my hips.

I leaned in as if I were about to kiss her then whispered, "Because you're my everything."

Then my mouth met hers.

I'd tasted every inch of her, felt her body quiver around me and heard her moan then cry my name. And I did it twice before I had to get up and meet Deck and the guys.

I leaned over her and leisurely kissed her, my hand slowly gliding down her side to her hip then to her ass where I squeezed.

She moaned and kissed me back, slowly and lazily. Her hand moved up my arm, over my shoulder to the back of my neck where it took a fistful of hair and drew me in deeper.

It was my turn to groan before I pulled back, bringing her with me to a sitting position. "I need to do something."

"I thought you were."

I chuckled. "Mmm, I was, but not the something I need to be doing."

She scrunched her nose and then her face fell as reality leaked its way back inside and I saw the devastation hit her again. She closed her eyes with a ragged sigh.

It was going to be a while before she accepted what had happened to her father. She wouldn't forget, but she'd learn to live with his loss.

I kissed her again then got up, bent, picked up my cargo pants off the floor and my T-shirt. "I'm meeting Dorsey." She swung her legs over the side of the bed, sheet held up to cover her breasts. "He'll tell us the location of the farm if we hand over your father's formula and the drug we confiscated from the lab." I walked into the bathroom and tossed my clothes on the bathroom counter then said, "It going down in three hours."

"Umm, Kai…" I raised my brows at the umm and she half-smiled, rolling her eyes. "I've been looking at the formula in my dad's notes and there are some powerful drugs in there. I think I know why Connor would do whatever they wanted and he probably doesn't even know it."

I leaned my shoulder against the bathroom door and crossed my arms.

"Scopolamine. It's from the seeds of a plant in Colombia."

"Jesus Christ. Devil's breath." Dangerous drug and could be administered pretty much in any form, but the most fucked-up way was just by breathing in the chemically treated seeds that had been made into a powdered substance. Looked like cocaine, but much deadlier.

She nodded. "It steals your consciousness, your free will and your memory of what you've done. He's mixed it with other chemicals though, one being steroids to make Connor feel stronger. I haven't identified them all yet. But Kai, in the form he's using, it's not easy to get. And my dad… he said one component was hard to get."

I stood up straight. "And he would've needed a contact in Colombia to get it for him."

She nodded.

"That's where the fuckin' farm is. That's where he is." Jesus, Colombia.

I stalked toward her, ripped the sheet out of her hand and threw it aside, bent, picked her up, hands under her ass and started carrying her into the bathroom. "You're fuckin' brilliant."

She bit her lip, legs curved around my ass.

"And I need to fuck my brilliant scientist in the shower."

I kicked the door shut and had my way with my girl.

CHAPTER
THIRTY-THREE

Kai

I SAUNTERED INTO THE diner, the bells above the door alerting my presence, although the place was empty, even behind the counter. I'd been here before and we were meeting here because it had excellent food and I was going to eat.

An hour earlier, before Deck and I left with Dr. Westbrook's files for the meet, I'd been heading for the door when London stopped me.

Chess, Tristan, Josh, Tyler, Vic, Georgie and Deck all stood in the foyer as her hand curled around my arm, pulled me to a halt and swung me around. Then her arms came up, hooked my neck, fingers bunched in my hair and she yanked my head down to hers. Then her lips met mine and the whole thing was fuckin' hot.

I never realized how erotic it was kissing a woman. Never did it before London. Never wanted to or cared to. Kissing was personal. It was more than raw, unemotional sex. It held much more power because it connected you in a way that sex didn't. You could fuck a girl and not care, but to me, you couldn't kiss a girl and not give a shit about her.

Maybe I was alone in thinking this way. Guys kissed chicks all the time, knowing they were there only for a quick fuck. But I wasn't like most guys.

I didn't care that everyone was watching her kiss me. Didn't care about anything at the time except her coming to me and kissing me. But when our mouths finally came apart, it was London telling me she loved me and to be careful that hit the hardest. I'd replied. "Always, baby."

I'd never had anyone give a shit if I came back from an assignment. If I lived or died. London gave that to me. London made me feel alive. Her breath was mine. Her heart. Her body. Her mind. All of her was in me and belonged to me. I'd do anything for her and her kissing me, everyone watching and her not caring they were, then me leaving and seeing the tears in my girl's eyes... fuck, that was the greatest gift she could've given me.

Now, I slide into a booth, the red plastic crinkling as I did, the waitress's shoes clinking on the linoleum as she came out of the back and sauntered toward me with a pot of coffee in her hand. Her half-bitten-off fingernails and dry hands passed me a menu.

"Need a moment, handsome?" she asked in a high-pitched voice.

I leaned one arm on the table and smiled up at her. She was in her forties, straw-blonde hair with dark, one-inch roots showing and styled in a bob that made her face appear rounder than it was. She wore too much makeup and there was a red smudge on her front tooth from her lipstick she had probably just re-applied when I walked in and no one was behind the counter.

"Been here before and know the omelet is good. Greek." The bell went and she looked over her shoulder. I didn't. I knew it was Dorsey because I'd positioned myself at a window where I could clearly see cars pulling up and a limo had ten seconds ago. I flipped over the coffee cup on the opposite side of the table. "Another coffee, darling." I winked and she cocked her hip smiling, a slight blush creeping into her cheeks.

"Sure thing, handsome."

Dorsey's dress shoes tapped as he treaded toward me and I got a lot from that. Even. Steady. Unconcerned. Which meant he was pretty damn confident. But then so was I. More so now that I had an idea where the farm was. Tyler and Vic were currently researching every known big-time drug dealer in Colombia who had been known to have Devil's breath.

The waitress moved away as Dorsey slid into the booth, his one hand immediately wrapping around the coffee mug. It was a crutch, a subtle sign of insecurity that had me inwardly smiling.

Dorsey had two men in suits standing at the car, both with their arms crossed and watching through the window. He also had a man who came in the door behind him and sat on a swivel stool at the counter. Yeah, he was insecure, as he should be. He knew how I was trained and what I was capable of.

I skipped the pleasantries as I sat back, my arm resting on the back of the seat. "Ernie?"

Dorsey took a sip of coffee then nodded. "In the back of the limo." I didn't let the relief show. He put his mug down and took a serviette from underneath the cutlery and dabbed his thin lips.

He wore a suit with over-priced cuff links glittering like a beacon, and a tie, silverfish grey with a light striping and done up tight to his neck. I never wore a tie. Hated them for the simple reason that a tie was a noose around your neck and could easily kill you in the right hands. I didn't need my wire when a man wore a fuckin' tie.

Dorsey was handsome enough for mid-sixties, dignified appearance with sharp features and short, salt and pepper hair. He didn't have an issue getting the girls he wanted and according to what I knew about him, he liked brunettes, tall, and a quarter his age.

"He'll die if he doesn't get the drug." He was talking about Connor. "Hand him over and he'll live."

"Not my call."

His brows rose. "Suddenly, you aren't calling the shots? Interesting. And a step down for you."

I grinned. "I call it a vacation."

He laughed and it sounded like the low roar of a motorboat starting up. "I always liked you, Kai. Thought your mother gave you too much rein, especially with the situation concerning the girl."

"You're under the assumption I have reins, Dorsey." I lowered my voice. "I don't."

The waitress slid my omelet and hash browns in front of me. "Can I get you anything else?"

"No. That's good, thanks."

"Sir, anything for you?" she asked Dorsey.

"No," he replied and the waitress moved off. "You were asked to bring her in. You hid her away in a house no one knew about." He paused when I didn't say anything because there was nothing to say. I did exactly that. Mother found out and shared the info with Dorsey. "And then you burnt it down."

I dug into my omelet with my fork, the cheese, tomato and olive leaking out the sides. "You care what I did to my house?"

"I found it ironic, actually," Dorsey said. "Seems fire follows the girl around."

I'd been trained for shit like this. How to keep my cool when I wanted to punch my fist through his chest and rip out his heart. He knew about the fire at London's house at university when I dragged her out, half-conscious. He fuckin' knew and I was betting I knew why.... He was responsible.

I shrugged and took another bite. "We done talking about bullshit? I'd like to enjoy my meal without you."

Dorsey shook his head. "The farm wasn't my idea. It was your mother's originally."

I knew that. Dorsey wouldn't like paying money out to feed kids and farm handlers for years before seeing any results. No, it would be someone much more patient who saw the long-term rewards.

He continued, "He thinks he runs this organization ever since he took over the farm. Your mother started it in Afghanistan, but when that kid escaped," *Tristan*, "he took it over. Gave him more control and he uses the kids for his own purpose." He tilted closer, lowering his voice, not sure why when no one else was around. The waitress was busy chatting up his bodyguard who wasn't paying attention to anything she said. "The drug is the new direction. Less time wasted and more control."

By the look of Connor right now, control was the wrong word. I reached in my front jeans pocket and slid the USB across the table toward him. "Do whatever you want with it. I don't give a fuck, but I want the farm and who runs it."

He nodded to his bodyguard who came over, picked up the flash drive then went back to the counter and plugged it into a small laptop he had on the counter. Dorsey gestured to the car and one of the guys opened the back door and Ernie staggered out. Another guy followed him and he didn't look too willing. Well, he was, but he was a quivering mess of a five-foot nothing skeleton.

My eyes went back to Ernie. Christ. He was beaten to a fuckin' pulp and had a bandage on his right hand. I barely glanced at him though and took another bite of my omelet.

"Location of the farm?" I kept my eyes on the guards, on their hands and on Dorsey's movements. If he were going to do anything, it would be now.

The bell dinged and the quivering mess guy came in and stood beside the bodyguard and looked at the laptop. Dorsey's eyes were on him. It would've been a sweet-ass time to reach under the table and slice across his femoral artery, but murder in a public joint caused problems. Dorsey knew that, too.

He turned back to me. "I could walk away right now."

I laughed. "You could. But you wouldn't make it to the car."

His eyes shifted around the diner, but he'd never see him. Deck was good at what he did, almost as good as me. Josh was the better sniper, but I didn't know him enough to use him as back up. Deck I'd had my eyes on for years.

"Killing me would end your chances of finding the farm."

I stabbed a few hash browns and put them in my mouth, taking my time answering. "Maybe. But I was always fond of killing assholes. And you're at the top of the list."

He stiffened, the grip on his mug tightening and his brows twitching. "You'll never find it and one word from me, he'll come after the piece-of-ass scientist you're so fond of."

I pushed my plate aside, leaned forward and lowered my voice. "Mention my girl again and my knife is cutting off your dick." He flinched, but the asshole had the nerve to sneer. "Then... I'll shove it down your throat until you choke on it."

He did have the smarts not to say anything more about London.

From the corner of my eye, the quivering five-foot nothing guy nodded to Dorsey. The bodyguard let go of his arm and he fucked off out of the restaurant. "Now, are you going to tell me the name of the Colombian who oversees the farm?"

Dorsey's eyes widened.

I smirked. "Yes, I know it's in Colombia."

"Then why meet me?"

He shifted in his seat and his eyes blinked more than usual. He knew his power had been stripped away.

"Because it takes time to find out his name and I don't like wasting time. I have a plane ready to take me to Colombia tomorrow."

"If I tell you, you can kill me the second I do."

I chuckled. "Yes. But you know me better than that, Dorsey. A messy, public killing is your specialty, not mine." I leaned forward lowering my voice. "Name."

"Moreno. Carlos Moreno. But I don't know where the farm is. None of us have ever been there, but he lives in Medellin."

I didn't need anything more, so I tossed a hundred on the table and got up.

"You'll take him out?" Dorsey said before I was five feet from the table.

"Yeah, I'll take him out."

"How long before it's done?" he stuttered and it really didn't suit him, but I knew why. He was scared of Moreno and he had a good reason to be. I knew the name and he was a drug lord with connections and enough money to pay off anyone looking at his illegal activities.

I kept walking. "Thanks, darling," I said to the waitress.

"You're welcome, handsome." She smiled and the lipstick on her front tooth was gone.

I pulled out my cell and typed a text to Deck.

Ernie?

He texted back.

Safe.

I walked outside, the cool air doing nothing for the internal heat radiating through me. Dorsey was slime. He wanted me to do his dirty work dealing with Moreno and he'd sit back on his throne, probably sell the drug or use it. Whichever way he went, it was about making a shitload of money.

Not happening.

I texted,

Take him out.

There was no need for him to reply and I folded into my car and drove away. As I turned the corner, I caught a glimpse of Dorsey getting into his limo.

Then a loud boom.

The ground vibrated and fire and smoke billowed into the air.

CHAPTER
THIRTY-FOUR

Connor

A BLIND RAGE RIPPED through my insides like an out-of-control inferno, tiny red-hot pinpricks piercing me over and over again.

I couldn't fuckin' escape it.

The handcuffs trapping me to the pipe cut into my wrist as I fought to get free. Blood dripped off the tips of my fingers from the damage I'd done to my wrist. The pain was nothing compared to the burning.

My flesh was melting. My reality was messed up and I was choking on the tightness in my chest; it was strangling me.

If I'd been given a knife, I was pretty sure I'd cut off my own hand to escape. My mind was so fucked up that I wouldn't have felt anything. I'd do it because it was better than being contained again, better than burning alive.

The clash inside me was destroying the coolness I'd been living in for years. Although, lived was the wrong word. I didn't live. I existed.

I was buried beneath a sea of darkness. I no longer knew who I was or what the fuck I was doing. I had no memories. Each day it was like they'd been blacked out. Some days I started to catch glimpses of what I was doing and then I disappeared again.

I never woke up. Days. Weeks. Months. I had no idea what I did or how long it'd been.

But since I'd been here, flashes of memories from my past hit me. They came and went like snapshots. It fucked with my head because I didn't know if they were real or not. It was easier in the dark. The darkness didn't hurt.

But each day was worse. My head, a jumbled mess of paint splatters, spread out as if they were soaking into my burning skin.

The rage was so powerful that it splintered my insides. I craved something and I didn't know what. I knew I was supposed to take…. They told me to take…. I had orders. I followed orders but now I couldn't.

"FUUCCKK!"

I yanked on the handcuffs so hard that a low agonizing sound tore from my throat at the pain. My hand hung limp. I'd snapped the bone.

The door opened.

I glared in the direction, the pain forgotten as I watched.

"Shit," a man said as he entered the room. "Connor. Jesus."

I racked my brain, recognizing the voice, but unable to find where it fit. I hated being trapped, defenseless against whatever was happening to my body. It was like I'd been dead for years and suddenly, I was waking up, but only pieces of me were.

My eyes darted to the girl with pink streaks in her hair who followed in after the guy with the gun on his hip. An overwhelming sense of… something… plowed into me. I shook my head trying to clear the fogginess, but all it did was send shards of pain through me. Pain. I'd been numb to it for years and I wanted that back. Cool. Numb. No memories. Just do what I was told to, but I couldn't even remember that.

"It's the withdrawal. Maybe he needs another pill?" Another girl stood in the doorway behind the girl with the pink streaks. "He looks like he's burning with fever. He needs to be cooled down."

"How the fuck can we do that?" the guy said. He crouched and rolled a water bottle toward me. Smart. My legs were free and I could easily break his neck if he came too close.

"Deck and Kai should be back soon and then we can give him a pill." I had no idea who the girl was. Never seen her before.

But the name Deck.... Fuck, Deck. Deck. I shut my eyes and my stomach rolled as the memory tried to bust through the barrier in my mind. I growled low in my throat as it pounded and pounded, but nothing broke.

"You sure this is a good idea, Georgie?" the guy asked.

The girl with the pink streaks answered. "Nope, I'm not sure, cupcake. But if there's a chance he'll remember something of who he was...then it's worth it."

"He can't have the pill then," the other girl stated. "He has no idea what he's doing when he takes it and he has no memory of what he did. As the drug wears off, he'll start to remember the present and the past. Although, I don't know if he will remember what he's been doing for the years he's been on it."

"He could kill a few people and not even know it?" the guy asked.

The girl nodded. "Devil's breath makes someone do whatever they're told. But my feeling is he's been conditioned to do whatever a particular someone tells him."

"Kai's mother, maybe? A goddamn deadly machine," the guy said.

I watched pinkie move across the room and my body stilled. It was the way her shoulders were held, the way her hips swayed, the way her steps were quiet and careful. It was a combination of everything that sent the blunt agonizing lash down on me.

I fell to my knees, my one free hand holding my head. I growled a low, deep scream as my body fought against letting whatever it was in.

"Connor!" Footsteps ran toward me.

"Georgie. No."

I glanced up as the pain faded and saw the guy grab her around the waist and haul her back.

She struggled in his arms, which pissed me off and I didn't know why. I felt... protective of her.

"Tyler. London. Out," a deep voice ordered from the doorway. "Georgie. I told you to stay the fuck out of here."

The guy, Tyler, still had Georgie in his grasp, but he put his hands up and let her go then he and the other girl left, leaving the door ajar.

"Deck."

I stiffened as she said his name. It was so familiar, yet it was like trying to lasso a dark cloud. My mind failed time and again to latch on to any reason why I'd know him. No, I did know him. I knew her, too. But my mind fought me every step.

She held out a small leather-bound book and my stomach cramped. I clenched my jaw as the memory of the sound of the pages turning flicked across my mind, but it wasn't a gentle flicking. It was so loud I wanted to tear out my eardrums. A pen scribbling across the pages. My pen. My hand.

"We've found nothing in it, but maybe we weren't meant to. Maybe it's just what it is, his thoughts." Her back was to me as she walked confidently toward Deck still in the doorway. "What if I read it to him?"

"He's not even lucid, babe."

She glanced at me and I glared back. "London says as the drug wears off, he should start to remember things from his past. It can't hurt."

I wasn't so sure about that. I hurt with her being anywhere near me and I hurt hearing her voice and I hurt every second they kept me here.

The guy, Deck, stared at me and I stared back. I took several deep breaths and calmed the anger before I smiled. "I'm going to fuckin' kill you."

Georgie gasped.

Deck stepped toward her and wrapped his arm around her abdomen, dragging her back against his chest. My eyes narrowed as uneasiness shifted through me. Why did I give a shit whether he was holding her close to him?

Ice cream.

The clank of a spoon as it settled in the bowl before it slid across a table toward her. The girl. She sat with her legs crossed at a kitchen table and he was there, the commando guy, and he gave her the bowl of ice cream, a soft, gentle look in his eyes that didn't match the commando who stood in the room now.

My breath quickened as the memory filtered through the burning. Through the pain. Through the rage. Then it was gone and darkness.

"Read it, babe," he said as he guided her over to a chair on the opposite side of the room. He sat and pulled her into his lap. She flicked open the book and read.

My torture began.

CHAPTER
THIRTY-FIVE

London

I RAN DOWN THE hall, my heart racing, nerves shooting off like misfiring electrical wires. I pushed open the guest room door and he was standing with his back to me, his shirt off and the muscles flexing as he placed it on the hanger then reached to hook it on the metal bar in the closet.

I knew he knew I was there because his head slightly turned in my direction, not enough to look at me, but as if he were listening. I loved that about him, so perceptive to everything around him. It settled a deep calming blanket over me.

"You going to stare at my back or come in and shut the door so I can fuck you?"

My breath hitched and my belly flipped. He closed the closet doors and, still, without looking at me, he undid his belt buckle then I heard the zipper.

I shut the bedroom door.

"It was okay? You're okay?" He was standing, no blood that I could see, but I still had to ask.

His pants fell to the floor, his boxer-briefs following. He stepped out of them and only then did he turn to face me.

And when he did, every worry dissipated because he had that twinkle in his eyes and that cocky grin pulling at his mouth.

"Were you worried, braveheart?" He didn't wait for a reply as he prowled toward me. And it *was* a prowl, his muscles contracting with every step. "I like that you were concerned for my wellbeing."

I was still trying to catch my breath when he cupped my chin and tilted his head down and mine up. "Never had that." His thumb stroked back and forth over the dip in my chin. "You doing okay?"

He'd just met a dangerous man who could have killed him, probably wanted to, and Kai was concerned about me. I melted. "I'm glad you're back."

"Not what I asked." His brows rose as he waited for my answer.

"Okay, well, not really." I tried to look down, but he wouldn't allow me to pull my gaze from his. "But better now that you're back." His naked body was so close to mine the heat radiated off him and sank into me. "Guess I'm not feeling too brave right now. With my dad dying and you leaving, I was so scared you wouldn't come back. I hated that feeling. It's like I'm suffocating. Like my lungs aren't getting enough oxygen until I see you again. It's debilitating and I don't like feeling that way. I want to be strong like you."

His knuckles stroked down the side of my face. "Baby, don't you know, I feel that, too." I melted some more. "You're brave as hell. You're a survivor. And being scared doesn't mean you're weak. It means you're alive. It means you care." His other arm slid over my shoulder to the back of my neck where it settled. "Don't ever lose that. It's part of the reason why I had to have you."

He dipped his head forward and lightly kissed my lips. It was barely a touch and made my belly drop at the anticipation for more. "I want to go home, Kai. One day. Back to your house. I liked it there. I liked that everywhere I touched, I knew your hands were on it. Will we get that one day?"

"No," he answered.

I frowned, body tensing. "Why?"

"When I came back and you were gone, I burned it." I gasped. He hadn't told me that.

Kai, with his hands on my hips, backed me into the wall then kissed the side of my neck. "Didn't know at the time if it was compromised or not, but I couldn't take the chance."

"But you built it."

"Yeah, baby." His hands ran down my arms, then latched onto my wrists and brought them up above my head. "I'll build another. For us."

He nuzzled my neck. "Kai?"

"Babe, can we talk later? I want to fuck you right now." He ground his hard cock into me and I moaned, closing my eyes.

"But…." I shut up when he raised his head and looked at me. It was a warning look. It was the 'be quiet and let me fuck you' look. It was a look I was going to obey because I wanted him to fuck me, and knowing Kai, if I didn't, he'd walk away and let me suffer wanting him for hours. So, my question on whether I could help him build a house would wait.

That was when his mouth claimed mine and there was nothing gentle about it. This was Kai making it clear that I was his.

CHAPTER
THIRTY-SIX

Kai

LONDON FROZE AND gasped. "Ernie?"

We were walking into the dining room where the guys were gathered discussing the next move. London and I had slept in, something I never did, but after meeting Dorsey and staying up half the night with my cock in my girl, and my tongue tasting her pussy, I'd slept in.

I quirked a half-smile when I saw Ernie's face drop then red inflame his cheeks. "Hey, beautiful."

After spending a year watching London, another two years helping me find her, it was obvious Ernie was attached to her. He'd used that four-letter word a few times, too, when talking about her. I knew he saw her like a daughter, and it fuckin' killed him to see her so broken because he knew her before Raven. He knew her smile, her kindness, her generosity. Only a few would take the time to chat with a homeless guy and give him coffee and breakfast every morning. It also killed him that he'd been lying about being a homeless guy.

She looked up at me then back at Ernie. "Ernie. I don't understand." Her eyes came back to me. "You know him?"

"After the fire, I hired him to watch you. He's an ex-Navy SEAL. Knows what he's doing and had eyes on you when he could."

"You had Ernie watching me?"

I nodded.

Her eyes shot to Ernie again. "You owe me years' worth of coffees and croissants."

Then she stepped from my arm and ran for Ernie, who was looking rather uncomfortable and guilty. Tyler, who was beside him, stepped away with an amused look on his face.

She stopped a foot from Ernie then threw her arms around him. It took a second before his arms found their way around her and he hugged her back, lightly lifting her off her feet when he did it.

"Where have you been? How have you—" She jerked as his hands slid down her arms and she noticed his bandaged hand, minus a finger. "Oh, my God. What happened?"

Ernie looked at me and shrugged. It was up to him if he cared to share what Dorsey had done. London had been through hell, but I'd never lied to her. If she asked me, I'd tell her the truth.

Ernie didn't like bullshit. He was pretty straight up, so he shared. "Dorsey. Decided to feed a snack to his pet shark." London's mouth gaped, her hand going to his chest. He put his overtop. "Thought he'd take my trigger finger. Fucker, picked the wrong hand. I'm a lefty." He chuckled.

London didn't. Instead, she pulled him into her arms again. I saw her whisper something, but I didn't know what. I did see Ernie's cheeks flush again.

Georgie and Chess sauntered in carrying mugs and a coffee pot. They set them down on the dining room table. Georgie then went to Deck, and Chess to the laptop where she started scrolling. Tristan, who'd been lounging against the windowsill, frowned and strode over to her, his arm snaking around her waist and pulling her up against his side.

She ignored him as her fingers typed furiously across the keyboard. "The media says the car explosion was an accident."

"I told you I'd make it happen," Deck said.

"Oh, Deck *always* makes it happen," Georgie proclaimed, eyes flickering to his crotch.

Chess looked up from the computer screen and laughed. She stopped abruptly when she glanced at Tristan. The fuckin' guy was staring at her like he wanted to eat her alive.

London moved in to me and I settled my hand on the back of her neck before I said, "With Mother and now Dorsey dead, proclaimed accident or not, Moreno will have his guard up."

"Colombia," Josh muttered. "He's careful. Word is you can't even get a sniper on him."

"Why did he need Vault?" Deck asked, his leg half-hitched up on the edge of the table. "His drug business is solid. Doesn't need contacts, he already has them."

"But he needs drugs smuggled," I said.

"Jesus Christ, the kids," Tyler said. "He's using fuckin' kids to get the shit over the border."

"That's why the farm was moved to Colombia after you escaped." I chin-lifted to Tristan. "I'm betting he paid my mother and Dorsey a percentage. He had his pick of kids from the farm to use for his smuggling, and Vault had a place to train killers."

"But Dorsey wanted out," Deck said.

"Men don't like other men having more power," Georgie said. "Not greedy meatloaves like those guys."

"We need to get the kids out before he moves them." Chess closed the laptop. "We have to go in now."

This was where shit wasn't going to be easy. We were leaving today, but not all of us.

Tristan, I realized, had fuckin' balls because he didn't make it sweet. He just told Chess what was happening. "You're going to Greece."

Chess scowled. "Excuse me?"

304

I was getting to like Tristan, despite his arrogance. He wouldn't take shit from my sister and my sister was going to be a handful. Her heart had always been her weakness and she'd go down to Colombia and run into a fray of bullets in order to help those kids.

Deck and I discussed it. Brought Tristan in and discussed it, then decided on a location. Tristan wasn't a mark for Moreno, so his house in Greece was ideal. Fuck, no place was ideal, but it was as ideal as we were getting in this situation.

"You heard me," Tristan said calmly.

"Tristan," my sister retorted. "Don't think for a second you have the right to tell me what I can and cannot do."

Georgie started to say something when Deck sent her a warning look that had her snapping her mouth shut and frowning.

"You're not going near this shit. It's fuckin' Colombia," Tristan growled.

"This is so not happening." Chess crossed her arms, stance wide, defensive and ready to take on the CEO. He, of course, looked unconcerned that she was pissed off or that she'd be pissed for a very long time.

"My plane is scheduled to leave in two hours." And he was smart to leave it to the last second to tell her. "We're leaving for the airport in ten."

"WHAT?" she yelled. "Tristan. No." She looked around the room as if for help, then settled on London.

London shifted uncomfortably beside me and then her eyes were on me. "Kai?"

"Moreno will come after us with everything he has when we go after the farm. He won't take a hit lightly." I glanced at Deck and he gave me a subtle nod. "Chess, London and Georgie go to Greece. Josh will go with. Along with Connor who will be sedated for the trip." I addressed London, "I need you to continue weaning him off the drug."

Chess marched from the room. Tristan wasn't far behind.

"Deck—," Georgie started, but was cut off as he interrupted.

"Not having you near this any longer." Deck looked unconcerned that Georgie was fuming, her eyes glaring, her cheeks heated and red.

"I can help, damn it. Kai, tell him."

I shrugged. "No choice. I said I'd support him on this, Georgie."

Her mouth dropped open and I knew why. I never called her Georgie. She'd always been Chaos, but shit had changed. She was Deck's girl now and I didn't work for Vault. This was about respect and I had it for Deck.

"What? You trained me. You made me into *Chaos* and I know what I'm doing. I can help."

"Maybe," I said. "But I don't call the shots. Not when it comes to you. Not anymore."

Her eyes darted back to Deck. "You're really doing this?"

He nodded and his scowl deepened, but his gesture contradicted that when he tucked her hair behind her ear and said in a quiet, calm voice. "Need you safe, baby. And I need you to do this for me. I can't do my job if I'm worried about you." She opened her mouth, but he wasn't done yet. "You could be the best assassin in the world and I'd still send you to Greece. This isn't about what you're capable of, babe. This is about letting me protect you."

London moved in closer to me, and when I glanced down at her face I caught the tear slipping down her cheek to drip off her chin.

I saw the moment Georgie gave in to him when her shoulders slumped and she sighed. Then she said, "Looks like you only have ten minutes to rock my world, sweetpea."

Deck snorted while scowling, but his lip twitched as he snagged her hand and pulled her from the room.

London had yet to say anything about going to Greece and I knew why. She understood why this had to happen this way because she'd been immersed in bad shit. No matter how brave and strong she was or pretended to be, she needed to be far from this.

"You good?" I asked her.

She stood on her tiptoes and lightly kissed my lips. "I don't want to go to Colombia, and I don't want you to either. But I know you have to do this." Her hand slid down the front of my chest, over the scars that she'd kissed and licked last night. "You'll come back to me?"

"Told you right from the beginning I'd never lie to you, so I'm not starting now. Can't promise that. But I'm good at what I do, so yeah, I expect I will."

Took her a bit, but then she smiled and I put my hand on the small of her back to guide her toward the door. "Ernie, give me ten."

"Later, London," Ernie said.

She suddenly bolted from my arms and ran to Ernie, throwing herself into his. I heard his oomph as he staggered back a step. I grinned. Ernie laughed.

"Be careful. Love you."

She kissed him on the cheek and came back to me. I linked our hands and started heading for the stairs when I heard the rush of water draining through the pipes.

She didn't notice, nor did Tyler and Josh who were arguing over whether it was cool to fuck a chick on the first date. Tyler thought it was. Josh didn't.

"What is it?" London asked, her hand on my arm.

It could've been someone showering, but it wasn't a gentle flow of water. This sounded too powerful like—"Fuck. Connor."

Jesus Christ, he broke the fuckin' pipe he was cuffed to.

"Tyler," I shouted. "Take her. Josh, get Deck. Ernie, side door. Connor's free." I made certain Tyler had London before I took off for the basement. I heard Josh running up the stairs yelling for Deck, and a door slam. Ernie headed for the side door. The shattering of glass breaking solidified that we were too late.

I busted through the basement door into the room he'd been in and dove for the window. My hand grazed his ankle, but he was too quick and slipped from my grasp.

"Connor. Shit. You need the drug."

The bastard had the nerve to turn and crouch before the basement window and I saw the journal Deck had shown me on the plane, clutched tightly in his grip. Did he remember? Why the hell would he take that?

"Get Georgie clear of this." Fuck, he remembered her. He jerked his eyes to the right and I knew it had to be one of the guys coming out the front door. I slowly withdrew my knife.

"Connor," Deck yelled. "Damn it, Riot."

Connor's brows lowered over his eyes for a second as if he was in pain. I took the opportunity of his distraction and threw my knife, not to kill him, but to stop him before he killed himself. It pierced his upper thigh where the bullet wound had been, but he didn't even flinch. Instead, he glanced at me, smiled, then yanked the knife from his thigh and wiped the blood on his pants leg.

His wild eyes went from me to the direction of Deck then back to me. "The girl. Where is she?"

"What girl? Who are you referring to?" I asked.

"Riot." Deck's voice was closer.

Connor waved the journal. "She's not in here. Where the fuck is she?" His voice was rough and sweat dripped down his face. The guy looked as if he was burning up with fever.

I knew there were pages ripped out. Had he written about some girl? Deck said there were missing pages. But why would pages be ripped out?

"We'll find her," I said to pacify him.

He grabbed his hair with one hand, clenching his jaw as if he was in pain. "He has her. Fuck. I can't remember." His eyes narrowed and darkened and he looked murderous. "Catalina."

I heard Deck inching closer. I slowly pulled a knife from my boot, but Connor must have noticed because his body tensed.

"Deck. Now."

But it was too late.

Connor was gone.

CHAPTER
THIRTY-SEVEN

Medellin, Colombia.

Kai

You okay?

It was a text message from London. They'd arrived in Greece two days earlier and were safe at Tristan's place. According to London's text message when they first arrived, it was over the top extravagant. She sent me a pic of the pool overlooking the edge of a cliff, but it wasn't the pic I wanted. I wanted the bedroom where she'd be sleeping.

I got that later.

Yeah, baby. But I won't be able to contact you for a bit.

Okay.

She did a cute heart and an xxx. I'd never had that and I seriously liked it.

London was stronger than she'd ever been. There was no argument about me leaving, about her leaving, about us being separated. She knew this had to happen and she was giving me what I needed.

She texted again.

Love you. Be careful.

Always, London.

That had a double meaning and I knew she'd get that. I'd always love her and I'd always be careful.

I tucked my phone in my pocket as Tyler lowered his and said, "Got info on Catalina Moreno," Tyler said. "Moreno married her at age twenty and word is, it wasn't by choice."

Connor was going after Catalina. The question was why? And did he remember enough to know where she was? And who she was?

Deck snorted, shaking his head with disgust. "Family?"

Tyler sighed. "None left. She was payment. The rest of her family killed, a brother, mother and father. Father had worked for Moreno, flew one of his planes back and forth to Miami, drug trafficking route. Probably stole from him, lost a shipment, who the fuck knows. But his family paid for whatever went down. Catalina lives because she's beautiful and according to my contact, Moreno likes beautiful things."

I crossed my arms while leaning against the old wooden door of the house we were holed up in while waiting for Tyler's contact to arrive.

"Fuck." I'd seen that shit, saw it those two years I'd searched for London. Still, no matter how many times you saw girls forced into prostitution, or marriages, you never became accustomed to it.

Tyler continued, "So Connor met her. Where? When? Shit, it could've been last month or ten years ago before he was taken."

I shook my head. "He had the journal in his hand when he escaped the house. He gestured to it when he asked where she was. He had to have met her before he was taken by Vault and those pages were about her."

"His head is also seriously fucked," Vic stated.

True. His memory was screwed up from the drug and we didn't know what the hell was going on with him or even if he was still alive.

There was a light tap on the door and I pushed away, my hand on my knife. I heard the men behind me do the same. Weapons ready.

I cracked it open. A small, robust man, early forties, dark skin, and a heavily wrinkled brow as if he frowned too much, stood with his hat in his hands while he nervously shifted his feet. I grabbed his arm and hauled him inside.

Tyler had contacted an acquaintance of his who lived in Medellin, Colombia. This acquaintance had known Tyler's father who had been a DEA agent. Tyler's father spent a lot of time down in Colombia, talked about it to Tyler when he was growing up. It was why Tyler had joined the army.

"Moreno? The kids?" I asked.

"*Si. Si.*" He nodded several times.

Tyler rose to his feet, walked over and slapped the guy on the back, "Juan. Good to finally meet you. My father speaks well of you." Tyler switched to Spanish, speaking it fluently. The man responded, although he stammered, obviously either scared of us or scared of what Moreno would do to his family if he found out Juan was being a snitch.

But if he gave us what we needed, then he and his wife and daughter would be looked after. Deck had strings, but they weren't like mine. They were on the right side of the law and he'd organized to safely get Juan and his family out of Colombia.

Tyler translated what they were talking about. "Juan here delivers food twice a week to one of Moreno's buildings. He says last week there were sixteen kids and twenty watchdogs with assault rifles. But yesterday Juan was told not to bring food."

"They're moving," I said.

Tyler nodded. "It's been the same routine for the last three years he has supplied them. Every Tuesday and Friday, never missed a day."

"Need to make our move now." Vic started to gather up his gear as did Ernie. Tristan shut down the computer and packed it up.

"He knows we're coming," Deck said. "He gets those kids into the jungle, we'll never find them. No time for sneak and peek. We go in locked and loaded."

The kids were most important, but Moreno wouldn't give a shit about losing sixteen kids when he could pick up twenty more. Our plan was to hit it hard and get the kids out while Tristan and Ernie had eyes on Moreno's house and his movements. Because he'd make a move the second he heard his farm was being taken out.

"We don't leave Colombia until he's dead," I stated.

The men nodded. We were all in agreement on this. Moreno was too dangerous alive knowing we were after him. Vault's foundation was crumbling, but it hadn't fallen and Moreno was a building block we had to crush fast before he found others to replace my mother and Dorsey.

I walked over to my knapsack, unzipped it, and then pulled out a wad of cash. Ten grand. It was more than this man probably saw in his lifetime. "Half now. Half when you show us where." I tossed him the money and his mouth gaped then produced a smile, revealing his crooked teeth.

Tyler translated what I said. He'd show us the location of the building. Then he'd take his family to a disclosed location where Deck's contact was waiting to get them out.

"*Si. Si.*"

Tyler spoke to him a little more in Spanish and then slapped him on the back again.

"Let's roll," Deck ordered.

I wasn't used to working with other men on a job. Ernie was it and that had strictly been while searching for London, never anything to do with Vault missions.

Now I had Deck, Vic, Tyler, Ernie, and Tristan, who surprisingly knew how to handle a gun and a knife. But it made sense; he had spent years at the farm before Chess helped him escape.

The Moreno Cartel had a number of 'jungle labs' for his cocaine operation, but according to Tyler's contact, Juan, there was a building owned by Moreno a mile from his extravagant property where he resided.

Juan took us to a rooftop of an abandoned apartment building and pointed to the west across an alley. It was obvious which one he was pointing to as it had barbwire above the eight-foot brick walls. It looked like a fuckin' prison.

"Fuck." I strode to the edge of the building, eyes on 'the farm.' Hell happened in that place. Darkness for days. Food deprivation. The pit. Torture techniques used to make certain we didn't break if we were caught during a mission. If we failed or weren't good enough, we were dead.

And my own mother started it. Sacrificed her kids.

Tyler was speaking quickly in Spanish and Juan nodded frequently. I had no idea what they were saying but I caught the odd word.

Deck and his men didn't fuck around and, on the flight over in Deck's plane, which was a cargo plane, we'd discussed all outcomes and who took lead on what. We'd had a blueprint of the building we knew belonged to Moreno, but couldn't confirm it until Juan. Now, we had confirmation.

Tyler shook Juan's hand. "Good man, Juan."

I opened my bag and passed him another ten grand and Juan smiled then took off.

"Not sure which is worse, back in the dry heat of Afghanistan or this sticky, humid shit," Tyler said as he ran his hand across his damp brow. "Thinking I like sand right about now."

"You might think differently sitting in a pit in the dry heat," Tristan muttered.

My eyes locked with his and there was a mutual respect gained between us. Tristan had spent years at the farm in Afghanistan. He knew what it was like and instead of burying what happened to him, he fuckin' uprooted it by spending his life making something of himself

313

in order to get Chess and shut Vault down.

Had a hard time respecting any man, but I was beginning to respect every one of them. I was beginning to give a shit about them, too.

"We make our move now. Not dusk," I ordered and brows lifted, all eyes shifting to me. "Moreno isn't going to give a shit about the kids even if they've been conditioned for years. He cares about how he looks to others. We take his farm, it damages his pride and makes him look vulnerable. That's what we play on."

"Agreed," Vic said. He crouched at the side of the building, his binoculars out as he surveyed the yard. "Give me an hour for habits." He was looking for vulnerable spots, finding the habits of the watchdogs in the compound.

Ernie was talking to Tristan and they were putting on their headsets. Ernie was good. He knew what this op entailed and what would happen if it went south.

Deck offloaded his gear. "Okay,"—he glanced at his watch—"two hours."

Tyler dropped his bag and took out his laptop and powered it on.

I stared at the building, and despite the heat, the cold wash of familiarity of this place hit me. "I can tell you where they will be the second the watchdogs radio trouble." Tyler stopped typing. "I know every inch of that place." I was sixteen when the farm moved here, so I spent two years here before I was assigned to Georgie.

There was silence for a few seconds. Then I turned, and Deck chin-lifted to me and started walking away from the group. I followed.

"You going to be solid?" he asked.

I stiffened, brows rising at his question, but I knew where it came from. Bad shit… really bad shit happened here. "I'm solid."

Deck nodded, his brows low as he continued to walk until we reached the opposite side of the building. "Don't trust you, Kai, and my men are going into this without much intel. And we are because there are kids involved and losing them isn't an option. Moreno living isn't an option." His stance was wide as he met my eyes, unflinching and direct. "You have anything to share, do it now."

Deck had men who had his back because he gave a shit. It was the complete opposite as to what I was accustomed. Operatives from Vault did missions on their own and we didn't care about one another because we were conditioned not to care. Getting an assignment or mission done took precedence over all else—even lives.

And that sat heavily on me. It rubbed me wrong and it was wrong.

But I did have something to share. "London." Deck nodded. "Anything happens to me, make sure she stays safe."

His scowl deepened. "Everyone gets out alive. You can look after your own fuckin' woman." He slapped me on the back and it was a surprising gesture coming from Deck. "Don't like you, Kai, but I get you now. So, I'll let you live and I'll have your back."

The corners of my lips curved up. "No invites to Sunday brunches at your place?"

Deck huffed. "Fuck, no."

Vic took out the two guys on the roof with his sniper rifle before we went in. Then he shot the grappling hook onto the roof with the crossbow and within seconds, we zip-lined onto the roof of the compound. Since it was daylight, we had no cover and no cover was shit, because we were visible to two guards.

Tyler and Vic unsnapped and dropped before we hit the roof and each took one out. We went in from this position because Vic said they were lazy fuckers who smoked too much and hadn't bothered to look up in the hour he'd been watching the compound.

"Landed," Deck said into his headset.

Vic responded, "Clear."

Tyler repeated, "Clear."

Deck and I kept low and made our way to the north side of the roof. I had the rope out and grapple hooked within seconds before I rappelled over the side. I hit the ground and had my knife in the side of the guard's throat before his finger flicked on the trigger of his rifle.

"Clear," I stated and Deck rappelled down and quietly landed beside me. I dragged the body in through the door and dumped it in the first door on the left, which was a classroom.

"I'm in," Vic said. He was coming in from the south while Tyler had eyes on the front.

"North clear," Deck said.

Dimly lit hallways, damp musty smell, and fuck-as-all hot with no circulation. I shook my head as the familiar smells hit me and I staggered, placing my hand on the wall. I'd been compliant by the time I was moved here, but the pain hadn't stopped.

I'd been dragged down this hallway, the bottoms of my feet bruised, and then beaten until I couldn't walk.

"Kai." I swung around as a hand came down on my shoulder. I had my knife to Deck's throat within a millisecond. Deck. Fuck. Not a handler.

"Shit." I shoved away from him, but he didn't seem concerned that I'd had my knife to his throat; instead, he nodded and gestured for me to lead the way.

"Two Jeeps leaving the house," Ernie stated. "In a hurry. Could be Moreno inside second vehicle. Serious firepower."

What the fuck? There was no way they made us that quick. There was no alarm. No gunshots.

"Eyes on the entrance," Tyler said into the headset.

Deck and I jogged along the corridor to the electrical room. Deck was taking out the power, so the guards would lock the kids up in one room until they investigated the issue.

Deck chin-lifted and went inside. I kept going, pulling my second knife from its sheath on my left hip as I drew closer to the door that led into the yard in the center of the compound where the pits were located and where we trained with weapons.

The lights flickered a second before a loud thump and whoosh as the power shut down.

I stood with my hand on the latch waiting for Vic and Deck.

My back against the wall, I heard light quick footsteps coming from the south, and then Vic was beside me. He wore black cargo pants and a snug black T-shirt that was covered by his vest. A pistol sat at his right hip and he held in his hands a kickass Combat Assault Rifle.

We needed to give enough time for them to gather the kids up and lock them down. Deck came down the corridor and joined us.

I held up my hand and counted down as I listened for the footsteps on the other side of the door.

One

Two.

Three.

I gave a short, abrupt nod to Vic then threw open the door and rolled to the right as Vic took out the first guy, Deck the second, and my knife the third.

I was on my feet and running toward a guard already shooting at us. I threw my knife while I ran. I didn't stop as I passed him, but yanked my knife from his chest and kept running. I knew this place like the back of my hand. Nothing had changed. I knew where the pits were and where I had cover. What screwed with me was the overwhelming feeling of dread that was fucking with my head.

The images. The feeling as if someone had a fist in my abdomen and was trying to rip out my guts. This place made me sick. It was sick and cruel what they did to us, what they were still doing. What they planned on doing with the drug.

"Jeeps headed your way. Two minutes out," Ernie stated. "We're one minute behind."

Vic was taking men out, keeping my path clear as I made my way across the yard to the door that led into a large room where they put us if there was any trouble.

I looked over to my right and caught a glimpse of Deck running on the other side of the yard parallel to me. It was the only time we'd probably ever be parallel, our paths in life the same and yet so very different.

"Yard. Clear," Vic said.

I gestured to the door with a chin nod and Deck positioned himself on the one side. Vic stayed where he was, watching for any incoming or overhead assault.

I kicked open the door and the wood splintered.

Deck and I stood clear of it for a five count and when there was no sound, I entered first, Deck covering me.

"Jesus," Deck muttered.

Some of the kids were terrified, thin as fuck, filthy, pale and I guessed from ten to fourteen years old. Other kids had no reaction to our appearance at all—numb. I knew the feeling. No longer caring. Time and fear no longer existent.

"Package located." Deck glanced over his shoulder at Vic who jogged toward us.

"Target has landed," Tyler's voice said over the headset. "Repeat, target has landed. Shitload of firepower."

I looked at the kids. "Move away from the door. Against the wall." I gestured with my hands, uncertain if they all understood English. But the farm hadn't been strictly about combat and pain and torture, we'd had intense schooling. We had to be able to communicate and inter-mingle with some of the most powerful men in the world, criminal or otherwise.

A couple of the older kids moved first then the others followed.

"Any more of you here?" Deck asked.

A young boy, probably the smallest, stepped forward. He didn't look Colombian and had blond hair and bright blue eyes. He also looked unafraid of us. "In the pit. Trick."

"Trick?"

The kid nodded and pointed to one of the pits on the left side of the yard. "Trick is bad all the time. He's always in the pit."

"Jesus," I muttered. Because I knew what it was like and depend-ing on what time of year, the pit was hot, cramped and suffocating. If you panicked, it only made it worse because you couldn't breathe, and screaming got you more days in the pit.

Deck was already moving to the pit the kid indicated. My head snapped up. Footsteps. Lots of them and they were running. I pushed the kids back away from the door. "Get back and stay down."

We planned on having time to get the kids out before Moreno

showed, if he showed, but he was here within minutes. No way could he be here within minutes of us taking the place.

Someone told him we were coming.

"Tyler, target confirmed?" Deck asked.

There was radio silence.

"Fuck. Tyler."

Nothing.

"Vic," Deck said.

"On it." Vic was out the door and gone.

"Deck. We do this. Now." He looked at me, paused, and then nodded.

Moreno was the target and he'd come here with a shitload of firepower. Firepower that Deck and I couldn't handle on our own and with kids potentially getting hurt in a shit storm of gunfire. We needed a controlled take down.

Deck ran to the wall, grabbed one of the ladders and lowered it into the pit closest to him. He gave me an abrupt nod and then disappeared inside.

I stood in the middle of the yard when Moreno's men barged in. I'd never surrendered before, but as I stood in the yard where I'd spent two years of my life, I realized I had surrendered—to Vault.

I tossed my knife to the right of me then held up my hands. Two guys covered the door while five took the perimeter of the yard and three surrounded one man—Moreno.

They walked toward me then stopped five feet away, guns aimed at my chest.

Moreno was tall and probably why he didn't look overweight, but he had a belly that hung over the belt on his pants. His hair was greased back and curled slightly at the curve of his neck. He also had a sharp, long nose with a notch in the center, and cruel, beady brown eyes.

His face was weathered from too much sun and made him appear older than his fifty-five years. He wore black pants and a white, cotton button-down that had the first three buttons undone and revealed his two gold necklaces, one with a cross and the other with an oversized emerald.

"Moreno." I lowered my hands and one of the men gestured with his gun and I put them up again.

I'd recognized the necklaces from when I was a kid. This was the man who'd stared down at me in the pit. The man who had stood with the other Vault members and watched my father tortured then killed by my mother. Who'd watched my sister beaten.

I practiced for years and years to conceal my anger and numb myself, but fuck, I wanted to kill the bastard. I wanted him to die the way my father did. I wanted to cut that smirk off his face and have him beg me to let him live.

I clenched my jaw and forced a smile. "How have you been? Been a while, Moreno."

"Yes. Since your sister's little… mishap." He clucked his tongue. "Such disloyalty you and your sister have shown to those who have raised you. Given you everything."

I had so much to say to that, but words had no meaning to him and it only gave him power. Instead, I ignored the guard's order to keep my hands up and lowered them to my side. They tensed and looked to Moreno who merely shrugged. Cocky bastard.

"You could've done better, Kai. I expected something a little more creative from you. Taking my wife and telling me to meet you here or you will kill her?" He laughed. "What…. Did you think I'd show up alone? That I'd let you live once you hand over my wife? What do you want? Money? Drugs? Power?"

I decided to play it off like I knew what he was talking about as it gave me an advantage. "Ah, the beautiful Catalina. A little young for you, isn't she?"

That pissed him off as the fingers on his right hand twitched at his side. "You think you come into my country, into my house, kill twenty of my men and leave with my wife?" His house? Killed his men? Ernie and Tristan had eyes on him. They weren't going in.

He laughed and the shrill sound echoed off the cold, sterile walls of the yard. "You dare to threaten me? My wife? You must not like your family very much."

I chuckled. "I killed my own mother. And as you know my father is already dead."

He took a step closer and so did the assholes with the assault rifles pointed at me. "And what about the girl... what's her name? London. And your sister. Both would be nice additions to my bed."

I glared, the twitch in my jaw and tension in my body sparking. I didn't even want her name to pass his disgusting lips.

There was a slight movement above me to the left on the wall surrounding the yard. I didn't look, to avoid drawing attention, but they were getting into position, Tristan and Ernie. I had no idea what happened to Vic and Tyler.

A man like Moreno didn't let something go down like this and let anyone live, and he sure as hell wouldn't give me money, power or drugs in exchange for the return of his wife. But what I couldn't figure out was why he thought I had his wife. But I had an idea who did.

"My wife, Kai."

I needed a few more minutes for Vic and Tyler, but I didn't know if either was still alive. "I very much doubt your wife wants to go back to you."

He smiled and it was a tight, cruel smile. "Grab one of the kids," Moreno ordered to the man on his right.

Fuck. Within seconds, this was going to turn real ugly.

Out of the corner of my eye, I saw movement in the pit or rather at the edge of the pit and it wasn't in the one Deck was in. Trick? But how the hell would the kid get to the top of the pit without a ladder?

Then I saw the rifle.

What the fuck? I kept my expression steady, but as the familiar eyes appeared over the edge, I suddenly knew what the fuck was going on.

Connor.

Jesus. He was here. In one of the pits. Waiting.

Catalina. He was the one who had Moreno's wife. He was the one who killed twenty of Moreno's men then came here and waited for Moreno to show up. What he probably hadn't expected was to see us.

Our eyes met for a split second. His were bloodshot, but the wild look had steadied.

I gave the signal knowing Deck, Ernie, Tristan, Vic and Tyler, if he was alive, could hear me in the headset. "It's time."

Then shit got real as I dove for Moreno, relying on Deck and the others to take out his men before I was hit. I felt the spray of dirt on my pants legs from the impact of bullets hitting the ground beside me.

It was chaos as Deck and Connor both shot up from the pits, and Ernie and Tristan came in from above.

Moreno made a dive for the door to where the kids were. I got to him first and slammed into him. We both hit the ground hard.

I grabbed him by the shirt, yanked him up, and spun him around before plowing my fist into his jaw. Then again. And again. Blood splattered my face and into my eyes, but it didn't matter because all I saw was red.

Moreno's fist crashed into my cheek and my head flung back. I reached for my knife in my boot. As my hand curled around the hilt, there was a stabbing pain in my side. I knew it was a knife wound, but nothing would deter me from ending this man's life.

I yanked my knife free and had it to his throat before he took his next breath.

He stilled.

I was on top of him, something sticking in my side and the warmth of my blood soaking into my shirt. "Been wanting to do this a long time."

He smirked. "You're no better than me, Kai."

It was my turn to smirk. "Actually, I am better. Because I'm the one with the knife to your throat. And I'm going to take great pleasure in killing you."

His smile dropped and his eyes widened. "I'll give you whatever you—"

I didn't care to hear what he'd trade for his life because nothing would stop me from killing him. But it wasn't the knife at his throat that killed him. It was the other one I'd grabbed in the dirt from where I'd tossed it earlier when I 'surrendered.'

I lifted my body inches off him before stabbing the knife up between his ribs.

He grunted with surprise, face twisted with agony. My hand still on the hilt. I jerked up further. Blood spurted from his nose and mouth and a screeching sound escaped his throat.

I climbed off him, but straddled his body while I peered down at him.

His hands went to the knife still lodged in his chest as if to pull it out. Then he went limp and his arms fell to his sides, eyes staring and blank.

"You guys done yet?" It was Tyler over the headset. "The body is starting to stink up the place."

Vic huffed then said, "Dragged his ass into a classroom."

"You good, Tyler?" Deck asked.

"Good, boss. A few pints short on blood. Fading out, so you might want to hurry the fuck up."

I stepped away from Moreno and noticed Connor beside me staring at Moreno, a murderous glare in his eyes. He walked over to the body, unsheathed his knife, bent and stabbed Moreno in the throat. Then he wiped off his knife on Moreno's sleeve and placed it back in his leather sheath.

"You have his wife?" I asked.

He nodded, but his eyes were still on Moreno. Hatred burned pure and steady from him. I was uncertain how Moreno and his wife played into Connor's life, but it wasn't good, and Connor obviously had some of his memories back, although I was uncertain which parts.

Vic had taken off to get Tyler while Ernie checked the bodies, and Deck and Tristan filtered out the kids and talked to them. Well, Tristan spoke, but his soft reassuring tone was nothing like the cocky playboy Georgie had complained about coming into her coffee shop when she'd been assigned to make contact.

When the last of the kids came out of the room, Connor's eyes deviated from Moreno to them. There was a flicker of softness before they hardened again. Tristan lowered a ladder into a pit on the north side of the yard and climbed down to get the kid, Trick.

Deck jogged up to Connor and me and said to him, "You remember?"

Connor's expression was blank. "Don't need to remember. Told you to leave me the fuck alone."

Deck stiffened, brows lowering. "Connor, it's over. You can come home. We'll get you medical—"

Connor's harsh, gravelly laugh had Deck stop short. "Too late for that." He glanced over at the kids. Tristan was crouched down in front of them speaking, his hand on Trick's shoulder. "She was good with kids."

"Who?" Deck asked.

Connor began to back away, his eyes never leaving Deck as if he were waiting for Deck to kill him. "She's in the sewer tunnels under his house. West wall. Get her the fuck out of Colombia." He'd backed all the way to the door and then his eyes narrowed. "Tell my sister I'm dead."

Then he was gone.

EPILOGUE

Six weeks later

London

THE BED SAGGED, and I instantly woke as Kai kissed the back of my neck and slid in behind me.

"Hey, baby," he whispered next to my ear then kissed the side of my neck.

"Is it time to get ready?" I'd fallen asleep after Kai fed me then fucked me on the dining room table before carrying me to bed and showing me how much he loved me.

His hard cock pressed into my ass and I wiggled back into him.

"Not going to Deck's engagement party. Told you that." His arm curved around my waist then squeezed. "Fuck. Love you in my bed naked."

"Kai, we have to go." I tried to turn over to face him, but he held me tight against him. "Georgie and Deck will be disappointed."

He snorted. "Do you think I give a shit if Deck is disappointed?"

"Okay, well, maybe not. But Georgie."

Deck and Kai would never be friends and in the six weeks since we'd been back in Toronto, we'd only seen him once. Tristan and Chess invited us over to show us the house Mason Developments was building for the kids rescued from Colombia. Deck and Georgie were there, along with Ernie who was overseeing the project.

The house was on a hundred acres and to be completed in a couple months. It already had thirty rescued farm animals, including a pot-bellied pig the boy Trick had named Bacon, and a three-legged goat who was an escape artist and refused to stay in the field with the horses. He'd badly injured his leg, attempting to jump a barbed wire fence where the farmer kept him. He had snagged himself on the wire and was left hanging for hours.

The farmer sent him to slaughter. Emily, who rescued horses, and Chess, went to the auction and bought him along with the pig and five horses. "Georgie would be. It's important, Kai"

"Don't like that shit. I'd rather stay in bed with you."

I moaned when his thumb brushed over my nipple. He was good at distraction. "Kai. We're going."

"Mmmm." He kissed my neck again and his hand trailed a gentle path down between my legs. I sucked in air as he ran his finger through the wetness, and sweet tweaks erupted in my belly. "We show late and leave early," he offered.

This was him, conceding. I smiled. "Okay."

He moved in closer and, with his other hand, he guided his cock down my ass to between my legs. Then agonizingly slow, he pushed inside of me.

"Kai." I arched back into him, eyes closed, breath stilled. When he filled me completely, I sighed. "This…"

He trickled lazy kisses along my neck. "Yeah, baby?" he murmured, settling inside me but not moving yet.

"Kai, this. You. You're my everything. You're my always."

"Fuck, braveheart." He abruptly pulled out and before I could contemplate why, he had me on my back and he was on top. He pushed my legs open none to gently with his knees, and then lowered his hips and thrust back inside me.

His fingers sifted through my hair then fisted a bunch of strands. "Mouth, baby. I need your mouth after you say sweet shit like that."

I bit my lip smiling.

And then any control he had vanished as his mouth took mine. Tasting. Owning.

I moaned beneath his bruising mouth, my legs hooking his waist to bring him closer. I had to feel every inch of him. Our mouths became a wild frenzy of need for one another with teeth clashing and lips bruised. My stomach whirled. Between my legs throbbed and I melted into the man who was my always.

He groaned, pulled back, and slid his hands down my arms, to lock on my wrists and drag them above my head. "Want you too much right now. So, I'm going to fuck you. And it's going to be hard. You good with that?"

"Yeah," I whispered.

He stared at me, those piercing green eyes flared with intense desire and need, his mouth inches from mine as he made me wait. His hands moved from my wrists to my hands where our fingers intertwined.

Eyes locked.

Bodies locked.

Our lives locked.

No key fit a perfectly ruined lock. Because that was what we were. Both ruined, but perfect together.

We were always and everything.

"Love you, Kai," I said.

His eyes flashed and his body tensed. "Always, baby."

His mouth crashed down on mine. At the same time he pulled out and thrust inside me hard. Then he thrust again and again, hard and without mercy. It was as if he were trying to convince himself I was there in his arms. That I wouldn't break and disappear on him.

"I'm here," I whispered. "I'm here and I'm never leaving you." He'd denied himself love his entire life, but love did conquer. It *did* prevail.

And now, his life was a fairy tale. It was one fucked-up fairy tale, but still a fairy tale where the prince gets his princess.

And this prince was mine. Kai was mine just as much as I was his, and he was making certain that was imprinted as he took every part of me.

I moaned as his mouth trailed kisses down the curve of my neck. Then he took my nipple into his mouth and suckled as he continued to pump into me, but slower, softer.

"Fuck, baby. You're so fuckin' damn beautiful." He flicked his tongue over my nipple then drew it back into his mouth, teasing.

"Kai." I arched my back.

He ground his hips, rotating against my clit. I gasped, feeling my tightness building.

"London," he groaned. "Damn it. I can't... fuck, come for me baby."

But he didn't need to tell me because I was already there. "Oh, God. Oh, God," I gasped. My body tensed. My insides clenched and waves of desire shot through my body over and over again.

Then he tilted his upper body up and thrust hard and fast several times. "Jesus," he yelled. His body tensed and shuddered for several seconds before he stopped.

He dropped his head forward in to my neck as his chest heaved in and out. "Fuck," he whispered.

Kissing my shoulder before he rolled to the side and onto his back, his cock slipped from me and warm liquid trickled down my inner thigh. He brought me with him so I was tucked into his side while his hand went to the back of my head to bring it to rest on his chest.

My leg thrown over his, sheet tangled at our feet, he stroked my hair as we both caught our breath.

He kissed the top of my head. "London." I tilted my neck so I could look up at him. "Loving you is like finding the light. I can't ever lose that again, baby. I won't."

I slid my hand up over his chest, the rough scars beneath my palms until my finger brushed his lips. "The light was always there, you just had to believe it was. And I'm not going anywhere."

He lowered his head and I moved up to meet his lips.

It was a slow, tantalizing kiss that caused goose bumps and quivers, and made me want him all over again.

When he drew back, his cocky smirk was there. I loved that smirk. I loved that he could change in a flash from serious to playful to intense. But most of all, I loved that he was resilient. Unyielding. Kai never gave up.

He never gave up on me.

"Hon?"

"Fuck," he muttered beneath his breath.

"What?" I asked, frowning and sitting up.

"Like you calling me hon."

"Oh." I liked calling him that, too. I lifted and threw my leg over his thighs so I straddled him. "I'll make you a deal."

His brows lifted. "A deal?"

I nodded then slid my hands down his chest and wiggled my butt on top of him.

His hands settled on my hips and he chuckled. "Another deal? You are brave."

"Mmmm," I murmured as I moved down his body, my hand inches from his cock and yet not touching.

"What do you have in mind?" He grabbed my wrist, stopping my hand that was about to wrap around his cock.

I smiled at him. "That if I can make you beg—"

He burst out laughing. I frowned.

"Oh, baby, you can try and I will enjoy you trying, but I don't beg—ever." He let go of me. Putting his hands behind his head, he appeared casual and completely relaxed as if he were going to enjoy this. "But please, go right ahead."

I slowly licked my lips and his eyes darted to them. I inwardly smiled, knowing he was already thinking about my wet mouth wrapped around him. "And if you beg?"

He shrugged. "Whatever you desire, baby."

I had him. "We arrive on time to the party and we stay until I want to leave."

He grinned. "Sure. But if you lose, then tonight I fuck you any way I desire."

I rolled my eyes. "You do that already."

"True. But I was thinking about something involving ice cubes and hot wax."

Shit. Kai may love me, but he still liked to push my limits.

"Okay. Time limit?" I asked.

He shook his head. "Nope. Take your sweet-ass time."

"Oh, I will," I whispered. Then I climbed off him and the bed.

His cocky grin faded and he frowned. "What are you doing?"

"Taking my sweet-ass time. And since I'm winning I thought I'd shower and save time. Multi-tasking, hon," I replied then strolled into the bathroom and turned on the light. I glanced in the mirror and saw him sit up. He could see my reflection perfectly. I bent and turned on the shower and when it was warm enough, I stepped inside.

I left the door open, glancing in the mirror. He was watching me, his cock jutting up between his legs, scowl fierce. Kai was patient, but so was I.

I reached for the soap then slowly lathered my body, taking my time, my hands caressing, stroking while I closed my eyes and lost myself to the intense pleasure of having his eyes on me while I touched myself. It was when I started panting as I circled the sweet spot that I heard him come into the bathroom.

He leaned his hard, naked body against the counter, ankles crossed to match his arms. Every one of his muscles were tense. By his scowl, he was unhappy, but by the intensity and the smoldering heat in his eyes, he was definitely losing the battle.

I leaned forward, palm on the tiled wall to support my quivering legs, water trickling over my skin as I played with myself. I was close to coming so I stopped. I didn't want to. Not yet. I needed to wait.

I ran my palm up over my abdomen to my breasts, then with my finger circled one nipple then the other. I knew Kai. I'd seen him lose control. And when I opened my eyes again and stared at him, I saw the wild, raw look in his expression. The flare of need. The tension ready to break.

I bent, turned off the water, stepped from the shower, and then took the two steps to reach him. I didn't touch. Instead, I trailed my eyes down his body then back up again. Then I smiled.

His brows lifted. "I hope you have more than that."

"Oh, I've just begun." I stepped closer, so the heated wetness from my skin sank into his. I lowered my voice, mouth inches from his. "You've taught me something, Kai. That getting what you want takes persistence and determination. That you never give up, no matter the odds." His brows dropped, and I ran my hand down the front of him, stopping when the pad of my finger brushed the tip of his cock.

He growled, but didn't move to touch me.

Then I stood on my tiptoes, my lips close to his ear, erect nipples against his chest. "All you have to do is say 'please, London,' and I'm yours."

His eyes narrowed. "You're already mine."

"Mmmm," I murmured. "True. And now I'm going to show you that you're mine."

Kai was unhappy.

We walked into the bar Avalanche an hour late with my legs still tingling and my cheeks flushed. Kai didn't actually beg, because he lost control and fucked me on the bathroom counter. It was decided we both won and so here we were. He was giving me two hours before he took me home so he could get his part of the deal—fucking me any way he chose—and, despite being a little nervous, it also got me really wet thinking about it.

"London. Kai," Chess cried over the loud music and rushed toward us. Tristan, whose arm she shoved off in order to get to us, remained standing at the bar, but his eyes never left her. He nodded to us, raising his beer.

Chess hugged me then stood on her tiptoes and kissed her brother's cheek. I smelled strawberry on her breath, and her eyes were glassy and bright. She'd obviously been into the alcohol already.

"You got him to come," she said to me.

Kai answered, "Yeah, several times."

She rolled her eyes at her brother then took my hand. "Come on, you need a drink. Brett makes the best strawberry daiquiris, although he complains while doing it. Oh, and you have to meet Catalina. She's working here now. Matt hired her a couple weeks ago." I'd met Matt, Kat's brother, when I'd been staying in Toronto before the Alfonzo shit went down. I hadn't met Catalina, but I'd heard about her. Heard who her husband had been and knew Connor and her had history, although I didn't know what that history had been.

Kai squeezed my hand. "Need to talk to Deck. Go with Chess. Be there in a sec."

"To congratulate him?"

He tugged me in to him, and my hand slipped from Chess's. Then he bent and kissed me briefly. "Business."

"It's his engagement party, Kai," I said aghast.

He shrugged while grinning, and then I watched him casually walk through the crowd, knowing he wasn't happy to be here, but doing it anyway for me.

He looked hot tonight, well he always did, but he dressed in fitted jeans hanging low on his hips with a white dress shirt. It was Kai being relaxed, and it was sexy as hell and all I could think about as I watched him shake Deck's hand, then Vic's, Tyler's and Josh's, was that he was mine. I had a feeling that leaving early was going to be my idea.

Chess nudged my shoulder. "Drinks. My brother has had you for weeks. We have sisterly bonding to do."

"Huh?" Sisterly?

She grabbed my hand and laughed. "You think my brother won't do everything in his power to make certain you stay his?" She tugged me toward the bar. "I give it a month before he has that piece of paper in his hand."

I laughed. "Kai doesn't care about a legal document saying I'm his."

She looked over her shoulder at me. "True. But he'll definitely want to marry you before Deck marries Georgie. That testosterone rivalry thing between them."

I laughed. That was more than likely, but, like Kai, I didn't need a piece of paper to say I was legally his.

"London," Tristan said and leaned toward me, kissing my cheek, and then reached for a fancy glass with red icy liquid off the bar and passed it to me.

I sipped the cool drink and we chatted about the progress on the house and Trick, one of the kids that Chess and Tristan were trying to legally adopt.

Soon, Emily, Georgie, and Kat came over and joined us. Tristan slipped away and left us girls to giggle and drink our daiquiris, which I soon discovered were rather potent. I wasn't used to drinking alcohol, so my tolerance was zilch.

It was nice. I hadn't had girlfriends in a long time, and it felt good to chat and laugh and drink. In a few months, I was starting at the University of Toronto to finish my degree, and I was already volunteering at a homeless shelter close to Kai's loft.

A hand settled on my hip and I smiled, tilting my head back to meet Kai's lips. "Baby," he murmured against my mouth. Then his arm came around my waist and he tugged my back into his chest.

"What were you men talking about? It looked intense." It had. I saw Vic arguing with Deck after Kai had said something.

"Business."

"Everything okay?" I took a sip of my drink.

He lowered his mouth to my ear and whispered, "Going into business together."

Daiquiri sprayed from my mouth and luckily no one was in front of me. I wiped my mouth with the napkin under the base of the glass then turned in his arms. "You're not serious."

But the second my eyes met his and I saw the spark with his grin, I knew he was. "That's what Vic was angry about."

He nodded. "One of the things. He thinks it's a bad idea."

"And Deck doesn't?"

Kai's hand on my lower back slid over my ass and back up again.

I was wearing a little black dress with a scoop neck and a low back. It was tight and stretchy, and I liked it because it was sexy, but not too revealing. But mostly I liked it because Kai helped me pick it out at the store. He swore it was the one and only time he'd accompany me to the mall.

"Deck knows I'm good at what I do. And changing Vault's direction is in his best interest. We merge and gradually shift those still involved with Vault to the way we want it to go." He cupped my chin and his thumb rubbed a spot at the corner of my mouth where I probably still had daiquiri. "Deck's morals differ from mine, so we'll clash, but we've found a common footing in that we want the same thing."

"Why else was Vic angry?"

He grinned. "I told him to go get me a drink."

I laughed.

"London." Georgie came up beside us with a dark brunette who had sun-tanned skin and dark, almost black eyes with long lashes. She was curvy, wide hips with average breasts. Her features were gentle and soft, except for her high-cheekbones. "This is Catalina."

I pulled out of Kai's arms, but he kept his hand resting on my lower back.

I reached forward and shook Catalina's hand. "Hi. Nice to meet you." Her grip was strong, but there was a hesitation before she took it.

Kai nodded. "Catalina." I knew that they'd met in Colombia and also what her story was. It wasn't a good one.

She glanced at Kai then back to me. "Hey."

"I talked to Matt. He said you can hang with us for a while," Georgie said. "Brett and Jen can handle it."

"Thanks, but I just started this job and want to make a good impression."

Georgie laughed. "No need to impress Matt. That sexy cupcake is sweet on all his girls."

But Catalina was already moving away and disappeared into the crowd.

Georgie turned back to us, sighing. "I want to help her, I just don't know how. I know she meant something to my brother. He'd want that."

According to Kai, Deck told Georgie exactly what happened in Colombia including Connor showing up and what he'd said. But like Kai, Deck would never lie to Georgie and I could tell from the strained look on her face that she was still struggling with the fact her brother had wanted her to think he was dead meaning he had no intention of coming back.

There was a loud commotion when the music shut down, and people started shifting around wondering what was going on when Deck stepped up onto the stage and grabbed the microphone.

"Holy crap," Georgie exclaimed, mouth dropping. "What's he doing?"

"Not my thing, standing up here," Deck said into the microphone and his deep, gravelly voice echoed through the room.

There was clapping and a few whistles and catcalls, but Deck ignored them as his eyes sifted through the crowd until they locked on Georgie standing beside me. The crowd turned to look where Deck was focused.

"My girl has agreed to be mine in the eyes of the law, but she's been mine since I first laid eyes on her."

"When she was illegal," Tyler hooted, and everyone laughed except Deck, but there was a slight pull at the corner of his mouth.

"We have history. Some not so good, but it's history and it's ours. She's been a pain in my ass for years." There was laughter. "And I suspect for many more." More laughter. "But there was never a time I didn't want her. Never a time I didn't love her. And there will never *be* a time." I sighed, along with all the other girls in the room. "I keep my shit private." There was a subtle chuckle from the crowd. "But the fact that I love her, that's not private. That's something I want everyone to know." I smiled and Kai huffed, but when I glanced up at him, he was nodding as he watched Deck, eyes showing admiration. "Love you, Georgie."

Georgie slipped past me, and I caught a glimpse of tears staining her cheeks. It was a lot for Deck to get up there and talk because he *was* private. But Georgie wasn't and Deck did it for her.

In two leaps she was on stage and in Deck's arms. He staggered back a step because she went full throttle into him with her legs wrapping around his waist and arms hooking his neck before her mouth was on his. She kissed him and then he took control and kissed her while everyone cheered.

"Sing!" Tyler shouted.

That got a mild laugh out of Deck as he lowered Georgie to her feet, but didn't let her go. "Thank you to everyone for coming. And I'm not going to sing but these guys made a special trip back to Toronto from their tour in order to play for us tonight."

That's when the crowd went wild as Sculpt, aka Logan, Ream, Crisis and Kite came out on stage. Deck relinquished Georgie to the boys as they each hugged her. There was a beautiful blonde girl on the side stage who had her eyes locked on Crisis. He turned and winked at her before he picked up his guitar.

Deck and Georgie came off the stage, and then the place went wild as the band hit it with their current number one song aptly named "Avalanche." But it wasn't about the bar, it was a love story of how a girl's heart shattered when the guy she loved died. Like an unstoppable avalanche, her life altered from joy and hope to suffocating in despair. It was haunting and beautiful at the same time, but it was the ending that brought tears to my eyes when the girl found a speck of light through the darkness and fought back. When she learned to live again.

I swayed to the music while Kai held me, and I'd never been happier. We stayed like that for two songs before I turned into him and tilted my head up about to ask him if we could leave because I wanted Kai to take me home.

But before my eyes met his, I caught a glimpse of Catalina up against the wall in the shadows of the bar. A man towered over her, one hand on her hip and the other above her head, his palm resting on the wall. They were fifty feet away from me, and there was a dim yellow light above them. It was obvious Catalina was in shock, because her eyes were wide and her body defensive as she had her hands up on his chest as if to ward him off.

He was talking rapidly, and from his tense, muscled body, he was angry, but I was unable to see his face. I gasped when he pushed back then punched the wall beside her.

Catalina said something then reached out, her hands curling into his shirt. He didn't move for a second, and then his shoulders sagged and he stepped back into her. His head bowed then dropped into the curve of her neck.

"Babe? What's up?" Kai asked, his arms giving me a gentle squeeze.

"I think Catalina is having trouble with one of the guests. Or not. I'm not sure."

His eyes darted to where I was looking and he stiffened. "Fuck."

"You know who it is?" I couldn't see the guy's face, but Kai obviously didn't need to.

"Connor," Kai said.

The End

Coming Early 2016 Connor and Catalina's story.
"Perfect Rage"

To the readers,

Kai and London (aka Raven) were first introduced in *Torn from You* two years ago and I've been dying to write their story ever since. Kai was such a mystery, but through writing *Perfect Ruin* I grew to understand him and love him more than any other character. This couple will always have a piece of my heart. I hope you enjoyed reading *Perfect Ruin* as much as I did writing it. I'm truly honored and grateful for your continued support.

Hugs,

Nash xo

Books by Nashoda Rose

Seven Sixes (2016)

Tear Asunder Series
With You (free)
Torn from You
Overwhelmed by You
Shattered by You
Kept from You (Kite's Story) 2016

Unyielding Series
Perfect Chaos
Perfect Ruin
Perfect Rage (Early 2016)

Scars of the Wraith Series
Stygian Book #1
Tyrant Book #2(2016)
Untitled Book #3(2016)
Take (standalone Scars of the Wraiths)

www.nashodarose.com

ABOUT THE AUTHOR

Nashoda Rose is a New York Times and USA Today bestselling author who lives in Toronto with her assortment of pets. She writes contemporary romance with a splash of darkness, or maybe it's a tidal wave.

When she isn't writing, she can be found sitting in a field reading with her dogs at her side while her horses graze nearby. She loves interacting with her readers and chatting about her addiction—books.

Where to find Nashoda

Newsletter: http://nashodarose.us7.list-manage1.com/subscribe?u=1e800ef9a8a22144c14399928&id=b12d168284

Facebook:
https://www.facebook.com/Nashoda-Rose-564276203633318/

Goodreads:
https://www.goodreads.com/author/show/7246093.Nashoda_Rose

Instagram: https://www.instagram.com/nashodarose/

Twitter: https://twitter.com/nashodarose

Website:www.nashodarose.com

www.ingramcontent.com/pod-product-compliance
Lightning Source LLC
Chambersburg PA
CBHW060226030726
47499CB00004B/1202